Once I Was Lost

Once I Was Lost

James Harlow Brown

First published in 2020 by Lorien Partners Pty Ltd

PO Box 280

Fairfield, Victoria 3078

Australia

www.lorienpartners.com

Copyright © 2020 James Harlow Brown

Publishing services provided by Green Olive Press
www.greenolivepress.com

US paperback edition ISBN 978-0-6489161-2-3

Australian paperback ISBN 978-0-6489161-4-7

Credits

Contents

Book 1   Neil's Story

"Dangerous Undertaking"

"Time is not real, Govinda. I have realized this repeatedly. And if time is not real, then the dividing line that seems to lie between this world and eternity, between suffering and bliss, between good and evil, is also an illusion."

Herman Hesse, *Siddhartha*

Chapter 1

Life is a quest, not a contest. Frank O'Connor showed me that. When I first met him on a night flight to Australia, I was driving my life in the fast lane. Perform, Achieve, Succeed—that was my roadmap. I didn't let anything get in my way, and I didn't slow down to think about unsolvable problems like global warming or worry about people's feelings. The world is a tough place. Life is a competition that doesn't have a happy ending unless you win. That was how I thought before I met Frank.

So what? you ask. Aren't there millions of people like me, trying to make it big in the world? You're right, of course, but I was lucky enough to meet Frank. He triggered my transformation when I had absolutely no reason to change. Think of me as being imprisoned in something like a cave.

Not a completely dark one—actually a well-furnished one—but a cave, nonetheless. Sometime in my past, I had unknowingly confined myself there. As a result, I could only see and move in very limited ways. If I had looked in the right direction, I might have seen a light that signaled there was an exit. It never occurred to me to look for a way out. My tight little universe met all my needs—and no one else's. Even now it's hard for me to explain exactly how I escaped. The best I can do is to tell my story and let you decide.

By the way, I'm Neil Armstrong Schmidt. Yeah, I know, like the astronaut. I was born on July 22, 1969, two days after the first moon walk. My father, in a fit of patriotism or desire for me to be great or something, named me after him. As you'll soon see, I'm not a hero like the astronaut, but I have been fortunate to meet a few heroes that I will tell you about.

I went to Australia several times a year to meet with our distributors and get them to push our products harder. On this particular trip, as always, I had flown from Washington DC to Los Angeles, coped with the usual two-hour wait in the Qantas Lounge, and finally boarded the 747. It was after midnight, Washington time, and all I wanted was to stretch out in business class and get to sleep as fast as possible.

LA to Sydney takes about fourteen hours, and I had a routine: tell the flight attendant I didn't want to eat or be woken up, wear the blindfold and earplugs from the courtesy pack, and—most importantly—*not* start a conversation with my seatmate. But that night I was restless for some reason, and I couldn't sleep.

The upper-deck cabin was dark when I finally gave up and decided to find a magazine. The man next to me in the aisle seat had his light on and was reading a book that must have been very interesting because he was busily underlining and making notes in the margin. I needed to get past but didn't want to break his concentration, so I sat, outside his little cone of light, waiting for the right moment.

My neighbor looked about sixty and was kind of weather-beaten, with short-cropped gray hair. He seemed quite tall and was slouched down in his seat with his legs stretched out under the seat in front of him. He had on jeans and a black sweater.

Suddenly, he closed his book, folded up his tray table, and stood up. Great! Now I could easily get out without the squirming, twisting contortions it usually took.

While I was unbuckling my seat belt, I glanced at the cover of the book he'd left lying on his seat. *The Homeless Mind.* Never heard of it. I got up and walked toward the rear of the cabin. He was standing there, waiting for a toilet. He *was* tall, probably six four. Even taller than me. I nodded to him and walked back to the galley to get a bottle of water from the flight attendant. I did some stretches for a few minutes to get the kinks out, grabbed a copy of The Economist and returned to my seat. He got up to let me pass, vaguely smiled at me, and then continued to read and underline his book.

After a few minutes, he turned to me and said, "Hi, I'm Frank O'Connor," giving me what I came to recognize as his Gandalf look. I like to use the wizard from *The Lord of the Rings* to describe Frank because that's how he affected me from the very beginning. Maybe he thought I was a little like Frodo too.[1]

He stuck out his hand. It was large and rough, like the farmer's son I learned he was. His handshake was firm. He was a management consultant, an American who had made his home in London. I introduced myself and told him what I did, and we chatted a bit. Then I asked him about the book he was reading.

Why did I do that? It wasn't like me—Mr Perform, Achieve, Succeed—to waste my time on conversation with a total stranger. Like I said, I can't explain why Frank was able to reach me inside my cave.

"I'm curious about the book you're reading. *The Homeless Mind*. How could your mind be homeless? It's part of you. Puzzling idea."

He gave me a searching look, maybe measuring my question against some criteria he had. Was it worth spending time to answer it? I must have passed because he immediately took our conversation to another level.

"Let me tell you what it's about, but not how you probably expect me to. It may take some time. Are you interested?"

He paused and waited for me to choose. I didn't actually care that much about *The Homeless Mind*, but I was intrigued by his response.

He must have seen the yes on my face because he quickly asked, "What are you thinking about, Neil?"

"That either you might be nuts or this might turn out to be a really interesting flight."

He grinned at me and returned my volley.

"I suppose, in a way, I am nuts. Like the authors of *The Homeless Mind*, I look at the world from a different perspective. Have you ever seen a 3-D puzzle picture? They look all garbled; you can't see anything but strange colored lines and shapes mixed together. Nothing coherent. But if you look at them in a certain way, you'll see surprising images emerge from the jumbled picture. That's what I do: look at our complicated human situation in a slightly out-of-focus way and find patterns that most people overlook."

"So, what have you found? Net it out for me."

That was Neil the Executive speaking. Impatient. Don't beat around the bush. Give me a sound bite if you want to hold my attention.

"I can't summarize for you. If I tried to explain the patterns, it would be like me telling you there are three dolphins hidden in one of those 3-D pictures. You need to see the dolphins for yourself. It's very difficult for most people to see the patterns in their lives, because their minds are stuck in a rut. They see the world in very limited ways. I help them find ways to get out of their ruts and see these important patterns."

It was obvious he was encouraging me to give it a go. He started working on the problem immediately.

"Remember the saying that we can't see the forest for the trees? Try this little exercise. Imagine seeing Earth from outer space—say, from the moon. Can you picture it? You can't see very much detail at all. Earth looks like a blue, brown, and white ball. Even when you're much closer than the moon, only a few hundred miles away, you still can't see anything man-made, not even large cities or the Great Wall of China."

"Now imagine you are on the surface, in some city. All you can see is detail. There is so much detail that you're in information overload. You simply can't see the world the same way you can from space. What I'm trying to say is that too much information blinds you to the hidden patterns and keeps you in a rut. You need to leave all this information behind, get some altitude above your ordinary life, so to speak, to be able to see the patterns. You follow me so far?"

"Yeah. We can't see patterns and details at the same time. What we see depends on our perspective." I still didn't get what he meant by patterns, but at that moment I was more interested in watching Frank's face than in what he was saying. His expression fascinated me. It combined intense concentration with a kind of peacefulness, like he was aware of something that I wasn't.

"So, here's a question for you, Neil. How do we escape from all that information?"

He waited for my answer. He reminded me of a teacher trying to make me use my mind more than I usually did.

Just then the 747 started to shake, and then it gave us a really good bounce. We must have been getting near the equator, where the captain had told us the winds would be a bit rough. The plane's computer smoothed out the flight as best it could, but the pilot kept the 'fasten seat belt' light on.

"That was interesting," Frank said. "Did you feel the autopilot kick in and get control of the plane?"

I had a thought. "Frank, what if our mind is in a rut because it's on autopilot too? What if, to get rid of all the information and see things from a fresh perspective, we have to turn autopilot off and, in a way, take control over flying our own mind?"

He looked at me with a big grin.

"That's a darn good way to put it. I like your autopilot metaphor. But the problem is still there. Where is the switch to our autopilot? How do we turn it off?"

He waited a moment, but when I just looked at him blankly, he answered his own question.

"Maybe something happens to us. Something completely unexpected grabs our attention and wrenches us out of our rut. It may be something simple, not out of the ordinary at all."

"There is a story about how something like this happened to the poet Dante. He once met a young woman on the streets of Florence who simply smiled at him and said good morning as she passed. He spent more than half of his life wrestling with the impact of that meeting. The young girl became Dante's heavenly escort Beatrice in his great poem *The Divine Comedy*. He was yanked out of his rut by that encounter. What happened? Maybe it was like a door opening very briefly, and he caught a glimpse of something through

11

the crack, something that fascinated him and wouldn't let his mind rest until he figured it out. Who knows?"

I imagined Dante meeting the young girl and walking around afterward with a stunned expression on his face. How did that fit me? I wasn't a poet. Poets are always seeing things that the rest of us don't. It felt like Frank was playing a game with me. I wasn't sure I wanted to play, but I decided to go along with him for a while.

Chapter 2

The 747 flew steadily southwest, somewhere near the equator, but Frank changed direction.

"Let me come at these hidden patterns from a different angle. You're a businessman, Neil. You like to get to the facts and the bottom line. Can you summarize the facts of our current world situation for me? Let's see if we agree."

I wondered what the global situation had to do with my mental rut, but to keep things rolling, I quickly summarized how I saw things. I probably showed my annoyance, but Frank didn't let on and listened intently.

"Things are pretty screwed up. The United States has a lot of power, but we can't do anything about the huge problems on our planet, or our own problems either. Poverty—the have-nots outnumber the haves by two or three to one. War and terrorism, the spread of violence throughout society—there's so much hatred on our planet among people who have fought each other for centuries, even thousands of years. Disease—look at how people ignore the basics of prevention. Famine—I've heard that thirty percent of the people on the planet do not know where their next meal is coming from. Global warming. I could go on. The Four Horsemen of the Apocalypse are destined to ride across our planet, forever spreading misery and destruction, and there's nothing much that you or I can do about it."

I stopped. He was smiling. What was there to smile about? It got under my skin, so I upped the ante.

"The facts of human nature are horrific, Frank, on a large scale and on an individual scale. The Holocaust, countless rapes and murders in our cities. What is there to smile about? The best we can do is to try to create a safe place for ourselves and our families. Those are the facts!"

"I'm not smiling at the situation, Neil. I'm pleased with how you get to the core of things. It makes our discussion easier. We can easily establish where we agree and disagree."

I wondered how he could possibly disagree with the facts I had presented, but I was starting to learn that he would come at things from outside the box.

"There are assumptions in your description of the current global situation. You're looking at the world in a particular way. Let me illustrate what I mean with a story.

14

Have you seen a movie by Ingmar Bergman called *The Seventh Seal?*"

I'd heard of it but hadn't seen it.

"It's the story of a medieval knight and his squire who return from the Crusades as the Black Death hits Europe in the fourteenth century."

What did a medieval knight have to do with anything? I wondered.

"Bergman is a master at creating a theatrical mood. Everything in his film is stark black and white. On the edge of a desolate ocean—on our world, but centuries earlier—Death comes for the knight. It agrees to postpone its claim over his life and play a game of chess for his soul. In the end, Death wins, but while the game is going on, the knight and his squire wander through the world, observing life on our planet at the time of the Black Death.

"They find themselves in a world gone mad with the fear of death. People practice outlandish religious rituals to ward off the devil, who they believe causes the Plague. Only the knight and the squire see their world as it actually is. Everyone else sees life through a strange lens and with fantastic convictions that drive them to do horrific things. Bergman was a great filmmaker with an ability to make us see this strange medieval worldview."

So what? I thought. "Where are you leading me, Frank?"

"Relax, Neil. I'm just trying to illustrate something about your assumptions of the world. The people in

Bergman's medieval villages lined the streets to watch processions of people carrying crosses and lashing themselves with whips. Soldiers in the town had captured a young girl that they believed had had intercourse with the devil. Everyone in the village thought it was right for her to be burned at the stake. Only the knight and the squire observed these things and were horrified."

"My point is that few people today see things like they really are. Ingmar Bergman is one. He observes our times through a different lens. Artists like Bergman are aware of the unseen assumptions in our lives. We're a lot like the people in the medieval villages, controlled by fearful assumptions that shape our everyday rituals. We are surrounded by circumstances and fears that we don't want to acknowledge or examine."

He was searching my face and must have read my mind: disbelief and defensiveness. I was struggling with all this negativism but looking back I realize that Frank wanted me to see the dark possibility that Bergman raised.

"As moviegoers, we're able to clearly see that medieval insanity, but it's far harder to see our own delusions. You're grimacing, but delusion is probably the right word. Illusion or mirage is even more accurate. I imagine that six hundred years from now, a future Bergman will make a film about our lives in the early twenty-first century, and people will wonder how we could ever have thought the way we do today. Our world doesn't make sense in many ways, yet we can't see it. We're stuck in our facts and beliefs. In the modern world, we are adrift on a sea of uncertainty without anchors or firm foundations, and this uncertainty creates fear at a deep level. That's what *The Homeless Mind* is about."

"Okay, enough for now," he said. "Let's relax."

Surely he wasn't done. I wasn't programmed by fear like the people in Bergman's film. He seemed to imply that, like those terrified people, I lived according to bizarre assumptions. What in *my* life could remotely be related to such horrific medieval insanity? Why did he tell me this awful story? One thing was certain: I wasn't going to get much sleep before I arrived in Sydney.

I thought about how Bergman filmed in black and white, and I had a brainstorm. Maybe the lighting in our lives was black and white, too! Maybe we couldn't, or wouldn't, let ourselves see other colors in life. Maybe that was what Frank was driving at. Seeing life's colors, the good and the bad, as they were, not just the usual images we allowed ourselves to see. The knight saw things the villagers didn't. Maybe I was afraid to see life as it actually is. For some reason, an image of a starving child in the Sudan I'd seen on TV flitted through my mind. Was that what Frank was hinting at? But I thought I'd pointed out those kinds of problems when I summarized the world situation.

"What are you thinking about, Neil?" he asked. "Still trying to connect Bergman with our global situation? Let it go for a while. If there are to be any insights, they will come on their own. That's the way insights work."

"I did have a thought," I answered. "I was thinking about how Bergman made us watch the medieval world in black and white. His use of lighting transported the audience

17

into an alien situation—to see things they didn't want to look at. Maybe a good metaphor for our situation is the lighting we use to see our world. What do you think?"

"Very good. I like it. Lighting and the theater of life. Maybe we play our roles on life's stage the way we do because we only see in black and white. If we changed the lighting, maybe we'd act differently. Who—or what—controls the lighting on the stage of our lives? Very powerful metaphor, Neil."

His compliments helped. He was telling me to keep going, I was on the right path; my insights were worthwhile.

For some reason I remembered the beauty of many of the cities I had visited. I recalled the spectacular views of the harbor in Sydney and the Hong Kong skyline at night. There was so much in our world to marvel at, so much human energy and level-headedness. Bergman's bleak story about *The Seventh Seal* didn't seem to fit the world I lived in.

Then I remembered a ragged beggar I'd once seen in Manila squatting in front of a ramshackle hut, watching my limo drive by with dull eyes. I was on my way from the airport to a five-star hotel in Makati. I might as well have been on a different planet than that wretched human being. The air he breathed was so polluted by the heavy traffic that I was afraid to roll down the windows and breathe it with him. I'd locked myself into a comfortable space capsule to protect myself from exposure to the beggar's alien environment.

If I began to see the world with different lighting, would I react differently and roll down my windows to let his life touch mine? Not very likely. I began to sense a hint of that hidden fear that Frank was pointing at. It kept me away from that beggar. I didn't know what I was afraid of, but at least Frank's story had triggered the question.

Much later, I realized that if I rolled down my window—at least metaphorically—and let in the misery of the beggar, I might have to do something about it. Get involved in his world and give up some of mine. That's what I was afraid of. Frank was encouraging me to be like the knight in Bergman's movie. Stay alert for things that are alien to your deepest sense of what is good for human beings. Do something about it. But something stood in my way. His next story shed some light on that.

Chapter 3

We flew on toward Australia in darkness, and Frank kept pushing me to get out of my rut.

"Neil, let's talk more about what it takes to see hidden patterns. Or better yet, why people can't see what's right in front of them. Let me illustrate this by telling you one of Chrétien de Troyes's stories. His tales were the foundation for the English legends about King Arthur, the Knights of the Round Table, and the quest for the Holy Grail. One of them is about Perceval, or Parsifal as he is often called.

"Parsifal was a Welshman, the only surviving son of a widow who lived in the Waste Forest. His two brothers had become knights and had been killed in combat, so his mother was terrified that Parsifal would suffer the same fate. She isolated him from any contact with the world, and he grew up incredibly naïve and innocent. He never asked questions or strayed far from home because his mother told him not to. One day he bumped into one of King Arthur's knights riding through the Waste Forest and was immediately consumed with the desire to become like him. For the first time, he disobeyed his mother. He followed the knight out of the forest to find the king and become a knight himself.

"Parsifal knew little about what was involved in becoming a knight, but that didn't stop him. He arrived at King Arthur's court with only the rudiments of training in the art of battle, and he immediately challenged the most experienced knights in Arthur's kingdom. That's why Chrétien called him Parsifal, which means 'innocent fool'.

"Surprisingly, Parsifal defeated them all and quickly gained respect as a mighty warrior. But that was only the beginning. After his initial triumphs, Parsifal encountered something that changed his life. While on a journey home to visit his mother, he found his path blocked by a deep river. He was searching for a way across when he noticed two men in a small fishing boat. He asked them if there was a ford or a bridge nearby. They told him there was no way to cross the river for some distance, but one of the men invited him to stay the night in his home, which turned out to be a great castle.

"Parsifal entered the castle and was welcomed by the man from the boat, who was now dressed as a nobleman and being carried by servants on a stretcher. The nobleman, called the Fisher King by his subjects, invited Parsifal to sit and dine at a sumptuous feast. A procession entered the hall, led by two servants carrying brilliantly lit candelabras. Following them was a beautiful maiden. With two hands she carried a golden wine cup covered with precious stones. It was the legendary Holy Grail, but Parsifal didn't know this. He sat silently watching the procession, remembering his mother's instructions not to ask questions. While they ate, the Grail was carried back and forth before them during each course of their feast. Parsifal never asked what the Grail was or who was supposed to drink from it."

Frank paused and looked at me. "Seeing any patterns in Parsifal's story, Neil?"

I nodded. "He sure wasn't very curious, was he? Never asked the Fisher King what was going on."

He smiled and continued.

"After the meal the servants prepared a bed for Parsifal in the great hall, and when they were done the nobleman left him, carried out by his servants on his stretcher. Once again, Parsifal asked no questions.

"In the morning, Parsifal woke up to an empty castle. Not a single person could be found. He went to the chamber where the nobleman had been carried the previous night. He shouted and knocked for a long while, but no one answered. Everyone had disappeared. Outside the castle he found his horse saddled, his lance and shield ready, and the drawbridge of the castle lowered so he could leave.

"As Parsifal rode away from the castle, he met a weeping maiden holding the head of a slain knight. She told him the story of the Fisher King, the nobleman who owned the mysterious castle. The Fisher King had been wounded years ago in both of his thighs by a lance and was consumed by pain. The only way he could bear the pain was to go fishing each day. The maiden asked if Parsifal had seen the Holy Grail procession while he was in the castle.

"When Parsifal said he'd seen it, but had asked no questions, the maiden was dismayed. If Parsifal had only asked the right question about the Fisher King and the Grail, he would have freed the king from his pain, and the entire kingdom would have been released from its curse! Upset by her accusation, Parsifal left the maiden and rode off in a state of confusion.

"From that point in Chrétien's story, Parsifal went on many more quests, but he never forgot the Fisher King. Finally, he decided to undo his failure to ask the right question in the mysterious castle, and he made an oath that he would engage in no more knightly contests until he found the Holy Grail and freed the Fisher King and his kingdom. He vowed not to abandon his quest for any reason.

"De Troyes never completed the story of Parsifal's quest. He left off writing mid-sentence, so we don't know how the story ended. Four other writers added endings later, each completing the myth differently. In one of the endings— the one I like—Parsifal eventually finds his way back to the hidden castle, sees the Grail again, asks the right question, and frees the Fisher King from his suffering.

"So Neil, does Parsifal's story help you understand more about what it takes to see hidden patterns?"

I thought about Parsifal arriving at a river he couldn't cross and meeting the Fisher King. That was unusual, but how was it connected to seeing patterns?

Out of the corner of my eye I saw the flight attendant hovering over us. She asked very softly whether we wanted any snacks. I think she was also giving us a subtle hint to be quiet. Frank glanced at me, and I shook my head.

"Parsifal's encounter with the Fisher King started it all," I said, "but I don't see what it has to do with seeing patterns, Frank."

"What do you think Chrétien was hinting at in Parsifal's failure to ask questions about the Grail procession?"

"I suppose he was saying that if you don't ask questions, you'll miss something that might be very important."

I wasn't used to this. People usually just explained things to me. Why didn't he just come right out with the answer instead of playing annoying guessing games?

He must have seen that he had pushed me far enough, because he let up on the questions for a moment.

"Let me help you. Parsifal had a very peculiar way of thinking. He didn't think for himself, and he didn't ask questions, because that's what his mother had instructed him to do. In effect, Chrétien was saying, isn't this odd behavior—encountering things without questioning them?"

He looked at me, gauging my reaction. I noticed little laugh wrinkles at the corners of his eyes and thought, This guy's on my side; he's not my opponent.

25

That helped, and I cooled down. "So, you're saying that Chrétien was trying to help us understand how important it is to turn off our autopilot. Otherwise, we'll never see new patterns! Is that right?"

He smiled broadly, and I knew I'd finally gotten his point. His way of teaching might work, after all.

"Bulls-eye! Chrétien knew that it's very difficult for us to see past our own peculiar ways of thinking. We invent rules about what we're certain and what we are allowed to question, and program our autopilot. Parsifal created the rule that he must be silent and not question his mother's advice. He was old enough to make up his own mind, and his mother wasn't with him anymore, but he still followed this outdated rule. Chrétien hinted that when we ask questions that go beyond the boundary of our thinking, it will change the way we see things. If we pursue these questions long enough, they will eventually transform us. And as we make the transformational journey, like Parsifal, we may even heal wounded kings and kingdoms."

Frank was finally beginning to make sense.

"I get everything except for that last part about healing kings and kingdoms. I have to be ready to question things, even things that I have known my whole life and am certain about. Otherwise there may be something important I'm supposed to find, like Parsifal, which I will never see."

Frank smiled again, then got up and walked to the back of the plane. I sat, almost like I was in a trance, and tried to come up with some things that I wanted to question. I couldn't think of any.

When he came back, the flight attendants were serving breakfast, and we didn't resume our conversation. Later, just before we landed, I asked Frank how long he was going to be in Sydney. I wanted to have dinner with him and talk some more. We agreed to meet at his hotel the following week.

As we were landing at Kingsford-Smith Airport, a strong crosswind made the plane bounce when we came down through the clouds. Just before touching down, a strong gust of wind tilted the wings over to one side. If that wing touched the runway, we would crash! I felt myself leaning, as if trying to help the pilot balance the plane. We landed safely, and I suddenly thought how lucky we were that the pilot had learned to fly *without* the 747's autopilot. It made me wonder if fear of crashing is why so many people stay on autopilot their whole life.

As I caught a cab into Sydney, I kept thinking about Frank. Why had he spent so much time with me? What was in it for him? Was I in a rut? Was it possible that I might encounter something that would change my life, just as Parsifal did? That *was* the question, wasn't it? Could there be some kind of fork in the road up ahead, some decision I would have to make about whether to go on a quest like Parsifal? I'd never asked myself such questions before. I had no doubt about one thing, however: Frank had me hooked.

Chapter 4

Sydney was spectacular, as always. I stayed at the Hyatt near Circular Quay, and early each morning I watched the sun bathe the Opera House in brilliant light. The ideas that Frank and I had talked about on the plane seemed out of place here. Sydney isn't thoughtful. It lives for the moment and doesn't seem to care about unanswerable questions. The average Sydneysider's view of life fit mine perfectly back then—no worries, so long as the property market keeps going up.

I was looking forward to seeing Frank. With his unusual stories and provocative conversation, he had caught my attention. I couldn't fit him into any category—casual airline buddy? Guru? New Age dreamer? I could usually size up people pretty quickly, but he defied description, which puzzled me.

He was waiting for me where we had agreed, in the ground-floor lounge of the Sheraton on the Park. I saw him first, sprawled out reading a newspaper with half a beer in front of him. When he saw me, he put the paper to one side and started to stand, but I waved him down. He shook my hand and seemed genuinely delighted to see me.

After we exchanged a few observations about our hotels and Sydney's incredible weather, I ordered a beer, and he began the same friendly cross-examination he had used on the plane. His approach made me feel vaguely responsible for achieving something, but what?

"So, have you had any more ideas about Parsifal?" He had an expectant look on his face, and looking back, I realize now that his curiosity and interest in my opinions created a kind of magnetism that drew me to him.

I said that I hadn't thought much about it; I had been really busy with work. We sat quietly for a moment, and he seemed to ponder something. Then, having apparently satisfied himself, he launched into another story.

"Well, let me tell you about someone like yourself named Elena. She was so busy that she almost met herself coming and going. Sound familiar?"

Busy is the name of the game these days Frank, I thought. I nodded and he continued his story.

*

"I first saw Elena right here, in this lobby, carrying a computer case in one hand and pulling what she called her 'wheelie-wheelie' with the other. I was waiting for someone, and she caught my eye because of her get-out-of-my-way stride. She had flowing red hair, was fairly tall, and wore a dark, serious suit. She was a real knock-out, and she held my attention until she got in the elevator.

"The next morning, I went for breakfast at the Cosmopolitan in Double Bay, and I saw her again, striding down the sidewalk toward the café. Didn't this woman ever slow down? When she sat at the table right next to me, I knew I had to meet her. I didn't have to figure out how to break the ice, because she looked over at my plate and asked me what I was eating. 'The Cosmo's special Ricotta hot cakes, the best in the world. And very crisp bacon. I have this breakfast every time I come to Sydney.' We ended up having a number of coffees that morning, and by the time our conversation was over, we'd arranged to have dinner later that week.

"Over breakfast I learned that she was an executive in a global corporation—like you—and traveled continuously. She was based in Hong Kong, but frequently visited Sydney, Tokyo, Shanghai, Singapore, and Taipei. Her computer was her office. She was in marketing, but she was a tech-head too. I especially remember one thing she said that morning. 'My goal is to cram as much into my life as three normal people.' She was a skier, a scuba diver, and a competitive sailor, and she had a personal trainer to push her to her physical limits. She intended to do the triathlon. She was studying yoga. She dated a number of men across Asia. She read three newspapers every day and surfed the internet constantly. Last of all, she was a workaholic.

"She told me all this in a rapid-fire burst of words, almost as if it was her standard practice to get past the introductions as fast as possible and into the good stuff. Maybe she was trying to see if the person she was talking to could compete with her. I told her about myself, but didn't try to match her accomplishments, because I couldn't. We became friends and still see each other occasionally. And I fell in love with her too, but from a distance. Courtly love, it used to be called. Elena taught me something important: a new meaning for meeting yourself coming and going.

"As I got to know her better over the years, Elena became a very different person. In fact, my theory is she *had* to change, because she experienced so many roles simultaneously: executive, athlete, adventurer, lover, and others. Have you read Thomas Merton? He was a trappist monk and a famous spiritual guide. He had an insight that I like: In our lives we go from innocence to experience and back to innocence. That's what I think happened to Elena. She found her lost innocence—collided with a long-hidden part of herself—among all her roles and experiences. I think she had to, to learn how to truly live."

I hadn't heard of Merton, and I didn't like the word 'innocence'. I wanted Elena's story to be about something that interested me, not naiveté or whatever innocence meant. I must have scowled, because he smiled at me.

"Merton's quote annoys you, Neil. What does a monk know about life in the fast lane, or running a successful business? Isn't success all about getting more and more experience? Knowledge is power. Knowledge is the ticket to wealth. Do I have it right?"

I thought, absolutely! In the real world, the people with the most power and knowledge win. Naïve people are losers. If you wanted to create really big ripples in the world, then the more smarts, information, and power you have the better. You needed to be plugged in, be turned on, and adapt to life at warp speed. That was how the real world worked, and how organizations had to operate to be successful. To believe anything else was nonsense.

Frank answered his own question. "But don't you agree that 'innocence' is an interesting word? It's used so rarely in our society that it's shockingly fresh. Makes you stop and ask questions. How can you go back to innocence once you leave childhood? Why would someone like Elena want to become innocent again anyway?"

I had no idea. Becoming innocent certainly sounded like an odd thing to do for a highly competent and motivated person like the woman Frank described.

Frank's mobile rang. He apologized but took the call anyway. He wandered around the lobby listening and responding to the caller's requests. I guessed he was making an appointment. When he'd finished, he sat down.

"Sorry about that, Neil. We don't really have much control over our lives anymore, do we? Anyway, about three years after we met in Sydney, I ran into Elena in Shanghai, and we had dinner in a German restaurant near the Bund. Have you been there?"

I'd been to Shanghai, but not a German restaurant. He continued his story.

"Elena didn't seem quite herself. I sensed she wanted to tell me something that was difficult for her to explain. She couldn't find the right words, she said. They would make what happened seem trivial. Words like 'finding herself' or 'getting in touch with herself'. She hated that pop psychology stuff. We sat there quietly. I didn't want to question her because that might've derailed her chain of thought. She was struggling to deal with a surprising insight into herself, and that took time.

"Eventually, she told me about a dream she'd had that was bothering her. I remember it exactly as she told it to me. She was sitting near the front of an old-fashioned theater, like the ones in London's Strand. Purple plush. Faintly musty. Worn seats and faded tapestries. There was only one other person in the theater, seated behind her, about five rows back. Elena could sense the other person watching her. She turned around and looked. It was a woman. Suddenly, Elena recognized that it was herself! She didn't actually see the face of the observer; she just knew the observer was another Elena. There were two Elenas in the theater!

"She turned away from Elena the observer and walked up the steps onto the stage. There was no scenery, but the stage was well lit, as if a performance was about to begin. She stood and looked out into the dark theater. The other Elena was still watching her and also seemed to be waiting for the show to begin. But the Elena on stage didn't know her lines or what role she was supposed to play! Then she woke up.

She told me she couldn't figure it out, but if she could, she was afraid she wouldn't like the explanation.

"I asked her what she thought it meant. She looked at me but didn't answer. I remember thinking how self-confident she'd been in Sydney, and I wondered how meeting herself in a dream could have such an effect on her.

"Finally, she responded. 'I actually have a lot of theories. I even looked up the images in a dream dictionary, and that gave me more ideas. The thing is, dreams conceal their real meaning. I read that when you dream, you're working to resolve something you can't or won't allow yourself to recognize in your waking life. The thing I can't explain is why did one Elena go up onto the stage and the other Elena just watch? What was supposed to happen?' Do you want me to take a guess? I asked. She looked at me very directly, as if she was calculating something.

"Then she replied, and the background noise in the restaurant almost kept me from hearing her. 'I don't know if I want you to. It might be better not to know what the play was about and why my other self was watching me. It's obvious that I need to know, though. I keep asking people what the dream means'.

"I decided to tell her my theory. All the demanding roles she played in her life were creating the Elena that was on the stage. I called her Role-Elena. The observer in the shadows I called In-Elena. [2] There are many different explanations that people have for these two sides of themselves.[3] I could have told her what they were, but the point of the dream seemed to me to be the distance she

35

sensed between Role-Elena and In-Elena. Not just a few rows in a theater, but a distance much wider.

"There was a chasm—and it couldn't be easily crossed—between the Role-Elena she was playing every day and the mysterious In-Elena. That's one reason why In-Elena watched her. She knew that Role-Elena could only see her in a dream, from a distance.

"Many people talk about being more integrated, as if that means managing their life better, keeping all their Role-selves in harmony. Balancing their work and their life and so on. But that's not what integrated really means. It means bringing these two very different sides of ourselves together, using processes that we hardly understand at all. There isn't any way to easily fit your In-self into your roles, like fitting a piece into a puzzle. It would be like trying to freeze-dry a mountain breeze and then, after adding water, expecting it to be there as it was in reality. Our In-selves are always outside our everyday thinking. They care about us and influence us, just as Role-Elena was touched by In-Elena, and they are amused at how seriously we take our roles. All this is generally hidden from us, however."

I broke in on Frank's story.

"Hold on. How did you know all these things? You were talking to her as if you had some special knowledge about In-Elena versus Role-Elena. How could you? She didn't understand, and she was inside her own skin!"

Frank grinned at me.

"Neil, sometimes you see things so clearly that I really am in awe of you. Great question. The answer is, of course, that I didn't—and couldn't—know precisely what was going on. If I had some secret knowledge, there wouldn't be any mystery connected to In-Elena, or In-Frank, or In-Neil for that matter. She was hoping that I could solve her mystery, but I couldn't. All I could do was provide her with some ideas about her dream that might be useful to her. It turned out that my explanation pretty much ended our conversation. Explanations usually do that to mystery. So we finished our dinner, walked back to our hotel, and parted."

I could imagine Frank and Elena walking slowly arm in arm and still talking. In my mind she was listening intently to him, hoping he had some answers. He was, well, being Frank, not really answering her questions, keeping things vague. I wondered how Elena felt when he left her that night. Frank kept going with his Elena story.

"The next time I saw her was about nine months later. She sent me an email saying she had a stopover in London, and would I like to meet her for dinner. Absolutely! I suggested a pizza place near my flat that I liked, and we met there on a late Sunday afternoon in May. When I arrived, she was already there, getting a lot of attention from a young waiter. He left after we ordered a bottle of Australian Shiraz— in honor of our first meeting in Sydney, I guess. She said she'd been doing a lot of thinking about my theory about her dream—Role-Elena and In-Elena.

"It had occurred to her that before she went to school, she was mainly aware of In-Elena. She was the one who lived every moment of her life, except for when she was in her Being-in-a-Family role. Her mother set the rules for that role, telling her how to behave as a good little girl.

"But she could still faintly remember what it felt like for In-Elena to wake up and have nothing to do—no agenda, no demanding roles, no performance standards, nothing. She was free to be who she wanted. She could imagine In-Elena walking outside early in the morning. She didn't have shoes on, and the dew on the grass tickled her feet. In her imagination she saw a blue jay chasing another bird. The clouds were incredibly white and fluffy. It was In-Elena who lived much of her waking life each day when she was a young child, experiencing things exactly as they were without trying to name them. She was fresh and innocent, not yet shaped by what she should do or how she should perform—except when she was around her mother.

"Thinking about her life now, it seemed that Role-Elena was the only one present. Her days were consumed by the demands of her roles and the need to be better or smarter or more beautiful or healthier. She couldn't remember the last time the dew had tickled her bare feet. What had happened to In-Elena? Maybe that's what her dream was trying to tell her; 'Hey, In-Elena is still here! Make time for me!'

"In-Frank nudged me as I listened to her. I remembered my own boyhood, growing up on a farm. As far back as I could remember, it seemed like young Farmer-Frank had chores. Not much time for In-Frank to be free like In-Elena. I was in the farmer role from the earliest time I could remember. But then I saw myself walking in the woods at the far corner of our farm and sitting in a clearing that I imagined no one else knew about. I saw tadpoles in the creek, and oak leaves were blowing across the ground and forming patterns, then blowing away. That was In-Frank; I knew how Elena felt.

"I tossed an idea at her. What if the demands from her roles were always far more intense than the dew or the birds? Wouldn't her life automatically become centered on meeting those demands?

"She thought about that. 'Yes, that's probably what happened. I went to school, and my student role began to shape my life. I spent more and more time with my friends, and we learned the rules of life together. You're right, Frank. That's how In-Elena disappeared.'

"I said, 'But In-Elena probably didn't completely go away. What do you think?' Elena didn't seem to want to talk about it anymore so we finished our pizza and wandered around the West End for a while, then went our separate ways. It was two years before I saw her again.

"We met again in London and went to a play. I think that evening was secretly arranged by our In-selves, in memory of the theater dream that had started her down a path toward meeting In-Elena. We saw a wonderful production of *Cyrano de Bergerac*. We could only get seats in the first row, which almost put us into the action on the stage. At the end, when Cyrano dies in the arms of Roxanne, the director used leaves falling from an autumnal tree in the convent garden to create a melancholy atmosphere. One of the orange and brown paper leaves floated off the stage and landed at our feet.

"After the performance I picked it up and gave it to Elena. The play must have infected In-Frank with Rostand's poetry, because I said to her, 'This leaf will remind you of Cyrano's In-self—his panache, his passion, and his hidden unrequited love.' She took it, and her eyes became shiny, and so did mine. She lightly held her Cyrano's arm as we walked out of the theater. Neither of us talked for a while. The play and the moment were too special for words.

"Later, we went back to the Westbury Hotel where she was staying and had a coffee in the lobby. She took the leaf from her purse. 'You know, Frank, this leaf has other meanings for me besides connecting Cyrano and our friendship. I haven't told you yet what has happened to me but leaves also remind me of In-Elena.'

"Elena looked down at the leaf for a moment, and then began her story. 'A year ago I went skiing in the Bavarian alps, near Garmisch. Such a wonderful, magical place. I was by myself and spent eight hours a day on the slopes. I got so good that I could get down the black runs with pretty good form. Then, in a stupid moment, I took a chance on a very steep slope and fell. I shattered my leg. A comminuted fracture, the surgeon called it, a fracture that results in three or more bone fragments. They had to operate and put pins in my leg. I was in the hospital at Munich for two weeks, and then they sent me to a rehab center in an old German mansion near Nuremberg. It used to belong to the IG Farben company but was taken from them after the war. I was there for two months. My leg was so weak that I had to learn to walk again.

"'Besides Physical Therapy twice a day, I had nothing to do. I didn't have my computer, so I couldn't work. All my Role-selves probably went into hibernation from boredom.

40

As part of the therapy, I took long walks in an ancient oak forest that surrounded the mansion. It was a mild winter and little snow had fallen in that part of Germany. The leaves from the old trees were everywhere. I used to wade through them as if they were waves in the ocean—and I'd meet In-Elena!

"'I guess it happened because Role-Elena didn't know what she was supposed to do. The only activities were physio, eating, sleeping, reading and walking in the woods. One day I realized that I was on that theater stage I had dreamed about, and there was no play because there was no role for me! I knew why the other Elena was observing me. She was waiting for me to notice her. In-Elena could make herself known because my Role-selves were asleep. So I began to have conversations with her. Do you think that's strange?'

"I smiled at her to let her know I understood. 'Here's another interesting thing. In-Elena didn't see things the way my Role-selves did. She hadn't been involved in their activities, and she hadn't learned the rules they lived by. She could still notice the leaves tickling her ankles as she walked through that German forest. In a way, she hadn't grown up, but in another way, she was wiser. Frank, I can't explain what it's like after so many years to suddenly experience things new and fresh. The leaves and the forest—and the leaf you gave me tonight too.'

"I told her that that was what innocence was all about. She nodded, but didn't comment. I realized later I should have thanked her for what she had said. Anyway, the moment passed, and she continued.

"'I spent a lot of time with In-Elena during rehab. She wanted to know what I did and what my world away from the forest was like. I learned much more from her than she did from me in those months. A lot of it I can't explain. Let's just say I learned what was at my center. The only word I can think of to describe In-Elena is lovable. That may sound odd to you. I always thought it was what I did and how much I achieved that made people respect me. In-Elena is lovable just as she is. You can't imagine how much peace and relief that gives me. And strength.

"'Frank, you can see why the leaf you gave me tonight means so much to me. It's a gift from In-Frank to In-Elena. That's intimacy, sharing our In-selves. Intimacy with others is the most real thing there is. I hadn't known that before I met In-Elena.'

"That's Elena's story, Neil. She and I still stay in touch. She keeps my leaf in her purse. Her stride has slowed a little, but not much. She says she isn't cramming so much into her life these days. She makes time to be with In-Elena."

Was that it? Didn't she change more dramatically? I shook my head slowly in disappointment and looked around the lobby, trying to avoid Frank's eyes.

"You're let down," Frank said. "What did you want her to do? Become some kind of Mother Teresa dropout and leave all her roles behind to work with poor people? She was changed—I saw it, and she knew it too. But she also stayed in the roles that she loved and was suited for. They were who she was too. In-Elena was right there with her, arguing about the autopilot rules she followed, asking provocative questions, giving her hints."

He paused to give me time to think of my own questions. I didn't have any. I was thinking about what Elena must have gone through after she changed, and what it must have been like in her hyper-busy life, trying to be successful and innocent at the same time, staying connected with In-Elena in the midst of organizational sound and fury. Much later, when I recalled her story, it seemed like I had seen a charming invitation in Elena, to know more about her. But at that moment I just felt unsettled, like a small part of my well-ordered world had suddenly become uncontrollable.

Chapter 5

The hotel lobby was still, as if, like me, it was waiting for what would happen next. Frank studied my face. I think he knew what was going on inside me; that's probably why he told Elena's story in the first place. He broke the spell by waving at the waiter and ordering two more beers. We waited quietly until the waiter brought them, and then Frank began again.

"Neil, let me tell you another story. It's about how I first met In-Frank long before I met Elena."

I was relieved; I needed to fill the uncomfortable hole that Elena's story had created in me with something. I nodded for him to go ahead, so he did.

*

"It started in Houston. I was a NASA engineer. It's important to understand some things about engineers. They are trained to think very precisely, work step by step, and not jump to conclusions. They test each new idea to see if it computes— is there an equation that can explain this? And they love puzzles, the harder the better.

"After I left Houston, I went to work for a consulting company as a project troubleshooter. Because I'd solved tough problems at NASA, they thought I could help other people solve theirs. They were right. I was pretty good at it. I had the ability to quickly see patterns—what was going on in complex situations—and I was analytical about finding the root causes of problems and their solutions.

"Two things happened that started me thinking outside the engineering box I had constructed for myself. One, I traveled all over the world to help clients, which gave me a lot of time on planes and in hotels to read. I probably got an informal PhD in philosophy from all that reading, searching for answers to a problem I could hardly see. The second thing was an insight I had. If I could see patterns in my projects so easily, why not look for patterns in the lives of people who had made a real difference? That's what I wanted to do in my life. I could find out why these people decided to do what they did. Suddenly, it seemed very important to me to get a firm idea about what made successful people tick. I had a sense that understanding this might be life-changing, so like any engineer I wanted to test my ideas thoroughly."

He stopped to give me a chance to digest what he had said thus far. I thought I understood. If you studied the biography of someone who had made a significant difference—someone like Lincoln or Churchill or Einstein—you could possibly find out why they did the things they did and how they were able to impact the future so dramatically. It made a lot of sense.

Frank continued. "I consumed stories about famous leaders; they were the ones who interested me in the beginning. Then I read about inventors and people who created long-lasting changes in the world. I'd started with the assumption that I would read about well-known people who had impacted the future in a major way. Then it occurred to me that there was another path, and I started to read about people whose everyday lives had undergone a profound change. What had happened to them? That's what led me to St Francis of Assisi—that, plus his name was Frank.

"I saw a film about him—*Brother Sun and Sister Moon*. There were two images in that film I couldn't forget: Francis stripping himself naked in the town square in front of everyone he knew and leaving everything in his old life behind, and the most powerful image, Francis dressed in rags rebuilding an old ruined church in the middle of a snowy winter. Doing it all by himself at first, then gradually joined by others who wanted to go on the same mysterious quest that Francis was on. Somehow, those images in the film seemed to be connected with me. I certainly didn't think of becoming a monk or dropping out of society. I just needed to figure out why Francis did such strange things.

"It might have been fate or something else, but I was assigned to do a project in Rome. You guessed it. I drove up to Assisi. I wanted to see the place where Francis had lived. It was very rugged, but beautiful: steep wooded hills with deep

47

valleys—unforgettable. You can understand why someone would want to leave everything behind and live a simple life in those surroundings. I went into an old church that had souvenirs for sale. I bought a plastic prayer card that showed Francis wearing a brown monk's robes and rope sandals. I still carry it in my wallet.

"When I left Assisi, I felt unsettled, like I'd forgotten something or left something behind. I tried to figure out my feelings as I drove back to Rome. Maybe it was the peace in Assisi I missed. The world I lived in was complex; Francis's world was much simpler. Of course, that wasn't really true. Medieval Italy had its own brand of complexity. Francis created his own space and time, simplified things, asked questions that no one could answer, and pursued innocence. Maybe that was what I yearned for. But Expert-Frank didn't want simplicity or innocence. He was recognized as an expert because he could see patterns in complexity; life had to be complicated for him to be successful.

"A question kept turning over and over in my mind: What had persuaded Francis to change his life so radically? He was the son of a wealthy merchant, and he had tried to join the Crusades. Imprisonment and illness had interfered with his plans, but something else led him to strip naked in the center of Assisi. What was it?"

He paused again to give me time to think. I heard Executive-Neil muttering, Oh boy. Here it comes. Frank's really a monk or something weird like that. But he wasn't; he was inviting me to imagine what he had discovered.

"My way of resolving this question was to throw myself into reading. I won't bore you with all the different ideas I came across, but I began to see a different pattern. In the modern world, unlike Francis' world, we are inundated with huge volumes of words and information. It's easy to float along in this surging sea of words and think you actually know something. But you only know *about* things through someone else's words. You don't actually know them yourself.

"As I thought more about it, it seemed that Francis had left behind other people's ideas of what life was all about to find out for himself. He wanted to know life—and God—directly, so he left all his roles behind. When Francis Bernardone was in his Son-Role, his father's words told him what life was about. But he left behind other roles too. One role he and his friends had invented was living a life of honor. They said life was about going to the Crusades and fighting and dying for a cause. He left behind Religious-Francis as well. Not that he rejected what the Church believed, because Francis remained a religious man, but he left behind rules for how to live his beliefs. He wanted to *know* God, not merely know *about* God. This last point struck me. Until that point, I had only wanted to know about life, not live it.

"In time, I gradually saw something else. We control our lives with our words about life. In the metaphor you and I are using, Neil, words are how we program our autopilot. Words are *about* things. Words are mind things. Suddenly, like Francis, I wanted to know real things, directly.

"That was the turning point for me. I had to leave words and books behind for a while. I didn't want to experience something and immediately say to myself, 'Oh, that's just like something I read.' I didn't want to answer questions using my autopilot. All of a sudden I realized that I had been keeping life at a distance by reading *about* it. Now I wanted to *live* it! My stripping myself naked was leaving books and familiar ideas behind, at least for a while.

"I continued to do my consulting job while all this mental fermentation was taking place. I didn't fully understand what I was seeking, but at least I stopped reading. I took long walks. I sat quietly on park benches. It was very hard for me not to analyze things. Expert-Frank was desperate to find some patterns and the root cause of my unease. But I refused to analyze my experiences, not wanting to add more words to the pile. So I simply waited.

"In-Frank was there waiting for me, but I had to strip away my equations and complex ideas to meet him. He didn't much care for mind things. It took a long time, but I finally found a good, simple, and—as Elena says—lovable person at my center. He's been present to me for almost thirty years now—and I still feel a thrill when he makes himself known to me!"

I felt uneasy. Why was he telling me these very personal things? I had only known him a few days. How did he want me to respond? I didn't want to change anything. I just wanted to listen to his stories. As he continued, he was so wrapped up in his story that I'm not sure he was even aware I was sitting next to him.

"Once I became conscious of In-Frank, I quickly realized I wanted to do something like St. Francis had done. The image of Francis rebuilding that tumbledown church wouldn't leave me, and then the idea hit—I would rebuild wounded organizations! In a way, I was already doing that by finding patterns and root causes for problems and helping people learn how to change their organizations. But I realized I wanted to go much deeper than that.

"I began to see problems in organizations that I had missed while on autopilot. Organizations of all kinds—companies, governments, schools, and sometimes even churches—were neglecting, even inadvertently hurting people who worked inside them. Managers didn't see their employees as special in and of themselves. They only valued them for what they contributed to the organization. I realized that organizations, at least in some ways, were inhumane. That was a shock. I had to do something about it! That's when I committed myself to creating a gentle revolution in organizations."

I must have had a grimace of disbelief on my face, because he interrupted his story.

"You don't see organizations like this, do you, Neil? Don't answer. I understand. Neither did I until I met In-Frank and discovered that there wasn't any place for him in the organizations where I consulted. If he is good—and I knew deep down that was true—why isn't he welcome? Something in organizations seems to oppose or at least make no room for innocence. That's another pattern I saw after a lot of reflection. Organizations become inhumane when the people in them become overly performance-focused, calloused, hard, unthinking, and uncaring."

All of a sudden I felt I couldn't continue down this path with Frank. He seemed to be demanding something I didn't want to give, almost manipulating me to agree to something outlandish. Of course innocence and his gentle revolution (whatever that was) had no place in organizations. My company wasn't a support group or social club! If that's what he meant by wounded or inhumane, I couldn't buy it. My company was a moneymaking system for its stockholders and owners who expected its workers to be focused on efficiency, not on having fun or caring for people. It was my job to make it work that way. And I wasn't being inhumane as Frank seemed to be saying.

"I know this is difficult for you," he said, "but stay with me. You'll begin to see this for yourself, I'm sure. If not, you can always disagree. Maybe the gentle revolution isn't your cup of tea."

Okay, Frank, I thought. I've come this far, and I suppose it's harmless to listen to your stories. After all, they can't change me against my will. So I nodded, but he knew I was struggling.

"I had a similar reaction in the beginning, but I finally understood that healing large and complicated organizations takes special people—innocent fools like Parsifal—who are willing to take on nearly impossible challenges. It's too hard for people in power. They think they need to keep things under control to meet the demands of the owners and the market. The gentle revolution I'm talking about seems to threaten their power. You need chutzpah to take it on. Most of us can only try to follow the lead of innocent fools, and even that's difficult.

"That's it, Neil. That's how I met In-Frank. You can probably guess by now why I tell my stories. I want to inspire people like you to meet their In-selves, maybe find out that they're a Parsifal and get involved with the gentle revolution. But it's only an invitation, not a demand. If I seem to be pressing you, I'm sorry. I have no right to do that."

We sat quietly for several minutes. His apology calmed me down. I didn't like the term 'innocent fool', and I didn't have the slightest inclination to bring Frank's so-called healing into my organization. I especially didn't like the word 'intimacy'. I thought it meant that you might have to give away some part of yourself to someone. What was the payoff?

But maybe Frank was casting a different light on it. Maybe intimacy was connected with intimations and hints—sensing and relating to the In-person in another person, like he did with Elena. That could be the payoff, a reason for sharing your own In-self with someone. I later recognized that In-Neil was inviting me to meet him in that insight. But I was truly stuck in a rut, didn't want to meet him at that moment, and didn't know how to go about it even if I did.

By this time Frank and I were hungry, so we went to dinner. We chatted more that evening about his story and Elena's, but I was still mulling over his suggestion that I might be a candidate for the gentle revolution. I thought of Frank sitting quietly on a park bench waiting for something he couldn't describe. Definitely not my style. Maybe our conversations had reached the end of the line.

We didn't arrange to meet again, yet for some unknown reason, I hoped we would. As Sherlock Holmes once said, 'The mystery is afoot, Watson'. Frank was slowly luring me into solving a mystery that I didn't even know existed!

Chapter 6

It's funny how our minds work. If something new comes to our attention, we begin to notice it everywhere. Suppose you see a red Saab convertible you really like. Suddenly wherever you look, you see Saabs. Something like that happened to me after hearing Frank's stories. Odd things appeared in my cave and demanded to be accounted for. I didn't instantly become a particularly thoughtful person, but I knew Frank had stirred something up.

About a month after I returned from Australia, I asked a young woman named Diane to head a change project. I approved the project because we needed greater efficiency in processing service calls. Our call centers were already excellent according to the benchmarks, but we needed to create ways to make them even better. One of my managers recommended I interview Diane to lead the project. She was bright and enthusiastic, and she wanted the job, so I appointed her. A week later she asked to meet with me.

She was tall, blonde, vivacious, and energetic, and she entered my office confidently with her laptop under her arm. Oh no, I thought, not another PowerPoint presentation.

"Neil, I want you to see something on the internet. Lend me your LAN connection."

She plugged in, searched the net for a moment, and then came around to my side of the desk so we could both see. She pointed at the screen to make sure I was paying attention. It showed a website about women in the workplace, with a graph of some kind.

"See this part of the graph, Neil? It shows that when women keep their children in day care centers at work, they don't worry about them as much and become more productive. We have about fifty women in each of our call centers who have children, and I want to help them start day care centers. It'll cost about fifty thousand dollars for each center, and I figure we'll get productivity improvements that will pay off in just three months. You're the boss, so I want you to approve it."

She looked at me with eyes that said, well, get on with it!

I stared back at her, probably frowning. Who reviewed this?

"Diane, has anyone checked your figures?"

I liked the way her eyes sparkled when she smiled. "I thought you'd ask me that. Yes, my team checked them. They're all correct."

Her team checked them? What about finance?

"We have a process for reviewing proposals like yours, a committee that meets once a month. This looks good. Why don't you present it to them?" I was trying to figure out how to get her out of my office.

She smiled confidently. "I thought you'd say that too. I talked to the guy who runs that committee, and he thinks this is a good idea. Says we should go ahead with it and present what we have accomplished at the next meeting, if you give the okay."

She pushed, but in a nice way. I folded and agreed with the expenditure, and she left. That'll get rid of her, I thought. But it was just the beginning. The next week Diane was back.

"Do you know some of our parts are made in a sweatshop in Indonesia?"

This didn't sound like it was part of her project. "Where did you get that idea?" I was annoyed.

"On the internet, from a site that tracks US companies who use sweatshops. I was embarrassed to find our company was one of them."

She looked at me expectantly, as if she thought I would pick up the phone and call someone to fix the problem immediately.

"Diane, is this connected with your project?" I don't have time for this!

She didn't smile this time. Her eyes narrowed.

"Yes. My team discussed it in our last meeting. We decided it was wrong, and I told them I'd bring it to your attention."

They decided it was wrong. Who was running things, anyway? I felt like saying keep your nose out of things that don't concern you, but I didn't.

"I'd like you to look into this, Neil. When are you going to be ready to discuss it?"

My face must have flushed, because she smiled, but I kept my cool and said,

"In a few weeks."

"I'll give you a call in two weeks. Can I tell my team that you think using the sweatshop is wrong?"

Now she was really irritating me. Who was *she* to question *me* about right and wrong? Then I had a thought.

"How did you and your team decide it was wrong? Do you know the facts about that factory in Indonesia?"

That smile again. I felt provoked each time she smiled, because I knew she was a step ahead of me.

"The website shows comparisons between local wages in sweatshops and more humane factories in the same region. I can get the figures for you, but my team actually discussed the issues about our factory on a different basis. If we have childcare here in the United States, why shouldn't they have it in Indonesia? Their productivity would go up too. That seems fair. People in our company ought to be treated the same way, no matter where they live. That's what my team decided."

Her team decided! She kept saying that as if it should carry some weight. Didn't she know things just didn't work like that? Then I thought of Frank's wounded organization metaphor. Was I missing something here? *Were* we doing something wrong in Indonesia? I couldn't see it. Moreover, I couldn't let Diane take control away from management.

But instead of my usual response of stop wasting my time, I said, "Well, let me think about it and get back to you."

"Will that take two weeks too?" she snapped. "Or do you think you can decide on right and wrong faster than that?"

She smiled again, and that took a little of the sting out of her question, but not all of it. I grinned back at her weakly and tried not to react. Somehow, she kept gaining the upper hand, and now I was beginning to feel less certain about what was right and wrong in my company. Come to think of it, I hadn't ever used those words about what our business actually did—ouch! Frank, I need to talk to you!

I had the opportunity a few weeks later. I was in London on business and sent Frank an email to see if we could meet. He invited me to dinner, along with a few of his friends. I found my way to his home using an intricate map he'd sent. He lived in a hard-to-find mews just south of Hyde Park.

His housekeeper served a delicious roast. There were six of us that night: a novelist named Lillian, and her spouse (I forget his name and never found out what he did); a gay couple, Greg and Darren, who were in some kind of technology venture; myself; and Frank. We had fun at dinner, trading airline and other travel stories. I liked Frank's friends, but I wanted to talk to him alone about Diane's question about right and wrong. I didn't get a chance until later.

As his housekeeper cleared the dishes, we moved to the study where Frank served port and coffee. I wandered around the room looking at his extensive library. I recognized a few titles, but most were scholarly works.[4] I sat on a large leather divan next to Greg, where I could observe everyone else. Remembering Frank's story about Elena, it occurred to me that we were in a kind of theater. The stage was set, and all of us were about to learn more about our roles in some mysterious play Frank was directing.

Frank, our director, stood motionless in front of his cast until we were ready to give him our complete attention. Once we were still, he began.

"I was browsing through a used bookstore once and found an unusual book with dozens of offbeat stories. I think one of them would be interesting to discuss. Let me summarize it for you."

I wondered if the others had heard his other stories, but I didn't ask because Frank dove right into his story.

"A woman was on a quest searching for truth. She approached a professor in a well-known university and asked him to explain the meaning of truth. He proceeded to give her a lecture, quoting liberally from research and noted authors to show his education and understanding of the topic. The woman listened for a while and then said, 'No, please tell me in your own words, not those of others. What is the meaning of truth?' He couldn't answer, so she left and continued her search. The professor, realizing what had happened, closed his department, quit his job at the university, and went on his own quest in search of someone who knew the meaning of truth."

Frank looked directly at me with a question on his face, but I didn't react. Was I to be the foil he used to make his points? I figured I'd wait him out and make him show his hand. I'm good at power politics, Frank.

Finally, he said to me, "Well?"

I acted puzzled. "Well what?"

He grinned. The others rustled in their chairs, probably embarrassed that I seemed to be acting rudely.

"Neil, you're thinking that I'm trying to lead you somewhere. You're also thinking this is a game, and he who makes the last move wins. You want to see more moves on my part to improve your chances of winning. Am I right?"

He was right; I was trying to win and appear intelligent to the rest of the group. Did I think there was a prize for winning? Or was this just my usual combative way of handling challenges? These thoughts took a few seconds to register and Frank made another move without waiting for my answer.

"You *are* right. I *did* tell this story for a reason. I have a goal in mind, but it isn't to win. The metaphor of teacher and student in the story fits us, but you might be surprised at who is in each role. Neil, you and I both are like the woman searching for the meaning of truth. We have each known professors of various kinds and asked them what they knew about truth. For a little while on our journeys, I have shared stories with you about some of what I have observed, for some purpose as yet undecided by the two of us. That's the game we're playing. Do you agree?"

No one moved. I kept my eyes fixed on Frank, embarrassed that he had outmaneuvered me. I had to answer quickly.

"I haven't been asking any professors for the meaning of truth. I think your metaphor fails on that point."

"Oh, I didn't mean you asked real professors. Don't you read? Watch television? Have conversations at work? Don't you ever have a mental dialogue with the author or the news reporter or your work colleagues? Don't you sometimes ask yourself if what they said is really true?"

I thought about this for a moment. I did talk back to the newspaper or to the TV when something struck a chord.

I answered, "I suppose I do that sometimes, Frank."

"Okay. What if I told you that evaluating truth was an unavoidable mental process that happens every time something catches your attention? Think of the human brain as a computer, although it really isn't much like any computer most people are familiar with. Doesn't your brain examine every piece of data your senses receive for truth? Every word in every book or TV program or conversation? Just because you aren't fully conscious of the process doesn't mean it isn't going on. Isn't every one of your actions the result of tiny decisions you make about whether the data fits your situation?"

Lillian, the novelist, broke into our dialogue. "Frank, is this a theory you read about somewhere? Is it scientifically valid?"

I looked around the room. Everyone seemed captivated by Frank, like they were watching a famous lawyer interrogate a witness. He looked at Lillian, but it felt like he was still cross-examining me.

"Lillian, suppose the scientist you think I'm quoting was here with us tonight. Suppose you asked him whether his theory was true. He would quote a long list of references and experiments that backed up his point of view. In asking your question, aren't you like the lady in the fable asking the scientist to define truth? Do you think you would learn the truth from him? More importantly, do you think he, as a scientist, would claim to know the truth?"

Lillian glanced over at me with a raised eyebrow, then smiled at Frank.

"I guess you're right," she said. "Where is this taking us?"

"I suppose the truthful answer is it's taking us toward 11 pm and some interesting debate."

He stopped. I felt like the mainspring of the conversation had been tightly wound, and I jumped back in. "Look at all the books in your library, Frank. Isn't there truth in any of them? Otherwise, why do you buy them?"

"Oh, that's easy. They interest me. The authors tell me their stories, and we have quite a good conversation."

I wouldn't let go.

"You mean you never ask the truth question about them? Or do you mean you never get an answer?"

"I can't stop asking the truth question, as you call it. My brain works just like everyone else's. But that isn't a very important part of my conversation with authors or scientists. What are far more important to me are the insights that come from the dialogue."

Insights. That surprised me. Isn't an insight a glimmer of the truth received from the unconscious or some other source?

Greg chimed in, "Frank, I think you're splitting hairs here. What's the difference between an insight and the truth?"

"Good question. Anyone else want to answer? I don't want to hog the stage. After all, I think we've established that I don't own the truth, and neither does anyone else."

Darren broke in, "When I have an insight, a 'now I see it' experience, it usually seems like I've discovered something new, something that might be valuable. This is a signal to me to pay attention to the idea, evaluate it, perhaps take action or change something."

Frank beamed at Darren. I thought it was a pretty good answer too.

"So when an insight happens," I joined in, "we start a mental process to see if it's useful or valuable. Sometimes when I'm working on a business problem I can't solve, I put it aside for a few days, and the solution comes to me. It just jumps into my mind. But I still have to see if it makes sense, and if I can actually use it, and how much it's going to cost to make it work. I never ask if the insight is true, only if it's useful."

The group seemed to withdraw into their own personal worlds, as if trying to recall if insights played any role in their lives.

Frank stirred the pot some more. "Now, suppose you read a famous myth, say *The Odyssey* by Homer. Suppose the story of that ancient sailor's journey resonates with you and triggers some insight for you."

He quoted the opening line from memory: *Sing in me, Muse, and through me tell the story of that man skilled in all ways of contending, the wanderer, harried for years on end …*

"Does the fact that for thousands of years, Homer's poem has created insights in countless numbers of people have any importance? Was Homer trying to teach us something very wise in recounting Ulysses' story? Should we give more weight to insights triggered by *The Odyssey* than say those from a Beatles song?"

Lillian answered Frank, "When I write, I'm trying to say something I feel is true. The story usually comes from some inspiration I have, but I don't think it has any more weight or truth than any other story. No, I don't think the fact that Homer's story has been read by so many people for so long counts for anything."

I looked out the window into the dark alley that ran through the mews. I thought conversations like this were probably vestiges of what they once had been in this very urbane city. TV ratings showed that any insights received by most Londoners probably came from sitcoms. I doubted there were many insights of any value from them, and then wondered why I had decided that.

Frank continued to stir us. "What about *The Lord of the Rings*? Why have fifty million people read such a complex fantasy, one that doesn't even directly relate to our world? Tolkien always said he wasn't writing a story with a hidden meaning, that he was only trying to tell a coherent history of an imaginary Middle-earth. Doesn't the fact that so many people seem to receive something special from his myth mean anything? I could also say the same thing about a Beatles song, by the way. Isn't popularity, at least when it's long-lasting, some kind of hint that a song or story contains a deep truth?"

I started thinking about myths I'd heard. Frank's Parsifal story. There definitely was some kind of special feeling connected to it, like I was looking through a clouded window at something that was very important. Did Frank's stories contain truth, or did they just trigger insights better than most stories because he was so clever?

Frank summed up the question for us. "The truth in myths or the usefulness of insights they trigger—which is more important?"

Greg said, "I think it's their usefulness. We could spend the rest of our lives arguing whether something was true or not, but if we never acted differently or changed our behavior because of our insights, they would be a waste of time."

Lillian disagreed. "Is it only what each individual decides is useful? Isn't that the height of selfishness? What about Nazi Germany? A small band of evil men decided it was useful to get rid of Jews. If I remember right, they quoted the 'truth' from ancient Aryan books to condone their genocide."

"But useful doesn't mean you can do anything you want," Greg answered. "There are obviously limits. Hitler violated what most people see as right and wrong."

I agreed. What happened after a person had an insight—the process we used to judge what we might do with the new idea—was very important. Every person had to test his or her insights against a wider set of standards than their own selfish interests. They might decide to go against what everyone else thought was right, but they ought to consider the effects of their actions on other people too. That seemed to me to be some kind of universal rule. I also wondered why insights sometimes switched off our autopilot, persuading us to fly our lives in new directions, like Francis of Assisi's story did for Frank.

Lillian looked at her watch. "It's getting late, Frank. Do you want to wrap this up?"

I thought I knew what he was going to say, that there was no wrap up or answer to these questions. But he didn't.

"Can you stay for just a few more minutes, Lillian? I want to discuss one more thing." He looked around at the rest of us. "Are you all willing to stay a little bit longer?"

We nodded. He offered more drinks, but we all said no. I guess we wanted to hear Frank's next question.

"You must have heard the famous quote, 'Give me liberty or give me death!' Patrick Henry of Virginia used those words to help ignite the American War of Independence. I imagine he stumbled across something, an insight that liberty was at the core of what it meant to be human, or something like that. That if he didn't have liberty, he might as well die because he would cease to be human. He must have gone through the process we are discussing, deciding whether this insight into freedom was valid and useful in his life. Obviously, he decided it was.

"Here's my final question: Why do you think certain people make profoundly difficult and dangerous decisions based on their insights, and many others don't? Remember, many colonials in North America were loyalists, happy with their lives under the king. Unlike Patrick Henry, they had different ideas about liberty, and they weren't willing to risk very much to pursue it. Was it only the usefulness of the idea of liberty that triggered his passionate commitment to the revolution?"

I thought I saw where he was heading. He wanted us to wrestle with what creates courage—or foolishness—and commitment to dangerous undertakings like the gentle revolution he had told me about in Sydney. It reminded me that I wanted to ask him more about why he decided to repair wounded organizations.

Darren interrupted my thoughts. "Greg and I went through something like that. Should we openly tell people about our sexuality or not? It really wasn't anyone else's business. Telling people would probably be risky. We talked about it for a long time. I hadn't thought about it this way before, but maybe what Patrick Henry said applies to us. Give us liberty or give us death. Life lived as a lie is sub-human. I think we probably decided to tell people because not to do so would have been life-threatening for us. We might not be able to find truth, but it sure is easy to recognize lies!"

Frank smiled at Darren and nodded. I wondered whether I would ever feel so passionate about something that I would risk everything for an idea.

There didn't seem to be much more to say; Greg had summed up the evening. We all sat for a few more minutes chatting politely, but the party broke up soon afterwards. I hung around because I still wanted to talk to Frank about Diane.

After everyone left, I told Frank how Diane had pressed me about what we were doing in Indonesia, and how she demanded a response. He listened intently, now and then nodding his head. Was he agreeing with my reactions or with what Diane had done?

"My guess," he said, "is that Diane may be a Parsifal on some kind of quest. Why don't you tell her his story?"

Why would I do that? She was already causing me problems. Imagine if she thought I was encouraging her to think even more deeply about corporate right and wrong. Anyway, was it right for a boss to have such conversations with his employees? Somehow it seemed inappropriate and risky. Suddenly I felt like I was standing on very shaky ground. Tough for a guy who never doubted his decisions or competency before.

"Let me think about it, Frank," I said. "She's pushing me pretty hard already. If I encourage her, she'll soon be running the whole place!"

He gave me his wry smile again, his Gandalf look. He was inviting me to take a risk and commit to my own quest. I can see that now.

"Neil, let me tell you a quick story, one about change. It has some bearing on the questions we discussed tonight at dinner and also on your difficulties with Diane.

"Have you ever heard of John Hersey? He wrote *Hiroshima*, a grim account of the first A-bomb and its effects."

As usual, he had read something I hadn't.

"No matter. I want to talk about another book he wrote, called *White Lotus*. Heard of that one?"

Nope. I felt embarrassed, like I was disappointing him because I read so little. I know now that that wasn't true, but that's how I felt at that moment. He summarized the story for me.

"*White Lotus* is a story about change, but non-violent change, not like ending the war by dropping an A-bomb on Hiroshima. The story takes place in an imaginary future right after China invades the United States, conquers it, and makes everyone a Chinese slave. Hersey wrote it in 1965 at the height of the civil rights movement in the United States. Its purpose was obvious: to make white Americans really understand what it was like to be black.

"Hersey's heroine is a young American woman whose Chinese name is White Lotus. She's captured as a young girl in Arizona and marched to the sea in California to be sold into slavery in China. Her first owner is a powerful Mandarin who is kind to her. For various reasons he sells her to another farmer who then quickly sells her to a poorer farmer. The poor farmer is pitiless in his treatment of her. She finally escapes to a 'free' province in China but finds that her life there is still not free like the Chinese. As we read her story, we learn what it means to be without dignity and hope.

"But White Lotus, like Parsifal, is an innocent fool. She decides to protest, disregarding the risks and the magnitude of the challenge. She goes to the local warlord's palace and stands outside his gate, waiting for her grievances to be addressed. She stands silently, in a position of utter humility—on one leg with her head down, like a bird. She remains in that position day and night in front of his palace for weeks, until the warlord finally takes notice and has pity— on her and on all the former American slaves in his so-called free province—and agrees to begin to change their living conditions.

"The symbolism in White Lotus' name is important. A lotus in China sometimes signifies purity emerging from mud. White Lotus's purity and powerlessness before the warlord is what persuades him to act and allow the Americans to get out of the all-enveloping mud of slavery they're stuck in."

Frank stopped there. He hadn't exactly solved my Diane problem, but I got his point. I felt edgy, so I summarized what I thought the story meant.

"Frank, I think the warlord had the power, and could make any rule he wanted, but White Lotus's protest showed that some of his rules were wrong. I didn't think Chinese society consisted only of the warlord's rules, though. Chinese

71

society was structured into slaves and non-slaves—haves and have-nots—and there were unspoken rules for how you treated people in different layers of society. Those were the day-to-day rules that made slavery work."

He seemed pleased by my analysis, as if a star pupil had done his homework. But there was another point to his story he wanted me to see. There always was.

"Now think about your interaction with Diane. Does the story suggest how she might be changing the day-to-day rules in your company?"

Hmm, that was interesting. Diane said her team had discussed what our company was doing in Indonesia and had decided it was wrong. She then came to me, the boss, to get me to make changes. She seemed to think she and her team had the right to discuss and define what our company should or should not do.

"She and her team might be able to get the rules changed, but only if they worked with management. She did come to me to get my approval."

"What if she hadn't come to you? What if Diane had simply sent an email to everyone about what you're doing in Indonesia?"

That jolted me! What if she had done that? That would really challenge my authority. Everyone would watch to see what kind of leader I was—a strong one or a pushover. I couldn't allow her to do that! Suddenly, I realized I was thinking like Hersey's warlord! That also jolted me.

The analogy didn't fit, though. My company wasn't China, and my workers weren't slaves. And Diane certainly wasn't the silent, meek White Lotus. Weren't the people in Indonesia who worked for our company better off than most third world people, anyway? A fleeting memory flashed through my mind, but I pushed it away. It was that ragged Filipino man again, the one I saw squatting by the highway in Manila as my limo drove by with the windows up.

But what if I *could* trust Diane? What if she had the best interests of our company in mind, and understood as well as management what made us successful? Would it hurt to let her encourage everyone to discuss how we treat people? I would still have the power to say yes or no. Still, this approach—you could call it bottom-up decisions about right and wrong—could be confusing and get out of control. The email chatter would be chaotic and could take a lot of time away from work. It probably wouldn't result in any sensible rules either. Warlord thinking, I thought to myself. Then suddenly I had an insight.

"Frank, I think right and wrong in organizations always originates with individuals. It could be a leader or someone down in the ranks, even at the bottom like White Lotus. When someone starts to see that their organization— or entire society—is doing something they think is wrong, their conscience is troubled, and they act. That's what happened to White Lotus. And that's what's happening with Diane and her team! She's standing in front of my gate like White Lotus, and she won't budge until I do something about some unspoken rule we have that she believes mistreats our workers in Indonesia!"

73

All this came out in a rush. Like most insights, it wasn't well thought out, or logical. It even sounded a bit foolish, but I said it anyway. It was a burst of creative ideas. That hadn't happened to me before. I'd managed to keep provocative thoughts out of my cave. I had to do that to perform effectively as an executive—or warlord, I thought grimly. I sensed vaguely that this insight eventually would raise new questions I would have to weigh, and decisions I would have to make. It must have been what happened in the warlord's mind as well. Somehow, his conscience had gotten through to him when he saw White Lotus standing on one leg for weeks. He started to see, however faintly, that the rules in his wounded society were inhumane and needed changing.

This was *my* insight, not someone else's. No one tried to persuade me it was true. In a way it was what we had talked about at dinner. Now the question was would I commit myself to actions based on this insight? It was a 'Give me liberty or give me death' moment. If anything was going to happen, it clearly depended on me. I had an opportunity— possibly even an obligation—to act on my insight. I thought of what Frank had experienced after he had left Assisi, and his determination to enlist people in the gentle revolution.

Looking back, this insight triggered an urge to discover what the gentle revolution meant for me. It was the moment when I realized that I needed to begin a quest to find what was beyond my cave. I didn't know the way forward. I didn't even know why I had to change or what form it would take, and I certainly had a very long way to go before I would get actively involved in the gentle revolution. But I knew that evening in London, however dimly, that I wanted to be part of what Frank was talking about. I was like Frodo in *The Lord of the Rings* when he told Gandalf that he would carry the Ring of Power to Mordor to destroy it. I didn't want to be a hero, but I knew there was some sort of important task I had to complete. Something vital depended on me, even if I didn't yet understand what it was.

Frank must have guessed my thoughts were in turmoil, because he didn't say anything. We sat quietly in his study. I could hear the traffic on Kensington Road in the distance.

Finally I said that it was late, and that I had an early morning meeting.

He smiled and said, "Take it easy, Neil."

I didn't take that as a very profound statement but, looking back on what happened next, it was.

Chapter 7

I was promoted to general manager, responsible for two thousand people worldwide and five hundred million dollars in annual revenues. I quickly got caught up in the demands of my new role, and delegated Diane's concerns about Indonesia to HR. In other words, I ignored them. Any thoughts about starting my quest also quickly evaporated in the heat of my new job. Frank had foreseen this; that's why he told me to take it easy. He knew it would take time for me to find the way, and it did. Roles and power create potent forces that keep us trapped within our caves.

Almost two years later, Frank and I finally managed to coordinate our schedules and get together. We were both presenting at a management conference in San Francisco. I was speaking on global sales strategies, and Frank's talk was on viral change. The way people hung on his words seemed like they regarded him as something of a guru. I later learned he hated being called a guru.

We met for breakfast in the Hyatt Embarcadero coffee shop the morning after our speeches. Frank looked the same, but apparently I didn't.

"Hey, Neil, you look terrible! What have you been doing to yourself?"

Thanks, Frank, I need that right now. Then I remembered my much-delayed quest and felt guilty.

"I guess it's the job and the travel. Makes a man out of you. Puts hair on your chest and bags under your eyes."

He didn't smile. "No job is worth your health. When was the last time you took a vacation?"

You have to be kidding. If I did that, my division would fall apart. The warlord can't let his kingdom crumble, can he?

"I can't remember. I took a couple of days off the last time I was in Paris. Met a gorgeous woman on the plane going over, and we drove through the Loire Valley together." I couldn't remember her name.

He still looked worried. "Back up. Tell me about yourself. What's been happening?"

I rattled off my accomplishments. "After I was promoted, I immediatcly got rid of two weak people on my management team and visited every one of our offices in the United States and Europe. Sorry I didn't look you up when I was in London—too busy. Asia had to wait—it was only fifteen percent of the business. Everyone in my division heard directly from me about where we were going and what I expected of them. I focused on profitability, created a new performance scorecard, and personally ran workshops to get my management team to use it. I downsized the division and let two hundred poor performers go. My people realized they were in a highly competitive game. Shape up or ship out! On my boss's team I asked the tough questions. There were poor managers running other divisions that were holding back our company's share price, and I pushed them every chance I got. My boss didn't particularly like conflict, so we played good cop, bad cop, and I was the bad cop."

I paused, trying to think of what I'd missed.

Frank asked, "How did all that make you feel?"

"Exhilarated. Powerful. On top of the world. I'm using all my skills. I feel like I was born to do the GM role. I love going to work; every day is so interesting. The sky's the limit!"

But that wasn't the whole story, and Frank knew it.

"Has anything else happened?"

"Yeah. Things got tougher toward the end of last year. First, the US economy turned down, and our sales fell off. No matter how hard I pushed, my team couldn't close deals at the rate they had before. I lost several key people to the competition. It took time to fill those positions. The replacements were good, but their learning curve hurt our numbers. We had to downsize again. Another hundred people. They weren't poor performers, but we had to let them go to make the bottom-line numbers. One guy had been with the company for twenty years and had the guts to ask me how I felt about firing him. I told him it didn't bother me; the company had to survive. It actually still does bother me.

"The worst thing that happened was my boss left during all this turmoil, and I had to break in a new one. Unlike my previous boss, the new one wasn't afraid of conflict, and after the first senior team meeting he told me to let up on questioning the other guys on his team, that *he'd* run things, thank you very much. I felt he didn't trust me. This definitely added to my stress. I guess that's why I look a little tired. I'm juggling a large number of balls. My new boss is an energy-taker, not an energy-giver so the job isn't as much fun now. I feel like I'm meeting myself coming and going, a little like Elena I guess."

I realized I had just confessed some inner turmoil to Frank that I hadn't actually admitted to myself.

He'd been slowly eating his breakfast while I talked. One thing about him; he really listened. I always felt like I had his full attention. He finished his eggs, and I had barely started mine, so I ate while he described his past two years.

"My life has become more challenging too, Neil. I get more requests for consulting than I can handle from senior executives who want workshops to create visions or initiate change. They want someone with a different approach. New paradigm stuff. I usually spend two weeks with a company and use a canned process they all seem to love. See the patterns in what you do today. Imagine where you want to be. Create a metaphor for the change journey. Conferences want me to speak about change. You heard what I said yesterday. You can hear the same thing said by dozens of others. Still, it keeps my pipeline full and money in the bank."

He seemed a little wistful.

I stopped chewing long enough to ask, "Do you use your stories?"

He shook his head.

"No. They wouldn't sell in this market; too soft, too indirect, not directly linked to improving near-term results. And I don't want to use them anyway. The setting is wrong. I don't have a deep enough relationship with most of my clients. There's not enough time for the conversations we need to have. Too many alpha males and too much testosterone in most executive teams for them to learn from my stories."

He was describing me and my company! If he felt that way, why had he bothered to tell *me* his stories?

"So, you only tell your stories to certain people," I said. "Doesn't that limit what you're trying to do—get the message out about healing wounded organizations?"

Frank leaned back and looked up at the splendor of the Hyatt Atrium, watching one of the elevators descend.

"You may be right," he said. "Maybe I should use the stories. I just don't feel it's right, though. Only innocent fools seem to understand them."

He looked at me sharply.

We stopped talking and sipped our coffees. Frank was giving me his Gandalf look. He knew I had decided to make the quest several years ago, but under the pressure of my new job had backed away. He looked sad, like he didn't know what to do, but I was wrong. He knew exactly where he was headed.

"Neil, have you ever read a story that you couldn't figure out?"

I thought about it. No, not really. Even mystery novels finally gave you an explanation. It was hard to guess what was going on at first, but it always became clear at the end.

"Remember the story about Parsifal and the Fisher King? There's another puzzle in it that's worth thinking about. When the Fisher King was a young prince—young and reckless, caught up in his own personal strength and power—he stole a piece of roasting salmon from a poor man's fire and was severely burned. He was so badly wounded—some versions of the myth say he was stabbed by an angel with a fiery lance—that he was confined to bed in agony from that day forward. The people in his court could do nothing to help him. To keep up their hope, his subjects believed the wounded king would be released from his torment and the entire kingdom healed when an innocent young man who would know nothing about what he was doing asked a magical question. That, of course, was Parsifal."

I wondered if Frank was saying that I was like the Fisher King but didn't ask.

"Parsifal didn't ask the magical question when he visited the castle the first time. In Chrétien's myth, Parsifal

82

had to undergo a series of trials and adventures to make up for this failure. Finally, after many years he met the Fisher King again and, as a much older and more experienced knight, asked the magic question that freed the Fisher King from his agony."

Frank was looking at me with piercing eyes.

"Any idea what Parsifal's question was, Neil?"

I couldn't imagine. Frank was right. The Fisher King was a puzzling story.

"In some versions of the story Parsifal asks about the Holy Grail, and who drinks from it. In the one I like, Parsifal simply asked the king, 'What ails you?' Such an obvious question; everyone in the court must have asked it many times. You wonder why only a special person—an innocent fool—could ask it in a way that would heal the king's wound. Any insights?"

Insights? No. Maybe an idea, though. The king was a leader trapped in a painful situation of his own making. The people in his organization were trapped with him. They couldn't ask the magical question because they were wounded too. A special innocent fool, Parsifal, had to intervene to heal them. But why was Frank telling me this story? I didn't feel wounded or in need of a Parsifal to rescue me. I looked at him quizzically.

"Nope, nothing really occurs to me, Frank. Why did you tell me that story?"

He smiled at me mysteriously and leaned forward over the table. I knew what that meant.

"Let me answer you with another story. This one's about Aragorn, the heroic king in *The Lord of the Rings*."

*

"At the beginning of Tolkien's story, Aragorn is a wanderer known as Strider, a ranger who is something like a knight. Aragorn hides his true identity as a king. That sounds foolish, don't you think? Why hide your power, especially when you are a person who could use it to do good? He volunteers to guide an innocent fool, Frodo, to the heart of the evil kingdom of Mordor in order to destroy the Ring of Power. Aragorn passes an early test by refusing to touch the ring, even though it could make him the most powerful king in Middle-earth. He knows it will turn him into the evil Lord Sauron's slave.[5]

"Early in the journey to Mordor, in Lothlorien, the land of the Elves, Aragorn has a strange encounter with Galadriel, the elf queen. She asks him a magical question. Not Parsifal's question, 'What ails you?' but 'What do you wish for?' He doesn't answer her question even though he knows the queen has the power to grant his heart's desire. Aragorn tells her he cannot have what he wants until he first passes a test. He finally gets his wish at the end of the story, after Frodo destroys the ring.[6]

"Neil, do you see the parallels with Parsifal's story?"

I thought of the obvious ones. Each story had a king in it—Aragorn and the Fisher King—but one is a strong leader and the other is weak and sick. Obviously, the Fisher King wished to be free of pain, but I wondered what Aragon's wish was. Each story also had an innocent fool on a quest—

Parsifal and Frodo—but they played very different roles. Frodo understood his mission when he undertook his quest: to destroy the ring. Parsifal seemed to wander aimlessly and didn't see the importance of his role for some time. Power also played a part in both stories. The Fisher King misused his power to steal from the poor man and was wounded. Aragorn used his power wisely and in doing so helped an innocent fool defeat Sauron.

I still didn't get what Frank was driving at in my case. Later, it occurred to me that I didn't want to.

"I guess I must be dense," I said. "What does *The Lord of the Rings* have to do with *The Fisher King*? And what do they have to do with me?"

"I would have thought you would know by now that you have to answer such questions for yourself. But I'll give you a few clues."

He sipped his coffee and waved at the waiter to bring our check. I could tell I wasn't going to get much help from Gandalf that morning.

"Think about it. What do you have in common with the Fisher King and Aragorn? You possess power. What do you do with it? Another hint: Frodo was the key to Aragorn's ultimate success, and the Fisher King needed Parsifal to set him free from his wounds. That's enough clues."

He was suggesting I had to change how I used my power, and to do that I needed an innocent fool to assist me. Was it Diane? How could that possibly work? I was the boss. Warlord thinking.

The waiter brought the check and we split it—thirty-five dollars each for breakfast! Next time I'd recommend eating somewhere cheaper. I asked Frank how long he was going to be in San Francisco, and we agreed I'd drive us over the Golden Gate to Sausalito for dinner in two days.

Frank's provocative story irritated me. I didn't need any Parsifal or magical queen to ask me questions. I already knew the answers. What ails me? Nothing I can't handle. What do I wish for? I already had it: the power to make wealth for my company and myself. I was on top of the world, not wounded. I was in control of things. Except for my boss, but I could even handle him. Yet beneath my confidence, I sensed there was a hollow ring to my answers.

That was a big step forward for me!

Chapter 8

By now you're probably really frustrated with me. How could
I be so blind? Why couldn't I see the point of Frank's stories?
Stick with me. You need to understand how dark the path out
of my cave was. It may seem to you that Frank was shining a
bright light on things, but for me it was very faint. For a long
time, I couldn't see a way forward—and I didn't particularly
want to. I can't explain why I couldn't see more clearly, except
to say that something inside me was closed and couldn't deal
with what Frank was saying. But he was patient, and through
his stories and questions, he helped me find the key to
unlocking this closed door in myself. Nothing else was
possible until that happened.

As we had agreed, Frank and I drove a rented convertible over the Golden Gate Bridge to Sausalito. It was twilight and cool; July evenings in San Francisco can be downright cold, but this one was pleasant. We had the top down. Rush-hour traffic was slow and backed up at the bridge, but we enjoyed being together, so it didn't matter.

The view from Ondine's Restaurant was spectacular. The distant San Francisco skyline at twilight across the bay was almost too beautiful to be real. We ate poached salmon, and the Grand Marnier soufflé was a 'best in class' experience.

We didn't return to the Fisher King and Aragorn right away. We hadn't really had a chance to talk at breakfast and hadn't seen each other in two years. After dinner we walked along the wharf where the fishing fleet was tied up. I felt more at ease than I had for a long time. Somehow, Frank's presence calmed me. He helped me feel that things really were all right, no matter how stressful the world or my job was. That was one reason why I looked forward to seeing him. I trusted him and could relax my tight grip on managing my life for a while.

"Neil, I gave you a few hints about yourself when we had breakfast at the Hyatt. Did you come to any conclusions?"

I hadn't, but I did have one question for him.

"Why do you tell stories, Frank? If there's a message for me, why not just tell me in plain language? Then I could understand and act on your advice, if I agreed."

I could always tell when I made a move that Frank had already anticipated, because he grinned and made his next move right away.

"Did you ever hear the saying, 'In the kingdom of the blind, the one-eyed man is king'?"

"It means someone who sees something that others don't, doesn't it?"

He nodded. "There's a danger in that, you know. People desperately want to believe there are a few special people who can see the truth. Most of us—myself included—are suckers who want to believe some special guru has found the hidden wisdom of the ages. I call this Guru-ism. Stick with me, Neil. I'm trying to answer your question about why I tell stories. By the way, In-Frank is constantly needling me like a court jester to make sure I don't believe I'm a guru myself! When people treat you like a guru, you start to forget who you really are."

I suddenly had an insight. Frank was answering a question I hadn't asked, but should have: Why did I feel so special? Why did I see myself as the king in the Fisher King and Aragorn stories? I knew the reason. I sat in a big top-floor office, and people deferred to me as if I were a king. Maybe I needed my own court jester whispering in my ear. Frank and I were walking next to San Francisco Bay after eating a meal that cost us each over one hundred dollars. More than half the people in the world don't make that much money in a year! Didn't that make us special? I would have to think more about that later. Right now, I wanted to listen to Frank as he explained his concept of Guru-ism.

"Guru-ism poisons us. We're too ready to think what we see and work out for ourselves isn't as reliable as what some special guru tells us. I'm not saying there isn't wisdom—

there is. Scientists and philosophers and other scholars have special, focused knowledge. We can use their knowledge to test our insights, to make sure, as far as we are able, that our intuitions are in sync with the real world. There are other forms of wisdom too, like folk wisdom and tradition. Nevertheless, each person *must* work out what they believe for themselves. Some special guardian of secret knowledge can't do the hard yards for you.

"Guru-ism only exists because most of us are in awe of people who we imagine possess complicated knowledge that we don't. We tell ourselves that if a physicist says something about reality, it must be true; they understand theories that we don't. It doesn't matter if genuine physicists only claim to describe limited aspects of reality. We still insist on following them in other areas. Fundamentalists of all kinds also rely on Guru-ism. 'I know the *real* truth, and if you believe differently, you're wrong.' Be careful if anyone claims special knowledge; odds are they're playing at being a guru."

Frank was really wound up about this stuff. I wondered what it had to do with his telling me stories. Once again, he was a step ahead.

"Neil, I tell stories in order to respect each person's unique journey toward their own hard-won beliefs. I want to make sure they respect their own insights, not just accept what I or any other person tells them. If I told you what my stories meant or gave you advice, I would be acting like I knew something special that you didn't. My stories are just a starting point. You have a blank sheet of paper, so to speak, to find your own meaning from your own insights. They are the precious early fruit of your quest.

"After hearing my stories, you can wrestle with your own questions and insights, find your own patterns, test your beliefs for yourself, and finally decide to act. After dinner in London, we talked about Patrick Henry's speech. The ability to really mean and not say lightly, 'Give me liberty or give me death' doesn't happen overnight. This kind of commitment doesn't happen because a guru tells you what to believe. You need to struggle to find something worth hanging your life on. Or maybe you won't find anything—there are no guarantees. That's why I tell stories. They are simply invitations to make a quest and commit your life to something."

I had never seen Frank worked up like this. His face was tense, the muscles in his jaws were working, and his voice had a sharp edge to it. Then the reason occurred to me. He was trying to warn me about taking a wrong path on my quest, the easy path too many people accept. Climb on the bandwagon! Follow that guru! Maybe he was also helping me understand how difficult it was to begin a genuine quest. He knew that I wasn't yet fully engaged. Life was rushing at me, and I was reacting to it. I was on autopilot. I didn't reflect about life or long-term consequences. Was I a wise leader like Aragorn? It wasn't all that important to me.

"This is pretty deep stuff, Frank, but I think I'm beginning to get your point. I have to take my insights and life choices far more seriously."

But would I really? I didn't want to focus on that. It was easy to agree with Frank when I was with him. It was a very different story when I was sitting by myself in my top-floor office.

We walked farther along the wharf in silence. After a few minutes, Frank stopped and sat down on a wooden bench at the end of the pier, then looked toward the city. He chose a new tactic, upping the ante once more.

"Neil, you remember I said that I started my quest in Houston? I finally met In-Frank because of something that happened while I was working at NASA. Let me tell you about that. A guy I knew at NASA, another engineer on my project, discovered something that switched off his autopilot."

Frank smiled to himself as he began his story about the engineer, as if he were back in Houston in those heady days of no limits, when NASA was leading the way into space.

"For some reason known only to him, this guy got interested in time. You know, how time works. He began to wonder if NASA had found new facts about the universe that might change our ideas about time. The problem was, he quickly realized that time isn't only about facts. We each experience time differently, in our own personal way. Einstein, only half in jest, once said if you want to understand how time is personal and relative, think about two different situations: a guy sitting on a hot stove experiences time as moving slowly until he can get off the hot seat; a guy with a pretty girl experiences time moving really fast because he's enjoying himself.

"Anyway, this guy kept bothering the rest of us with questions about time until we began to look for some way to shut him up. One day I had a brainstorm. I suggested he try an experiment. Maybe he could research how ancient people felt about time and compare that with how we experience it today. I thought figuring this out would keep him busy for a while and out of our faces. It worked. Months went by with not a peep out of him. Everyone thought I'd done a great job shutting him up. Then one Monday morning he came into my office looking like he hadn't slept in a week. He closed the door and sat down.

"'Frank,' he said quietly, 'something's happened, and I need to talk to someone about it.' Meaning me, of course.

"No, this guy didn't discover time travel or something weird out of the past. None of that New Age mumbo jumbo. He found something far more interesting that got me reading and thinking as well.

"The guy leaned forward, to make sure I knew this was very important. 'Frank, one thing we know today that the Egyptians and Romans didn't know is that the Big Bang happened, and time and the whole quantum universe took shape about fourteen billion years ago. I was thinking about that last week while I sat by a pond in my neighborhood after work. A frog jumped into the water right in front of me. The ripples it made spread across the whole pond!

'I had a great idea! The ripples from the beginning of time, from the Big Bang itself, are still present in our pond! Look, imagine the Big Bang created something like a gigantic ocean that is still expanding. The ocean is space and time. Everything here on Earth is our own little pond inside that ocean. The thing is our pond here on Earth isn't smooth. It has ripples in it. The ripples from the Big Bang are still touching us. And we're the first people who ever understood that!'"

"Wait a minute," I interrupted. "Why was the engineer amazed by that? So all the atoms and stuff in space created by the Big Bang are still touching us—so what?"

Frank nodded. "That was my reaction too. I thought he was just another NASA guy falling in love with the 'music of the spheres,' as they say. But let me continue. You'll begin to see.

"As the engineer sat by the pond that evening, he realized that the frog's ripples were only some of the movement he could see on its surface. He started observing it very carefully. It was a muggy Houston evening with hardly a breath of air. Insects were flying near the surface and occasionally one would touch the water and cause small ripples in the pond. Then he saw a swallow swoop down and lightly touch the surface as it caught a bug, which created more ripples. Then a light breeze came and went, and it caused even more ripples. All these ripples interacted with each other and caused complex patterns in the surface of the water.

"The insight he had was that all these different events—the frog and the bugs, the swallow and the breeze—were writing their unique pattern on the surface of the pond. Their patterns *were* reality. He'd seen the frog jump in, and the birds catch an insect a few seconds later, but their patterns lingered there in the ripples. Then it hit him. Our whole world is the same way! The ripples of events on our own local pond, planet Earth, create an ongoing evolving pattern that *is* reality. We make ripples and create the future every moment!"

Frank stopped to see if I was beginning to get a glimmer of the engineer's insight. "You see that, don't you?"

Something was stirring at the edge of my mind. Things that happened in the past affected the future and affected me. Okay. I used books because Gutenberg invented a cheaper way to print them. That seemed pretty obvious, but not particularly interesting. Nope, I didn't get it. Frank had also said this conversation with the engineer had really had a profound effect on his life. My mind was spinning trying to make sense out of a lot of disconnected ideas.

I shifted in my seat on the bench, trying to get comfortable.

Frank began again, speaking more softly, as if he were awed by what happened to the engineer.

"The engineer paused and looked away from me. He seemed to be going deeper into himself, from one level to another. He glanced at me with a shy, self-conscious look that said, 'I'm not sure how to tell you the next part.'

"He realized, as he thought more about the pond, that he was watching it from a distance, as if he was outside watching others make ripples and couldn't see himself in the picture. Suddenly, it hit him that there was no bank to sit on outside reality. He was right *in* the pond where the ripples were affecting him, and where he was causing ripples too!

"That was the insight that changed the engineer's perspective about everything. Turned off his autopilot. Seeing himself as *part* of the pond—as a crucial part of creating the future of *everything*—caused questions to erupt out of some previously blocked area of his mind almost like a volcano. How was he affecting the pond? Was he just floating and being carried along by the other ripples? Was *he* creating any lasting ripples that would affect others? The engineer called creating the future 'dropping a pebble in the pond'. How would he drop his pebble in the pond? With scarcely a ripple, or with a more lasting effect?

"It was this sudden surge of questions that had brought him to me. He needed to find someone who could help him sort things out. Before, his life consisted of finding problems and solving them. Now, for the first time, he was faced with something beyond his skill as an engineer— deciding how to drop his pebble in the pond—and he desperately needed to talk to someone who he thought knew how to do that. Little did he know that back then I had no more of an idea than he had!"

Frank turned and looked directly at me, reading my reaction to the engineer's story. I kept my thoughts to myself to see what he would say. Actually, I didn't know what to think. I was adding some questions of my own to the ones the engineer had asked. Was reality actually as fluid and changeable as a pond? Wasn't it a lot more solid, like a slowly evolving glacier—or even a mountain range—that we couldn't actually affect at all? Could the engineer's metaphor be wrong? Maybe we couldn't create ripples in the pond at all. But I'll say one thing for the engineer's story: it got me thinking! Could I, more importantly, *must* I try to change the future? What kind of ripples did I want to make with my life?

"What happened next?" I asked Frank.

"After our talk, when I couldn't help him, he seemed to pull away from the rest of us at work. I don't know why. Maybe he thought we didn't understand his problem, so conversation with us was useless. I left NASA six months later, and he was still there, keeping to himself, probably trying to work out how to drop his pebble in the pond. I never saw him again. Any questions, Neil?"

I smiled at him.

"Not right now, Frank. I need some space to think."

He nodded and got up. "Okay. Let's head back, then. I've got an early flight to London tomorrow."

We walked back to the car and chatted a bit more about his time at NASA but left the engineer alone. We talked about meeting in a couple of months in London. I thought I'd be over there. Maybe we'd drive up to the Lake Country and Hadrian's Wall. We'd have lots of time to talk then.

None of that happened. Life isn't that straightforward.

Chapter 9

After I left San Francisco, my job continued to be hectic, and I pretty much forgot my conversations with Frank and creating ripples on the pond. I was on the acquisition team buying another company, and my division was also bringing out a number of new products. A lot of people were making demands and there were a number of issues that threatened me. My role as general manager didn't allow anything to interfere with my survival! That doesn't mean nothing was happening; Frank's stories were having their intended effect, shifting things deep inside me.

Who knows what triggers an avalanche or what causes a tropical storm? One too many snowflakes touching a vulnerable snowbank on a mountainside? A butterfly flapping its wings in South America disturbing a sensitive air current? It was the same with me. Something touched a tender spot inside me, and I finally met In-Neil.

I caught the flu and had to stay home for a few days. While I was off work, a senior manager on my team went to my boss and complained about me, about the way our division was performing, about everything. He damaged his reputation with both my boss and me, because my boss called me and told me about the conversation. When I got back, the guy knew something was up when he came into my office. I was furious.

"Why didn't you tell *me*? I thought we *trusted* each other!"

He tried to explain, but finally gave up and left my office with a grim look on his face. Two days later, he resigned. In retrospect, his complaints probably triggered my personal avalanche.

For some reason, I didn't feel right about what happened. Why had he gone behind my back? He said I didn't listen to anyone. I rode roughshod over people, was abusive. I couldn't see it. No one else had said anything like that. I recalled Frank's story about Aragorn. He had refused to take the ring because he wouldn't be able to resist its power. Had I grasped the ring and become power-hungry? Was that what this guy was trying to tell me? It didn't feel right. Sure, I was a hard driver, and I pushed people, but I was fair. I had power, but I shared it. Still, he said I didn't listen. I couldn't get him out of my mind.

Two weeks later I was off to Paris on business. I decided to go early and spend some time by myself. I didn't know why, but I just felt like walking the back streets and being alone. The Sunday on which I arrived was beautiful, a warm and clear September day. I walked over to Parc Monceau, and it seemed like every family in Paris was there. Children were running with their balloons trailing behind them, and couples were hand in hand, lost in conversation and in one another.

Out of the blue, it hit me. Not only was I by myself in this park, but I was truly alone in the world. There was no one—anywhere—to look into my eyes like those Parisian women did with their partners. No one to see In-Neil and love the person they saw there, if there was any In-Neil to love. I thought of Frank and Elena and their intimacy, and it almost overwhelmed me.

Executive-Neil had gone to the park for a purpose— to rest so he would be clear-headed for work on Monday. But the lovers and families were there simply to be with each other. I had no one, not even In-Neil. I had never experienced such emptiness before. It was almost too much. Tears welled in my eyes. Good God, was I going to cry—in public? I needed to get back to my hotel, close the drapes, and wake up on Monday when Executive-Neil would be back in control. I hurried back to the hotel, drank a few beers in the bar, ate dinner, and went to bed very early, by which time the emptiness had disappeared. But not for good.

When I returned home, I couldn't forget what happened in Paris. I needed Frank. He seemed to understand these things. I couldn't reach him by phone, so I sent him an email. He responded that he was in Australia and we wouldn't be on the same continent again for a while. Anyway, a phone conversation and email weren't what I needed. I wanted to *see* him. Maybe he had a story that could help.

I finally remembered a friend who might understand what I was feeling—Connie. We'd worked together before she left the company, and we'd exchanged Christmas cards to stay in touch. She was one of those people who seemed to ponder things and listen intently. So, I called her, and after she recovered from the surprise of hearing from me, she agreed to meet me for a drink.

She listened sympathetically to my story, but she wasn't much help. I was looking for something in that conversation that I had never wanted before. Not debate, not facts, but empathy and "I feel for you, Neil, even if I can't help". But she didn't say anything about what she must have seen in my eyes.

As we sat there, I thought about In-Connie. The way she gazed steadily at me made me wonder if it was her. Maybe she didn't share with me that night because there wasn't any In-Neil to relate to, only the wounded Executive-Neil looking to fix his problem. We promised we'd get together more often. She gave me a light kiss on the cheek and was smiling as she left. I think that's when I first became aware of my need for Connie as a person, not just a business associate.

I believed then that the emptiness I was experiencing was a mistake or a personal flaw, a condition I had to escape. I didn't know then that it was a kind of force or energy luring me toward the future. In-Neil was on the far side of a chasm that Executive-Neil was powerless to cross, yet I was being pulled toward the other side. It all seemed impossible. But Elena had crossed, as had Frank. Maybe I could too. But how? That question began to torment me. What if I couldn't cross? Would this emptiness last forever?

Don't let me mislead you. Getting past that chasm didn't involve self-improvement or finding a new way to think or anything like that. In-Neil simply emerged over time, in unexpected ways. It was as if he sensed my powerlessness to reach him and came in search of me. I filled my emptiness most days with the furious pace of my life. In-Neil only appeared occasionally, at unguarded moments. At four in the morning, when I was restless and couldn't sleep. At airports, when it was painful to watch a joyous couple greet one another. And especially on weekends, when a stream of questions wouldn't leave me alone.

Why had I gotten so furious at the guy who quit, and how was he making out now? What was I doing with my life? How was I dropping my pebble into the pond? I thought a lot about Elena's encounter with herself. Was In-Elena just a figment of her imagination? A friend told me to just 'live in the question', and things would resolve themselves. What did *that* mean?

In time, I got past the chasm. At first, I only caught fleeting glimpses of In-Neil in memories from childhood, but gradually he became more and more real, as alive to me as Executive-Neil. What's the big deal, you say, about meeting In-Neil? After all, he *is* you. But you don't understand; I only knew myself through what I did or accomplished, not through how I felt or who I really was. The lighting on my stage was definitely black and white before I met colorful In-Neil!

Before I crossed the chasm, people used to tell me, "Take time to smell the flowers." Executive-Neil would reply, "What good is that? I can put my time to better use." In-Neil goes out of his way to experience the fragrance of roses and lilacs, whether it wastes time or not. That's one of the ways I recognize him. He craves pistachio ice cream even though it might put weight on Executive-Neil, who is always on different health kicks. He listens closely when I talk to the people who work with me. He is delighted when I grasp the problems they bring to me and don't give them answers because it takes away their opportunity to learn. He grins a lot more than Executive-Neil, and my employees seem to like that. I don't tell them that it's In-Neil smiling and not their boss. Anyway, it was all getting mixed up in my mind. Executive-Neil seemed to be catching some of the smiling virus from In-Neil.

I can hear you asking, exactly how did this happen? People who haven't yet crossed the chasm usually want to know that. As I said, I couldn't seem to get rid of my emptiness, no matter what I did. My cave had become uncomfortable. It was missing something, an unknown something beyond my experience. Then one Saturday morning at my kitchen table, an idea occurred to me. Not an insight; just a flicker of an idea I hadn't thought of before. What if I actually decided to meet In-Neil? How would I go about doing that? Where would I find him?

This idea opened up some new possibilities. I could try sitting quietly to see if I could sense a hint of his presence.

Like Elena, I could imagine what he was like by recalling my childhood. I could even call my mother. She might remember some stories about In-Neil that might help.

Then it hit me. I was planning to meet In-Neil! I believed that he actually existed! Later, when I told Frank what happened, he said, "I used to think seeing is believing. Now I know it's the other way around. Believing is seeing. That's why you finally were able to meet In-Neil."

When I began to believe in In-Neil not as an idea but as an actual living being, I could sense his presence. That gave me a peaceful feeling that I had never experienced before. Somewhere among all the roles I played was someone who didn't care about my performance, someone who simply accepted that I was okay! I didn't need to become a good general manager, a competent boss, healthy, or achieve any result to satisfy In-Neil. If ever I went back to Parc Monceau—and all of a sudden I was filled with the desire to do so—In-Neil would be there, in his element, enjoying a very special moment, hopefully with a beautiful woman who also knew her In-self. You can sum all this up by saying that when I decided to take In-Neil seriously, he got in touch with me.

Once I had ventured outside my cave, there were an infinite number of new possibilities. I could almost hear Frank exclaim, "Congratulations, Neil! Welcome to the amazing world of innocence!" Remember however that I was still a general manager while all this was going on. No one at work knew about In-Neil, and I certainly wasn't going to tell them. I was afraid it would seem weird and upset their confidence in me.

I began to see things in a new light. Outside my cave, the way was open for me to seek a far more profound purpose for my life. That was the quest that Frank had been leading me toward. But no matter how hard he might have tried to persuade me to go in this direction (and he was wise enough not to try), I first had to encounter In-Neil and get past my own internal barriers. But now that I was ready to begin the real quest, Frank wouldn't be able to walk with me, because he became seriously ill.

Chapter 10

I received an email from Elena. Frank had given her my address and asked her to contact me. He was in the hospital and was very sick, but she didn't know any more than that. I needed to go to London on business, so I scheduled a trip immediately.

When I visited him, he tried to pretend everything was okay. He kidded with the nurse who was changing an intravenous drip to try to show me all the fuss everyone was making was nothing out of the ordinary. He showed me the gadgets in his room: the call buttons he played with to tease the nurses, the ECG monitor, and other instruments they used to 'torment' him. He had been in the hospital for two weeks, which didn't sound promising. The sister at the nurses' station didn't say much, other than he was doing well.

"How are you really doing, Frank? What's wrong?"

He grinned. "My ticker and my stomach. Both went at the same time. Probably too many rich dinners with you."

"Hey, I didn't *force* you to go to Ondine's and eat all that rich food. So, what do you have? An ulcer?"

He got a bit more serious because I wouldn't let him off the hook.

"I had a pretty serious heart attack, and while they were running tests, they discovered a tumor in my duodenum. That's my small intestine. They're trying to fix it now. Anyway, I'd rather talk about what's been happening to you since our last conversation. Anything changed?"

I did want to talk about what had happened with In-Neil, but I didn't want my visit to be too much for him.

The nurse, who'd been listening, must have sensed my hesitation and said, "You can stay as long as you like. He's bored out of his skin and needs to do something besides think about himself." She was prescribing a deep and meaningful conversation.

I told Frank about meeting In-Neil, and he was delighted, as I had imagined. I told him I was going through a stressful time at work. In-Neil had caught my attention, but at the same time I was more and more driven by events—and Executive-Neil. It felt like Executive-Neil's autopilot was constantly telling me to speed up and make quick decisions;

the job demands it! At the same time, In-Neil was saying slow down, be still and reflect, then act. The different parts of me seemed to be at war.

Something else bothered me. In-Neil wouldn't let me forget it, and Executive-Neil couldn't figure it out. Was it possible that the organization I led was wounded? Frank's story about *The Seventh Seal* implied that maybe I couldn't see all the effects of my actions, just like the fear-driven people in Bergman's film couldn't see what they were doing. It seemed to me that we were focused on being a highly competitive and effective business. I couldn't see much wrong with that. And even if that wasn't the case, what could I do about it?

I told Frank that I knew the story about Parsifal healing the Fisher King had something to do with healing companies, but I couldn't see how that would actually work. I didn't know where to go next.

Frank listened quietly to all of this. Then he pushed a button on the bed to sit up straighter. "Neil, there's something else you need to see—a wonderful, unmistakable yet hidden pattern." He began his story.

*

"Many years ago, like you, I didn't know which path to follow. I felt I wasn't getting anywhere on my quest, even though I'd met In-Frank. Without really believing in it wholeheartedly, I decided to spend a weekend in a retreat house. The old house and grounds were set at the edge of the Potomac River in rural Maryland, about forty miles south of Washington DC. It was spring, and the flowering trees—dogwood and red bud—were exuberant in welcoming me. I still smile when I think about what happened that weekend.

"I checked in and went to my cell, a tiny room with a steel frame cot, a chair, and not much else. No one else was around, and the big old house felt empty, not only of people, but of spiritual promise. I was already discouraged, and the weekend hadn't even started! I walked around the house, then sat in the library and browsed through a few old magazines. When it was time, I ate dinner in the common room by myself. There were only a few people there, and they also sat alone, silently eating, staring out into the woods that surrounded the house. The food was plain and tasteless—tuna casserole and soggy broccoli, as I recall. Oh well, I wasn't there for the cuisine. Afterwards, I went to see the priest who was assigned to be my spiritual guide for the weekend. We would meet three times during the two days, each time for an hour. The rest of the time I would be alone.

"Father Edward met me in his sitting room. He looked about seventy and had what I thought was a quizzical look on his face. (Later, after I'd known him for several years, I found out the look was one of pain; he suffered from arthritis.) We chatted briefly about my reasons for being there and my spiritual background. I had rehearsed my answers pretty well and thought I satisfied him with my responses. Then he asked me what books I had brought to read. I had a selection of five, carefully chosen to lead me deeper in my quest.

"Father Edward smiled. 'Frank, I think you should put the books back in your car. Just be quiet. Walk around the grounds. Be still.'

"My heart sank. I'd really been looking forward to reading those books. Worse, what would I do for two whole days when I couldn't talk, read, watch TV or, it seemed, do anything? Suddenly I was anxious. Maybe this wasn't such a good idea. Father Edward knew what I was feeling from his long experience with 'seekers', as he called them.

"'Don't worry,' he said. 'The time will go more quickly than you think. The woods and the river are beautiful this time of year. Relax and enjoy this place. Don't try to accomplish anything else.'

"His smiled calmed me. I went back to my room, climbed into bed, and quickly fell asleep. The sun woke me on Saturday morning. After breakfast I began my retreat. Funny word, retreat—to pull back from the battle. It usually meant you were defeated and were trying to save yourself. Maybe that's what made me want to be there.

I was getting restless. Frank had used the word 'spiritual'. That was definitely not what I had signed up for! As usual, he was ahead of me, and noticed my unease.

"Don't get stirred up, Neil. I'm not trying to be religious with you or anything like that. I'm trying to help you understand what you're experiencing on your quest. That's all."

I felt more relaxed, but the setting of his story in a retreat house still made me edgy as he continued.

"As I walked around the grounds, I began to experience what one philosopher called the difficulties of the art of silence. A jumble of questions grabbed my attention. What should I be doing? What time was it? And, over and over, why was I doing this? The whole idea of a retreat began to seem like a waste of time, and I almost gave up, went to my car, and escaped back to Washington.

"But I didn't, and after a while I began to relax and experience little surprises. Like when I almost stepped on a rabbit. Not Alice's magical rabbit lurking at the door to Wonderland, but an ordinary gray one with a white tail. It sat right in the middle of my path, very still, and watched me with its large dark eyes. As I detoured around it—after all, the rabbit was there first—I laughed out loud. That laugh was spontaneous delight. I hadn't felt pure joy like that for as long as I could remember. I still had to name my experience 'joy' to satisfy Engineer-Frank's obsession with explaining things, but I had glimpsed something beyond words and collided with a mysterious world. The rabbit was its messenger.

"Over the weekend I received other messages: a strange, spindly blue bird standing motionless at the edge of the river. I watched it for at least five minutes, and it didn't move once. What did it see? I walked through stunningly sweet fragrances that seemed to lie in pockets in the woods, but there were no flowers that I could see. What was on my path that lured me with such sweetness? Only the simple, unadorned experience of peace, and hours that went by without notice. Time without action but filled with a magical liveliness.

"I had an idea on Sunday morning that explained what was happening in these encounters. Back then I always needed to be in control and explain things, and this was no different. What I imagined was some mysterious unseen powerful being playing games with me. Have you ever seen those puzzles for children where objects are hidden in a picture? A picture of a tree might have all sorts of tools hidden in its branches—shovels, hammers, saws, and the like. Well, I imagined some kind of force in some other world had carefully hidden lots of surprises—like the rabbit—for me to find that weekend, enticing me to play the game. That's what Father Edward was trying to encourage me to do: experience the joys of the games of mystery revealed only in silence.

"It seemed to me that the world that had collided with my usual world was playful and bursting with messages that I usually ignored. As I drove back to Washington, I remembered a few lines from *The Tao* that seemed to sum up my life and why I had to retreat from it.

> *Numerous colors make man sightless.*
> *Numerous sounds make man unable to hear.*
> *Numerous tastes make man tasteless.*

"I had never understood what those words meant until that weekend. Delight and joy were rare in my life, because figuring things out consumed most of my time. That funny little rabbit became my symbol of that other world's playfulness—deliberately placed in my path, waiting, even demanding to be noticed. After that, In-Frank was more alert for that mysterious world's surprises."

The nurse poked her head in the door and checked us out. When she saw how intent we were on conversation, she gave me a look of thanks and left.

"Frank, why do you describe your experience as colliding with a mysterious world?"

"Before my retreat I couldn't see any mystery in a rabbit sitting in the middle of my path. Afterward, I sensed that rabbit had special significance. The limits I placed on my everyday world had changed. Something had collided with my mind, or you might say my consciousness and altered it—forever!"

"I guess I understand," I said. "Where do these limits come from?"

Frank elevated his bed a bit and continued.

"These limits have many origins, but one of the most powerful and pervasive sources of limits of how we think about life are the myths we believe in. The widely held myths in any era restrict how people see their world and their lives. They contain humanity's shared ideas at any particular time about how the world works and what life is all about. These myths change, and our limiting ideas change as time goes by.

"From our modern vantage point what we notice in ancient myths like *The Odyssey* is the major role that gods play. Today, Darwinian evolution is the popular myth, and 'survival of the fittest' is the great god Zeus that makes things happen.

"According to Darwin's myth, the human mind is simply an evolving part of an evolving universe. We evolved out of the Big Bang, and our consciousness originated in mindless, purposeless evolution. What *is* a human being? In the scientific myth, we are only a collection of chemicals and energy that somehow developed consciousness over millions of years. Many people today take Darwin's myth and scientific truth as gospel. For this reason, I call the modern world we live in the 'Mind-World' because our lives at present are almost completely based on a scientific myth that our minds have invented to explain and control everything.[7]

"The Mind-World and the scientific myth leave scant room for gods, religious symbolism, and mystery. We currently believe science can explain everything that the ancient myths needed gods or magic to explain. Physics or evolutionary psychology or some other as-yet-undiscovered science—just you wait!—has the answers. We may not know what the answer is, but we believe science does or soon will. We devour books like *The Cosmic Connection* by Carl Sagan to learn how close science is to the ultimate answers we imagine. The science myth seems so obviously correct that it doesn't make sense to believe there might be another reality beyond the limits of measurements and facts.

I interrupted. "Frank, are you going to explain this other world?"

"Hang on. I'm getting there. The collision has to do with another reality breaking into our Mind-World. On my retreat I felt like I was standing in a gap between two different worlds as they touched. But they didn't just touch. They *collided* and caused each other to change. And since I was standing in between them, their collision changed me too."

"I think I see where you're headed," I said. "Unconsciously you wanted to escape the Mind-World when you went to the retreat house. What do you call the world that planted a rabbit in your path?"

"I need to tell you another little story before I answer you. Imagine that you really are an astronaut, like your namesake Neil Armstrong. In my story you have been

115

traveling on a long journey to a distant planet, in suspended animation. But surprisingly, when you wake up, you discover that your spaceship has traveled in a big circle, and you've actually arrived right back on Earth instead of a strange planet."

I must have looked puzzled, because he continued.

"You've been asleep in space for ten thousand years, out of communication. How could you recognize that you were really back home on Earth?"

I thought for a moment. Suddenly the hospital chair was uncomfortable, and I shifted to find a better position. I thought about stepping out of an imaginary spaceship onto a future Earth.

"If I'd been gone a very long time, things might have changed tremendously. I might not be able to recognize very much at all. So, in a way, Earth wouldn't seem like home anymore, would it?"

"Bravo! You're close. What makes us feel at home on Earth? Do we only feel at home because things are familiar?"

Even though Frank was sick, I was getting very impatient with him. The astronaut story had gone on long enough.

"Frank, let's get back to that other world. Are you implying that once I believe in it, I won't feel at home on Earth anymore? If that's true, then why should I take the risk of searching for your strange world?"

I couldn't take sitting in the hard chair for one more moment. I got up and stretched. Frank asked me to tuck the blanket in around his legs.

"Neil, that's the point! Why take the risk? The answer is connected with the name I give the other world. It's a world that frees life from its all-too-familiar limitations. I call it the 'Yes-World.' Why? I guess because when it collided with my everyday Mind-World it said, 'Yes! Frank, you are fundamentally good all the way down. Everything is.' The Yes-World lures us out of our autopilots and invites us to open ourselves to incredible possibilities. It places rabbits in our path to catch our attention, and it promises limitless surprises."

"The Yes-World is thoroughly good. When we are able to believe that the Yes-World is actually present, always colliding with our Mind-World, this knowledge brings awe and wonder into our lives. We can never go back to the sterile, scientific, facts-only, limited Mind-World."

I leaned forward and held up my hand for him to stop. "Wait a minute! How do you *know* your Yes-World is good? Maybe it's bad as well. You're just hoping that it's all good, aren't you? Maybe the Yes-World is just something you've imagined."

"There isn't any absolute answer to your objections, Neil. The Yes-World is what it is. Our map of it isn't the territory. What we are able to see of the Yes-World is a matter of believing is seeing. All people have their belief—their story—about the Yes-World that enables (or blocks) their quest for what it means to them. My story is that the Yes-

World exists and is completely good. Another person might believe the Yes-World is a mixture of good and evil, or even all evil but they probably wouldn't call it the Yes-World. Many others choose to believe that only the Mind-World is real. You can find any and all of these beliefs in human myths of one kind or another. Our story about the Yes-World shapes our hopes about our individual purpose on this planet, and the human purpose in the universe."

Frank paused. I had to chew on the Yes-World for a while. I could almost feel my mind at work, rearranging my thoughts into new patterns.

"So, when you say the Yes-World is good, you're telling me about a myth that you accept. Is that right?"

"Yes, that's right. My ideas about the Yes-World being good come from a myth."

"Which one?"

"I'd prefer not to tell you. That would make me a guru. And I don't want to turn this into a debate between you and I about which Yes-World myth is correct. Each person must decide for himself."

"So, tell me, why do you think it's so important to get in touch with the Yes-World?"

"I believe it's about finding our way home. The sad thing is that when people lose touch with the Yes-World, they actually are on an alien planet, even though they haven't left Earth. That's why I use the astronaut story. Things are familiar, so we think we are at home in the Mind-World. What is actually truer is that we have become accustomed to living in an alien Mind-World. We've forgotten the lost world we came from originally, the Yes-World that innocence can believe in and see. I believe that every serious quest begins when we become uncomfortable with the 'facts' of our life and begin to look for something we seem to have lost. That's when the Yes-World begins to change our lives in earnest."

He looked at me intently. This was the crux of everything he had been pointing at, the ultimate pattern he wanted me to see. I sensed how important it was to him, and I followed his lead.

"So how does this happen?" I asked. "You seemed to have accidentally stumbled into your collision with the Yes-World. What would be your practical advice to someone like me seeking it?"

He smiled at me like I'd finally gotten to the place he hoped I would.

"Neil, I know you're a Mind-World person like I was. Everyone is at first, even after we meet our In-selves. Let me see if I can help.

"What can you do? Well, you could forget about the Yes-World and stay where you are. After all, my story about the Yes-World is only a story. You can choose to remain in the Mind-World of facts. Maybe that's the best you can do. But you could also try to imagine that there might be another world—one where things cannot be explained by science, whose presence you might be able to sense in myths or, like me, in silence.

"If you choose that path, in the beginning you'll probably feel like you've deluded yourself. Your mind

119

continues to crave facts and certainty. Then it may occur to you that when you are thinking like that, you are still on autopilot, testing evidence for the Yes-World using your Mind-World story. You begin to see how slippery the Yes-World is. Its hints are very delicate, wispy, and ephemeral. You remain skeptical. Are these unusual experiences hints from another world or electrochemical phantasms in your brain? You could get the same results from psychedelic drugs like LSD. You realize that such thoughts are your autopilot using fact-based knowing again to judge these experiences.

"Eventually, you might see that you have to choose what to believe in—a Mind-World where seeing is believing and only facts have meaning, or a mysterious Yes-World with its subtle clues. To find the Yes-World, you must commit yourself to search for a world beyond facts. In other words, you must take a leap of faith.

"This is a very difficult choice; one we're not prepared for. Our culture molds us into Mind-World people who make rational choices, not people who leap across a chasm of non-Mind. Once you make the choice to search for the Yes-World, you must ask questions and wait, because that's all you can do. If you wait, I believe that the Yes-World eventually will collide with your world, but in a manner of its choosing, not yours.

"After a while, you may begin to see that you are wrestling with another question—*who you believe you are*. Your search isn't about understanding philosophical concepts. It's about deciding what kind of limits you place on who you are. Are you just some form of advanced animal with an evolved computer-like mind, or are you something more? Can you be described by science, or are you yourself a mystery, always unable to answer the deepest questions about who you are and where your true home is? That is the paradox of human knowing. You can never know such things, yet you have a deep hunger to know them. The Yes-World and who we truly are flee from our grasp when we pursue them. And they come to us when we wait. That is the reality of being human."

"But what's the answer, Frank? Why have you brought me to this point?"

He changed the bed's position again, lowering himself down a bit.

"Like I said, you have to choose what you wish to believe if you want to be able to answer such questions."

"But what if I choose to believe in facts—period? Does that mean I can never know the Yes-World? Am I stuck?"

"I think so. There is no mystery—for you. The Yes-World may remain lost to you."

"But what if it turns out there isn't any Yes-World?"

"I'm not prepared to be a guru and guarantee anything about the Yes-World. It's truly your choice and your experience that counts. You'll have to become an amateur astronaut yourself. Search for the Yes-World. Wait. See what happens. There's no cookbook recipe for discovering it."

"So, you want me to take the Yes-World literally. Is that what you mean?"

"You've got it. That's the astronaut's risky experiment."

"But will most people actually do that? Aren't most of us caught in our everyday roles, just trying to survive?"

I was thinking about my reluctance to take on the problems that Diane had raised or to see my company as wounded. Even though I'd met In-Neil, I was still immersed in a complex and demanding situation. Suddenly I realized that after I'd met In-Neil I *had* become an adventurer in a way, because nothing looked quite the same anymore. But now Frank had added another challenge, another chasm that I had to cross. A quest to find a mysterious Yes-World I knew nothing about. I felt jangled, exposed, and ill-prepared. Frank must have seen the anxiety on my face.

"You're on the right track, Neil. Stick with it! These are tough questions to answer. How do we recognize hints and insights from the Yes-World? How do we fly our lives and our organizations differently based on these insights, once we see our human situation as it actually is?"

I could see he wasn't going to tell me anymore that day. His face was drawn, and he looked very tired. The nurse had walked past several times in the last few minutes, signaling it was time for me to be off.

My mind was whirling when I left Frank that afternoon. When I got back to my hotel, I couldn't concentrate on work, so I went for a walk and eventually found myself in Hyde Park near Kensington Palace. Somehow, walking calmed me as I tried to make sense of it all. Frank was right about one thing: I didn't feel at home anymore. I'd been caught in a tornado of some kind, swept up like Dorothy and carried away to Oz. It occurred to me that I didn't *want* to go home to the Mind-World where Executive-Neil was comfortable! I think I was hoping that afternoon to meet my own magical rabbit in Hyde Park, a sign that I was on the right path. It didn't happen, but I was beginning to hope that someday it would. That was definitely a Yes-World hint.

In the end, though, I felt like I was being pushed too far, too fast. Maybe what I was missing was something like the strange Yes-World Frank was talking about. But right now, I wanted to hold onto the world of 'seeing is believing'. I wasn't ready to choose then and there.

I phoned Connie when I got back to Washington, but she didn't answer. I wanted to talk to her about what had happened. Maybe she'd have some insights. I left a voice message with my number, but she didn't call back. In-Neil said I should try again, but I didn't, not for many months.

Chapter 11

After he got sick, Frank began to write letters from his hospital bed to explain his ideas a bit more. I wondered at the time whether he was worried that I might not get the point of our conversations. Now I think he wanted to expand my horizons about the larger dimensions of the gentle revolution and my role in it. Whatever his reasons, his letters give you a window into his vision for the innocent fool's quest.

I received his first letter via email before I returned to London for another visit.

Dear Neil,

I am scribbling this on a yellow pad. The sisters have very kindly told me they will type it and send it to you. Deciphering my handwriting is their penance.

You and I have been circling around a larger issue in our conversations. Organizations—our own creations—ignore important human needs. Why precisely does this happen? Bad leadership? I don't think so. The answer lies deeper, at the level of organizational DNA.[8] Of course leaders influence this DNA, but there are other, more potent forces at work too.

Organizational behavior at the deepest molecular level isn't easy to understand because we are used to thinking about organizations in very simple terms, like teams or process flows, not as complex living things. Such simple models may work in some cases, like Newton's Laws work for simpler problems in physics, but we live in the age of quantum physics where nothing is as it appears on the surface. Why should living organizations be any different?

To understand their DNA, you need to start by assuming that organizations are not very much like anything you are familiar with. Scientists call them complex, adaptive ecosystems, and not one person in a thousand knows what that means. Most of us aren't scientists, so it's difficult to understand organizations in such terms. If you will be patient, I'll give you the ten-minute tour of organizations as complex ecosystems.

First, you need to understand that the mere fact that ecosystems are complex causes many things to happen. There are so many interactions and relationships among the parts of an ecosystem—whether a jungle or an organization—that everything seems to connect to and influence everything else. Scientists say highly connected ecosystems emerge. They evolve and change in hidden ways that gradually become evident over time. Jungles gradually evolve because they are highly interconnected. Organizations also change and emerge due to their complexity and the hidden interactions deep within their DNA. Even the planet Earth is an emerging ecosystem!

A good way to picture emergence in an ecosystem is to think of a kaleidoscope. When you slowly turn it, tiny pieces of colored glass continually rearrange themselves to make new patterns, helped by mirrors inside the tube. The combinations that emerge constantly surprise you with their novelty and beauty. Organizational ecosystems are like kaleidoscopes, continually shifting in their depths to form new emerging situations and behaviors.

Second, because they are complex, organizational ecosystems cannot be simply controlled like using a switch to control a light bulb. Very small changes in their depths can cause huge uncontrollable effects in ecosystems. The movie Jurassic Park dramatized the uncontrollable effects that took place across an entire island because of an error in one scientist's judgment. Similarly, because organizations are complex, management cannot completely predict how to control them. Many interactions in their depths have unanticipated side effects. Because of this, people like Diane have the power to trigger major changes in organizations. The small actions they take—however naïve and foolish they may appear to people in the power structure—can cause major effects.

Neil, I can hear you saying, isn't it better not to have Diane disrupting things? The answer is no, because Diane is a key part of the long-term survival and health of your organization! Her small actions can help your organizational ecosystem to self-organize to a new and healthier state that you probably can't create. How does this happen?

Many—but not all—ecosystems recover their health because they are able to learn and adapt. You can see this in rivers. They are able to revive and cleanse themselves despite being polluted for hundreds of years. Through relatively small changes in industrial waste disposal, the entire Thames ecosystem recovered much of its original health. How? Each small local part of the Thames—small regions of river water, individual plants, and bacteria—sensed and responded to small changes in its local area. When any small part of the Thames became clean, it influenced the parts nearest to it to also adapt and become clean. The sum of all these local small changes combined, and the whole river adapted and cleansed itself. Scientists say the Thames 'learned' how to become clean again. Diane and her team may be making their small part of your *company healthier, which can spread to your whole organization, like the Thames healing itself.*

Neil, you're objecting: "Surely I have the power to control what happens in my company." Yes, you do, but so does Diane and her team. Why? Because they, like you, are connected and can influence other parts of the organization. Innocent fools can trigger an avalanche of learning, which leads to bottom-up healing. That, very basically, is another way of describing the gentle revolution.

The mechanism that carries this avalanche of learning across your organization involves what biologists call 'tags.' [9] *How does this work? As an example, viruses like colds or the flu use tags to move from person to person, persuading them to be a host, then changing the host's health to allow the virus to grow. Cells in the victim's nose or throat attract the tag of a virus, and the virus sticks to the cell, once inhaled. This enables a virus to multiply and survive for a very long time, moving from victim to victim.*

Tags in organizations are anything attached to important ideas that make them attractive and enable such ideas to move from one person's mind to the next, like a virus. Innocent fools create powerful new tags, which act like healthy viruses to create an avalanche of change that can heal wounded organizations. That's why you don't have as much power to control things in your company as you think, Neil. Unless you can create tags that can compete in the 'meaning competition' with tags from other sources, you lose your ability to influence the hearts and minds of the people in your company!

Now we come to the important question I raised at the beginning of this letter. Why do organizations—human creations—ignore important human needs? This arises because of some very powerful tags in our Western culture that influence all of us to ignore many human needs inside organizations. These cultural tags continually bombard us with the following common idea: Single-minded focus on economic success is essential for everyone to live what we call 'the good life.'

Many tags in organizations carry this idea and make it very meaningful to us: higher salaries, corner offices, and other perks for people higher in the power structure. These obvious signs constantly reinforce the common cultural rules for success based on economic achievement. The end result is that we are all infested by this economic-focus virus and play our roles, conforming to a general rule that leaders use to control people in organizations: Don't do anything that interferes with economic success, including bringing your humanly sensitive In-self inside our organization!

Nonetheless, our In-self is always present in organizations because we can never leave it behind (although, as you and I both know, we can ignore it). Innocent fools like Diane bring their In-selves and its *human concerns into otherwise purely business and economic conversations. In some local part of your company, Diane's people are talking about their feelings and human dignity. These topics are probably becoming important tags to them because they are meaningful and relevant. Such awareness helps them begin to see gaps between their actions in organizational roles and their inner values. New tags begin to compete with the economic success tags. In this way, they are beginning to change organizational DNA in their group.*

Building on this awareness, Diane and her team begin to take simple steps to act more meaningfully and more consistently with their values. Using their new tags, they tell stories that are deeply meaningful to them, like treating working mothers in your company better. These personal stories—carried across your company—may ultimately have far more meaning than the 'organizational vision and purpose' tags created by leaders or culture. When that happens, innocent fools begin to win the meaning competition in their organization—and the gentle revolution is underway! The avalanche begins. A new, more humanly sensitive organization begins to emerge deep within its DNA.

Actually, Neil, the gentle revolution is already present—everywhere. It's just generally overlooked. The next time someone smiles at you, is concerned about you, helps you when they didn't have to, think to yourself, why did they do that? The answer is they were just being good.

Such actions hint that in every human situation, in every organization, deep down there are tiny forces of goodness transforming it.

There is of course a key difference between a natural ecosystem and an organization. Natural ecosystems simply evolve and change in response to their environment. There is a built-in rhythm to nature, a succession of species and ecosystems driven by fluctuations in the environment. That isn't how human ecosystems evolve. We can see and understand what we are doing. Unlike nature, we are morally responsible for altering the evolution of our organization and our planet—and ourselves in the process!

Because we have this moral sense that nature does not have, we have a moral obligation to choose what kind of future we wish to create. This, stated perhaps too simply, is the 'Green' message. We have a moral obligation to learn how to control our connectedness with sensitive parts of the ecosystems in which we live so as not to cause catastrophes such as global warming, the destruction of rainforests, or the injustices of inhumane organizations. Why? Because in the end, morally evil choices may destroy us! I'll discuss the very unpopular and counter-cultural word 'evil' with you when we next meet.

I suppose all that I'm really saying to you is that leaders of organizations need to assist these tiny forces of goodness to grow. Innocent fools like Diane need your help.

Can you now begin to see your interactions with her in a different light, Neil?

Kind regards,

Frank

Chapter 12

On the flight to London, I read Frank's letter again and thought about it. It was disturbing to imagine that there were hidden things going on in the depths of my company. Could Diane actually be changing the DNA in my organization? That felt bad, like a loss of control. I had lots of questions, but I was more concerned about Frank's health than about understanding his letter. When I entered his hospital room, he was propped up in bed, looking like he couldn't wait to get going.

"Neil, before we talk about that letter I sent you, we need to discuss a major challenge that innocent fools face in transforming organizational ecosystems. Okay?"

I nodded. He had obviously been waiting for me, and he had this conversation all planned out. It seemed there was something urgent he needed to tell me, like he wanted to pack a lot into our time together.

"I want to use *The Lord of the Rings* to help you better understand the gentle revolution. The central theme of Tolkien's myth is the conflict between good and evil. That's also the central conflict in any organizational ecosystem, at the level of its DNA."

I flinched, because I didn't like the words 'good' and 'evil.' They sounded almost medieval, like words the villagers in Bergman's *The Seventh Seal* would use. It didn't seem like good versus evil was what my company was all about. Frank ignored my reaction.

"Let me illustrate. When I was a kid, we only had radio, not TV. One of the programs I really liked was *The Lone Ranger*. I think it was broadcast on Wednesday nights at seven thirty. My whole family used to listen to it. It was about a masked hero and his sidekick who rode into small towns in the American West and rescued people from the bad guys.

"Now think about *The Lord of the Rings*. It's also about the good guys versus the bad guys. Frodo and a small band of companions against the evil Lord Sauron and his vast army of Orcs. The same basic theme as *The Lone Ranger*. There's a big difference though. Can you guess what?"

Frodo defeating Sauron. It did sound a lot like *The Lone Ranger.* I couldn't think of any big difference.

"I don't know, Frank."

With a sigh, which said Neil you should be able to figure this out, he began his explanation.

"The difference is the scope of the conflict. The Lone Ranger fought the bad guys in small towns in the old West. He could defeat evil in half an hour on Wednesday nights. In *The Lord of the Rings,* Sauron is attempting to enslave an entire world. Tolkien took eleven hundred pages for Frodo to win out over Sauron. In his myth, the scope and power of evil is almost too great to overcome. The Lone Ranger always seemed to know how to defeat the bad guys. But in *The Lord of the Rings* even the smartest people—Gandalf, Aragorn, and the wisest leaders in Middle-earth—couldn't defeat Sauron. The most unlikely hero, Frodo, the innocent fool, finally had to do it.

"Today, like Middle-earth, it's not the good guys versus the bad guys. It's the good guys versus the bad system. Things are so complex in our world that they seem about to overwhelm us. We can't see any easy solutions. That's why we love to see little guys like Frodo defeat the complicated evil of Sauron. *The Lord of the Rings* promises that there might also be solutions to our world's crises.

"Tolkien's myth rings true because most of us recognize Earth *is* being threatened, like Middle-earth. Wars, terrorism, ecological decay, and other evils of almost mythical scope confront us daily. But is some Sauron doing this to us? Are evil leaders behind these threats? The conspiracy theory people would say yes, but I don't think that's a likely explanation. I think that far more than bad guys threaten our planet. Organizations—corporations, universities, governments, even churches—are helping global threats increase their power, and their leaders are largely blind to this reality. Wounded organizations play a major part, however inadvertently, in supporting an evil system that is trying to enslave our Middle-earth!"

I finally had to speak up. Frank seemed to be going off the deep end. Our planet wasn't Middle-earth, and the organizations he was speaking about, my own included, were mainly doing good. Okay, they had a narrow focus on economic success, but they weren't evil!

"Frank, I can't buy what you're saying. All this talk about good and evil seems—I don't know—kind of simplistic. The real world isn't that black and white. Everything is so complex today. We don't think in terms of a battle between good and evil, or at least there aren't clear battle lines between good guys and bad guys. You made the point in your letter. The behaviors of ecosystems emerge out of many diverse influences."

Frank gave me his Gandalf look. He had me right where he wanted me.

"Are you saying things are too complicated for us to recognize good and evil?" he asked. "Or are you saying good and evil don't exist anymore? Neil, not to be too blunt about it, but if you believe either of those things, you believe in garbage. You know better. When a woman is raped or toxic waste is dumped indiscriminately into a river or a million people die of starvation, that is evil, and we all know it. How could things be too complex for us to recognize the Holocaust as evil? Let's call these things by their right name—human evil that needs to be opposed by all the goodness we can muster. My question is what are most organizations *doing* to combat these things? Relatively little, compared to their efforts to succeed economically. That's the challenge innocent fools must tackle."

He stopped to catch his breath. Then he changed direction again.

"Let me give you another clue about the conflict between good and evil in organizational ecosystems. Have you read *The Lord of the Flies*?" He didn't wait for an answer.

"It's about a group of schoolboys who find themselves completely free to decide their own rules. What do you think happened?"

"I guess they didn't just hold hands, sing *Kumbaya*, and decide to become little angels. Wouldn't be a very interesting book, would it?"

In-Neil nudged Executive-Neil in disapproval, and I grimaced, but Frank didn't seem to notice.

"They forgot the civilized rules they learned at home and reverted to the most primitive behaviors imaginable, including murder. Then there is the story about Weary Dunlop. He was an Australian doctor captured by the Japanese in World War Two. He was sent to the actual prison camp written about in *The Bridge on the River Kwai*. He did just the opposite of the boys in *The Lord of the Flies*. He brought order and concern for others into a hellish situation. He saved many lives and was honored by his country after the war. What do you think *The Lord of the Flies* has in common with Weary Dunlop's heroic story?"

He frowned in pain as he waited for me to figure it out.

"Well, I guess both those stories make the point that what you're calling good and evil originates in individuals, not circumstances. Groups of people have something to do with spreading good and evil too. The group of boys in *The Lord of the Flies* cooperated with each other to make evil spread. The other prisoners cooperated with Weary Dunlop's ideals and helped him spread goodness."

He smiled faintly. I'd guessed right, and it seemed that the pain had passed. But I still couldn't swallow all this good and evil that he insisted on discussing.

"But Frank, I still have a problem. If we use words like 'good' and 'evil,' isn't there a danger we'll go back to the days of religious hysteria like Bergman portrayed in *The Seventh Seal*? Demagogues will use evil to get people to do horrific things in the name of good. Who gets to define what's good and what's evil in a complex world like ours? Isn't it better to talk about problems and issues rather than evil, and ideals and values rather than goodness? Who can say confidently whether something is good or evil? Don't we have to deal with people and situations that have both good and evil in them at the same time?"

He sighed. "I guess you're right, Neil. A story about good and evil is kind of black and white. It's easy to see the source of evil in *The Lord of the Flies* or a Japanese prison camp;

it's much harder in everyday life. If a million people die of starvation, who can we blame for that? It might be due to primitive farming habits, or tribal warfare that prevents aid workers from helping the starving people. A messy set of intertwined causes wrapped in human foibles deep in a community's DNA influence them to emerge the way they do. So how can we say confidently that evil is involved? So, in a way, I agree with you. Because the system that controls much of our life seems like a complicated machine—and machines aren't human—it doesn't seem right to use terms like 'good' and 'evil' to describe it."

He paused again and pushed a button to make his bed nearly upright. He looked like he was getting comfortable for a long discussion. I wondered if he had the strength. I should have known better.

"Nevertheless, I insist that human evil is at the core of many problems in our world. The tags that create meaning, beliefs and actions—good and evil—in organizational ecosystems are of human origin. They don't just originate with leaders, although they too are responsible for some powerful tags. Underneath all of this, there is something in organizations that enables evil to spread and goodness to be ignored. Can you guess what it is?"

I thought of Lord Sauron in *The Lord of the Rings*. Certainly he was evil, but was there something else in that story that allowed his power to spread? The peoples of Middle-earth were divided, isolated from each other. That blocked them from uniting and fighting together. The Hobbits didn't actually seem to be aware of the threat from Sauron until the wise wizard Gandalf warned them.

141

"Maybe I see what you're driving at, Frank. Because there are so many divisions and factions among people on our planet, it's hard for us to agree about these threats or to take action against even obvious evils. Terrorism is a good example. Some people see it as evil to be stamped out regardless of the cost; others think it's a social revolution whose root causes need to be dealt with. These divisions keep us from acting, and in the meantime terrorists gain strength."

Frank grinned at me.

"Darn good answer! Divisions among people are underneath the spread of systemic evil. They keep us apart until we finally see the full effects of powerful evil—its obvious horror like the Holocaust—and we take our heads out of the sand and unite in a common cause to oppose it."

"But what if there is something else in organizations that permits evil to spread, something that's extremely subtle? If there is such a thing, and I say there is, we all could keep our heads in the sand for a very long time and ignore it. We could take no notice of it, and it would allow powerful tags to spread and keep on multiplying, wounding us and our organizations and our planet until the evil destroyed us."

He rang for the nurse. He needed to get out of bed for a while. She found his bathrobe and helped him to his feet. We walked slowly down the corridor, Frank leaning heavily on my arm.

I was frustrated. There were so many threads to follow, so many confusing patterns. I was still very uncomfortable with Frank's relentless focus on evil. I

142

wondered if his illness was affecting his normally even disposition.

"Frank, in this one case please just *tell me plainly* what you mean. What is this hidden factor we ignore that allows what you call evil to spread?"

He stopped and closed his eyes for a moment. I think he must have been enduring a moment of pain. Then he looked at me. His eyes were full of kindness and sympathy, but there was something else too. Determination perhaps.

"No, Neil, I won't explain it. That will just bog us down."

This time I didn't give in.

"Well at least give me a hint."

He smiled mischievously. "Okay. Call it N.M."

That was it? Was I supposed to guess what those letters stood for? Give me a break, Frank! He continued to smile as though he could read my thoughts.

"Okay, Neil, I'll give you one more clue, but that's it. The letters N and M happen to lie halfway between A and Z. They are middle-of-the-road letters. That's why I chose them."

He kept walking, letting me struggle with this new puzzle. Then, as usual, he jumped to a new subject.

"See this hospital? It's a marvelous human invention for creating good. Not that all the people that work here are angels. They're just like the rest of us, a mixture of good and bad. But there's a difference between this hospital and most other organizational ecosystems. Can you guess what it is?"

I kept trying to figure out what this had to do with N.M. but knew he would tie it in sooner or later. I said I didn't know.

"The difference is everyone in this hospital knows how to make judgments about what is good medical treatment and what's bad. Everyone agrees to live by a set of rules for good patient care and avoid the evil of malpractice. They have routine processes for making sure the people who work in the hospital know what the rules are and ensuring that everyone complies. It's the opposite of *The Lord of the Flies*. People here try to follow the rules, and goodness generally wins out.

"The process that makes and enforces the rules is called medical ethics. It's a fine system for making sure the complexity of medicine doesn't mask good and evil. The problem is most other organizations have no clear ethical systems or rules that everyone must follow. Oh sure, you hear about business ethics and professional ethics, but they don't work nearly as well as medical ethics. Probably because the people in most organizations don't think they need such rules. I guess they think they aren't dealing with something as important as life and death, like hospitals do."

"Frank, are you saying that the answer to global systemic evil is ethics? That sounds like a pretty weak answer for some very powerful problems."

"It doesn't seem possible, does it?" Frank said. "But think about it, Neil." He began to explain.

"No one can make me, an individual, follow a set of moral rules. Ultimately, I have the power to choose whether to serve the cause of good or of evil. It's my choice, period. But when I'm part of an organization, my choices are different. They go beyond my personal beliefs about right and wrong. I must understand the prevailing ethical rules and abide by them. If I don't, other people can discuss my actions, compare them against the rules, and decide whether I'm acting ethically, regardless of my personal moral intentions. They can enforce consequences, and even fire me.

"For example, as a doctor I might believe it's morally right to kill certain sick people in this hospital, but the group of people who manage the hospital—and the medical system as a whole—has the power to decide whether my behavior follows the ethical rules, and they enforce them. Do you begin to see how systematic evil emerges? When there aren't any rules about good and evil, it's the law of the jungle, like *The Lord of the Flies*. This may sound incredibly simplistic, but I believe that a lack of serious organizational ethics is one key cause of the spread of evil in complex human societies."

I still couldn't see where he was headed. I wondered about the ethics in my own company. If you stole anything, you'd be fired. I knew that. It wasn't written down, but I was certain it was an ethical rule. I tried to think of other ethical rules we might have besides stealing. I couldn't come up with any right then, but I thought we probably had them. It suddenly occurred to me that as one of its leaders, I should certainly know my organization's ethical rules! I wondered about other organizations. Did they have ethical rules?

What about schools? Did School Boards use ethics to decide what to teach students? Was it ethical not to teach ethics to students? I couldn't remember ever hearing a discussion about this. What about churches? You would think they had to have ethical rules because of the emphasis they put on morality. I wondered about the ways men in power in some churches had handled pedophilia in priests. Were they following their own ethical rules? Who had the power to enforce those rules? Could people outside churches insist on that? If the law was being violated, of course we could. What was the relationship between law and ethics anyway? I had stumbled into a mother lode of questions!

"Frank, you say that ethical rules in organizations—or the lack of them—are a key source of good and evil on our planet. Isn't it morality, or the lack of it, that is the real source? Is that what N.M. is about?"

Frank glanced over at me. I wondered what was going through his mind.

"Neil, you'll have to get past this point on your own. I can give you a few more clues, but the rest will have to wait for another day."

He was really frustrating me! I wasn't even interested in all this theory about organizational ecosystems and ethics. Even though I couldn't think of the ethical rules for my company, it didn't seem all that important. I knew what was right and wrong, and I could make good choices as a leader. What was he driving at? And then there was his mysterious N.M. What was that all about? I was very confused.

Frank asked to go back to his room, and we slowly walked down the corridor. He grasped my arm, and I was surprised at the strength in his hands. The nurse asked me to stay outside while they ran some tests. I was the only person sitting in the waiting area. It was quiet, so I thought over what we'd talked about.

Frank believed that systemic evil was a central problem on our planet. Changing whatever caused this problem was the focus of the gentle revolution. Ethical rules were the key to overcoming evil in organizations. Organizations have DNA like ecosystems. The connections between these ideas stumped me. It was all very puzzling.

The nurse came by and told me I could go back to Frank's room. The bed was inclined, and he was sitting upright.

"Neil, you need to go soon, but let me make one more point. Powerful evil will triumph at least in the short run unless there are rules and sanctions that limit its spread. The sanctions we use today to stop the spread of the worst evils are financial penalties, war, and prison. Unfortunately, those sanctions are applied after the evil has already done substantial damage. We need to do something proactively to curb evil and allow goodness to increase in strength. My solution is the gentle revolution and organizational ethics. Ethical rules and laws must apply to everyone in our world, the strong and weak alike. Otherwise, might makes right. The strong impose their ideas about morality on the weak. Does that help you?"

It all seemed too big, too complex. What could I do about the entire planet? Frank's ecosystem story seemed to imply that I couldn't even control my own organization.

He closed his eyes and rested his head back against the pillow. I knew I had to end this conversation quickly. Even though I felt powerless in the face of planet-sized problems, I began, finally, to see his point.

"Frank, if we could somehow find and enforce a set of ethical rules, that might help keep people like Saddam Hussein and terrorists from imposing their personal evil morality on millions of people. The problem is doing it. How can we create a planet-wide ethical system and enforce its rules, especially on the powerful? It seems very utopian and highly unlikely."

He nodded to show that he heard me but didn't reply.

I can see now with the benefit of hindsight that I didn't think I was talking about myself. Back then, as I sat in Frank's hospital room, I didn't see much need for ethical rules. I was basically a good moral person, wasn't I? My organizational ecosystem wasn't anything like Saddam's Iraq. I couldn't see a pressing need to do anything about evil in my part of the planet. In-Neil was strangely silent.

I went over to Frank and patted him on the arm. He opened his eyes and smiled at me, then closed his eyes again. I hoped I hadn't overstayed my welcome.

I left the hospital and caught a cab back to my West End hotel. I didn't feel like dinner, so I had a drink and went to bed. My mind kept working on Frank's gentle revolution. How could ethical rules possibly change the complex mixture

148

of good and evil that seemed to characterize our modern world? I had given up thinking about N.M.; I knew he would explain that eventually.

Then I thought of his letter. Tiny forces of individual human goodness were already present and making themselves felt in my company's DNA? Diane and her team were a signal that new tags of goodness were emerging? Frank had said clearly in his letter that I needed to help them. How? How did ethics fit in? Was N.M. (whatever it was) opposing Diane?

I flew back to Washington the next day to handle a crisis. Not an ethical one; just business as usual. That seemed to be the norm. *My* management team never seemed to face any ethical crises. I wondered why.

Chapter 13

A few days after I arrived back in Washington, Diane made an appointment.

"Neil, would you give a talk to my team? We're going away for a couple of days next week for some team building, and I thought they'd get a lot out of interacting with you. But if this isn't a good time …"

Without hesitation I said yes. She looked a bit nonplussed, as if she'd been expecting an argument, and then she left.

She sent me a short list of topics she wanted me to cover. My vision for the company and where we were going.

No problem with those; I had my story down pat. But there was one topic where I didn't have a standard speech: 'Tell us your views about the role of teams in improving our company.' I thought of Frank's letter on ecosystems, and of my ethics conversation with him. How many of those ideas should I use—or did I have the courage to use? I couldn't make up my mind and decided to wing it.

The following Tuesday I drove up to Cunningham Falls in the Catoctin Mountains in Maryland, where Diane had rented space at a conference center. The team had arrived Sunday night and had done a team building, hug-the-tree exercise on Monday. Judging by all the noisy chatter and laughter coming from inside the conference room, they were having a lot of fun. Somehow, my topic didn't seem interesting enough to provoke that kind of excitement, and I felt a little nervous. I needn't have.

At the break Diane introduced me to the team, and they seemed a little awed at meeting the head honcho. That made Executive-Neil feel better.

There were twelve of them, an equal number of men and women, young and middle-aged, all dressed very casually and sitting around the outside of a U-shaped table. I was the only one in a suit. I stood at the open end of the table. No place to hide. While I waited for them to settle down, I noticed some flip charts taped to the walls that described various draft visions for the group, lists of important issues and actions, and some marked-up process diagrams. Nothing out of the ordinary, yet there was something in the air. They had a lean and hungry look as they waited to hear what I had to say. But maybe I was imagining things.

I told the usual opening jokes and insider anecdotes and brought them into the picture of the company as I saw it. I was very accomplished at telling people where they fit into our plans, and I sensed I'd made a good beginning. They asked probing questions, and I scored some points with my answers. I was feeling pretty good when I got to the importance of teams in the company. That is where things got sticky.

I'd decided during the drive up to give them a pep talk on team performance. I'd read that in the time of the caveman, human beings had banded together in hunting groups to survive. The better hunting groups not only survived but took control of their territory. Team success was built into our cultural DNA, so to speak. I wrote three phrases on a flip chart at the front of the room: (1) Agree on what you are hunting; (2) Develop good hunting skills; (3) Focus intently on the hunt.

I'd just begun to elaborate on these points when a young man raised his hand. I wasn't ready to take questions, but he was insistent, so I said, "Yes?"

"Mr Schmidt, I don't think your caveman metaphor works anymore. We're not in survival mode. There's a lot more to life now than hunting for food." He stopped to see what I'd say. Of course, we weren't cavemen anymore, but the metaphor was about team alignment, learning, and focus. Couldn't he see that?

Diane broke in, "Neil, my team has agreed that anyone can question the assumptions that we base our work on. That's what Phil is doing, just so you understand."

Oh, I understood all right. Diane had set me up! This explained those lean and hungry looks. But I was ready to handle their challenge—I thought. In-Neil tried to break in and say something, but Executive-Neil's competitive juices had begun to flow.

"Phil, I take your point. I'm not saying that survival is all there is to life. I'm just pointing out the basics of a high-performance team."

Phil's eyes lit up as if he'd found a vein of gold to explore. "But isn't our performance linked to hunting something we believe is important? If we're focused on survival, we'll act a certain way. If we're focused on something else, we might perform differently."

A young woman interrupted. "Phil, what do you mean? What else would we focus on except survival? That's what business is about. Jack Welch and other respected leaders tell us that constantly."

Phil frowned at her. "Lucy, you and I have had this discussion before. I want to hear what Neil has to say." The others nodded and looked at me expectantly, but Lucy wasn't going to drop her point that easily.

"Neil, just a minute please. Phil and I need to resolve this." I was happy to let her continue; it gave me time to collect my thoughts. I shouldn't have relaxed.

"I think our group's assumptions are certainly influenced by what our leaders and managers think," she said. "But we are the ultimate decision makers on that score. I don't want us to just blindly follow their ideas." Phil nodded in agreement, and then they both looked at me. I had center stage again.

Great! Now I had *two* challenges to deal with!

Then I heard In-Neil clearly say to me, "These people aren't competing with you. They want to know what you actually think. Stop being so defensive."

I must have had a blank look on my face as I was listening to In-Neil because Diane added, "Neil, you may feel a little bit like I've set you up, but I haven't. This is the way this group is all the time. We bring things out in the open so we can see clearly what they really are. I told the group you are a very unusual executive, a person they can relate to. That's why they're treating you like you're a member of the group." Her conciliatory explanation relieved the tension in the room—and in me too.

I smiled at Diane and thought, I like it when you appreciate that your warlord is trying to be a different person. I also liked her saying I was a person they could relate to. Maybe I was a hit after all.

There was a lively give-and-take for over two hours. I learned a lot about what happens when a group of people seriously tries to take control of their own values and outcomes. They learned what it means to fit into a large, success-driven organization, and what it means to be a general manager. I didn't yet have enough courage to tell them about In-Neil.

Toward the end of the session, I decided to ask them a question about ethics.

"Who do you think decides what is right and wrong in our company? Or put another way, do you think there is a difference between personal right and wrong, what is right and wrong in your team, and what is right and wrong in the larger company?"

They all seemed to shrink back a little; to go into themselves. I looked at Diane. She was watching her team wrestle with the question and didn't say anything. There was silence in the room for what seemed like five minutes, but I'm sure was really only thirty seconds or so. Then one of the women who hadn't yet said anything shyly raised her hand. I nodded at her to go ahead.

"Mr. Schmidt, this is a question we talk about a lot. I'm not sure we've reached an answer as a team, but here's what I think. Most people have common sense and can tell right from wrong. So, if one of us sees something we think is wrong in our team or our company, we have an obligation to bring it up so the team can decide what to do. That's how we decided we had to do something about the unequal way our company treats the people in Indonesia. But our team can't force the company to change, just as no individual can force our team to change. That's how I think personal, team, and company ideas about right and wrong fit together."

I thought that was a pretty good answer and was about to tell her so when Phil broke in.

"We're still debating that issue, Natalie. I think our team has an obligation to change the company if it's doing something wrong. I know you feel senior management has the last say, but I disagree."

Phil was a bit of an agent provocateur. He worried me. I waited to see if others had different opinions. A gray-haired man named Jeff spoke up.

"I guess you could say Natalie and I represent the sane majority in this group. We cool down the firebrands like Phil. Our team has agreed to a rule that if there is a serious issue, we try to find a win-win solution that satisfies all of us. So that's why we can't give you a firm answer to your original question about where right and wrong comes from. It all depends on the situation and our debate."

Diane beamed like a proud mother when he said that.

Executive-Neil interrupted, "How much time do you spend in these debates? Isn't it taking time away from your real jobs?"

That caused a buzz. Diane broke in.

"Neil, many of our discussions are about how we can do our jobs better, but sometimes we need to bond with each other and have a deep and meaningful discussion. That's part of our job too. We can only become a high-performance team if we get to know how each person thinks and feels."

In-Neil nudged Executive-Neil. Diane has things well in hand, don't you think? She certainly seemed to. My respect for her grew every time we interacted.

Time had run out. I thanked Diane and the team for being so candid and told them to keep going; they were on the right track. Diane walked out to the car with me. Her face was flushed with excitement.

"I wanted you to see for yourself the dynamics in our team, Neil. I feel that sometimes you think we are wild-eyed revolutionaries threatening the existing order of things. I hope you can see now that we are responsible and care about the company."

I smiled and nodded. Yes, on the whole I saw that. Phil, the agent provocateur, was a concern, but the team seemed able to control his fervor.

She continued, her passion for her beliefs shining in her eyes. "I also wanted you to experience the commitment in our team. We're bound together by a strong belief that every human being is worthy of respect, no matter how insignificant they may be. We'll continue to try to influence the company to see things like we do. Oh, I know the company already feels it respects the individual, and to an extent that's true. Maybe our team is just more sensitive to the feelings of *all* people. The issue we raised about Indonesia is an example. How do the women there feel, not being able to care for their children? I wanted you to understand how committed my team is to people everywhere, inside the company and outside too."

I knew she'd rehearsed that little speech, and I understood what she was trying to tell me. But looking back, it took years for me to really appreciate what she and her team were getting at. At the time, it still seemed obvious to me that feelings weren't what business was about, unless you meant the feelings involved in customer satisfaction. Maybe that was the basic difference between Diane and me. Back then I needed a business case for deciding how to treat people, and she didn't.

Shortly after my meeting with Diane and her team, 911 happened. It stunned me and brought home the presence of evil in the world like no other event I had experienced. I had dinner with three bright, thoughtful women executives shortly afterwards. Over several bottles of wine, we searched for some explanations for what had happened in New York and Washington. Every possibility we discussed inevitably led us to questions we couldn't answer. How had things gotten to this point? Why hadn't leaders anticipated and prevented global problems like terrorism? We found no satisfactory answers.

Near the end of the evening I asked them, "Is the world at a dead end where the only possibility is violent revolution?" The sad thing was we all seemed to share a similar ominous premonition of an inevitable downward spiral into chaos, upheaval, and revolution. The striking thing I remember about our discussion was how helpless these three talented women felt. They knew how to make things happen in organizations and had been successful in their own careers. But now, although they wanted to do something about the world's crises, they were at a loss.

At the time, I felt I needed to give them hope, but was afraid to bring up Frank's stories and the gentle revolution. It didn't seem like Frank's emphasis on personal, local bottom-up change could do anything about preventing future calamities like 911. Also, how could I bring it up when I was a long way from committing myself to making it a success? That's what Frank began to work on next.

Chapter 14

Later, as I thought about Diane's team, something else occurred to me. Their project would only last for a year, two at the most. To change the DNA of our entire company and make it think and feel differently about people and global issues—assuming we needed that—was a long-term undertaking, probably far longer than management would allow her team to stay together. How could they lead the gentle revolution if the team ceased to exist?

When I got back, I sent Frank an email and asked him that question. I knew the sisters at the hospital would print it out for him and then forward his response. It only took a few days to receive his answer.

Dear Neil,

You asked me how individuals and small groups like Diane and her team who come and go like smoke in the wind can transform large organizations. It depends on the power and persistence of the tags they create. If the tags are sufficiently meaningful, they can outlive the groups who create them and go on and on for decades, even centuries. Think of St Francis, his Franciscan followers, and their brown-robed community, whose message about simplicity has lasted for over six centuries.

Human history emerges from the actions of dedicated individuals like Francis and Diane and their supporters. But there's something else going on as well. Darwinists say it's only chance and survival of the fittest. I disagree. I think somehow, mysteriously, the Yes-World also guides how human history is shaped. Yes, I assert that even in view of the evil in 911. (From now on I will refer to the Yes-World's actions in human society as 'Influence,' to distinguish them from all the other political and cultural factors that people use to describe how history emerges.)

To help you understand how the Yes-World's Influence works in everyday situations in companies like yours, I want to tell you a story about a woman I know called Hannah. She started a gentle revolution within her organization by changing her team's conversation about

Yes-World Influence. She was no saint, just a woman like Diane who decided to change things.

To get her ideas across, Hannah used a metaphor for an organizational ecosystem—a forest, and its trees and leaves. Organizations are like forests. Teams are like trees. When trees are healthy and growing, the forest expands. Similarly, when teams do their work well, the organization succeeds.

Each individual in a team is a leaf on the tree. There is something special about an individual leaf. It has a unique capability, although it's only a very small part of a tree and a forest. Leaves create food for trees. Each leaf has the power to transform light from the sun and carbon dioxide from the atmosphere into food for the tree through a unique process called photosynthesis. The leaf also releases oxygen into the atmosphere. Without leaves there would be no trees, no forest, a lot less oxygen, and probably no other life on Earth for that matter. Leaves have the ultimate power to grow forests—just as individuals have the ultimate power to grow and heal organizations.

In her metaphor, Hannah was describing how the Yes-World's Influence works through individuals to transform the DNA of organizations. Imagine that the Yes-World is like the sun. Just as photosynthesis works with the energy of the sun through leaves to enable trees and forests to grow, there is collaboration between the Yes-World and individuals to create special 'food' that organizations need

163

to grow and heal themselves. Even though a person is only one leaf, if she is in exchange with the Yes-World she can bring something powerful—new ideas or, in a way, new food—to nourish goodness in her group, and ultimately the entire organization.

The point of this metaphor is that human collaboration with the Yes-World is a vital part of changing the DNA of organizations. Hannah's simple story helps people begin to see that they aren't alone or powerless to change things in large organizations. Together with the Yes-World's Influence, they can transform the way human needs are addressed in their team and organization. Innocent fools can succeed only if the Yes-World's Influence is present. It's that mysterious presence that makes all the difference in the gentle revolution.[10]

Like you, Hannah wondered how she could change things if it would take a very long time. "If the gentle revolution means changing my entire company, and perhaps other companies too—healing entire forests— how can I create teams that are capable of sustaining such major change? The gentle revolution might be a very long-term undertaking. I would have to find highly motivated groups of people committed to making an extended and difficult journey." Hannah began to see that finding and shaping humanly sensitive teams to collaborate with the Yes-World was the work of a lifetime, perhaps even her own life's work.

And so, Neil, I come back to your original question. Organizations change, and people come and go, so can the gentle revolution persist? Incredible long-lived persistence arises when a group led by an innocent fool begins to understand its ultimate purpose. Unless people believe the team's contribution to the world is of the highest importance and is in a way more important than the team itself, their energy will gradually erode, and the gentle revolution will eventually die out in the organization.

So, at some point every team must focus on a moral choice. We can use our energy and knowledge in service of strictly short-term economic ends, or we can also serve short and longer-term human ends. There is a big difference between the two. One treats people as objects intended for economic or political ends, period. The other challenges the inhumane use of power because every person, no matter how seemingly insignificant, is of lasting value. When they adopt the latter view, a team begins to take on an additional risk in their journey—achieving both the group's assigned organizational tasks and supporting the fundamental belief they share in the ultimate value of human beings.

Unfortunately, teams can also decide to serve purely economic or politically focused purposes rather than include human needs. After all, each of us is free to decide what to do with our energies and who to serve with our efforts. Therefore, teams can also be the primary source of amplifying the power of the status quo or the evil system, and indeed most teams are doing so today. This is why the gentle revolution always involves a search for wisdom and moral choice.

I think the term 'community' rather than 'team' is a better description for groups who are focused on human values. (If I was bolder, Neil, I would say focused on love.) Together with the Yes-World, communities create powerful, long-lasting Influence. With this as their focus, diverse human beings, each with their own unique purpose, each on their own journey, create deep bonds within a community that can endure and carry them toward a larger purpose that may even lie beyond their own lifetime.

As a final point, think again about Hannah's metaphor. How can we tell if a forest is healthy? By looking at its results. Are the trees growing, and is the forest thriving? The same holds for organizations. If an organization competes successfully and survives, it must have a number of relatively healthy groups. But this is too narrow a description for organizational health. The organization's growth may still serve only economic or political purposes, so how can we recognize truly healthy organizations that also serve human values?

As part of the gentle revolution, I propose that organizations begin to use a second test for health in addition to economic success. Wise leaders must require each community in their organization to use its own value *system to determine whether it's becoming a healthy tree, as judged by its own standards. Communities must be free to hold up ethical ideals and standards for themselves, measure their actions and results against these, and take corrective actions based on their own judgments. The community needs to have conversations about how much progress they have made toward their ideals.*

Both the economic and ethical tests of health would give communities their organizational report card. Communities would report to leaders on how well they have progressed on their ethical journey, and also how well they have performed against the other organizational tasks.

Neil, my vision is that in being faithful to their ethical standards, the people in that community, in the wider organization, and in the outside world experience a tiny bit of healing of the wounds in our culture and a lessening of systematic evil. Obviously, if an entire organization gets to the point where it holds up ethical standards and measures itself against them, and safeguards human values no matter what, then this would go a long way toward healing the world on a much larger scale. That's the ultimate purpose of the gentle revolution.

I sense that Diane and her team have set off down this road and are becoming a community. They probably aren't aware of that yet. In fact, that might be your role—to expand their thinking about what they are trying to do. But don't worry about that just yet.

I hope this letter has helped you. I'm working on another and will send that to you soon. See you in a few weeks (I hope). Frank

When I finished reading Frank's email, I thought, he's answered my question, but somehow the gentle revolution just doesn't seem possible. Why would anyone in an organization run such risks? Could there be many people with that much faith in the Yes-World? I vaguely realized that I was asking a 'Give me liberty or give me death' type of commitment question that might come back to haunt me.

In-Neil whispered, "Why don't you ask Diane? Maybe she can help you understand." So, the next morning I called her and scheduled a meeting in my office.

I was running late, so she had to wait fifteen minutes. I apologized, and she nodded.

"No worries, Neil. What's on your mind?"

I offered to get her a coffee, but she declined.

I told her I really enjoyed the discussion with her and her team, but that after I left a question occurred to me.

"What makes you and your team want to continue challenging the status quo?" I hadn't told her about Frank, and I didn't think I should get into his story about Hannah and the Yes-World. In-Neil tried to persuade me it would work out, that Diane would appreciate it, but I decided to take a low-risk approach.

"Are you asking how we decided what to do about Indonesia?"

"No, I'm more interested in what makes your team tick. Where did this appetite to change things come from?" I realized this sounded a little like an interrogation, but I decided that keeping Diane a little off balance was a good thing. I still wanted to keep things under *my* control.

"Oh, I see. Hmm. Well, I think it's because we have been discussing the way the world is today. Things seem to be more and more chaotic. Our feeling was that there had to be a way for smart people like us to make a difference. That's how we thought of Indonesia. Maybe if a US company began to treat a Muslim country's people differently, that might spark something good. 911 just emphasizes that even more." She paused to see if that answered my question.

"I see. Do you and your team think you can take a small step like that and affect something much larger—like our company or the United States' relations with Indonesia?" I assumed she knew nothing about Frank's ecosystem ideas, but I was curious to see how she would react.

"Definitely. It's a bit like encountering questions you can't answer. Once you start thinking from a new perspective, you never know where it's going to lead you."

I looked at her sharply. Had she heard Frank's story about Parsifal? How could she have? I became irritated that someone may have gone behind my back and introduced

Frank's ideas into my company without me knowing. In-Neil whispered, "'Warlord thinking," but I ignored him.

"So, you believe you can change this company? Why do you want to do that? Do you think I'm not up to it?" Whoops. That last bit slipped out, and I was embarrassed. Diane grinned at me.

"I think you're probably as good a leader as can be found these days." I started to relax, when she added, "Of course, there's only so much you can do. That's the problem."

Now I was convinced she *had* heard Frank's stories. She was referring to the gentle revolution! I didn't feel much like continuing the conversation.

"Okay, Diane, thanks for coming to see me. I've been thinking about things a lot lately, and this has helped."

She frowned and, after hesitating a moment, left my office. I felt foolish ending our talk so abruptly and almost asked her to come back. And, after a while, I felt even worse when I realized she was actually on my side. I remembered the mysterious N.M. that Frank had referred to and wondered if that was why I reacted as I had with Diane. I would ask him about that next time.

Chapter 15

My conversations with Frank and my uncomfortable relationship with Diane continued to trouble me. I was wrestling with a number of questions. Why did I react to Diane so defensively? As its leader, I was responsible for everything that happened in my division. Why take the risk of changing its DNA? Suddenly, another question came to me, this time from In-Neil. Why couldn't I accept that the Yes-World was working to transform my company?

All the answers to these questions seemed to depend on my beliefs—about the gentle revolution, the Yes-World, other people, and, most important of all, myself. What did I believe? Whatever it was, did I believe it strongly enough to truly commit myself to the gentle revolution? I couldn't find answers to those questions, and I had no choice but to wait, as uncomfortable as that was, for them to emerge.

I called Connie again, and this time she answered her phone. I was nervous, but we got through the chitchat and arranged to meet at a local restaurant. She looked spectacular, and I felt like a teenager on a first date. We filled the awkward opening moments with small talk, but she left the direction of the conversation in my hands. What did I really want to tell her? In-Neil saved the day.

"Last time we met," I began, "I wondered what you thought after you left. Do you remember? Would you mind telling me?"

She smiled that mysterious smile again, but gave me a look that said, I've been waiting for you, Neil. Of course, I'll tell you. And she did.

That night, I fell in love. That's another story, but I need to tell you a few things about Connie and me, because they have a bearing on this story. My struggle to become a different leader intensified because Connie was an honest critic. I told her all the stories Frank had told me and the conflicts they raised. Like Frank, she didn't try to solve my problem. She didn't say, "Live in the question," either. Connie simply stated—and kept stating—what she believed about each person's obligation to improve the life of every other human being.

I had heard the old saying, 'No man is an island,' but I never really understood it before meeting Connie. It states a fundamental truth about life. In-Neil thrived on intimacy. His ability to influence Executive-Neil didn't draw strength from self-reliance or self-development. It grew strong from receiving and giving love. The exchange between In-Connie and In-Neil (and the Yes-World too, as I later discovered) was one of the fundamental forces of nature, like gravity and energy.

In many ways, Connie changed my life far more than Frank did. This story, however, is about Frank and how his ideas changed me. But I will tell you that Connie and I quickly discovered that although we were lost on the same alien planet, we were truly at home with each other. Exploring together what that means has been a wonderful adventure!

I received another email from Frank just before my next trip to London but didn't have time to read it until I boarded the flight. In it Frank also seemed critical of my leadership, more so than at any other time in our friendship. I tried to imagine what triggered his criticism but couldn't come up with anything.

Dear Neil,

This will be an especially challenging letter for you.

The people concerned with globalization seem to be asking, "Do we need powerful leaders like you and large organizations at all? Wouldn't we be much happier, and wouldn't everything work better, if things could be kept small and simple?" People who think like this seem to want to return to some imaginary and idyllic place. "Let's disassemble organizations, or at least vastly curb their power. Doesn't their size and power cause many of the problems we face?"

That's not my point of view of course. It's obvious that leaders and organizations are vital parts of the human future, but the size and complexity of global organizations do cause unintended side effects. As organizations grow in size, they require leaders who can effectively manage awesome power and ensure their organization's survival. The problem is ambitious people are generally the ones who fill these roles. These powerful people, most often men, end up pursuing organizational success at any cost and become very skilled at hiding this truth from themselves.[11] Men (and women too) who are sensitive to moral issues outside their work roles actually begin to ignore human welfare in their own organizations. Leaders like you, Neil, who are beginning to sense a need to heal wounded organizations, must find a way to deal with this personal power issue, or else the gentle revolution may only remain a dream.

Can the management gurus and teachers help you? No, because they are generally emphasizing the wrong things. Why is that? Because there isn't a market for the ideals I'm proposing. The conventional culture of leadership determines what the teachers will teach. The gentle revolution has a radical idea at its center that the consultants believe simply won't sell. What is this radical idea? Basically, that leaders must give up their unhealthy dependence on power if the gentle revolution is to succeed!

Leaders who truly desire to support the gentle revolution must accept a servant leadership role.[12] That doesn't seem so radical, does it? Some management scientists have been saying that for years. The fact is, however, servant leadership has never been a hot seller in the leadership coaching marketplace.

I'm sure you won't be surprised if I say that handling personal power differently involves a difficult decision that only you can make. To help you to understand this decision better, let me tell you a story. It's a story whose origins will always remain a mystery because they involve a man's private dialogue with himself. How did a promising young German architect, Albert Speer, become a principle director of Hitler's war machine? It happened because Speer was caught up in momentous events, apparently without the strength of character needed to resist Hitler's offer of power. He succumbed to "the unlimited opportunities Hitler offered him."[13]

What up-and-coming young executive hasn't experienced the attention and sponsorship of a powerful person offering advancement in exchange for loyalty? Which of us would question the motives or the morality of such a person giving us a leg-up over our peers? When Speer was asked the question, all he could think of to explain his attraction to Hitler's offer was the background of the times in which he lived. "The formative experience of his early years, he claimed, had seen a general sense of decline in values and a feeling that the ground was shifting *wherever one stepped. Everything was doubtful, nothing secure."* Which of us wouldn't use the same excuse, living as we do in our own confusing times?

Why didn't Speer sense Hitler's evil and turn away? The explanation is one that we surely can identify with: He ignored Hitler's lack of character and immorality and grasped the opportunity being offered because of the rewards it promised. Like Faust, he made a deal with the devil. He was twenty-eight, and all of a sudden, he was being offered important jobs and earning a reputation, even fame. Speer succumbed *"to the temptation of the opportunities which unexpectedly presented themselves to him."*

There is no need to continue Speer's story in detail or to list his crimes. We all know about Nazi evil. What is interesting is Speer's own lack of insight into his own actions. As part of the trials, he was confronted by a young Jewish American Captain named Klein: *"Mr Speer, I don't understand you ... You knew all this [horror] and yet you stayed, not only stayed, but worked, planned with, and supported them to the hilt. How can you explain it? How can you justify it? How can you stand living with yourself?"*

Before I give you Speer's response, Neil, think for a moment about your own life and your investment of time and energy in personal achievement, balanced against what you have invested in human growth and goodness. How many of us could stand a rigorous interrogation on *that subject with all the evidence about our lives assembled like Nuremberg? "After a moment of embarrassed silence, Speer began to answer. He said the captain did not understand him. He did not understand anything about life in a dictatorship, nothing of the ever-present fear, and nothing of the game of danger that also went with it. Above all, he understood nothing about the charisma of a man such as Hitler. When Speer had finished Captain Klein got up and left the room".*

Do you find my comparing you with Speer offensive? I understand. I can see similarities in my own experiences, and I feel horrified. I believe any leader, if he or she is completely honest, would see parallels. There is something immensely seductive about being admitted into the inner sanctum of power. It changes you. You harden your heart in order to make tough decisions. You shield yourself from the effects of those decisions. You have to fight to survive in a very complex world, where false steps or weakness give your competitors an advantage. I could go on, but you get the idea. Accepting that something like this has happened in your own life is essential in making a personal decision about using power wisely.

Neil, leaders like you are the absolutely indispensable allies of innocent fools in the gentle revolution. But you have a serious problem. Because of your status and power, you have lost contact with what's really happening in the company's DNA, and thus you are blind to the consequences of your actions. You are addicted to using power! The antidote for this addiction is people like Diane confronting you, asking, like Parsifal, "What ails you?" Once she does that, and not before, you can freely commit to support her. From what you tell me, I think she may have already asked you that question.

With kindest regards,

Frank

After I finished the letter, I turned off my light and sat in the darkness of business class, for some reason remembering my first interaction with Frank on the flight to Sydney. What had he seen in me? Why had he spent so much time with me over the years? Even after meeting In-Neil, I hadn't really changed. I was still pretty much the same person with the same beliefs. Frank's blunt statement that I had a problem with an addiction to power and that I needed Diane as my coach grated with my belief in my own competence to fulfill my executive role.

My mind swirled with questions and doubts about Frank's gentle revolution, and the Yes-World, which I still couldn't quite accept. In-Neil said, "Be patient with yourself" and Executive-Neil said, "Things are too hectic; there are too many demands and crises. I'm not an addict, but I'm no hero either!" I was glad I was seeing Frank the next day!

Chapter 16

Before I visited Frank, I had a meeting near the Tower of London with our insurance brokers. As I walked through London's curious mixture of very old and ultra-modern architecture, I thought about the implications of Frank's gentle revolution for this place. The complex global system of finance, which London epitomizes, depends on the shared goals and rewards of people around the world. This system would be very resistant to Frank's ideas. The hard facts about profit and loss and individual wealth seemed inevitably to conflict with soft fuzzy ideas about goodness. I couldn't see a way to reconcile these opposites. In fact, if I were being honest with myself, I didn't want to resolve them in my own life. I loved the power the system gave me.

After my meeting, I took a cab to the hospital. As the driver wove through the early afternoon traffic, it struck me that the vast majority of people in this energetic city were caught in a kind of trap, and it took all their skill and focus to survive. There wasn't much space left in their world for goodness. First you had to survive, then you had to excel, and then—if you had any energy left—you worried about the other guy or higher purposes. The prayer most of us said every morning was, "Please, God, let me survive one more day." The gentle revolution seemed only to increase the risk of survival without a tangible payoff. By the time I got to the hospital, I had plenty to talk to Frank about.

I stopped at the nurses' station. The sister didn't say much except that Frank was holding up well. He didn't look like it. He had black circles under his eyes and was noticeably thinner. Still, he was sitting in his chair, and I spotted the old Gandalf gleam in his eye when he spotted me.

I told him of my misgivings about changing the system and transforming leaders. People were too busy keeping their jobs to worry about the deeper meaning of good and evil in organizations.

"I agree, Neil," he said. "The need for organizations and leaders to change has been said over and over in the last century by people far more learned than I am. Nothing much has changed."

"So, what's the bottom line?" I said. "Why hasn't the gentle revolution happened up to now?"

"Two reasons. First, there is the immense weight of the old ideas about power that stifles the new ideas. All of us believe in the conventional wisdom that says leaders ought to wield power. Second, leaders use these beliefs about power to control us and maximize their own gain. They aren't hesitant to use their clout to eliminate dissenting ideas, and they are also blind to the consequences of their actions. These two power-related issues block the path that innocent fools must take in spreading the gentle revolution's goodness."

"So, is there a way past these barriers that all those other people haven't discovered?" I asked.

"I believe so. Most of them were stuck in the old ideas about power when they thought about solutions. Many have tried to convince leaders to use their power differently, or to set up government or other controls on power. I think innocent fools can take a different path, one that has a better chance of working. They can help leaders learn a new role that only *they* can fill, one that is the key to helping the gentle revolution succeed. Diane can coach you in this role."

"Oh, so I *am* needed in the gentle revolution after all! I was beginning to wonder if you even thought I was part of it."

"I never meant to imply that you weren't. But hold on; let me continue. You may be surprised by the role that I assign to you and other leaders in the gentle revolution."

"Assign a role to me? Who says that I or any other leader will accept this role? After all, as you said, we have the power, and conventional wisdom says that we ought to."

"You're a good foil for my argument, Neil. Let me continue. What if there were ways to initiate the gentle revolution and keep it hidden so that it didn't seem to threaten the success of organizations? What if the gentle revolution didn't cause defensive reactions in leaders and acted instead like a benevolent virus, infecting organizations before they knew it? What if, eventually, leaders could learn this bottom-up process from innocent fools and change their way of thinking about power and success? Could the gentle revolution happen then?"

"I don't think you could conceal Diane's team's ethical values from the leaders of an organization. She pushes too hard. No, I don't think the quest can be hidden."

"But the leaders of organizations aren't the ones I want to hide these changes from! I want to hide them from the external critics, the market analysts, the guardians of conventional economics, and the gurus who would pooh-pooh its beginnings and kill it before it even got started. The innocent fools who start a gentle revolution need to get through a stage of very tender new growth. Their ideas and moral power need a chance to mature and gather strength before they are attacked. That's the primary role I see for leaders in the gentle revolution. Like Gandalf and Aragorn protected Frodo, you need to protect and shepherd Diane and her team on their difficult quest."

"So basically, you're hoping that a person like me who has already firmly grasped power will somehow decide to let someone else exercise power and change the DNA in my company. Is that reasonable?"

Frank took a deep breath. "Many people I talk to sense that we are entering a new era of human history. We don't yet have a name for the new age, but 'things aren't the same anymore' is a constant theme in our conversations. Nine-eleven has emphasized this in a horrible way. Still, innocent fools like Diane believe we have entered a special time when perhaps the world will finally face up to the human and environmental conflicts we've ignored for too long. This special moment can result in rethinking the human-planet relationship, not just business-as-usual problem solving. Leaders are being exposed to this kind of thinking as the media and the internet make it a topic of conversation. Perhaps as a result, they may begin to see things differently, and be more ready to risk the gentle revolution."

I thought of my own experiences. I'd ignored these kinds of topics for many years but had to admit they were becoming a part of more of my conversations. I remembered my dinner with the three women executives after Nine-eleven and our feelings of needing to do something.

"The anti-globalization, anti-corporation people are another signal. You probably bristle because you believe your ideas about organizations are closer to the right track than theirs. You see the positive side of organizations. The achievements of global enterprises in the last hundred years are dramatic, affecting the lives of billions of people on this planet in positive ways. Corporations have created worldwide innovations in transportation, communications, computers, energy, agriculture, manufacturing, and entertainment. But leaders like you are beginning to see in the passion of the demonstrators, however faintly, that their organizations need to care more about human concerns and apply substantial resources to the issues the protestors are raising!"

I remembered Indonesia and that beggar squatting in the dust in Manila. My company wasn't doing anything about that, but at least I was now seeing things in color. Maybe that was a step in the right direction.

"Neil, surely you must see that the winds of change are blowing across our planet. That leaders need to change. Don't you agree?"

On the flight over I had read his letter repeatedly and thought to myself, I'm no hero. The gentle revolution requires heroes. That leaves me out. But I didn't tell Frank that. He must have sensed my turmoil, because he told me another story.

*

"Let me try to tie all these ideas together by using *The Lord of the Rings* again. Tolkien paints the conflict between good and evil in black and white. There are good leaders, like Aragorn and Gandalf, and bad leaders, like Sauron. As you and I discussed, however, our world isn't black and white. Most leaders aren't evil, just overly focused on economic success and personal power. They hold on tightly to the role that gives them power, and they think, probably with some justification, that they *are* doing considerable good for many people, including the shareholders who hired them. To support the gentle revolution, they must decide, like Aragorn, to not rely solely on their usual beliefs and power.

"There's a scene in *The Lord of the Rings* where a powerful leader who has already grasped the ring is defeated in battle. Saruman was the head of the order of wizards to which Gandalf belonged, but he became an ally of Sauron and, during the war in Middle-earth, was defeated by Gandalf and his allies. Afterward, Gandalf graciously offered Saruman his freedom. 'When I say *free*, I mean free from bond, of chain or command; to go where you will, even to Mordor, Saruman, if you desire. But first you will surrender to me the key to Orthanc [his castle] and your staff [his power]. They shall be pledges of your conduct, to be returned later, if you merit them.' Gandalf is telling Saruman that what he previously trusted in—his exalted position and his power—is what keeps him enslaved to Sauron. Gandalf's promise to Saruman is that if he leaves his power behind, perhaps only for a little while, and learns to make free choices away from its domination, he may then return to exercise power wisely, once he has been healed. Do you see where I'm headed, Neil?"

Of course. It was blindingly obvious. In his example, I'm Saruman, faced with a crucial decision. Choose freedom and a new leadership role, or hold onto my fortress of power. But I haven't been defeated! Why should I choose to leave my castle? In-Neil sighed, but didn't say anything.

"Remember my previous story about the critical decision that Aragorn faced? 'What is my heart's desire, and how much am I willing to sacrifice for Frodo's quest to succeed?'"

Frank stopped to rest. I thought I understood where he was going. Aragorn put supporting Frodo's quest first, and his own kingship second. Frank was putting it on the line for me. Was there anything important enough in the gentle revolution to persuade me to put aside my personal interests and support Diane?

Frank looked directly at me.

"Let's talk about the difficulties that Aragorn's decision poses for you. They point at the mysterious N.M. threat I that talked about before. What do you think the issues are for you, facing a decision like he faced?"

"Well, my first thought is why should I make this choice? What's in it for me? What's important enough for me to change my ways?"

I looked at him and he smiled faintly.

"Why do you think you can't imagine a good reason to change?"

Why did he always do that? I didn't know the answer to these 'why' questions. He must have known that, but there was no way forward except to try to think it through.

"I don't know. I suppose I would have to change if Diane really pushed me."

Wait for Diane to force me to change? That sounded pretty weak. I guess I felt that I couldn't invest much energy into the gentle revolution because there were just too many things driving me. Healing wounded organizations wasn't urgent. I was beginning to get a fuzzy idea about what N.M. was.

I said, "Frank, I think one of the problems for leaders is how familiar we are with the usual issues in our roles and how unfamiliar we are with what the gentle revolution is about. We just don't pay enough attention, because good and evil and ethical questions don't seem to have much effect on our organizations or our lives."

"You're getting close, Neil. But imagine for a moment that you have already made Aragorn's choice, to put the gentle revolution first. How would you go about supporting Diane and her team?"

"Well, I think I would go easy on the good and evil stuff. If there was a really important ethical problem in our company, I would encourage people to clarify what it was, and let them form their own opinions. I don't think I would announce I had just decided to change the company's ethics. That would only make things chaotic. I suppose I'd also become more serious about finding and helping more innocent fools in my organization. But the risk I see with people like Diane is that they may go off half-cocked and do something damaging to the company, or at least its profits."

"Is that really a risk? Can't you guide them, like Aragorn guided Frodo?"

"Yes, I suppose I could. Fine. That's how I'd begin. But there's another difficulty. What do I say to the other executives when it becomes obvious that people down below are driving changes into important parts of the company without the management team's okay? Even if they understood what the vital issue about good and evil was—and I still can't think of a real issue that would persuade me to go public in my company and support the gentle revolution—I'd never get a consensus from the management team about letting the people down below decide something so important. It's difficult enough to get them to agree about ordinary business issues!"

"Neil, are you beginning to see what N.M. is? Can you see why it's so dangerous? It's not dictators or terrorism or war that threatens our companies and our planet. It's what controls leaders and managers, familiar things that seem so important and reasonable—organizational and personal achievement and achieving short-term results. Imagine there's some good thing that an organization needs to do, but it has a temporary negative effect, financially. Most managers probably will decide to optimize short-term results and forego the opportunity to do the good thing. Can you see why this bias toward short-term results might have dangerous consequences?"

I still couldn't quite figure out what Frank was getting at regarding N.M. I disagreed with his statements about senior managers being short-sighted. On the contrary, I found them reasonably willing to balance short-term results against longer-term gains. That was one of their fundamental responsibilities. But in one way, he was right. If something was presented as only a long-term ethical gain without a business benefit, it would never fly. I doubted whether a case could ever be made for goodness in the business world.

"Do you think leaders can be persuaded to follow Aragorn's example?" Frank asked. "Put aside personal gain to transform their organization by supporting the gentle revolution?"

That was *the* question wasn't it? Are leaders able to put down the Ring of Power once they've grasped it? I thought, fat chance, but didn't say it out loud. What I said quite hesitantly was, "I'd like to believe I could do that, Frank."

He must have sensed the cynical answer I thought of, because he gave me the biggest grin I'd seen since he'd been in hospital.

"So, at last we come to the crux. What does In-Neil strongly believe, and can he persuade Executive-Neil to champion the gentle revolution? Have I got it right?"

He looked at me intently—challenged me is a better way to describe it. He was no longer my teacher; he was now my coach. Which game did I want to play? If I wanted to continue playing my usual general manager game, then all his previous stories had been little more than interesting diversions. Sayonara. Not interested in being your coach anymore, Neil. If I wanted to play the gentle revolution game, then I had to get on with it. I had to choose!

"I know it's hard, Neil. You're not the only one who feels like you do. In fact, N.M. is rampant in executive suites around the world. Leaders become incredibly resistant when confronted by challenges to their power. They block out dissonant views. They make it very painful for innocent fools. They also can be very persuasive. They promise rewards to those who don't rock the boat and who don't question their ideas or actions.

"There is no easy way for leaders to leave such feelings behind and learn to make free, creative, morally transforming choices. All leaders, including you, are addicted to power. The rest of us are codependent because we help leaders retain their power. That is the ultimate cause of the organizational wounds that I see. Leaders damage the healing power that exists in organizational ecosystems by opposing healthy ethical dialogue that has the potential to change things.

"So how can Diane help you once you've grasped the ring? The biggest danger you face is isolation. Being alone at the top maintains your addiction to power. It's too easy to be a power addict when everyone acts as if you are all-powerful. Leaders lose their way when their employees and lower level managers treat them as if they are different, like they're supermen. Innocent fools, like the court jesters of old, refuse to let leaders think they are special just because they have positions of power. They vaccinate them from the power virus by offering them honest conversation, one In-self to another."

"Is this possible?" I asked. "Will Diane have the courage to do what you're suggesting?"

"It's a chicken and egg situation. Which comes first, Neil? Your openness to undertake a potentially dangerous conversation or Diane's courage to start one before you're ready? There isn't a cookbook answer, but I suspect the collision with the Yes-World plays a key role here in bringing ordinary people and leaders together, encouraging them to take the first steps. It seems Diane has already started down that path with you."

Frank and I stared at each other. Though he was only a few feet away, suddenly I felt alone.

"So, Frank, the point of all this is that with the gentle revolution, timing is everything. If things are lined up, the right results will happen. If I ignore Diane, she bites the dust and the gentle revolution stalls in our organization. Is that right?"

"Well, yes. I'm afraid that's probably right. Diane mustn't let her expectations get out of hand. She really doesn't have much explicit control over events. I suppose the mystery here is why she keeps trying, knowing the difficulty. I guess she senses in her exchange with the Yes-World that it's the right thing to do. Who's to say what is loss and what is gain in that exchange? That truly is a mystery."

Somehow, this didn't seem like the way our conversation should end. I still didn't know why I ought to support the gentle revolution. Was the Yes-World saying something to me? All I could hear was the traffic outside Frank's window.

"Neil, what Tolkien was pointing at in the realm of mythic good and evil was an obligation that went along with being a true king. A king must prove that he is worthy to lead by the strength of his moral courage. I can hear you asking already, Does that apply in the real world? Am I right?"

"I was thinking that, yes. I suppose I can guess your answer too. Myths tell us deep truths about ourselves so that we can see things we miss in our usual surroundings. But to be honest, I'm lost. We've gone from the need for ethical transformation, to the crucial role of leaders, to my own choice, and now Aragorn's need to prove he was worthy to be king. I need help, Frank. It's all too confusing."

He nodded but didn't speak.

After a minute or so, I thought, that's it. He isn't going to tell me anything more. I have to figure it out myself, and there isn't anywhere else to turn for help. Then it hit me—this is precisely the challenge that every leader must rise to and overcome. He must deal with the extreme complexity of the situations his organization faces, and make difficult moral and ethical judgments where there aren't any black-and-white, good-versus-evil rules. If I chose the path of the gentle revolution, I was also choosing Aragorn's long journey to prove that I was worthy! Or I could forget it all and just hold onto my current kingdom, come what may. That was every leader's decision.

I could begin to see, very faintly, what N.M. was. It involved leaders with no sense of the importance of making wise moral judgments. The organizations that such leaders control will simply do whatever is necessary to survive. In my case, it was simpler to forget about the people in Indonesia because that made it easier to make a profit. That wasn't a huge problem, was it? Not unless you believe those people in Indonesia have In-selves too. If I believed that and still ignored their needs, then I would have to admit to myself that I was like the warlord in *White Lotus*. I suddenly realized that in all probability, I would remain a warlord and my organization would keep on ignoring human needs, unless I had a Diane standing at my gates confronting me, like White Lotus.

I suddenly saw the N.M. threat clearly. Our planet was trapped in a vicious cycle. The more powerful organizations became, the less concerned leaders would be about what humanity and the planet needed. And the less concerned leaders were, the more powerful their organizations would become! There was no way to break this cycle unless leaders could be persuaded to join the gentle revolution. Frodo could not destroy the ring without Aragorn.

It seemed one side of me wanted to be a warlord, and another wanted to be someone different. In that moment when In-Neil began to understand N.M., Executive-Neil made a decision, although he didn't feel very confident about it.

"Frank, I want to make a quest to destroy my own Ring of Power, but I don't know the way. I want to help Diane with the gentle revolution in my organization, but I don't know what to do."

This time Frank didn't smile. He got up slowly from the chair and walked over to me. He stood looking down at me and said gruffly, "Get up."

I stood and faced him. He was still taller than me, even in his slippers. Suddenly, he wrapped his arms around me. Now what?

"I need a hug, Neil. All this has worn me out. I didn't know which decision you'd make, but now I'm okay."

The nurse came in just at that moment and found two men awkwardly sharing their first hug.

It was almost the end of the visit. I finally asked Frank what N.M. stood for, and he grinned.

"Oh, all right. It stands for 'Not Me'—as in, 'Please don't ask me to make a moral decision and destroy my own Ring of Power'."

We hugged once more as I left. I had to go back to Washington, and I knew it would be a while until I saw Frank again. I hoped that next time he would be out of the hospital but sensed that wouldn't happen. I also suddenly had an urge to know a lot more about Diane, and whether she might be *my* innocent fool.

Chapter 17

I phoned Diane as soon as I got back to the office and invited her to lunch that day. She was surprised, but she readily agreed. We drove to a small French restaurant near the C&O canal in Georgetown. I'd chosen it because the tables were spread out and we'd have privacy. We each ordered salads, and I suggested a glass of wine. She seemed pleased, but a little on guard.

I didn't want her to get the wrong idea about the purpose of our lunch, so I immediately put my cards face up on the table.

"Diane, I've been thinking a lot about what you and your team are doing, and I would like to discuss it with you."

She tensed.

"No, I mean I want to know more about you. I like what you're doing. How did you get started down this path?"

I got the raised eyebrow treatment.

"Neil, what do you want to know?"

Why did I feel constantly off balance in her presence? What did I imagine she was trying to do? In-Neil reassured me that she was probably just being cautious. After all, I was probably still a warlord in her mind.

"Well, tell me about why you joined our company. Are you originally from Washington?"

"No, I grew up in a small town in southern Missouri. Graduated from St Louis University in marketing minoring in sociology. I worked for a small ad agency in Chicago for several years but decided I wanted to get broader experience. I saw an advertisement for this company and thought the electronics industry would have a future, so I joined and moved to Washington about five years ago. Is that what you wanted to know?"

She wasn't making it easy. Frank, how do you get people to drop their guard and open up? Had she met In-Diane? If so, why didn't she immediately relate to In-Neil? I must be doing something wrong.

She sat quietly and took a sip of wine. All of a sudden, the situation reminded me of the time when I first met Connie. There was something about me that prevented her from seeing In-Neil. Executive-Neil was keeping Diane at a distance. Not intentionally, but on autopilot. I remembered my concerns about her challenging my authority, about how bosses ought to treat employees. I must be transmitting 'be cautious' to her, and that's what I was getting back. I tried to change my approach.

"I didn't know you started out in marketing. I don't know much about that, but I heard somewhere that great marketing is really about touching people in new ways. Creating a bridge between a company and their lives." I stopped and took my own sip of wine. Would In-Diane appear in the space I created? I hoped so. I remembered Frank's pointed statements that Diane was potentially very important to me and our company.

I saw a tiny smile emerge in the corners of her eyes, and her face began to relax. In-Neil nudged me. I blurted out what was really on my mind.

"Diane, I have a very close friend named Frank O'Connor who is dying in London. The reason I asked you to lunch is that he and I have been talking about my challenges as a leader. I value your opinion and would like to hear what you think."

There. The fat was in the fire. No going back now. Was she a Parsifal or not? Did she understand the pressures I experienced as a Fisher King? Would she ask the magic question? Frank's story somehow seemed to fit our situation perfectly.

Her smile broadened.

"I was wondering why you asked me to lunch. And why you were so ill at ease the last time we met. Tell me more about Frank. He sounds like quite a guy. How are you feeling?"

That last question opened the floodgates. I had bottled up my feelings about Frank's illness and my own sadness. Everything came out in a long story as we ate our salads—about how Frank and I met, and our conversations over the years. I didn't tell her his stories, but I did tell her about meeting In-Neil. She listened intently. The obvious concern in her face triggered an emotion that I had no name for. I knew that Diane was a person I wanted to confide in and spend more time with.

She told me how she met In-Diane. She had been a nun for a few years. She had joined a church community and experienced a different form of spiritual growth. I wasn't alarmed by that side of her; she reminded me a little of Elena—a talented woman with a fast-paced job. Nevertheless, I guided the conversation back to what I wanted to discuss.

"Frank said that he had gone on a retreat and 'collided' with a different world. Did you ever have an experience like that?" I waited as she thought about the metaphor.

"Well, I wouldn't exactly say that I 'collided,' but I did have an experience that sounds vaguely like what happened to Frank." She opened up to me and told her story.

"While I was doing the marketing job in Chicago, I traveled a lot. One night around nine o'clock, I was waiting in the Kansas City airport for a flight to LA after a long day of work. If you've ever been to Kansas City, you know two things about that airport. One, it's practically empty at that time of night; there was only one other guy waiting in the gate area. Two, there is no direct flight to LA from Kansas City. I had to backtrack to St Louis to connect with an after-midnight flight to LA.

"I noticed that the other guy in the lounge was looking at an airline guide, and it suddenly occurred to me that there might be a better connection that would get me into LA earlier. I asked him if I could borrow his guide, and sure enough, there was a flight through Dallas that would get me into LA two hours earlier. Since I had only carry-on luggage, I went to the new gate, transferred, and got to Dallas just in time to catch the LA flight.

"The plane was nearly empty. I needed to sleep but couldn't. The woman in the seat in front of me was wearing an awful perfume that was giving me a headache. In frustration, I got up and walked toward the back of the plane and found an empty aisle seat. I sat down and immediately closed my eyes. Then I felt a tug on my sleeve. Now what?

"A small, very dark black man was smiling at me. 'Hello, are you my sister?' I just looked at him. He saw I was confused. 'You are a Christian are you not? Then you are my sister.' I saw what he was driving at, and to be polite I nodded hello.

"I still wanted to go to sleep. But he wanted to talk. 'Have you been to Los Angeles before?' I nodded and he continued. 'I have never been there. Can you answer some questions?' So I asked him what he wanted to know.

"That began a long conversation, mainly on his part. He was from Kenya, from a missionary sent to visit American churches. He was also collecting clothing to take back to the poor people in his church. He wanted to know how to find a hotel in Los Angeles (he had no reservation) and how much they cost (he had very little money). How did one get to the hotel? Was Los Angeles very big? And so on. It turned out that he depended on the people he met for help getting around the United States

"When we got to LA, I walked off the plane with him and showed him where his baggage carousel was. I didn't have any bags checked but decided to wait with him and help him find a hotel. He had *five enormous* suitcases! 'They are filled with clothing the good people of American churches have given me for my people.' Next, I helped him load two trolleys and pushed one over to the hotel courtesy phones. I could see he wasn't going to be able to navigate the airport's courtesy bus system. I found a reasonable hotel near the airport that had a vacancy and escorted him out to the bus stopping point. I waited until I saw the right bus and flagged it down. The driver helped him get his bags on the bus (I slipped him five dollars). At the end, I also gave the missionary all my cash, totaling forty dollars. I hoped he had some way to pay for the hotel. He gave me a big smile and a hug and said, 'You are my angel. Thank you.'

"Why did I do these things for a complete stranger? Probably because he was a truly naïve, well-meaning person engaged in a worthy mission who needed help. Most people would have done the same. As I thought about it later, I realized that an unlikely set of coincidences made our paths cross—my working late that resulted in a late departure from Kansas City, my unexpected decision to change travel plans, the woman with the perfume who made me change my seat.

Were these coincidences, or were they arranged? Maybe I was an 'angel' who was meant to cross his path. Of course, I could have turned away and gone to sleep, but I didn't. Something had collided with my world, as you said. The ripple effects from that meeting changed my perceptions of who I am. The man on the plane was right; I *was* his sister. I have innumerable brothers and sisters everywhere on the planet. I think that's why I feel so strongly about helping the women in Indonesia. They're family."

Diane watched my face to see my reaction. Truthfully, I didn't care much for her story. It seemed too pat. I didn't like the overt Christian content. Frank had always clearly drawn a line. He didn't like gurus who claimed they knew the truth and tried to proselytize others into following them. I hoped that wasn't where Diane was headed. It occurred to me that I wanted her to be someone I trusted, someone I could be safe with, who would help me ignite the gentle revolution in my company and not try to convert people to her religion. I was considering her as my coach—I didn't want to surrender In-Neil to her completely. All this swirled through my mind and must have been obvious on my face.

"Neil, you're frowning. Have I said something that offended you?"

It was the first time Diane looked uncertain. I wondered why her expression of vulnerability made me like her even more.

"Not at all. I was just thinking about your story. Something about it bothered me. I can't put my finger on it."

The old Diane quickly reappeared, a twinkle in her eye.

"Good. As my leader, I meant to stir you up a little. The implications of meeting that man from Kenya bothered me too." She didn't elaborate. I wondered if she was a distant cousin of Frank's. Like him, she was leading me somewhere by telling stories and refusing to explain them. Executive-Neil tried to reassert himself.

"Come on, Diane. What does your story have to do with my leadership?"

But she didn't budge. I had to figure it out myself. She was coaching me in servant leadership. I was learning to be a servant and she was asserting her leadership in one dimension of our relationship. Executive-Neil would never have put up with her before he met Frank.

The waiter came over and asked if we'd like dessert. I said no and asked for the check. Diane told the waiter to hold the check and bring the menu. She might want something sweet. She smiled at him and ignored me.

I tried to recover. "Diane, when you said you were that Kenyan missionary's sister, were you using a Christian term?"

She let me hold the initiative. "You can take it like that. But actually I meant I was his sister in a different way. I meant I began to see him as family. Seeing another person as your brother or sister means you have obligations to them. We may have lost that sense in our modern world, but it's very strong in some cultures, particularly so-called 'primitive' ones. It is inconceivable to members of many cultural groups that individuals can survive independent of the family or clan. That's what changed my view about who I am—and my role in my team and our company. I am part of a very large family and have obligations to it."

The waiter brought the menu, and I waited until Diane decided that she didn't really want dessert after all. I asked her if she wanted a coffee. She smiled and nodded. I ordered one for each of us. Now I didn't want the conversation to end.

"Funny, that was Frank's point too. The group or community is vital in the gentle revolution. I don't know, though; it doesn't feel quite right in business. You've heard the saying, 'Geese fly in flocks, but eagles fly alone.' Leadership seems in a way like it must be lonely. You can't have management by committee."

She looked at me very intently, measuring something. I had never seen her calculate anything before speaking. It reminded me of Frank when he was shifting gears, trying to find a way to get me to see things.

"You know a lot more about managing a large organization than I do, Neil. But I'm not sure that you need to be lonely to make decisions. Maybe it's a way of avoiding some of the dimensions of decisions, ones that might have risks and personal consequences you aren't ready to undertake."

She was sharp! She shifted the discussion from the practice of management to my personal motivation. Why did I isolate myself? For the good of the company, or for my own comfort?

"Neil, maybe you should examine that eagle metaphor you used. Do eagles actually manage anything more than their own and their brood's survival? Imitating the behaviors of geese might be a better metaphor for managing a large organization. Look how they support each other in making extremely long flights, which no goose could do alone. Why did you decide to be an eagle and not a goose?"

A goose? They're dumb birds! I should tell my senior team that we are going to imitate geese? Fat chance. I just looked at her.

"Well?" She wasn't going to let me dodge her question.

"I was just using that saying about eagles and geese to make a point. I haven't actually adopted the eagle as my ideal for management."

She grinned at me. "Oh, really? Why did your subconscious bring it up then?"

Now she's psycho-analyzing me! Executive-Neil felt the heat rising under his collar. In-Neil was saying, "Cool down. Maybe she's giving you an accurate picture of how you actually think."

"What do you think, Diane?"

Not to be outflanked, she just sat there and sipped her coffee.

After an uncomfortable ten seconds or so, I gave in.

"I like being in control, at the top, deciding where to fly. I never wanted to be in the flock. That's why I'm where I am. I'm not bragging; I'm just being honest about my motivation."

"So why do your conversations with Frank bother you?"

That was the question wasn't it? I told Frank I wanted to make a quest, commit myself to helping the gentle revolution, and even help Diane. But at what cost? I couldn't see myself as only one member of the flock. I loved being a leader! Did I have to give that up? It just didn't make sense, at least in the Mind-World I inhabited. The Yes-World may have collided with Frank's world, but it didn't seem to be close to colliding with mine.

"Diane, I just don't know. I can't seem to find a way to bring Frank's ideas into the company. I'm not even sure yet that it makes sense to do so. I want to help you and your team; that's about as far as I can go right now."

"Well, that's a start. Let's do it." And she gave me a thumbs-up and a big grin. I returned them.

"So, Diane, how do we work together?" She knew this wasn't one of my executive tricks to persuade a subordinate to do something; I actually didn't know what we should do. She chose exactly the right strategy.

"Think about it for a while. You have a lot on your plate right now. Let me know if you need to talk about Frank. That's enough at the moment. When it's time for something more, you'll know."

She was right of course.

I paid the bill and we left. We drove back to the office and went our separate ways. That evening, I realized that she had already taught me one lesson at lunch—to think of someone who genuinely cared about me and my purpose as my sister. Maybe she was my sister—and Frank and I were brothers.

Chapter 18

Several weeks went by, and when I didn't hear from Frank, I was worried. Had he lost the strength to write? I scheduled a quick trip to London and went directly to the hospital. As I entered the lobby, I felt gloomy. I was in one of the most interesting cities on the planet, yet Frank was desperately ill, and nothing else much mattered to me. When I got to his floor, the nurse waved me through, but I stopped to ask how he was. No change. She assured me again that my visits really helped.

Frank looked terrible. He was sitting in his chair, leaning into the pain, as they say. He told me it wasn't that bad, just annoying because he couldn't sleep well. His skin had a faint orange tinge, which, had I known more about cancer, would have signaled that the end wasn't far away.

He turned his head very slightly and looked at me when I sat down. His hands lay limply on top of the blanket that covered his knees.

"Well, Neil, we're almost at the end."

I wondered if he meant *he* was close to the end, not his storytelling.

He wanted to know how things were going with my job. About the same. Even though Executive-Neil had committed to the gentle revolution, he was still wrestling with In-Neil. I told him about my lunch with Diane, and he smiled faintly.

I wanted to talk with him more about leadership. I'd understood his message, and I wanted to change, but was it as simple as listening to Diane and others? Frank had used Aragorn, a man of wisdom and action, as his model leader. I saw the gap between how he led and myself. I now understood that I was a power addict and had to leave my castle behind for a while, like Saruman. But what did that mean in real terms? It was all very confusing. He listened carefully but didn't say anything. Eventually, I ran out of things to say. We sat in silence for what seemed like a very long time.

Finally, he stirred. "Will you get me a glass of ice water, Neil?"

I called the nurse because his carafe was empty, and she came right away. They seemed worried about him too. He sipped a little water through a plastic straw.

"I'm sorry, Neil, but I'm just not up to talking today. I've written another of my little missives to you though, so why don't you read it and come back tomorrow. We can talk then."

What could I say? He was obviously failing and too weak to have a conversation that day. I took the envelope he handed me, patted him on the shoulder, and left. I asked the nurse about him on the way to the lift.

"He's still holding his own, but the pain is getting worse. That's why he asked you to leave. He'll probably be able to see you tomorrow. It means so much to him, you know." She looked at me with sympathy.

I read his letter that night.

Dear Neil,

I often hear criticisms about the gentle revolution. "You are far too idealistic." "Shareholders won't stand for such risky investments in social experiments." "Ordinary people just won't do the things you suggest." "It just won't work." All of these objections arise from the deep sense of skepticism many people have today about global solutions for difficult problems. Some say that we have reached the end of Modernism. That we Postmodernists don't believe anymore in the possibility of better world. That we're stuck with the broken human race. "Utopia hasn't happened up to now, so tell me, why won't the gentle revolution fail like all the other impossible dreams throughout man's history?"

I don't believe that the quest for organizational goodness is utopian, although the emerging transformation of organizational DNA hasn't been very obvious up to now. The gentle revolution definitely stands on the edge of a knife, as Galadriel said to Frodo. Given the long human history of oppression of ordinary people by organizational tyrants of all kinds—kings, dictators, and tycoons—you can understand how our current mistrust of organizations developed. However, there exists a 'both-and' possibility we couldn't see before. The aims of both human beings and organizations can be accomplished if we begin to see the situation in new ways.

In his book The Great Work, Thomas Berry, a cultural anthropologist and former monk, has this fresh perspective. He looks at our planet optimistically, describing a number of sweeping social transformations in human history that affected the entire world. The first was the agricultural revolution ten thousand years ago. Another one we are all familiar with is the Industrial Revolution that created modern technology and the global corporation. A third is the global communications and internet revolution we are currently experiencing, which is helping to dismantle national boundaries across our planet and is changing our thinking about the human role in the planetary ecosystem. So, Neil, you can take it as a given that global social transformation is a historical fact. Perhaps the gentle revolution is the next one in line.

Berry defines the human challenge in the twenty-first century in terms of rethinking our assumptions about being the masters of the planet. We must begin to see our purposes and those of our institutions as part of the Great Work the planet itself is doing. "The Great Work now, as we move into a new millennium, is to carry out the transition from a period of human devastation of the Earth to a period when humans would be present to the planet in a mutually beneficial manner."14

Why do I hope that such a transformation is not only possible, but even likely in our times? Is this only the dream of old men like Berry and myself? Perhaps. But there are hints about the emergence of planet-wide transformation in our era that you might want to consider.

As a race, we have learned a great deal about our planet, and we are increasingly aware that some form of change is necessary. We have become conscious of the limits on our use of the biosphere. We know that in the past we have been indifferent to our connections with the planet and have caused significant harm. We now realize that our thinking and behaviors must change. Ecologists and others have been sounding the alarm for almost fifty years, and we are beginning to listen. Triple bottom line, sustainability, social responsibility, and other tags are increasingly applied to organizations by thoughtful people. These are clues that something is beginning to stir.

Berry suggests there are four areas of human life where this emerging transformation is close at hand. Indigenous peoples have an intimacy with the natural world that has been lost by modern man. Women enrich the dominant male rational approach with their wisdom. The traditional myths from various world cultures link us to what transcends our time in history. Finally, science demonstrates the unity and deeper workings of the universe to us.

Berry leaves it up to us to discover how to connect with these four sources in transforming our world. He refuses to be a guru with ready-made solutions. His insights are matched by other wise men, which also gives me hope. Edmund Wilson said, "We are entering an era where ... only unified learning, universally shared, makes accurate foresight and wise choice possible. In the course of it all, we are learning the fundamental principle that ethics is everything."15 So you can see that we're not alone in placing our hope in the gentle revolution.

Let me sum up. The gentle revolution is an emergent, creative, personal, and, past a certain point, mysterious process. In some ways, the deepest forces and urges that drive human and organizational transformation are beyond our reach. They are created by the Yes-World. Even so, we must reflect and act on these urges as we follow the quest for the gentle revolution. And we must tell our stories to others on our journey, enlisting them in the great work too.

That's all I have the energy to write now. I'm certain that you understand the importance of the gentle revolution, and I know that you will carry on my work and do greater things than I ever did. That means everything to me.

Warmest regards, Frank

Chapter 19

The next day, I returned to the hospital. The nurse beamed at me and waved me through to Frank's room. He was sitting in his chair again, and he definitely looked better. He smiled weakly as I pulled up a chair.

"How are you today, Frank?"

He nodded okay but seemed to want to get right into the meat of our conversation, as if he knew he had only a small amount of energy left.

"There's a scene in *The Lord of the Rings* that I love, Neil. Frodo and his company meet Galadriel soon after they arrive in Lothlorien. They tell her of Gandalf's death, yet she isn't disheartened. She looks directly at Frodo and says, 'Your

215

quest stands upon the edge of a knife. Stray but a little and it will fail, to the ruin of all. Yet hope remains while all the company is true.' Gandalf is gone, but there is still hope. I love Galadriel's immense strength and courage at that moment, and the way she infects Frodo and the company with her spirit."

Frank stopped for a moment and savored the scene, seeing it again in his mind. Sadly, my Gandalf would soon be gone too, and I had hardly begun my quest.

"Neil, I have told you about the gentle revolution and the transformation of powerful leaders and global organizations, and while I believe that these things are possible, the obstacles may seem insurmountable to you. You are right to be skeptical. Must you simply place all your hopes in Diane and voluntary, bottom-up, invented-on-the-spot ethical transformation?"

That was a good summary of my own misgivings. Could innocent fools carry the heavy load of the gentle revolution, even with leaders supporting them? Weren't the opposing forces in our modern world too entrenched, too powerful? Creating organizational goodness seemed a fairly weak outcome compared to pursuing profit and wealth. Frank didn't wait for my reply to his question and continued.

"I believe that the Yes-World gives us something that helps us in this quest, a source of energy and strength that gives us hope. I could simply explain what I think it is, like Agatha Christie solving one of her mysteries. As you know by now, I don't want you to blindly trust my explanations, but I am willing to help you see it. Let me get at it this way. Suppose

I was a doctor. How would you decide whether you trusted my diagnosis?"

I visualized being very ill, like him. "If I was sick, and I knew you were a good doctor, I would trust you. Of course, if I was *very* sick, I would get a second opinion."

"That's conditional," he said, "a look-before-you-leap kind of trust. Is there any situation where you would trust a doctor's explanations unconditionally?"

I thought, Frank, I trust you, but didn't say it out loud. Somehow, he didn't seem to want that from me.

"I suppose if we were marooned on an island, just you and I, and I was seriously injured, I would have to trust you, even if you weren't a doctor. Otherwise, I would die. I wouldn't have a choice."

"Correct. Another way to trust is to have it forced on you, to have no other way out of a life-or-death situation. But leaving that aside, is there any situation where you would trust me or anyone else unconditionally?"

"I suppose if I knew beforehand that you were absolutely trustworthy. I don't know how I would know that. Even if I knew you very well, it still wouldn't feel quite right to put myself *completely* in someone else's hands. I mean, aren't we taught to be self-reliant? A part of me would always want to stay in control, ready to protect myself from your mistakes."

"I take it then that you trust yourself unconditionally?"

"You have to, don't you? I don't feel comfortable trusting myself in all situations, but who else is there? This sounds like one of those no options, life-or-death situations. I'm forced to trust myself, even if I know I'm not completely competent or reliable."

Frank asked, "What do you think makes us so hesitant about trusting others, even ourselves? Is it our reason? Our feelings? Reason might tell us no one is absolutely trustworthy, meaning we have never met such a person. Our feelings might warn us through anxiety or fear about the same thing. It seems we learn during life that absolute trust doesn't make sense.

"This trust problem nags at innocent fools. How can I trust and commit myself to a dangerous quest when, according to everything I know, the odds against it are very long? What can I finally trust in when I decide to commit myself, no matter what, to the gentle revolution? Is it enough to simply hope it all works out? The great mythmakers down through the ages wrestled with these questions about trust. Homer addressed it at the end of *The Odyssey*. Let me briefly sum up that story."

Now it's Homer. Frank had quite a repertoire of stories! I would miss that. I was suddenly almost overcome by sadness, but Frank was speaking, and I had to concentrate on his story.

"When Ulysses arrived home at the end of his long journey, he found chaos. A group of evil men had taken over his household, stolen his wealth, and harassed his wife, Penelope. In a scene of bloody revenge, he killed them all, but his wife could not trust that the old man who suddenly showed up and saved the day was really her husband. So, she tested him.

Penelope asked the old man—Ulysses—to move her bed. Only she and Ulysses knew the bed couldn't be moved because it was rooted in an olive tree. When Ulysses told her that her request was impossible, he passed the test. Her conditions for trust had been fulfilled. Penelope came to him in tears. 'I could not welcome you with love on sight! I armed myself long ago against the frauds of men.'

"After reuniting husband and wife, how does Homer end the story? Ulysses must face yet another test, again involving trust. On his journey from Troy, Ulysses had met a prophet named Teiresias who had told him exactly what he must do when he finally returned home. He must 'Take an oar and trudge the mainland'. Ulysses must walk until he met a man who had never seen the sea or an oar and who would ask him an innocent question: 'Is that a winnowing fan on your shoulder?' That question would be the signal that his quest would be over. At that spot, so far from the sea that men wouldn't recognize an oar, Teiresias foretold that Ulysses' journey would end in peace. Sounds a little like Parsifal's magical question healing the Fisher King, doesn't it?

"But Ulysses doesn't trust Teiresias and so refuses to be healed. After reclaiming his home and wife, Ulysses does not complete his journey as Teiresias foretold. He trusts only his own judgment. He decides to search for his father rather than the man who would ask him the innocent question about his oar. As he looks for his father, the relatives of the men he killed pursue him, intent on revenge. They meet, and another bloody battle commences.

"Athena, the gray-eyed daughter of Zeus who had been behind Ulysses' trials from the beginning, asks Zeus, the king of all gods, what can be done to end the strife and bloodshed. Zeus replies that the gods will step in and save the day: 'We will blot out the memory of sons and brothers slain.' The myth ends in peace, but not because Ulysses trusted Teiresias's prophecy. Homer has the gods step in and rescue Ulysses from his mistaken choice.

"You are probably asking, Neil, what this has to do with trusting—and hoping—in the success of an improbable gentle revolution. Two things. If, like Ulysses, we trust only in our own judgment and skill to plan and carry out the gentle revolution, we will fail." He stopped and looked at me. It was almost like he was in my head, listening to my thoughts. He continued after a moment's pause.

"Second, the Greeks thought that quests and human fate and ultimate trust are mysterious and linked to matters beyond our control. If we ignore the Yes-World like Ulysses did (Teiresias' foresight about the future represented the Yes-World's insights in Homer's story), and if we trust only our own Mind-World logic, we will end up in conflict and failure. That is Teiresias's—and Homer's—warning."

"Wait a minute, Frank. Haven't we come a long way since Homer and the Greeks? Isn't Homer's story a bit out-of-date with all its talk about gods and prophets?"

He sighed and closed his eyes, but only for a moment. He twisted his body in his chair to look at me more directly.

"Neil, don't get caught up in the details of Homer's myth. The relevant question is about the Yes-World. Can matters like prophecy or destiny—forces that are obviously beyond the Mind-World—possibly be real? Isn't the central question really, 'Can I trust in anything beyond my own power?' Ulysses answered no, and that, according to Homer, was what caused his problems."

"So, what are you getting at?"

"A final mystery. Is the gentle revolution *destined* to succeed? But you must answer that question for yourself. I can go no further with you on your odyssey."

I thought, Frank, you're more like Teiresias than Gandalf. I hope my life doesn't contain as many bloody battles as Ulysses'. In-Neil said, That's your choice, isn't it?

"You're the storyteller, Frank, like Homer. You need to end this story!"

"I told you, Neil, you mustn't trust me to give you the answer. You face a decision, like every other human being. Do you only trust your own insights and knowledge, or do you also trust the Yes-World? I know it's difficult. Skepticism is our natural state in the Mind-World."

"Are you hinting that God will intervene in the gentle revolution?"

"Not exactly."

"But it does concern the collision between the Mind-World and Yes-World guiding innocent fools on their quest. Is that right?"

"Yes, but we already covered that a while ago."

"I give up. Frank, you're simply too hard to understand. What are you trying to tell me? I know you won't give me the answer, but I need help!" I immediately regretted losing my temper. I knew Frank meant well.

He sighed again. I think he was getting tired of jousting with me.

"You seem ready to toss in the towel, Neil, so here's one more clue. Why do you think the Greeks invented a whole pantheon of gods? Were they so very different than we are today? Not as enlightened?"

"No," I responded, "not if they were like Homer. They struggled with the same questions we do."

"That's right. There were too many unexplained things in their lives for the Greeks to feel at home. They used the gods to tie everything together in their stories. They loved order and hated chaos. Homer couldn't let Ulysses simply fight another bloody battle at the end of his quest. He wanted a neat and tidy end to *The Odyssey*. So did Tolkien; ironically, he had the creature Gollum accidentally rescue Frodo's mission to destroy the ring at the end of his story, and de Troyes' myth ended with Parsifal healing the Fisher King with his innocent question.

"That's the clue I'm pointing at, Neil. Order, not chaos. A proper end to myths and life. The good guys defeat the bad guys. Trusting that no matter what, things will work out. Happy endings. As near as I can tell up to now, no one has ever explained how the Darwinian universe will evolve into perfect happiness. Yet somehow that's what innocent fools crave, hope, and even believe is going to happen. That's my point."

"I still don't get it. Maybe things are supposed to be chaotic. Why should stories have a happy ending? Just to please me? Who am I that the universe should make me happy?"

He grinned broadly.

"That's very close to the ultimate question you need to ask yourself, the one essential, innocent, and foolish question upon which everything, including the gentle revolution, depends. You must discover it for yourself. Your In-self knows the question and its answer too, if you will listen." He looked at me briefly, then closed his eyes.

One final mysterious question? Executive-Neil (like Ulysses) rebelled against that idea. There are no final questions, no sweeping solutions like Frank's quest promises. You need to take matters into your own hands, day by day, and make things work. That's what being a leader means. In-Neil (like Teiresias) countered, you know Frank's right. Relax. The question will emerge, and you will find the way.

Frank opened his eyes. He had a forgiving smile on his face as he looked at me. He obviously knew my turmoil.

"Don't worry about it. I'm done with my stories. You don't have to struggle to understand anything else. I'm just happy you are here with me. That's the important thing. One other thing I hope is that you'll tell my stories to others. It's the best way. Tell them to Diane."

The nurse opened the door and an orderly pushed a gurney into the room.

"Time for your MRI, Mr O'Connor."

He slowly stood, and they helped him onto the gurney, then covered him with a blanket.

"Don't wait for me, Neil. This will take quite a while. I'll see you the next time you come through London. Hopefully I'll be out of this place by then."

I walked over to him, took his hand in mine, and squeezed it. I had forgotten how big and gnarled his hands were. A farmer's hands. He looked up at me and said as much to himself as to me, "It's been a long road." Those were the last words I ever heard him speak. They wheeled him away into the lift as I watched.

I heard from Elena a few weeks later that Frank had died in his sleep. I imagined that at the end In-Frank was keeping him company. At least that's what I hoped.

Chapter 20

Frank was constantly on my mind after he died. Once, I was certain I felt his hand grasp mine, signaling me, "I'm okay, don't worry." Then I received his final note, forwarded to me by Sister McMahon. It gave me some relief. It confirmed that he knew what I was going through and wanted to help.

> *To my dear friend Neil,*
>
> *Thank you for coming to see me. As always, our time together was stimulating. I hope your trip back to Washington was uneventful.*
>
> *I need to say a few more things to you. I haven't much time, perhaps only days. The sisters in this*

hospital are being very kind to me, helping a crotchety old man with his summing up.

You and I have had fascinating conversations over the years and in interesting places: Sydney, London, San Francisco. I treasure our friendship. I suppose what remains to be said is this: In every human journey there is a starting point, but really no ending point. I believe our journey together will continue and be limitless. As I lay here, I can remember past events in our friendship, like snapshots. But it's strange: I can't separate what I remember about you from my memories of myself. We have become a small community, you and I, in our shared quest. That is some kind of mysterious signal to me. We won't be separated, at least not for very long, whatever the future brings.

When we first met, you were impatient. You wanted answers, not my insistent questioning. Something persuaded me to probe and see if there was a different person underneath your hard-edged persona. There was. The fine man you are emerged over time, and you became one of my closest friends. I think that's how the process of becoming a person works. In its grasp, you aren't aware of any changes in yourself until someone helps you see them. You became my mirror and being yours was my privilege. Thank you.

I guess that's really all I want to say. Oh, and please take it easy, Neil. Don't strive to change people. Let them encounter the gentle revolution the way you did—tell the stories I told you, and your own too. That's all I have strength for today. Maybe I'll write more tomorrow.

[Added by Sister McMahon: Mr O'Connor didn't sign this or write any more of the letter, but I know he wanted you to have it.]

Gradually, things got back to normal, or whatever you want to call life after knowing Frank, but he left a huge hole in my life. I decided to adopt his advice and wait. Not do anything until I felt ready. He always said that was the right step when you faced unanswerable questions. Connie suggested that I write this book to get some closure.

Unlike Parsifal, I haven't yet found the way to the Grail Castle or how to heal the wounded Fisher King, who is actually me. Has the gentle revolution actually changed anything in my life? To be honest, my story is still incomplete and has several possible endings, like Parsifal's story. I'm still on my quest. You ask whether I believe there will be a happy ending. I'll give a 'Frank' answer to that: You need to examine *your own* myth concerning the Yes-World to understand that.

Frank said that all our experience, no matter how successful we are, doesn't prepare us for what happens when we turn off our autopilot. No one can explain it to anyone else; every person's way of flying is unique. Letting go was especially hard for someone whose true north had been 'Perform, Achieve, Succeed'. From inside my skin, life is complicated, and the gentle revolution isn't all that obvious most days. So, can I tell you anything about my experience of it?

Well, I'm still an amateur. Starting a quest is like learning to ride a bicycle. You wobble a lot and fall off, but gradually you get better at it. One day you let go of the handlebars and surprise yourself. You smile at everyone and shout, "Look at me! I'm riding a bike!" So, I'm happier, freer, and more aware—emerging out of my cave.

Thinking back, the first big thing I learned after Frank's death was how to act differently as a leader. Executive-Neil generally felt stressed and under the gun. I had to get rid of my warlike metaphors for work like 'having a couple of bullets one inch from my forehead'. Diane was an invaluable help.

In many of our meetings, I was still a warlord. Diane wasn't exactly the type to stand silently on one leg like White Lotus, so she let me know what was going on. She would inject a humorous line like, "Neil, you know you can duck and let issues go over your head. Then you might be able to listen to me." She had a sly smile that took some of the sting out of her chiding. I had this bad habit of motioning with my hand for her to speed up and asking her to 'talk net'. She would just frown impishly and wave back at me. Gradually, I slowed my pace. After a while I could even hear In-Neil when she and I were together! But I'm still a recovering power addict, and it's a struggle, day to day.

Another thing I learned can be understood in a story a friend in Australia told me. He worked as an internal change expert in a large government agency for a number of years.

He'd done good things with small groups, but no one in power really noticed or seemed to care. "Originally, my boss managed to sell the organization on softer forms of social change, but now our group has been disbanded because of budget pressures. I feel like we actually made a difference, and maybe ten years from now an executive that we influenced will change the agency. But I wonder if it all really means anything."

Underlying my friend's wistfulness was a subtle barrier that I had to get past too. We don't actually believe we can have much effect on large organizations—even as their leaders. Most people I know have an overwhelming sense about the world's resistance to change. Nothing we do seems to really make any difference. I used to argue with my Australian friend about the tactics he could use to change things in his organization, but it all seemed too improbable and too personally painful for him to keep trying. The funny thing was, I had the same limiting beliefs myself, and I couldn't see it for the longest time. That was where Diane was so valuable; somehow she believed she could change things! What gave her the courage to think this way—and to confront a warlord like me?

This question puzzled me for a long time. I finally saw that people face three choices when they consider making a difficult quest. First, they may decide it's all too hard and refuse to think about changing their situation or their organization's. Such people withdraw, become passive, remain victims, and wait for someone else to do something.[16]

Second, some people at least reflect on the situation they are in and begin to realize they do have power to change it. But then they become overwhelmed by the dangers of the undertaking. They hold on to the status quo, believing that the devil they know is better than the one they don't. You can recognize such people because they actually talk about what needs to be done and seem to understand that they might have power to influence and lead changes. In the end, though, they say that the idea that anyone can transform the deepest DNA of a large organization is only theoretical, or so improbable that it isn't worth the risk.

Then there are people like Diane. You can call her choice the heroic one because in the great myths, starting a quest was always seen to be an extraordinary act requiring great courage. The first step in heroism is imagining that you have the power to influence things. The second step is acting despite personal risk. The third is persevering despite difficulties and failures, because your vision is so vital and compelling. As Diane says, "Even if I am only one person, I might make a difference. Therefore, I must try!" Thinking like this, innocent fools set out to challenge the warlords in their organizations. Seeing Diane as a kind of hero was the thing that changed how I saw myself as a leader.

I began to see what Frank had been trying to tell me about Aragorn's choice. I had always seen myself as a self-made man. Now I began to see another force at work that was changing me, both as a leader and a man. It wasn't Diane alone; my learning was triggered by the Yes-World insights she brought into the company and exchanged with me. I didn't have to rely on In-Neil being a hero, at least not in the same sense as Diane. It was enough to be a servant of the Yes-World's cause.

Not that being a servant-leader was easy—it felt awkward most days. It meant swallowing my pride and honoring beliefs that I couldn't always understand or even agree with. Of course, I continued to fight the usual business survival battles—even Aragorn stayed a warrior—but I didn't have to do the most difficult task of destroying the Ring of Power. Diane could do that. In a way, I had to trust that she was in touch with the Yes-World, even when I wasn't. I know that sounds like I made her a kind of priestess, but it wasn't like that. It meant trusting that someone was wiser than me in some areas, that she knew where the gentle revolution was headed, even if I didn't.

I also understood more about why Frank often used *The Lord of the Rings*. Tolkien was describing the mystery of being chosen in a time of crisis and the necessity of action rather than passivity, no matter how unlikely the chance of success. As funny as it may seem, once I understood that, I received a great deal of the courage to commit myself to the gentle revolution from that myth. I knew I wasn't Frodo, and I finally admitted to myself that I wasn't Aragorn. I was just one of the warriors defending Middle-earth, helping Frodo succeed in his quest. But I committed myself to the battle between good and evil; that's what is important.

The final lesson I learned—but not the least important—was to take the Yes-World seriously. A few years after Frank died, I returned to Sydney on business. It was a trip filled with memories of Frank, and I went to the places he had described in his stories. I walked through Hyde Park and remembered another story Frank had told me. I could hear him as clearly as if he was right there with me.

"Mystery finds *us* Neil, not the other way around." It surprised me one afternoon as I walked through Sydney's Hyde Park, taking a shortcut back to my hotel. People were doing their own thing that fine Australian summer day. Some were exercising. Others were asleep on the grass. There were lovers lying in each other's arms, oblivious to the rest of us. I expected nothing unusual that day. My friend, a homeless man, was lounging on a bench where I always found him, near a wind-eroded sandstone statue of three figures.[17] As usual, I stopped for a brief chat.

"We'd met for the first time on a previous trip to Sydney. I'd assumed that he was homeless and offered him money. He'd smiled and said he didn't need any money right then but would let me know if he did. That was what caught my interest and made me stop each time I walked through the park. He looked to be in his fifties with a dark complexion and a thin beard. I assumed he was Japanese, but he might have been East Asian.

"He asked where I had been. I'd had a disappointing day unsuccessfully trying to close some consulting work. My pipeline wasn't looking too good, and I said honestly, "If you know any business gods, say some prayers for me." He smiled. Then he told me a poem he said he'd written. He looked directly into my eyes as he recited it. I remember some of the lines even today.

God, you must have heard me,
Shouting over the years,
Yet you never answered,
And gave me the gift of waiting.

"He waited for my reaction and probably sensed my surprise. My homeless man was more than he seemed. I asked if he would write his poem down for me and if he had published it. He said it wasn't published and that he would write it down for me, but only when the time was right. He smiled at me again, and that was the end of our chat. I continued on across the park to my hotel. For some reason, I thought of *Wings of Desire*, the Wim Wenders film about angels wandering in our cities, silently watching over us. It made me wonder, who are these creatures—like my homeless friend—that we walk past every day? Hyde Park suddenly seemed pregnant with mystery.

"Neil, mystery approaches us, but subtly. It usually sits on a bench at the side of our path and lets us walk by. You need to work on your awareness in order to see it, and not pass it by."

I remembered Frank's instructions as I walked through Hyde Park that day. I found myself looking for Frank's homeless man but couldn't find him. But I was on the alert for the unusual, something unexpected, someone—or some*thing*—different. And it happened.

I was walking in a fog of memories and stopped at a pedestrian crossing on Liverpool Street at the south end of the park. Traffic stopped and the red don't walk light changed to green. I started to cross without looking when suddenly, right in the middle of the street, I stopped for no reason. Almost instantly, a car ran the red light and sped past no more than one foot in front of me. Had I not stopped, I would have been killed, or at least seriously injured! Needless to say, I was rattled. Was it a coincidence? Did my unconscious mind see the car and signal me, or was I stopped by something that wished me well, and also wished I paid more attention crossing the street? Frank had told me I should be more aware of the Yes-World, and this was a graphic wake-up call! I decided the incident in Sydney was like Frank's rabbit, the Yes-World's invitation to me to be aware of it as a vital everyday force in my life.

When I got back, I told Diane what had happened in Australia. She was sitting at her desk working at her computer as she listened to me. When I finished, she began looking for something in one of her desk drawers. "Just a minute, Neil," she said, "I've got something you should read. Here it is."

She handed me a book. *The Upanishads*. "It's the ancient wisdom of India. When you read it, you'll see why I'm lending it to you." She watched as I leafed through the pages, then I thanked her and went back to my office.

I didn't read it for several weeks, and then only after I had a strange dream. I was in a large, well-lit room in the basement of a building. Across the room was a group of people with their backs to me. They were silent. A woman in the group turned and began to walk across the room toward me. I walked toward her. She was a tiny Asian woman, a stranger, not anyone I knew. When she got close, she stopped and looked up at me. I can still remember her sad eyes and exactly what she said: "You have lost your center." That was it.

The dream left me feeling rattled. So, probably looking for a clue about what it meant, the next day I began to read the book Diane had given me. I opened it at random and immediately read this passage:

Like two golden birds perched on the selfsame tree
Intimate friends, the ego and the Self
Dwell in the same body. The former
Eats the sweet and sour fruits of the tree of life
While the latter looks on in detachment.

As long as we think we are the ego,
We feel attached and fall into sorrow.
But when you realize that you are the Self, the Lord
Of life, you will be freed from sorrow.

The Lord of Love shines in the hearts of all.[18]

Suddenly, I saw what Frank had been hinting at all along. The Asian woman in my dream—some would call her my subconscious mind—and *The Upanishads* were pointing the way toward the deeper purpose of my quest. Once I was able to see it, I wanted to spend more and more of my time pursuing it. At least that's my hope.

Book 2　Elena's Story, Part I

"Initium est dimidium facti"

(Once you've started, you're halfway there.)

Latin Proverb

Chapter 1

I didn't know where Frank was buried. It was my fault; I hadn't gone to his funeral, at his home in Washington DC. Death was not allowed to interfere with my life. That was one of my firm rules. I hadn't gone to my grandmother's wake or funeral either—my parents had been disappointed but not shocked. They were very familiar with how tightly I managed my life. My grandmother, like Frank, had had a major influence on me—I was named Elena after her—but that was no reason to relax my rule. Now, on impulse, a year after his death, I wanted to see Frank's grave. I was in New York on a business trip from Hong Kong, and I decided on the spur of the moment to fly down to DC. The death notice in the newspaper had given me the cemetery's name but not the location of his grave site. That's why I was standing at the entrance to Glenwood Cemetery, wondering how one finds a specific grave among so many. How did the death system work?

I wasn't going to get an answer from the angel that guarded the cemetery entrance on Lincoln Road. He (or she or it) was writing something in a stone book, balanced on his stone knee. Maybe if there are angels, they might know where Frank was now—that was what the stone book meant. I think I heard once that our names are recorded in some kind of book for eternity. Sort of a social register. If you had certain credentials when you died, you made it into the book. If not, well, you had no status in the afterlife. You were a non-entity. Did that mean you didn't exist, or did it mean you were a second-class citizen? Maybe if I had attended a few funerals I'd know more about such things.

I walked over to a small house near the entrance. Why would anyone want to live inside a cemetery? Probably it was the caretaker's. Not much salary but the house is included. I knocked on the door and waited, impatiently. I suppose when you live in a cemetery, time moves a lot more slowly than the real world. Finally, I heard footsteps and the door opened. A fragile old woman in a housecoat looked at me with little interest. "Yes?"

"I'm sorry to bother you (not really) but I was looking for some help in finding my friend's grave. He was buried here a few years ago." She pointed over her shoulder. "Go see Sam in the back." I thanked her and walked around behind the house.

Sam was unpacking a wooden crate that contained a tombstone covered in paper and straw. He was pretty old himself, at least sixty. He glanced up as I approached him with an 'I'm pretty busy; leave me alone' look. Not one to care much about other people's problems, I ignored his look and repeated my reason for being there. He sighed and straightened up. "Come on down to the office and I'll look it up."

I followed him down the road from the cemetery entrance, about 100 yards to another small building. It had several stone statues in front: another angel with a lance in his hand (this one was probably a man) and an ornate cross with a vine growing around it. Sam walked into the front door and I followed him. Miracle of miracles, he had a computer! "What's your friend's name?" "Frank O'Connor," I said. "Hmmm," he said, and keyed in Frank's name. There was only one Frank O'Connor, thank God.

"He's in section B, plot 126." Sam gave me a map of the cemetery and drew a line from where we were to Frank's grave. I thanked him and walked out the door. When I got outside, I tried to orient the map so I could follow Sam's line but couldn't seem to get it right. Sam was still watching me and came up behind me and took the map. "Follow that road over there around the bend. Walk to the next crossroad and turn left. Then walk about 200 feet further on. Section B is on the right. You'll see a statue of Pope Pius the tenth." As if I could tell one pope from another. Then he seemed to have a second thought. "Come on, I'll show you where your friend is." Probably a chance to get away from unpacking the tombstone for a little while – and walk with a pretty girl. (Not that I'm 'pretty' exactly, but that's what an old man might think.)

We walked slowly down the road. "You from DC?" I glanced over at him and said, "No," then looked away. He got the message and we continued down the road in silence. I didn't want to talk; he was probably used to that. We arrived at Section B and he turned off the road without a word and I followed. We threaded our way between headstones. Julian Gantley, Mary Costello, Charles Lansdale. It's hard to walk through a cemetery without reading the names. Finally, Sam stopped and pointed. Frank O'Connor. June 3, 1925—April 25, 2005. 'Once I was lost but now I'm found.'

I don't mind telling you that my feelings were a jumble as I looked down at the slight rectangular depression in the grass that outlined his grave. I was sorry that Frank was here—although I still couldn't believe that he was actually dead. My body trembled with repressed sobs, more uncontrolled than the day that I found out Frank had died. Images of rot and decay tried to intrude but I pushed them away. I groaned out loud, Frank, help me!—and looked around to see if Sam or anyone else heard me. There was no one in sight. The silence and incongruity of this oasis of death in the midst of a living city had a strange effect of making me more alert. I strained but couldn't hear any traffic. It was almost like I had crossed some boundary and left planet Earth.

I felt claustrophobic, imprisoned by death. Then, for no apparent reason, I felt hope. I was sure that Frank was alive, somewhere. He was beckoning to me to go somewhere.

I didn't know where or the way. The experience suddenly reminded me of a story he told me once, about a friend of his, a NASA engineer. He had a life-changing experience at a secluded pond in Houston. Like Frank's friend, my life was stuck in a rut and I didn't even know it! Like him, I also received a signal, strange as that sounds, that I could (and would!) find my way.

Surprisingly, that insight cleared the jumble in my mind. I didn't have to do anything here and now. It was OK to just let things happen when they happened. Then, on impulse, I opened my purse and found the red and brown paper leaf Frank had given me years ago, from the London production of Cyrano we both loved. I looked for a secure place to put it on his grave but there wasn't any. So, I dug a little hole in the dirt at the base of his tombstone and covered it up. I would miss having it with me, but I knew I had to leave it with him. It symbolized my own small death and new beginning. In-Elena nudged me, expressing her admiration for my gesture.

I didn't see Sam on the way out of the cemetery. I managed to hail a taxi on Lincoln Road and arrived back at my hotel in Georgetown about four. Too early to eat so I walked around M Street for a while, not really noticing anything, just wandering. The shops and tourists were the same; I wasn't.

Chapter 2

Some people are thinkers; I enjoy action. Life feels perfect when I'm barreling down a black run or getting my ass wet on a trapeze, sailing. I was never one for thinking about the depths of anything, even after I met Frank. Oh sure, with his prodding, I met In-Elena and grew familiar with her, but that didn't instantly change my life, or make me a thinker. [19] I wouldn't say I was shallow; my attitude was there is so much excitement and challenge right in front of us, why complicate your life trying to answer unanswerable questions? Early in life, my success proved I understood the system pretty well and how to play my cards. But then, a few years after the GFC my deck of cards got incredibly scrambled and I, like millions of others, was forced to see the game of life differently. More about that later.

I'm Elena Gaunt by the way. Neil told you some of my story, but just the parts I told Frank. For one thing, Frank didn't know that I hate my last name. When I was younger that was almost enough to make me find a man with a better surname and marry him. Only kidding. I love my freedom too much. Another thing Frank never told Neil, although I think he surely must have known, was that I was ready to rethink my freedom, if Frank asked. He never did.

I met Neil for the first time in Kowloon, about a year after I visited Frank's grave. He was in Hong Kong on business and asked if I'd like to have dinner. I wanted to show him the city I loved. Seen from the mainland of China, Hong Kong lines the horizon with skyscrapers. Even though I have lived in on the island for over ten years, I enjoy taking the Star Ferry across the harbor to Kowloon, having drinks at the Aqua Spirit bar on the thirtieth floor, and watching Hong Kong's brilliant lights. That's where I took Neil.

He had written his book about Frank and wanted to check a few things in his manuscript before publishing it. I think we were also both hungry that night to bring Frank back to life in conversation. We had no trouble recognizing each other when we met, and we gave each other a lingering hug. We knew each other through Frank. I guess you could call us The Frank O'Connor Fan Club. As we sat at the bar before dinner, Neil described his book. He told me that there were some things about me in the book and gave me a quick rundown. Since I had told that part of my story to a number of people, it didn't bother me.

I liked Neil right away. Or, more precisely, In-Elena liked In-Neil. I think our executive and high-achiever roles would have gotten in the way otherwise. I worked for a guy who was a lot like Neil, who seemed a typical 'I'm in charge here' guy. Unlike Neil, my corporate boss in New York obviously hadn't met his In-self, and I was handling him by keeping my distance. Neil and I didn't talk work that night but, several years later, at another dinner in London we did, although under very different circumstances.

During dinner we chatted about trivia. Afterwards, Neil was curious about whether Frank had broached the gentle revolution with me. When I said that my conversations with Frank seemed to go in a different direction, he seemed pleased, almost like that made him feel special.

"So, Elena. How about you and Frank?" He had a grin like a teenager asking his buddy about his girlfriend. Typical male insensitivity. I stared at him and didn't reply.

He knew from my icy look that he had stepped on my toes, and quickly backtracked. "I mean Frank and you were close friends." Better. I wasn't ready to forgive, yet. He paused, trying to figure out what to say next. I figured that I had inflicted enough pain to keep him on track, so I told him about Frank.

"Frank was one of a kind. He sort of grew on me. When we first met in Sydney, I was curious about his days working at NASA and went to dinner with him. Later, it was his 'out-of-the-box' way of looking at things that drew me to him until, at last, he became my confidant. We were very close, even though we seldom saw each other, with me living in Asia and Frank in London. I was with him the night before he died."

I still got teary when I talked about Frank, and I could see Neil was affected too. We sat silently for a short while and Neil broke the spell by reaching for the menu.

"I still miss him too," Neil said quietly. "No one else seems to have figured out life the way he had. There was a kind of, I don't know, maybe it was authority he possessed. He wasn't theorizing; he was reporting—a scout coming back to show us the path toward some mysterious horizon that he had located up ahead. Now I have to find my own way." He paged though the menu to find the desserts. "Is the gelati any good here?"

"Everything's pretty good." I was thinking about the mysterious horizon Neil mentioned, which Frank had been leading him toward. That sounded a little like what had happened to me as I stood by Frank's grave.

Neil waved at the waiter, who ignored him. "It's not polite to do that in Asia," I told him, and simply looked at the waiter and nodded. He came over and Neil ordered pistachio gelati and I passed.

"Neil, you said Frank and you discussed a quest, a journey toward some kind of horizon. What did you mean?" He looked away for a moment, then, surprisingly, reached out and awkwardly took my hand.

"Elena, Frank told me your story early on, a long time before he helped me meet In-Neil. You were part of his way of encouraging me. He said you are a busy executive who found the way to live." He squeezed my hand in thanks and let go. His smile said, "Who are you kidding Elena? You were close to Frank. You must already know where you are going." But I didn't, and was too embarrassed to tell him.

Neil finished his dessert and that was it. We both knew it would be a while before we saw each other again so we hugged again at the end of the evening and went our separate ways.

Later that evening, back in my apartment, I thought about our conversation. I knew that there was a lot more I could have told Neil about my relationship with Frank, but I realized that I didn't want to, at least not right then. I didn't know if it was too private or I just wanted to have a part of Frank that was only mine, and no one else's.

Chapter 3

Time passed. My memories of Frank become less painful. Then I had an experience that raised deep questions, just like Frank might have posed. I was on a 747 from Hong Kong to New York City. About three hours into the flight, strangely enough in a book on self-development, I read a poem and reflected on it. Very unusual for me.

Reading poetry is one of my least favorite pastimes. In school, I liked literature but couldn't seem to get the hang of poems. The teachers tried to make me find something in the words that wasn't there, for me. 'Analyze your reactions.' Boredom, puzzlement? But, at 39,000 feet that night, something finally spoke to me in a poem by George Meredith.

Dirge in Woods

A wind sways the pines,

And below

Not a breath of wild air;

Still as the mosses that glow

On the flooring and over the lines

Of the roots here and there.

The pine-tree drops its dead;

They are quiet, as under the sea.

Overhead, overhead

Rushes life in a race,

As the clouds the clouds chase;

And we go,

And we drop like the fruits of the tree,

Even we,

Even so.

"Overhead, overhead rushes life in a race." That sure sounded like me. But the next line jolted me. "And we drop like the fruits of the tree." OK, I know we all die; but why do I need to know about my future date with the dead pine needles? Suddenly, I wondered what I had experienced in the cemetery when I sensed that Frank was still alive. Was that just my own pathetic wishful thinking? I stopped reading and let my mind dwell on that question. "Do I really believe that Frank still lives, somewhere?" No answer came, just a sense that this question wouldn't go away. Frank's advice about unanswerable questions came back to me. Live with them. Eventually the answer will come. I smiled when I remembered how he always tried to persuade me to be more reflective, and I resisted! It pleased me that I had finally done what he wanted.

When I arrived at JFK, I was met as usual by Mikhail, my regular limo driver. He helped me recover my bags and loaded them for the drive into Manhattan. It was evening rush hour and we usually chatted about where I had been since the last ride. I think I was Mikhail's window into a much larger world—he rarely left New York City and hadn't gone out of the US since he and his wife had immigrated from Russia twenty-five years ago.

The question the poem raised was still on my mind. "Mikhail, do you ever get the feeling that everything is just temporary? This city, the world, everything?" I could see his eyes in the rear-view mirror and they momentarily left the road and looked back at me. Like most taxi drivers, Mikhail was an amateur philosopher and had opinions about most things and he wasn't reluctant to share them.

"Of course. Everything is temporary. Look at Soviet Union. Who ever thought it would come to such an end?"

"No, I mean something else. Moscow is still there. But someday it will be gone, like great cities in ancient times. People in the distant future will hardly remember that Moscow and New York ever existed. Is there anything that is timeless, that will last forever?" I was thinking about Frank.

We were weaving through buses and cars coming out of JFK, crowding onto the Belt Parkway. Mikhail was quiet for a minute, probably trying to think about which route to take to Manhattan and my question as well. Finally, he answered, in a surprising way.

"When I lived in Soviet Union, I was engineer. But I wasn't happy. My family didn't have what I wished them to have. I didn't know what it was but I knew it wasn't in Soviet Union." He glanced back at me and I nodded. "So, I thought maybe we can find it in America. My wife didn't want to leave her mother but finally we got permission to leave and even bring her mother. So here I drive a limo, which is better than a taxi. So, am I happy now? Does my family have what I wanted?"

He paused. We were in heavy traffic in Queens and I was glad he was paying attention to his driving. "In Russia, we have saying, 'Every seed knows its time.' Here my family's seed is planted in a place where it can grow. In Soviet Union it couldn't grow. My family is free to grow, but am I happy with this? Yes and no. It is good to be free and grow in America but there are many, many weeds here. I don't want my children to be choked by weeds. They are grown up now, but I still worry about them."

I could see his eyes in the mirror, but they weren't looking at me. He seemed to be starring out the windshield, beyond the traffic at some private picture of his family.

He shrugged a little. "Look, what do I know about forever? Living everyday in this country is complicated enough. My children need to choose for themselves. That's why I came here. I shouldn't be complaining about American weeds."

We were moving a bit faster now. Maybe it wouldn't take an hour to get to Manhattan after all. I was tired and wanted to take a shower and go to bed. But Mikhail's story intrigued me.

"Mikhail, how old are your children?"

"My son is twenty-four and my daughter is twenty-two. They both grew up in America. Both went to university and have good jobs."

"You must be very proud of them." I could see his eyes smiling. "Why do you think your family was able to grow differently here in America?

"It is expected. Everyone wants to be someone here, be a success, make more money, have a house, two cars. Go to Disneyland. That is different in Soviet Union. You didn't believe your children could achieve so much there."

We both sat silently for a couple of minutes. Mikhail was right. Why worry about forever? During my life, things would pretty much stay the same; why be concerned about what might happen in the distant future? Then In-Elena said to me, "That's what's bothering you. Why do you care about forever?" I remembered Frank's story about the NASA engineer again. That man saw, in an insight that changed his life, that he was part of the future, part of a giant universal becoming. He could create ripples in that future by 'dropping his pebble in the pond.' Was I trying to figure out how to do that too? Maybe that was part of it, but there was something more, something I couldn't see that bothered me.

Mikhail interrupted my thoughts. "We have another saying in Russia. I think it applies to your question about forever. The answers to such questions are 'written with a pitchfork on flowing water.' They keep changing, the more you think about them."

"So, do you think I should just stop trying to write with a pitchfork? That doesn't seem right."

He nodded. "Writing on flowing water is difficult. I don't say you ought to stop. But don't expect to see an answer. Many possible answers will appear and disappear before you find what you seek."

I looked at his eyes in the mirror, which briefly flicked back to mine.

"Thanks Mikhail. You have been very helpful. I'll have to keep thinking about this question. Tell me more about your family."

He told me what his children did and what he and his wife did, now that they were alone. He didn't mention the weeds that worried him, and I didn't ask.

We finally arrived at my hotel on West 52nd Street. The Bellman recognized me and took my bags from Mikhail. I signed Mikhail's trip ticket—the company would pay him—and patted him on the arm before I went into the hotel. I was lucky he was a friend, a kind of an avuncular Russian oracle.

That felt comforting, to think someone might understand how answers about forever could be found. I certainly didn't.

Chapter 4

The next morning, I caught a cab to our corporate offices on Sixth Avenue. It was a mild mid-July day, and summer had briefly given New Yorkers a badly needed respite. I loved Manhattan—it was all I really knew of the city—because it had a certain order to it. You could get to know and become known in its neighborhoods—their shops and restaurants at least. You needed money to create your own special place in cities. Luckily, I had it.

The meeting I was attending had been called suddenly. I normally came to New York twice a year for marketing strategy meetings; in the spring, to kick off the strategic planning cycle and again in November to finalize the budget and plans for next year. Corporate usually wasn't all that interested in Asia Pacific; we were a relatively small percentage of the business. I liked that because it meant I got to run marketing pretty much as I saw fit—so long as I stayed within budget and followed the corporate brand rules. But this meeting was unusual and worrying, what with the growing impacts of the GFC on our business results.

As I rode downtown amid a throng of yellow cabs, I wondered what my boss would be dreaming up. He loved to create situations to 'stretch his team.' He thought it kept us sharp. We thought it was inane but of course we went along. I don't think he ever understood our nonverbals of crossed arms and grimaces as he gave his pep-talks.

When I arrived, I took the elevator to the twenty-sixth floor. As I walked onto the floor where Corporate Marketing was located my antenna suddenly went on full alert. It was too quiet. I passed several people I knew and they didn't look up or give me the usual "Hi." I felt my stomach contract.

My boss' secretary saw me and waved me over with a smile. She'd smile if the building was on fire I thought. "Bob asked me to tell him when you got here. He'd like to see you before the meeting starts. Is that OK?" I nodded. OK? What did she think I was going to say? No, I don't want to see Bob? I hated pseudo-genuine questions. You couldn't actually answer them honestly, and the sham courtesy pissed me off.

Bob stepped out and led me into his office. I sat down facing him and looked at early morning Manhattan south of the Empire State Building. I loved this view! Then I looked back at him and was startled. He wasn't smiling and was looking through some papers on his desk. Now I was really on the alert. What had I done? I searched my mind quickly, but everything seemed in order in Asia Pacific. We were ahead of plan, under budget and there weren't any 'red flag issues' (as Bob called them). He looked up.

"There's no easy way to say this Elena. We have to let you go."

Looking back on it, my life changed totally at that instant but honestly, my mind didn't grasp what Bob said. It might as well have been, "A Martian just landed on that building behind you."

"Excuse me?"

He leaned back and put his hands behind his head. Strange posture for executing someone. "We are terminating you, effective immediately." He looked me straight in the eye. That took balls.

"You're firing me?" I heard my voice quiver. Damn.

"No, we want a mutually agreed separation. If you agree to resign, we'll give you a separation package. But you have to decide today."

"But why?" Now I felt the anger, flushing my face and gripping my chest. I'm sure he saw it too.

"We're reorganizing worldwide. There isn't a position in Asia Pacific for you. Your group will report directly into New York."

"Who decided to do that? Why wasn't I consulted?" I knew the answer of course. Bob had been directed to cut his budget and took the easy way out. Get rid of people outside New York. I wondered if I could go to his boss. No way. He reported into a hard-nosed cost-cutting SOB who never really understood why the company spent so much on Marketing. Checkmate. No way out.

Did I have any leverage? I wondered who else was being let go, if there was any chance of showing some kind of bias or lack of due process on the company's part. But I knew Bob was within his rights. As an executive, I actually had no rights like ordinary workers. The bastard!

Bob sat there quietly. To give him credit, he must have known what a shock this was, and that I needed to get my head around it. Finally, he said, "Look Elena, this isn't all bad. The package is generous. You have great experience and plenty of options. It could be a great opportunity. Here, take this letter that spells out the details and think about it. Don't bother coming to the meeting at 10 o'clock. I'll see you after lunch. Please don't talk to anyone else about this." He handed me the letter and escorted me to the door of his office.

His secretary didn't look at me. Neither did anyone else, as I walked back to the elevator.

As I got on the elevator, my mind was reeling. Everything seemed surreal, like I was on another planet. I stood and mindlessly watched the floor numbers change. Thank God no one got on and the elevator went straight to the ground floor. In the lobby, In-Elena finally said something. "You handled that really well, don't you think?"

What did she know? What was she comparing my performance to? I had never failed at anything, never lost a job before. Her comment was typical In-Elena, loving me no matter what, not a realistic assessment. "Yeah, sure," I muttered to myself.

I went across Sixth Avenue to a Starbucks. I ordered a Grande Mocha and I'll take the whipped cream! The people around me, all obviously corporate New Yorkers, were chatting about anything but work. I wasn't one of them anymore! New York didn't seem special either, just heartless. I took my tall paper cup, piled high with whipped cream, and found an overstuffed chair facing the street. My mind just kept repeating what my boss had said, almost like mantra, "We have to let you go. We have to let you go."

An attractive guy sat down opposite me and smiled, then began to read the Wall Street Journal. My eye caught one of the column headlines, 'Unemployment Forecast to Rise.' Boy, was that right! I was now one of the statistics. All at once, I understood what not having a job felt like—a chasm. Imagine, millions of newly unemployed people feeling like this. How did they cope? How would I?

A voice broke into my bleak world. "You look upset. Can I help?" It was the attractive guy. My immediate instinct was to shake my head but I didn't.

"Yeah. Thanks. I just lost my job." His face fell. "Wow! That's awful."

"It sure is. The funny thing is, I didn't see it coming. It was a complete surprise."

He nodded in agreement. "That's always the case. We just do our work and lose track of what's going on. The economy is real shaky right now." It was obvious to him why I had been let go. It wasn't my fault. That's how I would explain it to my friends and family.

"You're probably right. I was an easy person to let go. I work in the Hong Kong office. No real connections with the people here in New York." It wasn't about me, or my failure.

He shifted gears. "Hong Kong. Wow, that must be exciting." I was thinking, I do love Hong Kong but now…Would I stay there? Could I stay there? There weren't a lot of jobs for expats these days. You had to live on a local salary and Hong Kong was incredibly expensive, if you lived a Western lifestyle. In the past ten years, I had gotten used to luxury I wouldn't be able to afford.

"Yes, it's great. Have you been there?"

"No but I want to go someday." That's what all Americans say about Asia and Australia, but they rarely make the trip. The seven hours to Europe is time enough on a plane.

"You should." Suddenly, our conversation had run out of pleasantries. Even though any other time I would have liked to get to know him better, today I didn't feel like it. "I have to go."

He looked a little disappointed, but I was glad that he didn't ask me where I was going because I didn't know. I just wanted to be by myself. I walked downtown on Sixth Avenue and, on impulse, turned left on Forty-third. I suddenly remembered that the New York Public Library was only a few blocks away and decided to go there.

The lions guarding the front steps somehow seemed friendly and, after going through security, I found my way to the main reading room. I walked along the bookshelves looking for something to kill time with. Then I had an idea. I'd see if Neil's book was here yet. The older woman at the desk looked in her computer but couldn't find it. Damn; I really wanted to read it. I'd have to ask Neil where I could get a copy.

Then I remembered the letter my boss had given me. I went over to a long wooden table and found a place next to an older man with a stack of books in front of him.

My boss was right; the separation terms were generous. With ten years of service and my accumulated vacation, I would be given a check for over a year's salary, less Hong Kong taxes of fifteen percent. If I watched my pennies, I could survive for well over a year without touching my savings! Plus, they would pay to ship my personal effects back to Australia, my home country. The company would also pay to break the lease on my flat in Hong Kong. That meant I could only stay there for another few months. I'd have to decide where I wanted to live and work more quickly than I wanted. I'd talk to Bob about that. And also, about the four weeks for each year of service. Maybe I could get more by playing on his sympathy. He owed me, the bastard.

I crumpled the letter in anger. Suddenly, I was gasping for air, like a fish yanked out of water, caught on a hook set by an unknown adversary. How had this happened to me? How would I survive? My body said 'run away' from this threat so I left the library and walked aimlessly between Manhattan's uncaring office buildings. All the time, some part of me was saying, "You stupid bitch! What did you do to screw up?" In-Elena said, "Who is saying this garbage to you Elena?"

After wandering around a bit, my head cleared. By the time I got back to the office, it was almost time to meet my boss again, but I waited in the Starbucks across the street. I didn't want to have to talk with anyone in the office.

When I got there, his secretary smiled at me again, which irritated me. I didn't acknowledge her and walked into his office and sat down on the couch against the wall rather than at his desk. He looked at me with a question on his face but then came over and sat down at the far end of the couch, keeping his distance as if he was afraid I'd slug him. That would be fun, I thought, but I just smiled and said nothing. Let the bastard make the first move so I could see better how to play the little game he had set up.

"Elena, you look upset. Are you OK?" I nodded.

"Good. Well, what have you decided to do?" He was clearly ill at ease.

"It all depends on you Bob." Pause. "This is a completely unwarranted action on your part." Let him figure out if that was a threat or not.

He looked a bit irritated. I wasn't going to be easy. That was my leverage. He hated conflict. I wondered how badly he wanted to avoid it. Unresponsiveness was one of my weapons. I had another but I might not use it.

"We had to cut costs. Asia Pacific is a small part of our business and its costs were out of line with the profits it generated."

I thought, whose fault is that Bob? I tried each year to recommend ways to grow Asia Pacific but the company was so US-centric that no one listened.

"So, I was just a cost to you Bob?"

He grimaced. "You know that's not so Elena. You accomplished a lot. I'm proud of what you did. I hope you are too."

Not so proud that you fought to keep me, you bastard.

"So, if I resign, you'll be happy to give me good recommendations?" He relaxed and I saw that I had made a wrong tactical move. References were something for the end of our conversation not the beginning. I immediately tried to reclaim the advantage.

"Bob, I don't want to dance around all afternoon. I read the letter. It's a start but obviously it doesn't recognize my accomplishments as you put it." Pause. "For starters, I think four weeks' severance per year is pretty cheap."

He sighed. "Elena, those are our standard provisions. You know that. We can't set a precedent."

I knew I had to use my other weapon. I reached for my purse and took out a hankie.

"Bob, you know how hard it is these days to find jobs. You're basically throwing me out on the street. That's not fair." I dabbed at my eyes gently. He couldn't tell if I was crying or not.

He looked panic stricken. "Wait Elena. Let me see what I can do with Legal. You're right about the GFC changing things."

Boy was he a lousy negotiator! "Bob, if you want me to sign this letter this afternoon, let's you and I agree what's fair and change the letter. Then you can get Legal to okay what you think is fair."

"So, what do you think is fair Elena?" He just missed his opportunity to set the framework for negotiation.

I mentioned an outrageously high number. "I think it will take me two years to find another job. That's one hundred and eight weeks with no salary, or eleven weeks of severance per year of service."

He groaned and shook his head. "That's impossible Elena. You know it too." I didn't say anything. He had to make the next move.

"With your accumulated vacation, and the four weeks' severance, you'll get almost a year's salary."

"Bob, I earned my vacation! It has nothing to do with this."

He tried a compromise. "If I agree that two years' salary is fair, and you agree to cover part of it with your vacation, do we have a deal?" I breathed a sigh of relief. I had won!

"Maybe, if we agree on one or two other small details."

From that point onward, he basically folded and gave me what I wanted. We marked up the letter and both signed it. I asked when I'd get my check and he said he have it couriered over to my hotel tonight. So much for Legal's approval.

As I stood to leave, he stuck out his hand. For a moment I thought of just ignoring it and walking out, but he had given me more than I expected so I shook his hand. But I didn't smile, and I didn't say anything other than "Goodbye Bob."

I decided to walk uptown to my hotel. It was only about fifteen blocks and a nice way to unwind. When I got back there, I went up to my room and changed out of my business suit. I was still too keyed up to sit and wait for the separation check, so I walked up to Central Park and, on impulse, went for a ride in one of the carriages that lined the south edge of the park. There weren't many tourists and the gentle motion of the carriage and the clopping of the horse soothed me. The woods in Central Park reminded me of the time in Germany when I spent two months convalescing after a skiing accident. That's when I met In-Elena. I remembered how proud I'd been when I told Frank the story. God, I missed him!

When I got back to the hotel, an envelope was waiting for me at the Front Desk. I carried it to my room and then tore it open. It was a big sum of money, the largest single check I had ever received! Maybe things wouldn't be so bad after all.

I didn't yet realize what a roller coaster ride my life had now become!

Chapter 5

I decided to return to Hong Kong immediately. Even though I loved New York, and had planned to see several plays, I needed to be in my own place, immediately. Luckily, I was able to get a flight the next morning. Mikhail was surprised when I called him to go to the airport three days early.

He loaded my bags in the boot of the limo in front of the hotel. "Is everything OK with you?" This was the first time I had to answer that question, so I tried out my cover story.

"My company is closing their Hong Kong office due to the global financial crisis. I didn't want to move to New York so I resigned. They're taking care of me financially so

I'm fine. Going to take a few months off and enjoy myself." Sounded pretty good. I almost believed it myself. Anyway, it was mostly true. No one had to know that I was the only person that Bob had let go. Why did he do that? It was a tender nerve.

Mikhail looked at me as he held the door. I got the idea that he only half-believed me. Or maybe he was just worried.

"It is difficult time. For everyone." He closed the door after I got in the limo.

As he got in the driver's side I said, "Yes, it is hard but you know the old saying: when one door closes another opens." I hoped that was true. Who opens that new door? If it was up to me, I didn't have much energy right now for starting a new career. I felt washed out.

"So, what new door are you going to open?" Ouch! I didn't really want to talk about that right now, but Mikhail was a friend. I couldn't just clam up for an hour while he drove to JFK. It wasn't like me. He'd know something is wrong.

I let my mind wander and started to throw out possibilities. "I may go back to Australia for a while. See my friends. Or go to Nepal and do some hiking." Those sounded plausible, even interesting. Maybe I would do them.

"That sounds like excellent idea. I'd love to have the time and money to do what I wanted. What will you do afterward? The same kind of work? In Hong Kong?" He wasn't going to let me get off the hook with just vacation-talk.

"Well marketing is my field. So, I'll probably look for a similar position, starting in Hong Kong. My network is there. But I'm flexible about where I live." As I listened to my answer, I felt strangely ambivalent. Marketing didn't seem all that important right now. What *did* I want to do? Where did I *really* want to live? I realized I hadn't ever thought about these things and now I had no sense of where I wanted to go. In-Elena said, "This is good. You can decide what's important, not just about a new job."

"In Russia, we say that there is a time for everything. Perhaps it is your time not to know. Then you can find something new. If you know already, you won't find anything." He actually turned and looked back at me. Keep your eyes on the road I thought.

"Thanks Mikhail. You may be right. But I'll be happy when I know what I'm doing. Right now I feel unsettled, edgy."

He shook his head slowly. "No, you feel what is happening. You are not settled; you are on the edge of something new. That's what you feel. That is good."

I think both of us had to digest those deep thoughts because we were silent all the way through the tunnel and well into Brooklyn.

Then I said, "Mikhail, I don't know when I'll be back in New York again. My company brought me here twice a year but now, I don't think I'll be back for a while. I'll miss our conversations."

"Oh, don't worry. Someday I hope you'll be back." He paused and thought. "Because you like New York so you must return. And I want to see you be happy."

"Well I hope that comes true Mikhail. I'd like to come back."

The rest of the drive was small talk, about Hong Kong and Australia. Mikhail gave me a big bear hug when we got to the airport before the security cop made him leave.

I liked flying in the morning. I could read, eat, watch movies and not be exhausted, like on a night flight. But I must have been emotionally tired because I fell asleep shortly after takeoff.

I had a strange dream, as meaningful in retrospect as the one I had told Frank about years ago. I was in a large room, which had bits and pieces of various things scattered all over the floor. Someone—I didn't know who—had ordered me to sort out the 'good' stuff from the trash, and to get it done by a deadline they had set but didn't tell me. There was too much stuff and the time was getting short! I was immobilized by the task. The clock was ticking and I was unable to move. Suddenly, there were tiny animals or robots in the room with me, I couldn't see them distinctly. They were sorting everything out while I watched. Suddenly I knew I'd meet the deadline after all. I felt carefree, enjoying watching this work going on rather than having to do it myself. I never saw the work completed because I woke up.

The feeling of peace and enjoyment in the dream carried over to the flight. I watched several movies that seemed just right for my situation. Women overcoming adversity in different ways. The meals and wine were excellent. It was a memorable flight all the way to Hong Kong, even including the connection in San Francisco. We landed around 9 pm Hong Kong time. I was feeling pretty good, the long trip and everything else considered.

Chapter 6

As I rode to Central Station on Hong Kong Island on the
Airport Express, the reality of what had happened to me
finally hit and suddenly I began to feel down in the dumps.
The people around me were excited about returning home
but I realized that I wasn't actually going to be able to stay in
Hong Kong very long, when the company stopped paying for
my apartment. I was free to go anywhere but there wasn't
anywhere I wanted to go!

My depression got worse as the taxi wound its way
through the city traffic, up toward The Peak where I lived in
a high-rent expat district. Probably one of the nicest places on
Earth to live and now I was an outcast. I couldn't afford and

didn't belong in this fashionable neighborhood anymore. The taxi dropped me off at the lobby of my apartment and I wearily dragged my suitcase into the elevator. Thank God I hadn't felt like this in New York! I never would have made it back to Hong Kong.

Did you ever crash and crawl into bed, without a reason to get up the next morning? It's scary. I was used to a highly active life, driven by work, exercise, social life and travel. My calendar was packed; I color-coded different activities in Outlook to keep everything under control. All of a sudden, I had mentally deleted everything from my schedule. I didn't want to see anyone or do anything, just stay in bed. There were a few things I knew I had to do, involving wrapping up my 'old life,' all colored the same depressing gray in my imagination. Just like the fog that surrounded my apartment sometimes. The night I got back from New York, and for several weeks afterwards, I believed my personal fog would not lift, at least any time soon.

Actually, although I felt like it, I didn't remain in bed for more than twelve hours. I went to my office late in the afternoon after I got back to Hong Kong, to say goodbye and pick up my personal things. That wasn't pleasant. My own team had obviously been notified by corporate and kept their distance. It was as if I had the 'lost job' virus and they didn't want to catch it. Everyone feels insecure when, for no discernable reason, someone at the top of their game loses their job. Uncertainty plus anxiety equals discouragement and fear. That's what my mental state was and my former team, picking up my signals, pulled away from me. That made me feel even more disheartened.

When my friends called, obviously not knowing what had happened, I dumped on them. I got lots of "Oh you poor thing" and "Those dirty bastards." It was nice that they commiserated but it didn't help much. They wanted me to go out with them and get smashed, prescribing alcohol and partying. I wasn't up to it and stayed in my apartment. Somehow that felt safe—until I remembered that I had to move within sixty days according to the agreement I had with the company. I certainly couldn't afford almost $10,000 US a month in rent! I avoided the obvious and put 'Where am I going to go?' out of my mind.

I only went out of my apartment to get groceries. I didn't even exercise, which deepened my funk. I watched my DVDs—I had hundreds of them—and escaped into romance, science fiction and murder mysteries. No real-life dramas; too close to the bone. Eventually, In-Elena got through to me. "You're OK. Life goes on." I saw an ad for some European auto that proclaimed: "You were born screaming; what happened? Live life again!" Being a marketing person myself, I wondered who their target market was—but I also knew their advice was spot on. I had to get on with life, find a new place to live and another job.

It was in the midst of this when I found the letter from Frank O'Connor leaning against my door one morning.

It was a dirty white envelope that obviously had taken a beating, with a number of postal forwarding labels stuck below the original address. Whoever had mailed it originally had sent it to Elena Gaunt, Shanghai China rather than Hong Kong. They had the correct street address but the wrong city.

I turned it over to see who had mailed it. It was Sister McMahon, from the hospital where Frank died. Why had she put Shanghai as my address? One of the forwarding labels had sent the letter back to the hospital from Shanghai, so someone there must have forwarded it to Hong Kong. But it had taken over two years to reach me. That was puzzling. It must have rattled around the Shanghai mail system for a while, or the hospital mail room or somewhere else.

I sat on my couch and, though I was curious, didn't open the envelope immediately. It transported me back to the last days I had with Frank in the hospital. I could see him clearly, lying in his hospital bed, with his head and chest slightly elevated and his eyes closed. In my memory his face was extremely thin but peaceful. Occasionally he would open his eyes and look around, until he saw I was still there. We didn't talk much. When he would awaken, I asked if he needed anything and fetched whatever he wanted. Water, the nurse with painkiller. He never mentioned giving me anything. I wondered what was in the envelope.

Inside I found a letter from Frank and a note, from Sister McMahon.

Dear Elena,

Frank's lawyer found this letter addressed to you among Frank's papers and brought it to the hospital about a month before he died. Frank gave it to me to hold, and to mail to you after he died. I am terribly ashamed to say that I put it aside and forgot to mail it for several months. Please forgive me.

Sincerely

Sister Gwen McMahon, RRN

That explained part of the delay. I wondered why Frank hadn't given it to me himself, while I was there.

Then there was the letter signed by Frank. My heart jumped!

Elena

If you're reading this, I am dead. I don't know how long afterwards you'll receive this; I've asked Sister McMahon, bless her soul, to mail it to you. I have written a book, about my 'spiritual journey'. After you read it (if you do), please decide what to do with it.

You need to know that it's a true story but told as an allegory, to highlight certain points about my journey.

I'll tell you in advance: there isn't much about you in the book. I think you'll forgive me for that when you read the story.

Knowing you'll read my manuscript means a lot to me.

As always, with love

Frank

I don't know how long I sat with his letter on my lap. It was classic Frank. It felt like he and I were having one of our rambling conversations. I wondered why he wanted me of all people to read his story, since he knew how I would feel about things like 'spiritual journeys.' But he obviously had some reason. Why didn't he talk to me while I was with him? And where had he left his manuscript? Just like Frank; either he forgot to tell me or he wanted to create another puzzle for me to solve.

I wasn't sure I wanted to read his story. Frank and I had been—still were in a way—intimate friends. Why risk upsetting something so precious? It was weird. I sensed some kind of danger if I read Frank's manuscript. I was beginning somehow to feel excluded from Frank's life, by not being a character in his manuscript. That wasn't surprising though. Why should he make me part of his 'spiritual journey?' And yet, I wanted to be part of everything in his life, even now.

Enough of that I thought. I went to bed.

Chapter 7

The next morning it occurred to me that I was sitting next to Frank on the day before he died but he didn't say anything to me about what he was thinking, or his book. I had a thought. Frank knew he had to do the process of dying, by himself. That must be tough, knowing you must do your death alone, regardless of who is sitting in the room with you. He must have felt loneliness. No, that's not it. Aloneness. Maybe that's why he withdrew at the end. I was experiencing that aloneness now. It might turn into loneliness if I let it, but aloneness was neutral, an awareness that, ultimately, the answers one needs can only be found by oneself. Others must be left behind.

I was in a dark mood. In a way I was dying because everything I knew was in the process of disappearing. I no longer had any place to live because there was no one I wanted to live with. Suddenly aloneness wasn't just an idea; it was a hollow pit inside me. I missed Frank intensely.

I remembered a night in London when I sensed that Frank had come close to letting go of his tight control. We had seen *Cyrano* and he had given me the leaf that fluttered off the stage when Cyrano dies in Roxanne's arms. I remembered exactly what he said when he gave me that leaf. "This leaf will remind you of Cyrano's In-self—his panache, his passion, and his hidden unrequited love." We were standing close together outside the theater, as the crowd chattered about the play and other things. I was looking up at him, with my head tilted back, and he had this little smile on his face as he spoke. I knew he was talking about himself and me. I looked at him and wondered if he was going to kiss me—but then the moment fled and he asked me where I'd like to go for an after-the-show drink. I said I was tired and could we just go back to the Hilton where I was staying?

When we got to the hotel, I told him about my encounter with In-Elena after my skiing accident at Garmisch, over a coffee in the lobby. As I told the story, Frank was quiet, listening intently. He knew of course that this had been an important moment in my life. Years earlier I had dreamed about it, and he had given me his theory about our roles getting in the way of our intimate relationships. So when I told him at the end that I finally understood what he had been pointing at—that In-Elena and In-Frank had a deep relationship—he nodded and said, "I sensed you were

286

different tonight." For an instant, I thought he was going to move toward me again, and I would certainly have responded, but I was wrong again. His controls were back on. Sitting here now in my aloneness in Hong Kong, I wondered why I hadn't moved toward him. Certainly I knew how. I had played the role of 'temptress' before. But that night at the Westbury I experienced another kind of intimacy that somehow made that role out of place. Did I regret that? Not really. My friendship with Frank towered over all the other relationships in my life.

As I write this chapter years later, I realize now (but didn't then) that my black mood that morning in Hong Kong signaled a turning point in my life. I went from one way of being to another, even though I wasn't conscious of that then. The old Elena, intent on experiencing life at top speed, began to be eclipsed as some unnamed and unseen planet began to block out her accustomed sun and certainty. A new Elena had a chance to emerge from the shadows because the old Elena could no longer find her way.

My mind was swirling, trying to rationalize the Frank I knew and the Frank that had written about a spiritual journey. Why had he been so careful not to bring religion into our wide-ranging conversations and then ask me to read an apparently religious document after he died? Why hadn't he told me about this side of himself when he was alive? I thought we had been close, even intimate in a non-sexual way but now I wondered if that had only been my own wishful thinking.

I searched my memory for clues about this unfamiliar and somewhat off-putting side of Frank. We first met in Sydney in 1988. That would have made him sixty-three then and seventy-nine when he died. He was much older than I, about the age of my father. But he was also much younger than his chronological age, with an agile mind and enthusiasm for life that fascinated me right from the start. The first time I noticed him was when I sat near him in an outdoor café in Double Bay. It wasn't hard to strike up a conversation with him. We both knew that there was some kind of connection made and we agreed to meet for dinner later that week, at Big Mama's in Woollahra.

Big Mama's was a small family-run Italian restaurant with tables crammed together in a small dining room. It had two walls covered with graffiti, left by people over the years. If you go there now, and look just across from the bar, you'll find 'Elena and Frank; great food and great conversation!' which Frank wrote as we waited for the bill. He was right but I can't remember anything we talked about except that it was an even match, with Frank lobbing new ideas at me, and then both of us maintaining an extended volley of point-counterpoint. We were evenly matched, which made Frank attractive. I was confident that he hadn't ever raised religious ideas with me because I would have slammed them back at him, hard. I have this thing about religion—I don't actually know why—but I didn't like, and still don't, the weird out-of-date language that many religious people insist on using.

I decided that, if there had ever been an opportunity for Frank to bring up spirituality with me, it would have been either when I told him about meeting In-Elena or when I sat with him as he lay dying. He hadn't, either time. Why? He must have intended to, eventually, because he took pains to make certain that I read his book after his death. That irked me too. Why hadn't he trusted me enough to share this side of himself with me directly? OK, I would have probably reacted negatively. Still, he could have told his story in some way that I could have simply listened and not felt he was trying to persuade me to believe. It was his fault not mine. Somehow, I felt guilty that he hadn't been comfortable enough with me to reveal such an important part of his life.

All of a sudden, my life seemed empty of promise. I wanted to believe that, in due course, something better waited in my future. I didn't even know where I wanted go when I left Hong Kong. So I occupied my mind with solving that pressing practical question. Where did I want to live? I knew where I *didn't* want to live: back with either of my parents in Australia. Not even as a last resort. I'd become homeless first. I hadn't talked to my father in over fifteen years since the divorce and I wasn't going to start now. I only talked every few months to my Mom. She didn't know I had lost my job and I felt no pressing need to tell her. All that conversation would produce is a lot of stress for both of us.

In the end, I decided not to decide. I would store my belongings in Hong Kong until I knew where I wanted to live, and sent an email to my boss asking the company to agree to defer payment for shipping them to wherever I moved for a period of up to two years. I got an email back confirming that in twenty-four hours. I was glad I had left without burning my bridges.

I wanted to leave Hong Kong as soon as possible. I went to lunch with Molly, an acquaintance who was a travel agent. Obviously, she was delighted to help. We had a long Yum Cha and a number of glasses of champagne (which she paid for) at the JW Marriott. I had only a few constraints about the trip. I wanted to go to London to see if I could find Frank's manuscript. I didn't want to return to the US—my company had soured me on New York right now, which was the only place I actually liked to visit in the States. I didn't want to go to Australia, China or India. Other than that, I was open to her suggestions. I told her I wanted to get away for a few months, do some thinking and not bounce around a lot. She said she'd look at what specials were on offer at this time. Money is a factor if you don't have a job. She didn't actually say that but I knew she was thinking it.

Several days later Molly phoned and asked me to come to her office. She laid out a three-month trip, with three focal points. Initially I would stay in London, then Dublin, and lastly Rome. She recommended that I return to Hong Kong afterwards because I didn't know where I actually wanted to live after my trip. British Airways had a series of off-season specials, combining flights and hotels that Molly had strung together, which added up to an amazingly low cost. I thanked her and she booked the trip while I sat there. I would leave in one week, on August 15th. That would get me back to Hong Kong before the holidays. I especially liked the idea of visiting London first, so I could find Frank's manuscript.

Next, I had to wrap up my life in Hong Kong. The movers agreed to come in four days, pack my things and put them into storage. I had to sort through everything and decide what I would take with me on my trip. Because it involved two seasons, summer and autumn and because I wasn't bouncing around too much, I took two large suitcases and my carry-on 'wheelie-wheelie.'

I went out to dinner with several friends the evening the movers emptied my apartment. We went to Aqua Roma in TsimShaTsui where Neil and I had gone. Paul and I had been lovers (briefly) and had survived that experience to become reasonably close friends. He was obviously worried about me and kept asking me what I was going to do after I returned from my 'holiday' abroad as he called. I created a slight air of tension by my vague answers. I think he was concerned more about who would replace my role of confidant in his life. Li was a woman I had known for almost ten years and my conduit into the Chinese community. She was busy chatting about some exhibition that would open soon at Pacific Place. It probably didn't much matter to her whether I returned or not. And, finally, there was Rivka, the only one that I would really miss.

Rivka was a free spirit. She supported herself by a succession of odd jobs and lived in a tiny apartment, which had her living room, office, bedroom, and kitchen crammed together into about a four-by-five-meter space. She was a really good listener and, over the years, had supported me without demanding too much of my time. We had been there for each other. Tonight, she mainly watched the rest of us. Once she told Paul that I needed space to sort things out. I felt as if she would like me to return but had resigned herself to the likelihood that I wouldn't.

Those three people were all that tied me to Hong Kong. I was ready to set sail toward an unseen destination. I was optimistic and used to trying new things. I believed the next three months would be like starting yoga or trying to apply *The Secret* to my life. I had always domesticated change, cut it down to size. My personal transformation was under control. Three months of travel would take care of everything.

During the evening a nagging question kept diverting my attention from my friends. Why hadn't Frank given me his manuscript in person? Obviously, it had been finished well before he died. He could have easily given it to me when I was with him in the hospital. Not only hadn't he given it to me; he hadn't even told me it existed. Neither had he ever hinted over the years about his spiritual journey, as he called it. He obviously wanted me to know his story but, just as obviously, didn't want to discuss it with me. Why had he been so circumspect? The only reason I could come up with was he didn't want to open the subject of 'God' with me, face to face. He must have felt that I wasn't ready to have that particular conversation. That, somehow, it would be better for me to read his story than hear the real thing directly.

The truth was I *wasn't* ready to read Frank's story *precisely* because it revealed something about him that I didn't want to hear. He had a spiritual life! He hadn't wanted to change our relationship by introducing what was, for me, a discordant topic into our conversations. So, he had hidden a very important (to him) part of himself from me, even as he lay dying. That hurt! But he wanted me to encounter that side of himself, so he left me his manuscript. I sensed, somehow, that In-Elena knew why he did that, and where it would lead but she gave me no clues.

I sat with my three friends, pretending to hold up my end of the conversation, while this interior dialogue played out. I couldn't share that conversation with any of them! That was sad I thought. I wondered if they could tell that I had already left them. I was a lot quieter than usual. Maybe they thought I was a bit depressed about losing my job. I realized that I didn't really care what they thought. My life in Hong Kong, such as it was, came to an end that night.

The next morning, I left Hong Kong.

Chapter 8

At this point, someone else was writing my story might explain what happened to me as a shift in my self-awareness. But I wasn't aware of any shift. Deep within me, something was slowly heating up. Small bubbles of awareness began to float into my conscious world. Part of me recognized this and tried to name it, as feeling unsettled or something. But now I know that something more than feelings was involved. On that flight to London, I began to reflect not just act.

The lights were out on the upper deck of the 747. I turned off my reading light and pressed the full recline button on my business class bed. Being able to sleep was worth all the Frequent Flyer points I had used to upgrade my economy ticket to London. I took a Melatonin and lay quietly, waiting for sleep to arrive as it always did. Images from the past rolled through my mind, like a Flash Player on a website. Frank and I in London, at *Cyrano*. Frank and I when we first met in Sydney. Why was Frank attracted to me? I fell asleep with that question wandering around my mind.

I dreamed I was sitting next to Frank's bed in the hospital. His eyes were open and focused on me. He reached over and opened the drawer on his bedside stand, then beckoned for me to come over and get something. I looked into the drawer and it was empty. Then I looked back at Frank but he was asleep. What was he trying to tell me?

I caught a London cab into the city when I landed. I had decided to splurge and stay in the West End for a week, near Belgravia where Frank had lived. Suddenly, I wanted to revisit the places he and I had frequented. The Hilton could only give me a room for three days so I ended up in Marriott's Grosvenor House, a grand old hotel on Park Lane at the East side of Hyde Park. Because I had so many Marriott points, they upgraded me to a suite. Somehow, the universe knew I needed some TLC!

As I unpacked, I remembered my dream on the plane. Frank had beckoned for me to get something out of the bedside stand but there wasn't anything there. Of course! My unconscious was assuring me that I would find his manuscript here in London, connected to someone very near to Frank, whom I didn't know. A person that didn't involve nostalgia and visiting 'our' places but going some other place where I hadn't been with Frank, something that was important to him. How would I find such a place?

I was pretty good at solving puzzles so I went the lounge in the hotel and had a cup of tea to think this one through. How would I find out about Frank's life here? I actually didn't know any of his friends. In fact, the only person I knew that knew Frank was Sister McMahon at the hospital. I decide to start there. She might know who had visited him. Even though I had flown almost eighteen hours, suddenly I felt a surge of energy. I went back to my room, grabbed a light jacket and caught a taxi to Royal Brompton Hospital. Frank had been able to afford the best medical care in London, and the Royal Brompton had been fairly close to his home. I checked at reception and Sister McMahon was on duty. I wouldn't have to wait for days to begin solving this mystery.

"Hello dear. It's so nice to see you again." Sister got up from her seat at the nurse's station on the same ward that I had visited when Frank was dying. The sights and smells thrust me back to those painful days but her smiling face made them recede into the past.

"Sister, it's nice to see you too. I am here in London for a little while and thought I'd drop by to see you. Can I buy you a cup of tea? If not, I can come back." I thought I'd wait to ask her about Frank's friends when she had time.

"Oh, this is a good time and I'd love an excuse to have a break." She told another nurse that she'd be gone for fifteen minutes or so and we took the elevator down to the hospital coffee shop. I had a coffee and a pastry and bought a pot of tea for her.

She had a bright smile on her face. "How have you been doing dear? Did you get the letter I sent you? I'm sorry that it took so long to mail it."

I told her it had been sent to Shanghai instead of Hong Kong but didn't mention just how long it really took. "Thank you, Sister, for your kindness in mailing it."

She looked at me kindly. "He was a fine gentleman. It's hard to lose someone like that."

She waited for me to respond, probably to see if I needed to talk about Frank. Actually, I did.

"I miss him a lot, Sister, but I'm ashamed to say that I actually didn't think about his death that much until I visited his grave in Washington DC a year ago. Since then I have felt a bit empty. I recently lost my job and that has deepened that feeling. I feel that there's something that Frank's trying to tell me."

She was a good listener, nodding but not saying anything, so I continued.

"I need to find something here but I don't know what it is. Closure maybe. Maybe to convince myself he isn't alive and hiding somewhere."

She nodded, as if she knew exactly what I meant.

"I came here to ask you if you can give me any clues about where to look for the manuscript he wrote. His friends' names, for example, if you feel comfortable giving me those. Anything you remember would be really helpful."

She looked up at the clock on the wall.

"I only have a few minutes before I have to go back to the ward. Let me just give you what comes to mind and then, if you want, we can meet again while you're here."

"That's nice of you. Is it OK if I take a few notes?" I took out my small leather notepad and pen that I always carry in my purse.

Sister described people that visited Frank. It was surprising that she remembered anyone; because many people passed through the ward she supervised. He must have made an impression on her. She couldn't recall their names but there had a gay couple, and a married couple that visited regularly. A priest too but she couldn't recall his name either. He visited him and he had given Frank the last rites. Most of her memories were about Frank himself. He had been a good patient. Had a good sense of humor. All the nurses were glad to do things for him.

"Oh, and there was that American gentleman, Neil somebody. He and Frank had a number of long involved conversations. It occupied Frank's mind, writing those long letters to him between visits. Helped take his mind off his illness. He wrote them out on a yellow pad and we typed them up and emailed them to Neil. And you too, dear. You were a great help to him. He was always more peaceful when you were there."

I felt a pang of regret or jealousy that Neil had received long letters from Frank. But then, I had received his letter. I made a mental note to ask Neil if he would share some of his conversations with Frank. Maybe they were part of his book.

Then Sister had an idea. "I think I have Frank's lawyer's name and address. He brought that letter I mailed to you and left his card in case we had any questions. Let's go back to the ward and I'll look in the files."

She found it with very little difficulty. I wished I was as organized. She gave me his business card and I copied the details in my pad. Stephen Moorcroft. Weymouth Street. West End. His phone number. Great! I could contact him. He might be willing to share something with me. I felt like I was a detective, tracing a missing person.

"Thank you, Sister. You have been very helpful. I'll give you a call. I'd love to have another chat. Perhaps we could go to dinner." She agreed that would be nice and then I left.

Jet lag was beginning to catch up with me and I went back to my room. I took a nap and I called Frank's lawyer late that afternoon. After a little hesitation, he agreed to meet with me the following afternoon. I had room service bring up some soup and a glass of wine and called the housekeeper to turn down my bed. I slept very soundly and had no dreams. I had forgotten about myself and was focused completely on finding Frank's manuscript.

Chapter 9

The next afternoon, I walked over to see Frank's lawyer, who immediately cleared up the mystery of why it took two years for Frank's manuscript to reach me in Hong Kong. After he shook my hand and ushered me over to a sofa in his office, he apologized.

"Elena I'm delighted to meet you. Frank always said nice things about you. I'm afraid I didn't do my job very well. Sister McMahon called me this morning about the mis-addressed envelope and told me what happened. I realized that, somehow, I got Shanghai into my mind as your home instead of Hong Kong. I'm sure Frank told me Hong Kong.

I apologize for any inconvenience or upset my mistake might have caused you."

I told him it was perfectly okay. In fact, it was probably fortuitous that I received the letter from Frank when I did. I briefly summarized what had happened to me in the last month for him.

"I know a number of people who have had their careers shredded by the aftermath of the GFC. It's very difficult."

We chatted a little about Frank and it felt good to see Frank through his eyes. They hadn't been close; it was strictly a business relationship, but Stephen was an acute observer of people and remembered some of Frank's quirks. That he always seemed to take a contrarian point of view in any conversation. His habit of asking questions. The kindness in his eyes and that he seemed to suffer fools gladly.

I asked him if he knew who had Frank's manuscript. He was surprised as I was that Frank hadn't told me. Then I asked why he thought Frank wanted me to have the manuscript, instead of some other of his friends. He paused and thought about it, trying to remember what Frank had said when he instructed him.

"I can't remember anything unusual in Frank's request. In making his will, he asked me to dispose of a number of personal items for him. He left the bulk of his estate in a bequest to charity. He told me he had written a book and wanted you to have it. He didn't tell me why, or what it was about. I'm sorry but I don't have it. Oh, now I remember. He did say that he once thought of giving it to Father McEvoy over at the Farm Street Catholic Church in Mayfair, but he thought you'd get more out of it. That's exactly what he said. 'Get more out of it.' I'm sorry but I can't remember anything more. So maybe Father McEvoy has it."

We chatted a little more and then I left and walked slowly back to Grosvenor House, lost in thought. It was about 5 pm and the traffic was getting heavy as people drove home. What had Frank meant when he said I would get more out of it than Father McEvoy? Was there something hidden in it I was supposed to get? Wouldn't it have been a lot easier if Frank had just come out and told me, who had the manuscript in the note he sent? Why was he so damned mysterious? My head buzzed with questions and I wanted to have a drink in the lounge at the Grosvenor House when I got back.

As I walked into the lobby of the hotel, I decided to ask the concierge where Farm Street Catholic Church was located. He got out a map of Mayfair from his drawer and circled the location, smiling at me as if I were a typical pious woman. "They have a 6 pm Mass every day. You have plenty of time to get there." I frowned at him and thanked him curtly. I went to the lounge and ordered a Bombay Sapphire gin and tonic in a tall glass.

I looked at the map the concierge had given me. Farm Street Church *was* really close by, just a block down Park Lane to Mount Street then three blocks down Mount to the church. I wonder why they called it Farm Street Church and then noticed that Farm Street ran parallel to Mount. The main

303

entrance must be on Farm Street. I had never been to a Catholic Church but all at once I thought I'd like to see what a Mass was. And I'd certainly like to meet Father McEvoy, who was a close friend of Frank's. I decided on the spot to go there that evening. I drained my drink, freshened up in the Ladies, and left by the Park Street entrance.

It was 5:45 pm when I found the entrance to the church, at the end of a garden path off Mount, and walked in. I came into the church at the front, near what I assumed was where the Mass would be held. The seating in the church was facing a raised platform like a theater stage. I suddenly remembered the dream that I told Frank, years ago, about being on stage in a theater and not knowing what I was supposed to do. Being here made me feel that way again. I had no idea of what kind of performance went on in this place. What would I be expected to do if I sat in the audience? But there was no audience. The church was empty. Had I gotten the time wrong? I decided to walk around and look at the inside of the church.

It was actually quite a beautiful building: a high arched ceiling with columns on each side and statues off the side aisles. The most prominent statue was of a marble man slumped on an eight-foot marble cross with two stone people looking up at him. I assumed the man was Jesus. I had no idea who the others were. Luckily, they had small signs saying who they were. A man who looked like a priest with his arms raised held the sign 'Saint Francis Xavier, missionary to Asia.' I wondered if he had ever visited Hong Kong. Halfway back, there was a strangely touching statue of a woman in a long brown dress with her arm around a young girl. 'Saint Frances

304

of Rome.' Toward the rear of the church was a powerful but kindly looking woman with a black cloak, holding a long staff. 'Saint Winifred of Wales.' I liked her instinctively.

A few people started arriving and sat at the front near the platform. I glanced at my watch and saw it was almost six. I sat down at the rear of the church to see what would happen. Saint Winifred was watching over me. She had a mysterious smile carved on her marble face, as if she knew I hadn't a clue.

A small bell rang somewhere and a man—I assumed it was the priest—entered through a side door, walked on to the platform at the front of the church, bowed toward a table on the platform and then faced the few people in the audience. He was dressed in an unusual costume: a long white floor-length gown with a green cape that came to his knees. He was a short man who, from my position at the rear of the church seemed ancient. He began by saying something like, "The Lord is here" or something, to which the people upfront responded. I couldn't hear what they murmured in low voices.

I won't try to describe the rest of the service. It was unlike anything I had ever experienced. I had no idea of what was going on, no reference point to compare it with. The priest read several selections from what I assumed was the Bible and led the people in the audience in praying for different things and some sick people. At one point, the priest lifted a round white object above his head and said softly but distinctly, "This is my body," followed by a gold cup, saying "This is my blood." I remember that specifically because it was so odd.

The whole ceremony took only thirty minutes. At the end, the priest came down the center aisle and stood at the door at the back of the church. The people filed past him and he smiled and shook their hands. I hesitated but then decided to ask him if he knew Father McEvoy.

As I approached, he looked up at me—he was very short and very old and reminded me of someone I had met once but couldn't recall—and smiled at me. I inquired about Father McEvoy and he replied, "You're speaking to him. And who might you be?" I didn't answer.

He grinned broadly. "I have that effect on people, with my imposing stature. Let's try again. Have I met you before?"

This time I answered. "Father, you don't know me, but you knew a friend of mine, I'm sure. Frank O'Connor. I'm Elena Gaunt."

A number of expressions passed across his face in rapid succession: puzzlement, then surprise followed by delight. "Elena! Of course. Frank spoke of you often. How delightful. Do you have time to chat?" I told him I would love to chat and he suggested I wait at the back of the church until he put his vestments away. That only took two or three minutes; Saint Winifred was still smiling at me but this time I felt some kind of kinship with her. I had no idea why. I'd have to ask Father McEvoy about her.

He came back down the side aisle and I joined him at the main door. He put his hand into a marble fount, took some water and touched his forehead, chest and shoulders with it. Then, he turned to me and grinned. "Schoolboy habit."

We walked slowly up Farm Street. "Do you have time for dinner? I am a regular at a decent pub restaurant near here. We can get a booth with some privacy and have a nice talk about Frank." I didn't have any plans and wanted to hear about Frank.

After a short walk, past Berkeley Square, and onto Bruton Place, we came to a small but inviting restaurant called The Guinea Grill. A jolly doorman boomed out, "Hello, Father Mac" and led us over to the proprietor who greeted us again and led us to a booth. I thought to myself that Father Mac must bring a lot of guests here for 'chats.'

"What will you have Elena? I'd like my usual." This was directed to the proprietor. I said I'd like a Bombay Sapphire gin and tonic, my usual. While we were waiting, Father Mac asked about me where I lived, what I did, was I married? I gave him my two-minute tour rather than getting into the complexities. "Right now I live in Hong Kong but I'm going to have to move because I lost my job, and can't afford the expat life style. My parents live in Australia but I am taking three months to get some rest and relaxation before I decide what I want to do next. That will determine where I live."

He nodded. "A lot of that going around right now. People in my parish who worked in the city and thought they were secure are suddenly out of work for the first time in their life. It's a real shock." He paused and waited for my reaction. "Yes, it was a shock but I'm past that now. I decided to go with the flow and see where it takes me. I haven't spent much time thinking about the future actually." I thought to myself, as if I ever thought about the future. I didn't plan; life just happened.

"And London is where the flow brought you first?"

"Yes. I thought I'd spend some time here in London because it reminds me of Frank."

Father Mac smiled. "I envy you young people. The world is your oyster. You have money, freedom and the spirit of adventure. I wonder what I'd do in your situation."

I think it was a genuine question because he looked a bit wistful. But then he continued. "Actually, I did my exploring early, before I became a priest, and have no regrets. I'm exactly where God wants me to be."

"Father, do you mind if I ask you something about Frank? He was a dear friend and sent me a letter about a book he wrote and wanted me to read. He didn't tell me where he had left the book. And I'm puzzled why he never spoke to me about it, even when I was with him at the end."

At that moment our drinks arrived. Father was having a schooner of dark beer, or perhaps Guinness. After taking a deep swallow, he looked directly at me. "I told Frank he ought to talk to you before he sent you that letter. I read the manuscript and liked it of course. Still I felt that he needed to explain to you why he wanted you to have it. Let me clear up one mystery. I have the manuscript and will give it to you."

What a relief! I could hardly wait to plunge into it. But, since Father Mac had already read it, I thought I'd get a preview.

"What did you think of Frank's book, Father?"

He took another sip of beer and looked around for the menu. He didn't answer immediately. "I knew what Frank had gone through in real life and I thought his description was quite honest, although allegorical. He and I debated how to get some of the ideas across, so I feel comfortable with his views."

I returned to his earlier statement about Frank needing to talk with me before he sent the book. "If I may ask Father, why did you think Frank should talk with me before I read the book?"

He smiled mischievously. "Now we're getting into dangerous territory." Then he added with a wink, "My memory's not so good anymore," and reached for one of the menus the proprietor had left and handed it to me.

"We better order before the crowd comes in. Everything here is pretty good."

I was thinking, Father, you are a clever dodger of questions, but I read the menu and ordered a Chestnut, Leek and Mushroom Pie with a Caesar Salad to start. He just told the proprietor he'd have his usual.

I still wanted to know what Frank and he had discussed about me, but I decided to take a different tack. "Father, how long have you known Frank?"

He took another sip of beer and told me a brief history of their relationship. It went back twenty years, to when Frank first moved to London. He had been coming to Farm Street Church since then. They first met at the greeting after the Mass, and then began to go out for dinner occasionally. "Our friendship was based on the fact that both of us loved the cut and thrust of debate. We discussed topical issues and deeper philosophical ideas. Over time, Frank shared his personal life with me, which I don't feel comfortable discussing with you. Not because of the seal of the Confessional, but because intimacy is private and special. I'm sure that you agree with that Elena."

I did, recalling the dinner I had with Neil in Hong Kong. I hadn't wanted to share the details of my friendship with Frank with him either.

"One thing I can tell you Elena. Frank thought you were special. That's the exact word he used. Special." He smiled at me.

That jolted me. Not because I was surprised that Frank though highly of me; I had sensed that when we were together. It was his telling Father Mac that and not ever telling me! He had discussed me with this priest, who wouldn't answer my questions about Frank. I was getting hot under the collar.

Father Mac must have read my surprise and anger on my face because he didn't say anything. Instead he just sat quietly and sipped his beer and let me make the next move.

Finally, I managed to calm myself with the thought that Father Mac isn't the one I'm angry with. It's Frank! He died and ended our relationship. We never had a chance to share more about ourselves.

"Father I'm sorry. You really shook me up just then. I didn't realize that Frank and you had discussed me. That's not what a girl wants to hear." There I said it. Father Mac knows how I feel about Frank.

He nodded. "I know it's difficult to lose Frank. Just so you don't get the wrong idea Elena, he never discussed his relationship with you. He only said in passing, when he was trying to decide what to do with his manuscript, that he thought you ought to get it because you are special. He didn't elaborate. You asked before why I thought Frank should have talked with you before sending you his book. I actually told him that at the time. 'If Elena is so special to you, why not discuss it with her?' Frank just shook his head and said, 'No. That's the wrong thing to do.' I saw that he had his mind made up, so I didn't press the point. Now, with your obvious unhappiness, I'm a bit embarrassed I didn't." He stopped to let me absorb what he had said.

So Father Mac was a bit peeved with Frank as well. Somehow that made me feel better. Just then our dinners arrived so we put the conversation on hold.

After a while, I asked him, "Do you have any theories why he didn't want to talk to me about it? It's been driving me crazy."

He shook his head. "Not really. I think it has something to do with Frank's aversion to telling people what they should think or do. He wanted you to experience his ideas allegorically, not as a firsthand account that you could ask questions about. He respected every person's life journey and didn't want them to model theirs on his. Come to think of it, that's one thing he probably meant when he said you are special. You have a unique journey to make, one that he didn't want to shape. He loved you too much to take your adventure away from you. That's my theory."

He said the magic words. 'He loved you.' I could live with Frank's strange way of treating me if I believed that. And because Father Mac had known Frank so intimately, and had no reason to lie to me, I did believe him. He gave me a wonderful gift that night!

I wanted to read Frank's manuscript, so we walked back down Farm Street and he went into to his office. It only took him a moment or two, and he came back out and gave me a manila envelope containing the manuscript. He asked me to drop by tomorrow morning at ten because he had something else to give me, and he would like to see what my early reactions to Frank's book were as well. We said good night and I walked back to the hotel. I desperately wanted to begin reading, knowing that Frank meant for me—a special person—to find something he had hidden in it.

Book 3 Frank's Allegory

Before you speak of peace, you must first have it in your heart . . .

We have been called to heal wounds

To unite what has fallen apart

And to bring home any who have lost their way.

—St. Francis to the first Friars

PROLOGUE

Gradually, my hospital room fades from sight and I find myself standing on a grassy hillside in a mountain valley. Down below I can see the river that someday I knew I would encounter again. Everything is incredibly bright, not at all dreamlike so maybe I'm really here. Clouds float across a brilliant blue sky, their shadows touching me briefly then moving on. Off to my left is a green meadow as dazzling as an emerald, dotted with slate colored granite and carpeted with red and orange wildflowers. The air feels chilly, like early spring, and is fragrant. There is silence except for the river whispering softly in its canyon.

I often thought about what would happen on this day as I got older. I feared the process but not the idea of dying, but now I feel relaxed and curious. Soon I must cross the river

317

down below to get to the other side and I sense that it isn't time yet. The other side of the river appears just as Francis described it to me before he crossed over, many years ago. I wonder if someone will come to greet me and help me cross over, as Francis' father came for him.

This peaceful mountain valley reminds me of something else that happened in my past. When we were young and first married, Rachel and I drove through a breathtaking part of Western Colorado that looked much like this place. We planned to return someday but now Rachel is gone, on her own path to the river.

I recall other times in the past, moments of insight when I sensed, fleetingly, that something mysterious lay just at the edge of everyday reality. I realize that today the door to those indescribable experiences is about to be flung wide open and never closed again. How strange it is to be finite, on the verge of infinity.

Suddenly, my vision shifts. Suddenly I'm back where my journey toward the river first started…

Chapter 1

The beginning of my journey

One summer, more than a few years ago, I encountered a mystery. I don't mean a whodunit that poses a puzzling crime and at the end shows you the solution, but a very different, weird and wonderful kind of mystery. One which has neither an adequate problem description nor any possibility of a solution. In fact, I'm writing this story as an allegory because that is the only way I can describe how this astonishing mystery suddenly thrust its way into my life and changed it.

My journey started with a situation that many people encounter in intimate relationships. After living with me for twelve years, my wife encouraged me to get away, to find myself, as she called it. She needed space. So, one Saturday in early August, I left on a four-hour drive to a mountain resort we had once visited, to be by myself, relax and think. I was going to a familiar place to do things that I enjoyed. I ended up experiencing something unplanned and not at all enjoyable. That also happens to many people. But now, I must leave the commonplace and tell you the story of the journey that was suddenly thrust upon me.

As I was driving on the interstate highway to the resort, a violent summer storm forced me to pull over onto the shoulder and wait. When the worst of the wind and rain had passed, the highway had flooded and become impassable, so I pulled off onto a narrow side road that seemed to go in the right direction. My strange journey began when this road ended abruptly at the edge of a deep canyon. I thought it must have been washed away by the storm.

In frustration, I got out of the car to investigate and saw that that the canyon was, in reality, an incredibly wide chasm. I couldn't see the other side; there was nothing but mist as far as I could see. It was goosebumps time. What is going on? Roads don't just end; you can always see the far side of a canyon, even the Grand Canyon. I tried to turn around and retrace my path back to the main highway, but in the deepening twilight the narrow road I had been on now faded away and disappeared. You can imagine how frightened I was! I was lost in an ominous place without a clue of what to do.

320

Just before the sun set completely, I saw a small farmhouse at the edge of the woods a short distance away, so I hurried there to ask for help. No one answered my knock, so I entered the empty house. All at once I was exhausted, probably from the stress of the situation, and sat down to rest on a worn sofa. I soon fell asleep. I don't know how long I slept, but a rattling in the dark jolted me awake.

Even now I can clearly recall the two spirits who visited me that night in the farmhouse, perhaps in a dream, perhaps not. I will call them Adversary and Pilgrim although they have had many other names throughout history.

I had been awakened by Adversary, which appeared like a shapeless black form lurking near the ceiling of the not-as-black room where I slept. There was nothing human about Adversary except its voice which was a hoarse whisper. I sensed a menace in Adversary that you might call slyness.

"Can you see me up here Jacob?

I was shaking with fear. "What...Who is that?"

"Don't be afraid, I won't hurt you."

I could barely whisper, "Who are you?"

"I am the most real thing that exists. You know me, but like most men you refuse to see me."

"What do you want?"

"I am here to explain the chasm you encountered today. Watch."

I had a vision of groups of people I didn't know coming over the hills surrounding the house I was in and then, shockingly, walking off the cliff all along the chasm's edge. I watched them fall into its dark depths until they vanished from my view. Each person seemed to be sleepwalking and peaceful as he approached the edge yet, just before stepping off, each awoke, and his face took on an expression of horror and dismay. Suddenly, I too was standing at the edge of the cliff and I knew it was my time to step into the abyss. I was filled with dread, a feeling of being lost, of hopelessness, but somehow something even worse. My face contorted in terror and became rigid like a mask. I stepped off the cliff and fell into the abyss. As I fell, I turned and looked back toward the top of the chasm. I saw it expand until the entire Earth was consumed. Still I continued to fall, and the Sun and finally the stars and everything disappeared into the chasm. Although I fell on into nothingness, I was alive and aware.

Suddenly Adversary reappeared, and I was back in the farmhouse. "Would you like to know what your vision meant?"

"I think I can guess," I replied.

Adversary's voice was an intrusive, rasping presence in my mind. "I'm sure you recognize the chasm as death, but that is only part of its meaning. The chasm also is what truly exists beyond death. All men fall out of existence into nothingness."

A question occurred to me. "Why did the people appear peaceful then suddenly horrified just before they stepped into the chasm?"

"It happened because, at the end, they realized that they had wasted their lives on Earth and that there would be nothing else."

Something didn't make sense. "But I was still conscious as I fell into the abyss. That contradicts what you've said about there being only nothingness after death."

Adversary dismissed my question with a sneer. "That isn't important. All you need to know is that your life is all important because only nothingness follows it. Make the most of life; experience all you can before you die and cease to be."

I was clear-headed enough to probe into Adversary's advice. "How do I know I can trust your explanation about life and death?"

"I have the authority of the One who sent me, the great unknowable One who never approaches men. It is of little concern to It whether you believe me or not."

With that Adversary's dark shape seemed to expand and then blur and disappear into the general darkness of the room. I looked around the room to see if it was still lurking somewhere else.

[Elena's note in the margin of the manuscript] Frank, this is over the top, even for you. Where are you going?

As my eyes anxiously darted around the room, I saw another dark figure standing near the door. This one looked human and his form became lighter and more solid as I watched. He looked something like the pilgrims I remembered from childhood Thanksgiving stories, so I'll refer to him as Pilgrim, He was about my age and height.

I must have been getting used to having conversations with ghosts because I asked, "Who are you?"

"I am a traveler much like you Jacob. Once I was lost but then I found the way. Now I help others by coming here to explain the meaning of this experience, after Adversary explains the chasm."

I instinctively trusted him. He didn't seem to like Adversary. "What was Adversary?"

"It has many appearances. Once it was a friend of God. Then it rebelled against Him and was defeated. Now God permits it to interact with humans and tell its lies about the chasm. Unfortunately, many people are satisfied with what Adversary tells them, because its explanations actually make them more comfortable with their lives."

This interested me. "So, if I knew the whole truth about death, it would cause me some discomfort?"

"Excellent question! But you're getting ahead of yourself. Let me begin with how you arrived at this place. How did you come to be on the road that ends at the chasm?"

I didn't tell him about my wife's suggestion that I needed to find myself. "I accidentally got on it when a storm blocked the highway I was on."

"Marvelous! An unmistakable invitation! Tell me about the trip you were on when the storm forced you off the main road."

I sensed that Pilgrim must know about me already somehow, so I told him the whole story. "I had been trying to get away from business for years, but it was always one crisis after another. Even my family started to complain that they never saw me. There were too many things pulling me in different directions; it all became too much for me. I decided to get away and take a vacation by myself for a couple of weeks to get my bearings. Think about my life, and where I was going. My wife needed time alone too."

He sighed. "I had a burden like that in my life also, and I had to leave my family for a while. But we were better for it in the end. It's true that a person must be alone to encounter the chasm."

"Why am I having these fearful visions?"

"We didn't have psychology in my day, so I'm not good with your modern jargon. But I think it comes from encountering something which won't fit your nice, secure image of the world. You think you have everything under control, and the chasm tells you that you really don't. This realization finally happens to everyone. Adversary had that part right: The looks of horror on the people's faces when they saw that all their planning and attempts at control had been useless in the end. The chasm is a shock to you modern men. It says that your way of thinking is wrong and that you are truly helpless to control your death. That's frightening. Nowadays you think you can overcome anything because you've cured so many diseases that used to kill us in the past, you've gone to the moon, and so on."

"So why am I here? To be shocked into doing something differently with my life?"

"That's part of it."

"But why this strange place?"

"In my personal experience, which goes back only about three hundred years, every person I have met or heard of started his journey by first losing his way and finding the chasm. Why this must be I cannot explain. Maybe you'll find that answer on your own journey."

Now I was really alert. "What journey?"

"The mysterious journey that all men make, which begins in this place."

"So, you're saying that my being here is part of some plan?"

"Precisely. Think of the plan this way. You were on a highway filled with people hurrying to get somewhere. Sadly, you and they never had time to think about where you were going or why you wanted to get there. The dead-end road which ends at the chasm gives you time to think about these things. Everyone's ordinary road ends at the chasm, which is death, because there's no way for anyone to go past that point alone. There is a way past the chasm but you need help to find it."

"Is death really nothingness like Adversary said?"

"That's what he would like you to believe. There's really no way to say, in words, what is beyond the chasm because everything is different once you enter it. But death is *not* nothingness; I can assure you of that!"

I remembered the strange mist that covered the chasm. "I couldn't see across to the other side of the chasm, only a gray mist. Can you tell me what is over there?"

"In my day people saw a river representing death instead of a chasm. We could see the other side back then too: Beautiful castles surrounded by marvelous gardens. Today most people can't see anything on the other side, or even the river itself."

"Is Adversary from the other side?"

"It was once. But now…well, I guess the chasm is its home. But let me continue. When a person takes the side road and encounters the chasm, Adversary and I visit him. We explain to each person what you have heard. Each person then decides for himself."

My ears pricked up. "Decides what?"

"Whether to search for the way past the chasm or to go back to the highway you were on before."

"But the road ends at the chasm. How can anyone go farther?"

"Another excellent question! In fact, it is *the* question! There is a way to the other side of the chasm, but you can find it only when you go through a very special gate."

"Where is this special gate?"

"Watch."

I dreamed of a man in prison who resembled Pilgrim. But this man did not appear peaceful like Pilgrim. He was obviously in pain, kneeling in his cell, and weeping. But as I watched he abruptly stood up and straightened himself as if he had decided something. He opened the cell door, walked out of the prison, and left the city where the prison stood. I saw him climb a small hill and approach a gate in a high wall. He had some difficulty getting through a swamp on the way, but when he got to the gate he knocked. It was opened, but I lost sight of him as he passed through the gate. The dream faded.

When I awoke, I looked for Pilgrim to ask him about the dream but he was gone. The sun was up, and I went outside the farmhouse. My car was there, and the road; but more wonderfully the chasm was gone! I felt exultation and got into my car to drive away from this fearful place. Then I remembered what Pilgrim had said about the decision to return to the highway or not, and I didn't start my engine.

I sat in the car for a long time before I went back into the house. Several times I got up and started back to the car, in mounting frustration and anger. "What do you want from me?", I asked no one in particular. Only silence answered me. I wrestled that day with the visions and especially with Pilgrim's dream that pointed to the mysterious gate. Of all the possible meanings I considered, only one made any sense: "I can avoid death. I'll find Pilgrim's gate and walk through it."

It seemed that this was the clear message of the dream, but it made no real sense to me. Why the mysterious way that the message was delivered? In fact, Adversary had tried to mislead me. Why? Why was the gate hidden, not right out in the open where anyone could see it? Try as hard as I could, I did not have satisfactory answers to many troubling questions. I discovered that I had spent the day struggling with these questions. Tired and hungry again, I found some bread and honey, ate it and fell asleep again.

This time I dreamed about my wife and children. But not as they were when I left for my vacation. In my dream they were celebrating someone's birthday or having some sort of party; they were lively and laughing. I hadn't seen them so happy in a long time, and I was envious that I wasn't there and irritated that they were having a party without me. And then it struck me like a blow! They were free to have fun; I was away on vacation and not spoiling things with my presence! The scene shifted, and I watched my wife and children walk out of our house and toward the same gate that I had seen Pilgrim enter. To my horror I then saw myself run up the hill, roughly grab my wife and drag her away from the gate. The children ran after us crying and frantic because they thought I was hurting their mother. But the final horror now emerged. I pulled my wife by the arm, past our house and over a small hill, where I saw the chasm! I dragged my wife down toward the chasm, with the children following, and I had a look on my face that haunts me to this day. I was asleep and peaceful. I was doing this terrible thing as a sleepwalker! There was no hope that my wife's or the children's cries of terror would bring me to my senses before I dragged them all into the chasm.

I woke in darkness; in an agony of…not fear this time, but realization. The truth of the dream was obvious, and it almost was more than I could bear. In reality, my family would not be celebrating now. More likely they were quarreling or ignoring each other, following my example. And the beautiful, tender girl I had married had become a dry, stressed woman. I helped to make her that way by keeping her on a starvation diet of attention and care.

> [Elena's note in the margin of the manuscript] Frank's confession about how he had treated his wife is awful. It doesn't seem possible that the kind man I knew would have done that. He was a caring person, although he was a bit unemotional. I think that there must be two sides to the story of his marriage.

My situation in the dream seemed beyond hope. I could hardly move under the weight of the guilt I felt. I was truly sorry and wished that I could tell my family how I felt if they would listen. I knew that wasn't very likely, the way things were at present. I wanted to change my life, treat my wife and children with kindness, though I knew with shame that I had little love to give.

A knock at the door jarred me. When I opened it, a burly young man carrying a lantern stood outside. He was dressed in rough work clothes like a farmer or a laborer and looked over my shoulder to see if anyone else was in the house.

"Are the Goodmans at home? Who are you? A friend of theirs?" Despite his blunt manner he seemed friendly.

"I've been staying here for a few days after... my car broke down. I haven't seen anyone else. Do the Goodmans live here?"

"Yes, but I guess they're off visiting again."

He looked at me thoughtfully. I think he saw something of my pain and turmoil because he came several steps into the room and put the lantern on a table.

"Do you mind if I stay for a minute? I had a long walk getting here, and I'd like to sit for a minute. You look as if you could use some company right now."

All at once I needed to unburden myself of my pain, and although he was a stranger this man's sympathetic manner invited me to open up. So, with a broken heart about my family's condition, I told him the story of the past few days and confessed in embarrassment the ways I had wronged my wife and children. I felt relieved because of the attentive way he listened, without interrupting or criticizing me for what I'd done. I had never met him before, but something made me feel he was my friend. When I had talked myself out, he told me he could take me to the gate Pilgrim had entered in my dream. He asked whether I would like to go there with him. I had not yet made up my mind, but I felt a strong urge to go with him and see this wonderful gate past the chasm. But I hesitated; things were moving too fast.

I stuck out my hand. "We don't know each other; my name's Jacob."

"Good name. Suits you somehow. Mine's Evan. How about it? Why don't you come with me to the gate? Even though it's still dark we can find it with this lantern."

Because Evan was insistent, I agreed, and we left the house, walking slowly—in a circle of light from the lantern which showed us the path—down the road away from the highway. As Evan and I walked we discussed the gate.

"How did you find out about the gate, Evan?"

"I found it many years ago, after getting lost like you. I was on a trip and a brilliant light, lightning I think, knocked me to the ground and blinded me. Thank God good people found me and cared for me until my sight was restored. I found the gate shortly after that."

He was smiling, remembering something.

I asked, "What will happen when I enter the gate?"

"It's not that simple. I can show you generally where the gate is, but you must find the last few steps yourself. Once you are through the gate you will find many paths open. But there is only one correct path for you. I continued to journey all over the world; Pilgrim had a more solitary path to follow, although he now meets many people on the way. There are some who simply return to their homes. Some disappear from the world completely. You must find out from God which path is yours."

I didn't like the sound of this. "Find out from God?"

"The one who shapes everything. He sent me here tonight."

"Then God is behind all my experiences in this place?"

"Just as he is in everyone's life, Jacob."

I was frustrated. "But why is all of this so mysterious? Why didn't God just tell me directly where the gate is and what it's all about?"

"I can see you are a typical American. Show me the problem, and I'll put a plan in place and solve it. Jacob, the point is that you can't enter the gate on your terms. It must be on God's terms, and one of them is that you must give up your desire to control events and make everything happen your way."

This didn't make sense to me. "Why? God gave me a brain. I think he expects me to use it. What you're suggesting sounds weak and foolish. Quite frankly it repels me."

"Nevertheless, that is God's condition. Even God's own Son went through a similar struggle during his life on

Earth. Adversary tried to persuade him to use his power selfishly and not as God would have him use it. But He flatly refused to do what Adversary suggested. He obeyed God and entered the gate on God's terms."

I didn't like where this was headed. It sounded too religious for me. "I'm not certain that I'm ready to go that far. I've always been self-reliant, and I'm darned proud of it."

[Elena's note in the margin of the manuscript] You and I agree about that Jacob!

"Well, we're at the point where I have to leave you. What do you want to do? The gate's just up ahead."

I glanced at him, and he was looking at me intently. I could see a wall a little way up the path and I knew that the gate must be nearby. I was resisting; I hadn't had time to think this through. But as I stood there, I remembered the peace I felt as I unburdened myself to Evan in the farmhouse. Somehow, I trusted him as a friend who wanted only the best for me. This broke down my resistance, and with an increasing desire to see the path that God or something wanted me to follow I gave up trying to hold myself back.

"I want to go through the gate if I'm able."

"Are you willing to trust God with your life?"

This felt strange. I didn't know God; how could I trust Him? But I wanted to see the gate that led out of this strange place. I hesitated and Evan noticed.

"God is asking you to decide: Beyond the gate, will you trust him with your life? There may not be another chance to decide."

Again, I hesitated. What would happen to me? I stood in thought for only a short time. I had come to this point because I had been brought to it by some mysterious force, perhaps even God. I wanted to trust him, but I really couldn't. There had been only one person in my life up to now that I had trusted—myself. Finally, giving in and wanting to trust but not having much trust to give, I made my decision.

"I do want God to change my life because I have made a mess of it. If he can help me find a way to do that, I will trust him."

Evan said nothing more. He smiled and pointed up the path toward the wall. He handed me the lantern and walked back down the path and out of my sight. I waited only for a moment, and then I walked up the path. I immediately saw the gate, but it was closed, blocked by a massive wooden door. Nothing could batter this door down, I thought. I took a deep breath and knocked. Nothing happened. In disappointment, I decided to sit and wait to see what might happen.

As I sat I thought about my decision. I certainly had made the logical choice. It seemed logical that God or some mysterious force had brought me to the chasm in order to bring me to this gate. But why, now that I was here, didn't He open it? Again, I felt my impatience growing. But I remembered my promise to trust God with my life, so I said to myself, "If it is really possible to know you, I want to. I'm going to wait here for as long as it takes." So, I sat there rather peacefully and thought of all the things that had happened to me during the past few days and nights. After a time, as the sun rose, I heard my name spoken. I glanced over at the gate and saw that the door was now wide open! With a feeling of relief, I got quickly to my feet and walked through the gate to the other side.

Chapter 2

A New Place

After I came through the gate, at first everything seemed the same as before. But as the sun emerged from behind the hills in a particularly glorious sunrise, I began to notice differences. For one thing, I seemed to be more aware; the intricacy and beauty of everything around me caught my attention and delighted me. I heard birds rejoicing at the sunrise, and I felt the slight touch of the dawn breeze. I smelled the fragrance of this place beyond the gate. It was if before I entered, I had been encased in an invisible plastic bag, which had suddenly been torn away, letting the full beauty of the world reach my senses.

I was also aware of an inner sense of newness and potential and joy that I had not known since childhood. I wondered when I had lost these. And beyond this there was more. At first it seemed only that the burdens I carried from the past had become lighter. But somehow, I knew it was more than that. I had been given an awesome and mysterious gift, beyond my understanding. On that first day inside the gate I called the gift peace. Much later I began to see that it was infinitely more.

The beauty around me seemed unspoiled and almost unearthly. Yet not far away I could see the same hills I had driven through on the way from the highway to the chasm and Goodman's farmhouse. Beyond those hills was my home and family. Evan said that God would show me where He wanted me to go from here on; I wondered how he would do that. Then I saw an old man and woman approaching me on the road. They were engaged in animated conversation, obviously enjoying each other and the morning. As they came nearer the man greeted me pleasantly.

"Morning young man. Beautiful day isn't it? We're the Goodmans from down the road, Martha and Peter."

"I think I stayed in your house the last few days. I apologize for intruding, but I had some trouble. Oh, I'm Jacob Newman."

"That's perfectly all right, Mr Newman. When we're off visiting we always leave our door unlocked for just that reason."

I noticed how they held hands and that Martha was standing close to Peter. I felt the remorse of the previous night begin to return. These days my wife Rachel and I maintained distance between us as if each wore a high voltage warning. I thought I saw a glance of sympathy on Martha's face as she looked at me.

"Would you care to join us, Jacob? We live alone out here and love the company."

I walked with them back to the point where I thought I had entered the gate but there was nothing there. I must have had a question on my face when we arrived back at their house, because Martha said, "The gate's real Jacob but you pass through it only once. Peter and I entered a long time ago and have never seen it since. But we believe strongly that we are still in God's kingdom beyond the gate."

As we entered the house, Martha suggested to Peter that he and I sit and talk while she prepared a meal. Peter motioned me onto the sofa where I had slept the previous nights and sat across from me on a straight wooden chair.

"What did Martha mean? She said that you two believe you are in some kind of kingdom beyond the gate."

He answered with a smile. "Being in the kingdom means God's power and life is here with us. Have you never heard the message Jesus preached? He said that the Good News is that 'The kingdom of God is close at hand'. In our modern terms he said that people had to wake up! and change their way of thinking to be able to believe and see that God's kingdom begins here on Earth. That is what Martha meant. I gather that you have entered the gate just recently?"

I was getting in deeper and deeper. I wished Peter hadn't brought up Jesus. I was wary of Christians trying to convert me. I was just trying to go where God led me.

> [Elena's note in the margin of the manuscript] I almost stopped reading at this point. I don't like the references to God and I especially don't like the reference to Jesus. What is Frank trying to do? Convert me? I hope not. But I don't think Frank and Father Mac would have cooked up such an elaborate way to convert me. Frank knew me better than that. Oh well, I do want to see what happens and I'll just have to put up with a little God-talk.

"Last night, after I talked to a man called Evan, he led me to the gate. But he didn't say the gate led into the kingdom of God. He talked about the gate leading where God would show me the road that leads past the chasm of death."

"Same thing. In a sense you're past the chasm and in eternal life as soon as you enter the gate to the kingdom."

"You mean I'm past the chasm already?"

"That's correct. Oh, you'll have to cross the river of change when God calls you, but you shouldn't have any problem there."

I was really perplexed now. "But does that mean I'll avoid death altogether?"

"No, all men must die. Even God's own Son. But Jesus changed death. Now crossing the river isn't truly death, any more than going to sleep is death."

I was astounded. "So literally, not just in a manner of speaking, Peter you *really* believe that when you take your last breath that you only blink your eyes and are still alive?"

He looked at me with surprise. "Of course. But after crossing the river, alive in a new and unimaginable way that's different from our life now."

Peter seemed genuinely puzzled by my lack of understanding of what to him was such an obvious truth. I wondered if he had ever considered any other possibility or experienced a visit from Adversary and dreamed about men and women falling in terror into the chasm. Then it occurred to me that death might be just one of Adversary's lies.

"Peter, I have lived with anxiety about death at the edge of my thoughts for much of my life. To tell you the truth I still can't quite believe that what you're saying is literally true; it sounds like a fairy tale."

"Don't worry about it; you'll see soon enough."

I was curious about his description of death. "What is the river you mentioned?"

"It's at the end of the journey you make in the earthly part of the kingdom. It separates life here from eternal life in God's presence. After you have done God's work here, he calls you to the river and brings you across."

This was getting more and more perplexing. "But how do I know which road to take to get there? Or what work God wants me to do?"

He glanced back at the kitchen. "I see that Martha is ready for us. Why don't we talk more after we've eaten?"

We sat down at a table that Martha had laid out neatly, with cheese and more of their bread and honey. The two of them chatted about their recent visits with friends while I ate and listened. Then I told them how I had arrived at their house and about the chasm. They nodded but didn't comment. I told them about Adversary, Pilgrim, and Evan. Peter said he knew Evan well, and liked him, after a bit of a rough start. He had heard of Pilgrim but had never met him. They both had encountered Adversary, but not in the same way I had. They seemed to want to go on to other things.

Suddenly a new thought bothered me. "Why is there so much trouble in the world? If God exists, why doesn't he just change everything and defeat evil?"

"Jacob, you are wrestling with a mystery that always has puzzled men. Even Jesus' closest friends were disappointed when he didn't bring victory immediately and destroy all their enemies. In fact, some of the local clergy had Jesus killed when He told them bluntly that they had the wrong idea about God's power in the world. Today people in the world hate us for many of the same reasons. But God proved He was more powerful than evil by conquering death, and He guarantees us the same victory."

"So, the road I have taken through the gate is a dangerous one. Pilgrim hinted at that."

He nodded, "But the highway you were on before was far more dangerous. It truly ends at the chasm."

This gave me a jolt. "Are my wife and children on the road leading to the chasm? If so, I helped to put them there, and my dream was the truth."

"No man can throw another into the chasm. We each make that choice alone. Still, I think you may have made it harder for your family to find the gate than it need be. But you can try to correct that, God willing."

I began to think about my conversation with Evan. He had told me that there would be many roads inside the gate, and that I would have to learn from God which one to take. How did I find God to ask him? Obviously, Peter and Martha knew where he was.

"Peter, you know where God is. I want to find him so I can ask which road I should take from this point forward."

Peter just smiled. "You have already found him, Jacob."

This wasn't making any sense. "I haven't seen God. What do you mean?"

"When you entered the gate, what did you experience?"

"I don't know. Everything literally looked the same...but there was something different. I noticed the

343

newness of everything. I felt like a child again, as if the world was magical and waiting for me to discover its secrets."

"Why do you think you felt like that?"

"Well…I don't know. It seemed like I had been given a fresh start."

Peter smiled gently. "I know. Words can't express what happened to you. When we cross into the kingdom everything changes."

That made sense but it was still puzzling me. "I realize I'm inside the gate and that I'm different somehow. But where is God?"

"He is with us."

I was getting more and more frustrated. "You're speaking in riddles Peter. Where? Is he like Adversary, a hidden spirit we can only see when he shows himself?"

"You are avoiding the obvious, Jacob."

Now I was angry. "Why is everything so mysterious with you people? Pilgrim, Evan, none of you give direct answers. Tell me, Peter. Where is God?"

He just looked at me. I knew he would not—or could not—explain further. I was frustrated with the whole business. It seemed that everyone thought I was a child—a child who couldn't be expected to understand the truth. All I wanted to know was where to find God so He could give me straightforward directions about the road He wanted me to take.

"I want to help you, Jacob, but this is something you have to find out for yourself. I think perhaps if we took you on a brief visit it might help. Martha, do you feel up to going back to see Frank Simpson this afternoon?"

She nodded, and the three of us soon set off along the road where we had met that morning. We walked through rolling fields of wild grasses and flowers surrounded by wooded hills. The morning was alive with winged insects and birds in pursuit. There was a certain rightness, a sense of balance everywhere that made me feel at ease and relaxed.

After about half an hour we came to a high wire fence, an alien thing among so much natural beauty, and it brought me back abruptly to reality. It appeared to be a prison, and my guess was confirmed when a uniformed guard emerged from a low building next to the prison gate. How could there be a prison here? Peter left us and talked to the guard through the fence. Martha saw my puzzled expression and explained, "Jacob, this is one of the places we visit our friends. You'll understand when we go inside." I could see the guard listening to Peter and glancing over at me with an intense look. Finally, Peter motioned for us to join him.

"Jacob, you'll have to be searched before they'll let you in with us. Follow Sam here into the guardhouse." Sam gave me a nod, opened the gate, and led me into the guardhouse. While he frisked me, I looked around the room and read a sign on a wall that said I was in a federal prison for dangerous criminals. How did the Goodmans have a friend here? Maybe he was the Chaplain or another guard. But when I rejoined the Goodmans the guard led us into a wire-enclosed area in another building where prisoners met visitors under the watchful eyes of television cameras mounted in the corners of the room. The Goodmans motioned for me to sit in a chair next to them, in front of the wire screen, with a chair facing us from behind the screen. I turned to Peter, but he answered my question before I asked it.

"We come here regularly to see a prisoner named Frank Simpson. He is confined here for life. We first met him through the warden about three years ago."

Peter stopped and I saw a short balding man dressed in a gray shirt and trousers come through a door and walk toward us.

"Martha, Peter. What're you doing back here? I thought you told me you would be back in a couple of weeks." He was talking to them as he sat down but was looking directly at me. I couldn't read anything but curiosity in his look.

"Frank, I want you to meet Jacob Newman. We met him on our way home this morning. Jacob just came through the gate into the kingdom last night and is puzzled. We thought maybe you might help him."

Frank smiled at me but only with his eyes. His face didn't seem capable of bending into a normal smile; it was as if he had never learned how. He turned his chair more toward me.

He took his eyes off me briefly and glanced at Peter. "You could have told him Peter."

"No, he needs to hear your story from you. He asked us how he can find God, and why we're so mysterious about everything."

"So, Jacob. Tell me how you came to find the gate. Who showed you?"

He seemed so intent on hearing my story that I told him how I had arrived at the chasm and my experiences before I entered the gate. I was more open about my mistreatment of my family than I had been with the Goodmans. Perhaps I felt that somehow he would understand better. I described the meeting with Evan and my growing desire to find the road that God would show me. I ended by sharing my confusion about where this mysterious God was to be found.

"Peter said that God is with us, when we were back at the farmhouse, but that I would have to find Him myself. He said maybe a visit here might help."

His voice was unexpectedly soft. "Maybe it will. Let me ask you a question first. You know that Peter and Martha are special people from talking with them. Why do you think they brought you here to ask someone like me?"

I remembered my dream about Pilgrim in prison and wondered if that had something to do with it; but that seemed farfetched. He waited for an answer but when he saw I was stumped he turned to Peter and Martha. They said nothing and he turned back to me.

"I remember when I first came through the gate. God was so real to me. I'm having a hard time understanding how

347

someone can be in the kingdom and not know Him. I thought I was a hard case, but maybe I wasn't so bad."

I turned to Peter. "Peter, now I'm totally baffled. After we talked, I thought you knew where God is. But then you bring me here and we play more games. What's going on?"

My irritation was rising again. Peter saw that.

"Jacob, be patient. We're not playing games with you. It's just that no one can tell another person how to find God. He finds each of us in a unique way."

"Then why is He being so evasive? It seems such a waste of time."

Frank spoke up. "There's one thing I can tell you after being in prison for twenty-four years: Some things you can see only when you're ready. Now I know why you brought him here Peter."

Peter nodded. "Why don't you tell him how you entered the kingdom, Frank. That's what I thought might give Jacob some help."

With that Frank began his story. His father was an alcoholic and dead by the time Frank was twelve. His mother was not at home much, trying to make enough money to support Frank and his two sisters. He began to steal for spending money and left high school for his first stay in prison—for armed robbery—at sixteen. When he was released he became angrier and angrier looking for work he couldn't find. Soon he was back at robbery again. One night he had too much to drink and walking back to his room he spied an old woman and decided he needed some money. He went toward her on the dark street but she must have been afraid and started to scream before he got close. Rather than run away, in his drunken logic he decided to make her be quiet; he grabbed her mouth. Frank said that the next thing he remembered was her lying on the street while he ran away with her purse which he dropped after taking her wallet. He was caught two days later and convicted of second-degree murder. That was the first time he had killed.

Paroled seven years later, he was on the streets again without a job. He met a drug dealer who needed a delivery boy. Before he was caught again he had stabbed to death two addicts who couldn't pay. That's how he came to this prison for life. Frank told this story in a matter of fact manner with no emotion. But he took no pleasure in telling it. He remembered what he had done, yet he seemed to be at peace with himself despite the horror of his actions.

He paused, as if he were changing gears. I thought a different light came into his eyes and that his voice became richer than the flat monotone he had used until now.

"So, I was in prison at the age of twenty-seven, locked up for the rest of my life. I was always angry, in solitary more times than I care to tell for fighting. No one messed with me. After many years, one day the warden told me I had a visitor. That was strange. My sisters came only on holidays. When I got to this room there was Peter. I sat down, said nothing. He grinned and told me the warden asked him to meet with me to see if he could help. I found out later that Peter came to the warden and volunteered to work here if anyone needed anything. The warden decided to test him with the hardest man around—Me. I said, 'Forget it' and I walked out. He came back again; I refused to see him. One night I was lying on my bunk. The other guy in the cell was reading like he always does, and it came to me that maybe that visitor could teach me to read. I got word to the warden and Peter and I started to read together. This went on for about a year; I was getting pretty good at it. Then Peter gave me a Bible. He told me that reading this book would be good practice, but it also would help me get out of prison. Naturally, I began to read it. Tough book, but Peter explained it to me. After Peter and I had been reading for two years or so, he asked me one day how I got in here. I didn't want to tell him, so I said that I had done some things I didn't want to remember. He said that if I wanted to get out of prison I had to come to grips with what I had done."

Frank looked at Peter and grinned slightly, the first time I had seen his face become animated. "I'm witnessing, ain't I, Peter?" Peter smiled back at him and nodded.

Frank continued. "Well, I didn't want to talk about it. I had pushed it all out of my mind, the old lady in particular. And my drunken old man. One day we were reading the Bible for practice, and I came to the part about the prostitute. I knew a few of those in my day and I was surprised that they were in the Bible. So, I read that Jesus forgives a prostitute right on the spot. No questions asked. This didn't seem right and I asked Peter about it. Didn't she have to pay for all the things she had done? Like me? Peter said that Jesus looked into her heart and saw that she was truly sorry for the mess she had made out of life, so when she approached him, he forgave her. The other people in the story couldn't believe it either! She was such a bad person. It's like the warden deciding to let me out of prison. What uproar if he did that! But Peter said that was why Jesus did it. To show all those people what God was really like. Not some tough judge who can't wait to send you to prison. But someone who wants everyone to be OK again, and to be His friends. That night I couldn't stop thinking about what Peter had said. I dreamed that I was about to die and nothing could stop me from falling into a bottomless hole. And a man whom I didn't know came up to me. I told him who I was and what I had done, like killing people. He didn't seem to mind. He asked if I was sorry, and in my dream I let go and cried like a baby. The man then told me all I had to do was come with Him and I wouldn't die.

"The next day when I saw Peter I told him about the dream. He said it was from God. That God was telling me that He had already forgiven me for what I had done because he knew that in my heart I was sorry. Peter asked me if that wasn't so in my case; I said yes I was sorry, particularly about that old woman. Peter asked if I wanted to follow God like the prostitute had and I said yes. And then he asked me to pray with him, and I did. That's how I went through the gate. Let me tell you what happened next." Frank paused. He had become very choked up telling this and I could see tears in his eyes. I looked at Peter and Martha and they too were touched.

"I felt like I had never felt before. I can't tell you. It's like I was young again and my father wasn't a drunk, and it was Christmas with lots of presents. I wanted to jump and shout, only I knew the guards were watching me. Peter said it was like what happened to the Apostles when they first got the Spirit. And I can tell you from that day on my life changed. I don't fight. I'm reading the Bible to my cellmate, and anyone around me who will listen hears about God. He rescued me. I can forget about all the things I did because God has. And I'm out of this prison in a way. I'm free to follow Him inside just as I could on the outside, so what difference does it make? Ask the warden about me now. He'll tell you."

Frank stopped talking and watched my reaction to his story. I probably didn't let on, but suddenly I felt surrounded by love which is difficult to describe. Things are really good at their core and God brings this goodness to the surface every once in a while as a gift to us when we can only see badness. Like Frank, I felt excited as a child at Christmas, unable to wait to discover more of the surprises God had in store for me. His story left me with no doubt that God was friendly in unimaginable ways. Yet I still had not learned where God was hidden.

"Frank, thanks for telling your story. I'll always remember it. But can you tell me more about when you actually met God?"

"He was with me all the time. Only I had convinced myself He didn't exist, so I blinded myself to Him."

I still didn't get it. "With you? Where? Inside you?"

"Where is the wrong word, Jacob. God isn't inside or outside me. I can't really say. Somehow He fills me, and everything else too. Peter, can you help me?"

"You said it very well, Frank."

"So, when I ask *where* God is I'm trying to find Him in the wrong way?"

Peter spoke up. "Precisely. When you came through the gate you entered the kingdom and received the gift of seeing in a new way—seeing things with the light of God who fills everything and makes it shine. No one learns to see in the kingdom all at once. God grows your spiritual sight in you as you follow the road He leads you on. Why does God do it that way? Was that going to be your next question, Jacob?"

"Well, yes. Why does God let us stumble around, hurt ourselves and others, and generally make an unholy mess of things? It seems like the world would be a lot better off if we could clearly see God all the time and what he wants us to do. I know I wouldn't have acted so badly toward my wife and kids. And Frank sure wouldn't have done some of the things he did. Would you Frank?"

Frank didn't answer, but looked with curiosity at Peter, who answered my question.

"Jacob, again you're hitting on something that has always mystified men. Why did God make the world and us the way He did? Why doesn't He just wipe out all the evil and pain that is in the world if He is so good? Does He take pleasure in it or something? And so on, and so on. Don't you think that if there were an easy answer, you and I and everyone else would already know it? You have to find an answer that satisfies you, Jacob. That's part of what God will show you on your journey to the river, or at least some hints. God will teach you on your journey, just like He taught Jesus on his journey. But you'll only know completely on the other side of the river of change when you're face to face with God, and He finally explains everything. That's the only help I can give you."

Frank spoke up. "I can tell you from my own life that what Peter says is true. The past few years, since God rescued me, I have learned more than in all of the previous fifty years. I see things every day in this rotten place that show me God at work. Don't tell yourself God is only in nice places, like churches. He is in prison too, perhaps even more so, because here we really need Him. In fact as I think about it, Jacob, if you want the best chance to find God go look where most people would say: 'God is not in there, in that prison or that slum; it's too awful!'"

I felt relief. I didn't have to figure out where God was. Somehow, further along my path, it would come clear. I thanked Frank, "I think this visit has finally started to penetrate. Frank, I want to thank you again for helping me."

[Elena's note in the margin of the manuscript] But where is God? God isn't with me because my life is too comfortable? I don't get it.

Frank grinned at me and I could tell that the visit was a gift to him as well—but not just from Peter, Martha, and me. We said goodbye and the guard led us out through the prison gate to the road. As we walked back toward the Goodman's place, I was lost in thought about everything I had seen in the kingdom on the first day. My head was swirling with new experiences and suddenly I wanted to be by myself and think about them. But as I walked, I thought of my family and I knew I wanted to return and tell them what had happened to me.

When we got to the farmhouse, I lingered with Peter and Martha for a short time. In a single day these people had become genuine friends, seeming closer to me than any of my past friendships. They wanted nothing from me; they wanted only to give what they had. I think I began to understand the word 'love' for the first time on that day I spent with them.

Peter and Martha must have both sensed the way I felt; they each hugged me as if I were their son. When I drove off they stood and waved until I lost sight of them in my rear-view mirror. As I drove back to the highway I couldn't stop thinking about everything that had happened. A kind of jubilation filled me. Where would God lead me next on this new road? I could hardly wait to share this with my wife. I had forgotten completely the reality of my family and job. The drive home that afternoon was one of delight and peace as I savored my new life in God's kingdom.

Chapter 3

The Road to the Wilderness

I arrived home late that same afternoon. No one was there, and the house seemed empty. It had its own personality, which I had never noticed. It was well furnished and very neat but not hospitable. I suppose, unsurprisingly, that it had become like my marriage—everything in order on the surface but neither alive nor vibrant underneath.

I realized with a shock that the lack of love in my house was an accusation of failure. I sat down in the living room and tried to regain my sense of peace, but it could not be summoned back like a memory. In my heart, I asked God

357

to take this troubling remorse away, but it didn't leave me. My wife found me in this frame of mind when she returned.

Rachel is a striking woman, with dark hair and a tall slender athletic body. She is always in command. She must have been surprised to see me sitting on the couch and she looked tightly wound. I saw several greetings flicker across her face before she selected one.

"Well, surprise! I didn't expect you for another week. Trouble at the office bring you back?"

Like always she put me on the back foot. "I…How are you, Rachel?"

"Just fine. The kids are at a soccer game. I have to go back and pick them up in an hour. So, are you going to tell me why you're home from your vacation so soon? Didn't take very long to find yourself apparently."

I looked at her, and heard a familiar alarm go off. Her provocative questions usually led to a power struggle between us. I had no taste for that now. I wanted to tell her what had happened to me, and my new road, but I didn't feel safe enough with her to share my feelings. I expected a cynical response and her rejection of what had happened to me as 'neurotic' or 'crazy'. It occurred to me that I had already started the fight with her in my mind and was taking both sides of the argument myself! I looked at her and said nothing. I waited tensely for her to say something else. She walked out of the room when she saw I didn't intend to respond to her question.

Perfect, I thought. I'm home less than a half hour and the peace and newness I found in the kingdom has already disappeared. I want to follow God on a different road, not back here with a woman who is an expert at needling my vulnerable spots. Rachel returned and sat down next to me.

She wasn't as tense now and spoke more softly. "What's bothering you, Jacob? I want to help if I can."

"Do you?" I instantly regretted that.

She didn't take the bait. "Not when you pout. But I'll try to listen. We can't keep on like this. I've had time to think while you were gone."

"I can't...It's hard to explain. I'm afraid you'll feel too threatened."

She looked alarmed, even a little scared. "Now I *really* want to know."

Hesitantly, I tried to choose my words carefully. "Something happened to me, Rachel. I'm not the same person who left here a few days ago. Well, that's not completely true. A lot of me *is* still the same. But I've been...the only word I can think of is rescued."

I was hesitant to go further. Rachel and I both went to church sometimes, but we avoided talking about God. He was an awkward subject between us. I knew that if I told her about my mysterious encounter involving God and the kingdom, Rachel would be turned off, but I found it difficult to explain what had happened to me without relating the whole story.

She pressed me, her voice rising. "Were you in an accident? Are you hurt?"

"No, no. I meant rescued as a figure of speech. Rachel, to be blunt what happened to me is that I have decided to follow God. He confronted me on my trip with what I have done with my life up to now, and I have decided to follow His road from here on."

This came out in an embarrassed rush. It even sounded strange to me, as if I were some crazy convert to an offbeat religion. Rachel just sat and stared. For once she didn't react. I wondered what she was thinking. Her face was impassive although her foot was tapping the carpet.

Getting control back, she probed. "I don't understand. Are you having a nervous breakdown or something? What do you mean you're following God? What about the children and me?"

Her voice began to increase in intensity. "What the hell happened on your trip Jacob? Tell me, I want to know. Have you gone insane?"

I found it painful to discuss something so sensitive with someone I thought was ready to attack. But I managed to give her the highlights in a tense monologue that she didn't interrupt.

"So, if I understand you correctly someone converted you to some oddball religion?"

"No. That's not it. I'm not sure converted fits. Maybe it does though."

"This is just unbelievable! You, of all people! You always have been neurotic, ever since I've known you. Look, I can't handle this. I'm going to pick up the kids. Why don't you just clear out and take the rest of your vacation trip. By the time you get back, *if* you come back, I may have sorted out my feelings. Typical!"

With that final epithet, she grabbed her purse and slammed the door on her way out. I heard her car start and pull away. Nothing had worked. I didn't handle it right. She was stunned, repelled.

I needed to tell her that I was sorry for my part in the problems of our marriage; she probably didn't want to hear that either. Why hadn't I done that instead of forcing my recent experiences on her? My mind was racing, in confusion. How could I be such a poor husband? I sat there in an agony of self-doubt wondering if, indeed, as Rachel perhaps accurately perceived, I was a neurotic fool. I was so confused that I couldn't even utter a coherent prayer for help. After a short time, I felt some consolation in the fact that I honestly had told Rachel what had happened to me and had not become snared in a mutually destructive verbal battle as I might have previously. I sensed that she was right; I should leave, for now, and let her be alone to sort out what she wanted to do. I needed to say something more, and I found a pad in the kitchen and left a note for her on the refrigerator.

Rachel, I hope you will think of the good times we had. I want you to have your freedom and will live with any decision you make. Believe me when I say that I now am beginning to know what I have done to

*you and the kids and that I love you all. Say Hi to the kids for me. I'll
be back. Love, Jacob*

As I drove away from my home that evening, I was
depressed. I hadn't even been able to spend one hour with
my wife without an argument. Maybe if my defensiveness
hadn't gotten in the way she might have listened. As I drove
through the suburbs surrounding our house, I continued to
reproach myself. On the very day I had entered the kingdom
and experienced such joy, I now had become discouraged and
sad. What a fool I am I thought.

> [Elena's note in the margin of the manuscript] I have
> stopped reading because tears are blurring my vision.
> Frank was in real pain and I hadn't ever noticed. I
> wonder when this meeting with his wife had taken
> place, how many years before I met him? But maybe it
> hadn't actually happened. In his note to me, Frank had
> said this story was an allegory. But there was little
> doubt that he felt guilty about his marriage. Maybe
> that's why he didn't want to make a commitment to
> me. I realize I don't even know if he divorced his wife!
> Suddenly it seems that I haven't had much of a
> relationship with Frank after all. Chalk up another
> failure for me.

I needed a place to stay that night and checked in at a motel
on the outskirts of the city. I was hungry, and after leaving my
suitcase in the room I went to a nearby restaurant. Waiting
for my dinner to arrive I watched the people around me.

Mainly couples, having an evening out together. This deepened my loneliness. I knew that even if Rachel were here we would each be trapped in our own private anger. I missed the Goodmans and couldn't help but wonder if any of those people around me had entered the kingdom.

Whether it was my mood or something else, I perceived suddenly that all the couples around me were blind and isolated in their own selfish worlds. I felt frustrated and angry: Angry that they seemed so self-involved and frustrated that I couldn't do anything about it. I felt darkness hovering over this place; I quickly finished my dinner and returned to the motel.

I was afraid what I might dream about that night and watched television to postpone sleep. But the falsity of everything on television led me into more despondency. I wondered if I had somehow blundered and left the kingdom and was lost again. I asked God to give me some sign that He was with me then I lay down to try to sleep.

After struggling without sleep for what seemed like hours, I got up, dressed and took a walk to try to relax. The night was warm and pleasant, and I wandered along the shoulder of the quiet highway. It was an area of fast food, motels, and rundown businesses that stretched for miles on the main highway. Everything was closed and only a few trucks and cars passed me.

When I turned to go back to the motel, I saw a young woman standing in the shadows on the side of the road. She was dressed in dirty Levis and an old leather jacket. She held an unlit cigarette in her hand and was looking at me. "You got a match mister?" I shook my head and she put the cigarette back in the pack with a slight groan. "You a trucker?" she asked.

I didn't want to talk with her, but it was hard to ignore her directness. "No, I'm just driving through."

"What're you doing out this time of night?"

Her question seemed a threat. I looked around to see if anyone was with her. "Just taking a walk," I said cautiously.

She was a few steps away from me and I could see that she was about sixteen and had a thin prettiness that reminded me vaguely of Rachel when I first met her. But something else about her hinted at trouble. "Isn't it late for you to be out here alone?" I asked.

She grinned at me. "Don't worry about me, Pop; I can take care of myself."

I saw that she probably could handle me or anyone else she ran into. 'Pop' suddenly made me feel old and out of place.

"You want to buy me a drink? I know an all-night place right down the road where we can get one." She was still grinning at me.

"No, I don't think that would be a good idea."

She still didn't leave me alone. "Come on. I haven't had anything to eat all day. How about' a hamburger instead of a drink?" She wasn't grinning anymore and had a hard look about her. I knew I didn't want anything more to do with her;

she frightened me. I walked past her without saying another word. But she wasn't going to let me off that easily.

"What's the matter, old man? Afraid I'll bite? Lighten up. All I want is something to eat. Just give me some money; you don't even have to go with me."

I just kept walking and ignored her. When she saw I wasn't going to give her anything, she peppered my back with angry profanity, but I kept on walking. When I got to the motel driveway, I looked back but she had disappeared. I went back to my room to try to get some sleep; this time I succeeded.

My sleep was fitful. I had no coherent dreams, just images of people I didn't recognize in strange places. I woke up in the dark feeling completely alone and lost again. I thought about Frank in prison and how he must have felt at night before he entered the kingdom. Hopeless! I wondered if God was leading me somewhere in my despondency, but I just felt emptiness. As I dropped off to sleep, I saw Pilgrim.

He wasn't with me in the room this time, but he showed me a vivid message. I saw him walk from his prison cell—as he had in my first dream—and start toward the gate. This time however, I saw him fall into a swamp and in fear call out for help. A man came along and pulled him out of the thick mud in which he was trapped. I heard their discussion clearly.

"Friend, how did you fall into the swamp? Couldn't you see the path?"

Pilgrim responded, "I was afraid, and in my hurry, I fell in."

"I'm glad I heard your cry. You must be more observant from now on and stay on the path."

"What is the name of this swamp? Why can't it be repaired so it won't trap those who are trying to follow God's path?"

His helper looked at him. "It cannot be repaired because it is a result of the accumulated wrongs that men do on Earth. Each man tries to move toward God's path but then stumbles over his own personal contribution to this swamp. Then all of his doubts and discouragements confront him. It is called The Swamp of Despondency."

"But why can't it be fixed?"

The man shrugged his shoulders. "Oh, many have tried. Over the years God has sent thousands of workers to repair this place. They have poured millions of truckloads of helpful instructions into this swamp, but men still have this dizziness in their heads and ignore the advice and get stuck here."

That is when I awoke from the dream. I felt relieved; the message from Pilgrim helped. I was able to get to sleep and enjoy a welcome rest until morning. I ate breakfast in the same restaurant but now I felt at home among the early morning crowd, eating before they went to work. They reminded me of my own office; I decided to drop in briefly to see if I was needed.

I drove downtown to the building where I worked and parked in the underground garage I used every day. The elevator was packed with people hurrying to work. I entered the floor where my office was located and another shock greeted me there. My office now seemed as alien and unfriendly as my home. It seemed to question why I had bothered to return. I glanced at the papers on my desk. There were a few things I should do, but a feeling of incompetency suddenly seized me. Would I lose my role in the company because of the change in my life? My anxiety returned with a vengeance. I knew my imagination was running wild and that nothing probably had changed as far as my job was concerned. But my feelings of not fitting in anymore, of somehow being out of place were not imaginary. I sat behind the desk in my office feeling as if I had been cut adrift from everything secure—first, my family, and, now, my work. It was clear that I was stuck again in The Swamp of Despondency.

I left my office and returned to my car. I had no idea where to go. It seemed that the only place where I might regain the peace of the kingdom was back with the Goodmans, so I decided to go back to their farm.

As I drove toward the highway, I saw a young hitchhiker and on impulse picked him up. He wore a backpack and looked as if he had spent a lot of time outdoors. He tossed his pack in the back seat and joined me in front.

"Thanks, I've been waiting quite a while for a ride. How far are you going?"

I told him the exit where I would turn off the highway to get to the Goodmans and he seemed disappointed that I wasn't going further. He quickly began to make conversation.

"You on a vacation?"

"I'm going to visit friends who own a farm."

"You ought to try hiking into the wilderness that surrounds that area while you're visiting."

Being alone did sound good to me. Maybe that's what I needed: to get away and wait for some sign from God.

"Have you done much hiking?" I asked. He said he had and told me some of the off-the-beaten-track places he'd been. It sounded more and more exciting. I hadn't been camping since I was a boy.

"What gear would I need?" He said the less I carried the better. We talked for a while about equipment he would recommend. As we drove past a shopping mall he said that there was an outfitter there, and that I could let him out and pick him up again if he hadn't gotten another ride by the time I came out. He got out and I went into the mall.

As I entered, I noticed the shoppers. What especially caught my eye were their faces. Some were excited; some were intent. But also it seemed to me that everyone was anxious. I felt their anxiety sweep past me as I stood at the mall's center court and watched the crowds walk by. The image of the chasm came back to me and I imagined this crowd of shoppers walking down the hills and falling into the chasm. Maybe they didn't realize what would happen because they were under the spell of this place. Suddenly I saw that they truly were sleepwalkers! I wanted to shout at them: 'You're prisoners! Wake up before it's too late!' I sensed that it would do no good. If I tried to speak to that young man over there he would pull away in hostility—or think I was crazy. I remembered a street corner years ago where a disheveled man had been calling 'Repent' to the people who passed by. He had repelled me. I had been vaguely afraid to come near him. I knew that I would be seen in the same way here in the mall if I shouted out 'Wake up!' None of these people would believe that I had seen God, or the chasm or the kingdom either.

I bought the camping equipment I had come for and hurriedly left. I sat in the parking lot for some time and again I struggled with despondency. I believed that I had found the gate into the kingdom, but I thought of the millions who lived in this city and the billions elsewhere in the world who apparently hadn't. I wanted to trust God; yet how could he have allowed so few to find the gate? A shadow passed my car. I looked to see what it was. Suddenly I knew that these thoughts came from Adversary. I felt relief. Suddenly I knew somehow that God wouldn't let such a massively cruel thing happen to so many people.

I drove away from the mall with a renewed feeling of trust and hope. I saw the hitchhiker still standing where I had dropped him off; I picked him up again. His presence now had an air of mystery connected with it. Was he another messenger from God, like Evan or the Goodmans?

I asked him. "Have you been waiting for me today, or is it just an accident that I picked you up?"

"Nothing in this world happens by accident, Jacob."

"Did God send you to me?"

The hitchhiker had a quiet authority. "Why are you so impatient?"

"But…everything has been so confused since I left the Goodmans."

"Didn't the Goodmans warn you to expect trouble on the road?"

"But I thought they meant…attacks by evil."

"What would you call the trouble you have been experiencing from Adversary?"

"Not evil. I just became depressed. Pilgrim showed me it happens to everyone."

The hitchhiker smiled at me, and I recognized what I had said. I *had* done something wrong: getting mired in despondency and not trusting God as I promised Evan I would.

"Well, I didn't mean to. I just got caught up in my feelings."

"What about the young woman last night?"

How did he know about her? I replied defensively. "I didn't do anything to her!"

He grinned at me. "Precisely. She needed you and you walked away. God sent her to you for help."

Suddenly I remembered her asking me for food or money and I was ashamed.

"Don't worry, someone else helped her. Why didn't you?"

"I was afraid that she was…I mean that I might…"

He looked at me gently, "You are imprisoned in your fears, Jacob. Don't you realize that God gave you the gift of freedom from fear when you entered the kingdom?"

All at once I saw the hitchhiker in a new light, like the helper who pulled Pilgrim out of the swamp. He looked ordinary, not at all like I thought God's helper should look. I began to see that a lot of my perceptions about how God worked could be wrong.

"Jacob, before you try to follow God's path to the river of change, you need to be prepared. You were in the military once. Call it 'basic training'. That's a good analogy. You need to be alone for a while to learn what you need to know. Go directly to the wilderness from here." His last statement was a command that left no options!

We drove the rest of the way in silence. The command in his voice silenced my questions. I thought about what the hitchhiker had said concerning the preparation I needed; I agreed with him completely. My mind was filled with new experiences and questions that I had to sort out. It was not only a matter of finding out what God wanted but also understanding who I had become since entering the kingdom. The hitchhiker was right. I was imprisoned within myself and not truly free. I felt as if I had become an awkward mixture of old habits and new beliefs, at war within myself. I needed to be alone with my new self for a while.

At the exit ramp leading toward the Goodman's farm I pulled to the side of the highway and let the hitchhiker out. He wished me well on my journey and stood watching my car as I left the highway. It was late afternoon when I finally reached the farm. The house was dark and I didn't stop. I left my car, took my camping gear and began immediately to climb up into the hills behind their farm.

Chapter 4

Night in the Wilderness

The climb into the hills was difficult for me. The path wasn't steep, but it wound constantly upward through woods thick with underbrush. By the time I was high enough to have a view of the entire valley where the Goodmans lived, I was ready to give up. I sat down heavily and wearily took off my pack. What was I trying to prove? I looked around for Adversary but found no trace of it.

The air was fresher up here, and I again sensed how acute my perceptions had become since I had entered the kingdom. The wilderness seemed to console me with the promise of discoveries. I recalled a clearing in the woods on my grandfather's farm, a secret place beside a stream I had found as a boy. I had felt very safe there. If I closed my eyes I could imagine I was sitting in that same quiet place.

A shadow fell across my closed eyelids and I lurched back into the present. I saw nothing out of the ordinary. I was stiff from sitting and when I stood up to go on I felt exhausted. Discouragement caught at me again. Suddenly I was anxious about the approaching night. Although I had not come very far, I wanted to return to my car and find some company. Anyone would do; I rarely had felt so alone and isolated. But I argued myself out of leaving the wilderness and found a spot to roll out my sleeping bag and build a small fire.

I felt relieved when the small camp was ready, but the feeling of desolation returned as the forest darkened. The fire created jumping shadows against the encircling trees, and my mind became a nest of fears that seemed about to grow into something truly terrifying. With effort I again focused my thoughts on the clearing from my youth; it was a refuge from my fear and I fell sleep.

I was startled awake by someone touching me. I looked up and saw a man dressed like a hunter. As he gazed at me his eyes held no threat, but I felt shaky nonetheless.

"You lost?" he asked, giving my camp a quick inspection. "I don't see many people walking through these hills anymore."

I didn't answer. I didn't want to explain. He walked over to my pack to examine it. "Brand new. Your first time out here?"

"Yes. I used to go camping as a boy, with the Scouts."

The hunter put out his hand in greeting. I reached up from my sleeping bag and shook it. It was the roughest hand I had ever grasped, and I knew he must live with few of the comforts on which my life depended.

"My name's Jack Waters. Sorry I gave you a scare. I saw a fire in the woods and came over to put it out. But I see you know how to make a campfire safely."

I was pleased by his compliment and told him my name. I was suddenly glad to be with someone and wanted him to stay. I got out of the sleeping bag and joined him at the fire. Jack added a few small branches to the fire indicating that he was staying awhile. He looked at me and repeated his original question.

"Do you know where you are?"

I didn't actually. "I followed the path up from the valley. I think I could find my way back out of here."

"Good. This place is nowhere to get lost. I wouldn't get too far away from the path if I were you. How long are you staying?"

"I thought about a week. I've got some thinking I need to do and this place seemed like a good place to find…something I'm looking for."

I was wary of the conversation getting into an area which might offend him. Vaguely I wondered why I was worried about that. Maybe Rachel's reaction had made me edgy though that seemed like a lame excuse.

"You see a lot out here that gets covered up back in the city in a crowd of people. That's why I stay."

I was curious now. "Like what?"

"Things most people don't want to see anymore. That's why I don't meet many people out here these days."

Suddenly, I realized what he meant. He was another messenger. "I think I may need to see some of those same things. Would you show me?"

He looked at me intently. "Do you think you're ready? You look inexperienced to me. These things can be frightening for beginners."

I didn't feel ready. "I hope I am. I think I have been sent to see whatever is in these woods." I was thinking about the hitchhiker.

Jack didn't reply. He sat quietly for a bit, and then stood up. "Let's go. I'll take you where you need to go right now."

"Now? Can't we wait until morning?" I wanted the security of daylight.

"You must learn to deal with darkness where we're going. If you want to see what's there we have to go now." He looked at me expectantly. He probably thought I was going to back out, and to tell the truth I almost did. My life had not prepared me for danger or adventure, and I felt fear clutch at me. But, now, feeling Jack's strength somehow, I accepted his dare and motioned for him to lead on. We put out the fire and left my camping gear; Jack said I could pick it up later. As we left my campsite I felt like I had as a boy when someone told a ghost story. The storyteller always acted as if something truly terrifying might happen—but it never did. Only something *was* going to happen to me tonight! My heart rose into my throat as we walked away from the Goodmans and deeper into the wilderness.

Jack walked through the woods quickly and it was difficult to keep his shadowy form in view in the darkness. I began to breathe rapidly and finally had to call to him to slow down. "We're almost there," he called back and kept up the pace. Somehow, I managed to stay close to him until he stopped in front of a rock cliff that towered above our path.

He pointed to a dark opening in the cliff. "Here is a cave where you can find what you are looking for."

"Will I meet God here?"

He grinned at me. "You should know that I won't answer that. But I can see why you have been sent here."

"Who are you?"

"I am only a man living in the wilderness, preparing people to follow God's way. Only when someone goes through the darkness of the wilderness and enters this cave can he hope to find the right road to the river of change." He looked at me expectantly.

[Elena's note in the margin of the manuscript] This is strange. Does Frank mean that everyone must go through such strange experiences? I never heard anyone else mention anything like this.

There seemed to be nothing more to say. I thanked him for leading me to the cave and turned to leave when he stopped me. "Jacob, it will be hard for you in there, harder than you expect. Just remember that God has brought you here and is watching out for you. He won't let you be tested beyond your strength." With that he walked into the night and left me alone.

I hesitated for a moment and then walked into the dark mouth of the cave, feeling my way cautiously, step by step, on the rock floor. The blackness was total, and as I went deeper into the mysterious place I shivered in fear. Then I heard a sound—a blurred roar like a river rushing through a gorge, which gradually resolved into human shouting. I saw a faint light ahead and I began to tremble as the noise of an unruly crowd reverberated in the cave. All at once I could see that the cave ended ahead in daylight, and I could also see a large, excited crowd, facing away from me, watching something. The crowd was oddly dressed, like actors in a Greek tragedy. They were agitated, shouting in a strange language I had never heard before. Unnoticed, I stood at the rear to see what they were watching. I looked down over their heads into a huge stone stadium with a dirt floor surrounded by a rough wooden fence with several gates. It was what was happening on the floor of the stadium that had excited the crowd.

I looked for only a moment and then I turned away in disgust and loathing. But I have never forgotten the scene that

I saw in the cave that day. A small group of men, women, and children were standing at one end of the arena, tightly packed together, looking away from what was happening nearby. There, about twenty feet away, a pack of wild dogs was ripping at the bloody body of a man. The group of people was looking away from that awful sight toward a gate, from which a pack of lions and tigers, intent on their prey, were slowly stalking toward them. The entrance of these beasts was what had brought the excited crowd to its feet. I looked at the spectators' faces; they were beyond excitement; they were contorted with frenzy! I couldn't bear this place and closed my eyes to blot it out. The shouting stopped and again I was in total silence.

I opened my eyes and the crowd and the arena had disappeared. Now I was standing at the edge of a small clearing in a lush jungle. In the center of the clearing was a tall, swarthy man, wearing a long robe of bright colors. He held something over his head and was looking up at what it was. There were others who looked like primitive savages watching him. They were standing at the edge of the clearing staring at what the man was doing. I saw that he was holding a baby above his head. It was squirming in his grip. I heard its small cries. To my horror he flung the child into a gaping pit at his feet and watched it fall for a moment before he turned and walked toward the others. In revulsion, I closed my eyes again. What was happening to me in this place?

When I opened my eyes I was in a desert valley, surrounded by large boulders, with barren rocky hills on every side. About one hundred yards away I saw an old man and a boy about ten years old talking quietly near a small fire. The boy climbed up onto a nearby boulder, lay down, and spread his arms wide against the stone. The old man approached him and, to my shock, took a large knife out of his dirty cloak and raised it high over the boy's chest as if to stab him. I couldn't watch and tried to shout to the old man to stop, but no sound came. The man abruptly stopped as if he were held immobile by an unseen hand. He backed away from the boy and flung away the knife. I bowed my head in relief.

When I looked up, the scene had switched again. Now I was on an ancient city street in the midst of an angry crowd. To my dismay I saw a man who looked like a young Evan in the crowd, holding the coats of a group of men who were holding large stones in their hands. One man threw his stone hard. I saw it strike a handsome young man standing against a wall and knock him down. The rest of the men began to throw their rocks at the now unconscious youth crumpled on the ground. I saw Evan wince, but he didn't stop the awful violence of the crowd. This terrible revelation about Evan stunned me, and I turned away.

Then, abruptly, I was on another ancient city street, surrounded by a shouting mob. It looked like the crowd I had just seen but I realized that this crowd was watching a different man suffer. A group that looked like Roman soldiers was whipping a man brutally. He lay on the ground, and they tried to make him stand. One of the soldiers grabbed a spectator and shoved him toward the man on the ground. The spectator picked up a large wooden beam lying on the ground next to the man and hoisted it to his own shoulder. Then I knew what I was witnessing, and I hated the people around me for their stupidity and their bloodthirsty anger. I couldn't watch any longer and hid my face in my hands. When I heard the noise cease, I looked up and saw that I was in yet another place—at the edge of what appeared to be an American Indian village.

This time, however, I was not a bystander. I was dressed in a dusty blue military uniform, riding a lathered horse through the village with other soldiers. Some carried torches, burning the Indian huts. Others were shouting and firing their rifles at a small group of Indian women and children huddled in the center of the dirty village. What shocked me most, however, were my own feelings. I was burning with fury! The helplessness of the Indians only made my anger stronger. How I loathed them! I drove my horse straight at the crowd, savagely swinging my saber. I was in a blood-rage, releasing feelings that I had long kept bottled up. These were heathens and I was doing God's work! They would never kill another of my friends!

Then I was no longer mounted on the horse. The scene had changed, and I was now afoot in a small Irish village and under attack myself, being ridden down by other horsemen. But my rage continued to burn. I hated my own helplessness and that I had to watch my neighbors being killed by the godless English. Then I saw to my shock that one of the men charging toward me, with a wild look on his face, was the soldier Pilgrim. This was more than I could bear, and I closed my eyes again in fear and confusion.

Now I saw I was in a peaceful forest clearing but I still felt shaken by my previous visions, and my mind spun from the fear and anger. It was several minutes before I regained control. But I had no time to think because two young men were walking toward me across the clearing. They were dressed in animal skins and obviously arguing. One shoved at the other, picking a fight; his companion did not respond. To my horror the aggressive one stooped down, grabbed a large rock, crashed it on the other's head, and killed him before he could react or protect himself. It seemed as if he had been totally surprised that his companion had attacked him so savagely. He simply stood and took the mortal blow.

Suddenly, all the scenes I had witnessed made some kind of perverse sense, and I was disgusted with the human race. How bloodthirsty we are! I recognized in that moment that I was no different from any of these people. I had ignored this ugly reality until now. I had believed that I was special, unlike the rest of men. All my life, I had been comfortable with myself. My world appeared 'civilized' and so was I. But here in the cave, the events of my lifetime—wars, crime in the city where I lived, even my own family's petty quarrels—demanded that I admit the truth to myself.

The forest began to fade away and I was back in the city where I had seen the Roman soldiers beating the injured man. This time I stood outside the city on a barren hilltop. I felt no revulsion now; this time I was at home in the crowd and joined in their anger and hostility.

I shouted in derision as the soldiers raised the man and crucified him in the midst of other criminals hanging on that awful hill. He was naked and bloody but that made little difference to me. Who did He think He was? He had misled us; we hoped He had come to free us from the Romans, yet

He had ignored them, and meekly given Himself to them without a fight. So, let them crucify him. He was a fake, and I hated Him for it!

Above the sullen mutter of the crowd I heard the crucified man call out. I understood his words—although they were in a strange language—and they stunned me! In that instant I knew that God is a mysterious and puzzling God, challenging all of us by this man's cruel death. His words seemed to be about failure and disgrace. But then God gave me a gift and I understood that His words, uttered in human agony, were the beginning of a warrior king's poem of praise to God, thanking God for protecting his life from his enemies!

My anger vanished. In shame I recognized the unfathomable love that buoyed up the crucified man's determination to endure everything. He also had seen the awful things I had witnessed in the cave and, even so, loved the human race. And, over and against this love, I saw, bitterly, my own ingratitude and hardness in my life up to now.

> [Elenas note in the margin of the manuscript] I know what Frank is trying to say here but I feel like I'm being manipulated somehow. It's all so strange.

It is terrifying to discover, suddenly and surprisingly, that you are responsible for an awful crime. I felt as if I had awakened from a nightmare to discover that my dream of falling into the chasm was real. I could no longer distance myself from anything the human race had done. I saw that Adversary had been right, in one sense, when it said that all men deserve to walk into the chasm and be destroyed. But I knew that Adversary was lying also. The crucified man's death on the cross is the truth, demonstrating the absurd mercy of God's forgiveness for the broken human race!

That was a truth I learned in the cave that night. In my humanity I *was* guilty and broken and distorted by an ancient inheritance as well as my own up-to-date version of fear and anger. But the mysterious and puzzling God who sent that man to die on the cross had overlooked and even forgotten my offenses and had led me into the kingdom. I could hardly raise my eyes off the dirt path to thank him. Somehow my brokenness still seemed an insult to him. Then, as if the deep soreness was removed from deep inside me, I felt filled with peace. That was the first gift God gave me in the cave.

[Elena's note in the margin of the manuscript] How could Frank feel guilty for something that happened 2000 years ago? He was a good man, probably as good a man as I ever knew. OK, he had ignored his family and become a workaholic. Join the crowd. But somehow he felt as guilty as the murderers and scum he imagined in those scenes in the cave. I can understand he might feel regret, but broken and distorted? I feel like there is now something between Frank and I that hadn't been there before—a barrier or a secret he hadn't shared that damaged our relationship.

Almost immediately the forest began to darken; my doubts returned and drove away my newly found peace. What would happen now? Jack Waters had warned me of overwhelming difficulties. Gradually the light left the forest, as twilight fades after sunset. I stood again in utter darkness. I waited, hardly able to breathe

In the blackness I felt everything alter. Then I was transported into outer space, with stars and galaxies everywhere. It seemed I might be falling again within the chasm of destruction, and I was afraid. I heard a voice from everywhere and nowhere saying, "Jacob, I see your struggles and know you are an honest man. Now I will show you what you seek." I thought this meant that, at last, God would show Himself to me.

The stars began to move and accelerate away from me (or maybe I moved away from the stars, I couldn't tell). I saw the entire universe from a great distance; it appeared as a single brilliant flower of light in the midst of vast emptiness. I was shown all existence from a God-like vantage point, but still I could not see God—either in the universe or in the void. Then the universe exploded toward me and closed around me again.

I rushed throughout the universe seeking God. My curiosity was unrestrained; there were marvels everywhere, but I could not see Him in the stars or on any of the planets. Then, as everything rushed toward me and became immensely large, I became incredibly tiny. I was made smaller than any atom, and I could peer inside of everything and look for the hidden God. I understood many wonderful things that made the universe work, but I could not find God inside anything. Finally, back in the cave, I still felt the desire to search for God's last conceivable hiding place—inside myself.

I cannot describe how I looked inside myself; yet I did. I knew my body and mind as things apart, and I could not see God in them, although for a moment my mind seemed to hold an image like Him. I realized that I had dreamed that image, and that it wasn't God. I asked again where he could be hidden, and I thought a final answer had come to me. He might be in the very consciousness that I used to observe my body and mind and the universe. Maybe my mysterious awareness was God's presence within me. It seemed like God; my consciousness gave me God-like powers to see the universe. Perhaps God was part of my awareness, or maybe I was part of His. But my hope that I had found Him was short-lived; the voice from everywhere and nowhere again spoke: "I am not anything you can perceive, Jacob. Yet I am, and I am with you as I choose to be with you." And I was left alone in the dark forest inside the cave.

Thus did my utter helplessness to see God finally confront me. He was, is nothing that I can possibly see or grasp. No one I met could ever help me. That's what the Goodmans, and Jack Waters, and the others had been telling me! I then felt like the cave was infinite and that it imprisoned me like an impenetrable shell. It seemed that God was outside the shell, and I was inside. I experienced intense isolation and desolation—believing that God existed, but infinitely different and separate from me.

It suddenly seemed that all my ideas about the gate and the path toward God were absurd and that Adversary might be right after all. That what Adversary called the great unknowable One was only a spectator who sat outside the cave and cynically watched man struggle, without caring what happened to us. But in that moment of desolation and confusion I felt another power, the power of faith surge in me! Adversary's lies *would* have an overwhelming destructive force against men, except for faith. Through faith God is present to men. We, and the cosmos as well are 'in God', in his care. With the eyes of faith I could see His hand in everything—and I knew that only a man without faith asks, "Where is God?" Suddenly, I was confident that I could withstand Adversary's attacks of emptiness and cynicism! In that manner, I learned a second truth in the cave, about the power of God's gift of faith to me.

Calmed by this insight, I waited to see what would happen. The roof of the cave seemed to descend and narrow, becoming a dark tunnel which called on me to enter and continue. I walked into the dark passage and followed it only a short distance when it opened again into brilliant sunlight.

[Elena's note in the margin of the manuscript] I can see where Frank is leading me, and I don't want to follow. Faith is his answer—but to what question? He has been asking where is God? That isn't my question. In fact, I don't really have any questions. God, life and everything are what they are. My problem is to figure out how to make my life worth living, right now. Frank's 'Big Questions' don't bother me. Even if they were suddenly answered, I'd still have to figure out how to live. Frank was a thinker and I'm not. If fact, now I see that Frank is something like his God— distant. Maybe that's why he didn't give me this manuscript. He couldn't be close to me as I read it. He couldn't share love. I'm feeling sorry for him now. Or am I feeling sorry for myself?

Chapter 5

Francis and the Desert

A surprise met me as I left the cave. The green wooded hills behind the Goodman's house had vanished. I stepped from the tunnel into a barren desert. I was at the base of a high, jagged ridge of volcanic rock at the edge of a vast arid plain. After only a few steps from the cave I lost sight of it; its entrance seemed to disappear into the cliff. My next test, I surmised, was to find my way out of this forbidding place. I learned, however, that once again I misunderstood God's ways.

From the height of the sun I could tell that it was about mid-day. It was incredibly hot, and since I had taken no water with me when I entered the cave, I knew I had to find some quickly or I would be in serious trouble. I looked for some sign of water or of life. The ground was rocky and hard, with very sparse plant life, not a promising place to find water. Far across the desert, a range of mountains shimmered in the heat. I decided to go toward them rather than wandering aimlessly looking for water.

As I slowly walked out onto the desert plain and found no water, my thirst became painful and I became increasingly irritated with my situation. I was being lured into a journey and losing touch with real life, which was, for me, holding a job and providing for my family. It occurred to me that my life had not been all that bad. Wasn't I a basically good man, with a decent job and a normal marriage even though it had its problems? What did God want from me?

Almost in answer to my frustration, a small cloud crossed in front of the sun and gave me some slight relief from the heat. As I continued across the harsh desert I wrestled with my conscience. My struggle in the cave began to seem weird and self-centered. Ever since I had entered the kingdom I had become a dreamer, caught up in events that were leading me away from my job and family. Surely that was not what God wanted. I continued to walk and grumble to myself for quite some time, becoming more and more thirsty and exhausted in the process. I could not deny that God had led me here. Yet I could see little reason for the difficulty of this journey. My purpose was to reach the river of change and avoid the chasm of destruction. What was the point of this struggle? Wouldn't it be easier on everyone if God led us to the river directly?

> [Elena's note in the margin of the manuscript] This is more like it! I can relate to what Frank is saying. All his experiences in the cave didn't mean all that much, compared to his relationship with his family. I feel a brief surge of guilt as I think of my separation from my own mother and father, but it quickly passes. They had brought that on themselves. So, I'm beginning to understand what Frank is saying. How one walks the road of life is what matters, whether you have faith or not. No, that isn't what he is saying but maybe he will clear things up later on.

The more I thought about it, the more the process I was enduring seemed absurd, without any meaning that I could discern. Why was I being forced to endure these tests in order to learn? God could easily give me the knowledge I need to live a better life. In fact, why put mankind in the world at all? We could all be with God on the other side of the river from the beginning! Why did God's mysterious and subtle ways of doing things always leave me perplexed and distressed? It seemed that he provided only challenges, not answers or satisfaction. It was while I was lost in thought about these questions that I saw the old man. I was delighted to see another person and I immediately went over to greet him.

He was huddled against a rock with his face to the sky and his eyes closed. He was tiny, as small as a young boy, and he seemed asleep. When I touched him to wake him, he didn't move but his heart was beating; I felt a weak pulse in his throat. Then I noticed a waterskin next to him. Thank God it had water in it. I took a small drink and it was delicious. It took more will power than I thought I had to force myself to stop drinking. I poured a little water on his lips to try to revive him and his mouth opened automatically almost like a baby's.

Although I didn't think I was supposed to give him a drink because he was unconscious, I poured more water into his mouth. His eyes fluttered and I gave him more to drink, the remainder of the water in the bag in fact. I hope he knows where we can find some more, I thought. As he sat there looking up at me, obviously gaining strength, I observed him more closely. He was dressed for the desert wearing a loose white robe and sandals. His face was brown with age and the sun. Compared with other elderly people I knew he was easily the oldest person I had ever seen, probably over a hundred years old. What was he doing out here by himself? As if in answer, he smiled at me.

"Are you OK now?" I asked. He nodded his head and motioned for me to sit down. When he spoke, his voice was a hoarse whisper; I had to strain to hear.

"Thank you, young man, you're very kind to help me. I must have passed out. My name is Francis Wiseman. May I ask yours?"

"I'm Jacob Newman. Glad you're feeling better. I used the rest of your water. Do you know where we can find more?"

He nodded his head and pointed toward the hazy range of mountains in the distance. I wondered if we could reach them without water. "They look a long way off. Can you make it that far?"

"God willing. I've lived in this desert a long time and know its secrets."

He motioned for me to help him stand. We began to walk slowly in the direction of the mountains. I was curious why he was out here by himself. Where was his family?

"I try to help travelers like you cross this desert, Jacob. That is the work God has given me."

"But at your age what can you do? I mean it seems like I had to help you."

He turned and looked at me steadily. I felt he saw everything about me, and it made me uncomfortable. Then he smiled again, and that feeling passed.

"Jacob, you know that this desert is another test for you. Why do you constantly question the ways of God? He has sent me to you. Isn't that enough?"

We walked in silence, and I thought about his gentle rebuke. I remembered my doubts about what God was putting me through. I wanted to ask about the meaning of all this, but his attitude stopped me. He seemed to believe that I should simply wait for God to reveal His purpose. We walked without talking for quite a while, and then Francis suggested we stop and rest. We found a large rock and sat in its lengthening shadow.

"Tell me Jacob, how did you get here?"

I told him of the chasm, my entrance into the kingdom, and the difficulties I had been experiencing. I related my visions in the cave, and what I thought God had taught me thus far.

"So, what is left for you to learn, Jacob? Why do you think God has led you to this desert?"

I looked down, away from his penetrating gaze. "I don't know. It puzzles me why He is putting me through all this."

"Is God doing this to you, or are you putting yourself through these tests?"

That startled me. "What do you mean? I didn't decide to come to the cave or this desert. I was led here, first by a hitchhiker, then by Jack Waters. In fact, what I wanted to do was to spend a peaceful week in the woods thinking about the kingdom and God."

"So you want to find what God wants you do, but do it in your own way. I'm beginning to understand. It may help if I tell you about myself."

He began his story when the sun was low in the sky. When he had finished, the sun had set and we were in darkness. I will tell his story as I understood it then. Since then I have come to see a different meaning that I will tell you later.

Francis was born into wealth, and as a boy lived a life of happiness with his family in a beautiful garden. As he grew

394

older, he explored the grounds where he lived and found that, while they were extensive, they had limits. A high stone wall with a locked gate surrounded the garden. As a young man he once asked his father what was on the other side of the wall. His father advised him not to pry into forbidden things. Francis and his family had the garden and he should be satisfied with it.

He was happy there, but he could not forget the wall and what might be beyond it. His need to know what was outside was a kind of hunger gnawing at him. Finally, he decided to climb over the wall and told his parents of his plan. They were shocked at the idea and pleaded with him not to do what was forbidden. He asked who had forbidden something as normal as exploration. His parents could not explain it to him, beyond saying it was God's command. They repeated, over and over, that if he climbed the wall, he might not be able to return but Francis did not believe this. The next day he said goodbye to his tearful parents and walked to the edge of the garden. He hesitated, thinking of his parent's warnings and of the possibility that he might lose all of this. Yet his desire to see what was outside the garden was so strong that an irresistible urge pulled him forward. He climbed a nearby tree, inched his way out on a branch that hung over the wall, and dropped to the ground outside.

The world beyond the wall was not as beautiful as his parents' garden; it was different and yet seemed somehow to welcome him. He wanted to explore and know everything that was outside. He soon came to a small village where he was fascinated by the people, working and enjoying themselves in activities that were completely new to him. He remained in the village with a friendly man who taught him how to make shoes to earn his living. The man had a daughter whom Francis came to love and eventually married. Occasionally he thought about taking her back to the garden to visit his parents, but he was always busy and eventually forgot the garden.

Years passed and Francis felt his fascination with the world rekindling. What was beyond the village? One day he told his wife he wanted to take a trip in order to see more of the world. She told him tearfully that he might not return. He offered to take her with him, but she had no desire to leave everyone she cared about so she refused. Francis left the village, assuring her he would be gone only for a few days. He walked through the countryside and saw many wonderful things; these increased his desire to see even more. At last he came to a large city that had even more marvelous sights than he had ever dreamed existed. When it was time to return to the village and his wife, he knew that there was much more to see and experience in the city. So, he stayed and gradually forgot his promise to his wife. Over the years he became a powerful businessman, owning many shoe stores in the city and throughout the country.

One day a young man came to Francis' house and asked for work. The young man was obviously poor, and Francis took him into the house and shared what he had with the boy. From that point he began to look for others who had nothing and to share with them as well. This made him happy and also eased his conscience about his wife and parents. He became known far and wide as a charitable man and everyone respected his goodness. But Francis' old desire again began to burn. What was beyond this city? He heard of a group of adventurers who were setting off to explore the wilderness in another country, and he decided to join them. His friends and all those he had helped tried to persuade him to stay. The trip would be dangerous, and he might not return but he left anyway.

As Francis and the other three adventurers traveled, they got to know each other. They discovered that they were remarkably alike: Successful people who had experienced much in their lives and who felt they had done good in one way or another. And most strikingly they found that they all were willing to risk everything to satisfy a burning desire for exploration.

When they reached the distant country, Francis and the others set off across a vast desert. They wandered for months; their trip was extremely difficult, but they never faltered. They persisted because of their desire to see what was beyond the desert. At last they came to a massive range of mountains. They climbed into the mountains and, in an isolated valley, came eventually to a stone wall which blocked their path. All of them quickly scaled to the top of the wall to see what was on the other side and were astonished by what they saw. Inside was a gardenlike valley much like the one where Francis had lived with his parents. He recognized it instantly and wistfully knew that his lifelong desire to explore had finally brought him back to the only place where he could be completely happy. The others had similar experiences. They too saw the valley as a happy place known only in their youth and one where they finally could be completely satisfied. Francis noticed a group of people in the valley waving at the four men to join them. But the adventurers were unable to climb past an invisible barrier that held them out of the valley.

Then came another devastating vision. Francis saw his parents and wife among the people in the valley! Indeed, all the people the adventurers had left behind had somehow found their way inside. And now, though they longed to be with them, the barrier held them away. Francis told me that he knew instantly that he would have to retrace his steps to find a way into that valley. And so he did, leaving the other men and re-crossing the desert, returning to the city where he had been so successful and charitable, and the village where he had left his wife. His wife and all the people he knew in these places were now dead; he had been gone a long time.

He went back to his parents' garden and tried to climb over the wall but the same invisible barrier stopped him there too. He explored everywhere, looking for the way into that valley but found none. No matter where he asked he could find no one who could help him. In fact, many people thought he was crazy, a result of being out in the wilderness too long. They didn't believe such a valley existed except in Francis' mind.

What was he to do? At his wit's end, Francis prayed. He gave up his search and waited for God's response. Finally, God rescued him and showed him the gate into His kingdom. Francis was then led back to the desert, beyond which he knew lay the mountains with the valley where his loved ones waited. But he remained in the desert and did not try to reach the valley a second time. He told me that his work was in the desert: God would bring him to the valley when it was time. At the end of his story we both sat quietly and listened to the faint whispers of the desert.

> [Elena's note in the margin of the manuscript] I like Francis. He seems so humble. Frank was lucky. I wish I could meet someone like Francis. I wonder if Father Mac is my Francis?

Francis broke the silence. "We better sleep here tonight. The desert can be difficult unless you can see where you're going."

"Francis, tell me: Is your story an allegory, or did it really happen to you?"

"Both. I am the man in the story, but it is also true for many others. Did you see yourself in it, Jacob?"

I tried hard to think. "In places. Maybe more than I want to admit. You said that the valley was in mountains at the edge of a desert. Are those the same mountains that we are traveling toward?"

He nodded. "They are the same ones."

"One more question. You mentioned your work in the desert? What is it?"

"For one thing, I tell stories that God wants remembered. I'll tell you another tomorrow on the way to the mountains."

By now the desert had become cold. We lay down and made ourselves as comfortable as we could. Almost immediately Francis began to snore softly, but my mind raced with the experiences of the cave and of the desert. I lay on my back and saw the universe spread over me across the sky. The stars seemed empty tonight, as if some presence had left them after my vision in the cave. It was disturbing to look at the universe and sense only emptiness. Now I had to be satisfied with faith, without illusions. I thought about Francis' faith, how he was waiting in the desert for a call he was certain would come eventually. And I realized that I felt melancholy because I now realized that I had to wait for God to act! I was angry with myself for not yet trusting Him. Francis' example of trust seemed impossible to imitate. I fell asleep with my mind and emotions still in turmoil.

Adversary and Pilgrim visited me again that night. I saw them only as shadows cast by starlight against desert shrubs, but I recognized their dialogue.

Adversary spoke in a low growl, "Well, Jacob, I see you still are pursuing your dream of a God who cares for men. Are you beginning to see that it is futile?"

Pilgrim spoke quietly. "Don't listen to Adversary, Jacob. You have experienced the strength of faith. Adversary is probing for a weak point."

"Pilgrim, you are a fine one to talk. Jacob saw the truth about you: Killing those innocent people in Ireland."

I sensed that Pilgrim cringed at that accusation, but nonetheless he answered. "Jacob, you saw correctly what I did after I entered the kingdom. Let it be a warning to you that human weakness is a constant foe—even in the kingdom."

Adversary seemed to sneer. "A good dodge, Pilgrim. But you ignore the most basic reality. I still control the world. What men call 'God' stays remote from all this strife and watches man's ignorance and brutality create havoc."

"Jacob, can you see the desperate lie in what Adversary says? Adversary has been defeated and is now only a frustrated shadow. God's plan is the only true reality; men who pursue Adversary's lies find only the chasm of death at the end. Ignore Adversary. It is time for you to understand the wisdom of God's plan more deeply. Watch now what I show you."

The shadows of Pilgrim and Adversary melted into the darkness and again there were only the stars and the desert. Nearby, Francis breathed quietly in sleep. Yet, suddenly, there was a new tension electrifying this place. Abruptly everything was swept away and only nothingness remained—and my consciousness. Pilgrim, from wherever he was, showed me what my faith proclaimed—that in the beginning God was everywhere and nowhere, beyond time and space.

I saw that nothingness is the only possible human image for the infinite God, unless He approaches us. And, wonderfully, He does approach! The tension that was electrifying me was God's creativity, continually breathing the universe into existence. The subtle newness I experienced when I first entered the gate was the wonderful quiver of creation—new every moment! Creating constant newness for us is His delight! That is my understanding of what Pilgrim showed me first that night, although words cannot describe what I saw. I only understood that I was the result of some poignant divine yearning and I knew for the first time why humans are never satisfied with the status quo.

[Elena's note in the margin of the manuscript] I wish I could believe these things.

Pilgrim next showed me God's purpose in creating. But, rather than the beginning of time, I now saw the end. Again, I could sense only the same nothingness that I had seen in the beginning. At the end there was God. But I also knew somehow that, at the end of time, God's creative freedom was now shared among the billions of humans whom he had made. I was still Jacob Newman, the person I am, yet I was immersed in all humanity, aware of the uncountable individual realities of all other humans, encompassed and surrounded by God's own completeness. How can I describe this? It was infinite peace and infinite adventure at the same time. We, the entire race of humans, calmly yet busily creating gifts of new adventures in God's fullness—just as He had created the first gift of the adventure of human existence and life for us. Yet, despite the incredible risks of our adventures we were totally joyful. We knew that our gifts of creation would be unconditionally accepted by God and would delight him! I did not want to leave this dream ever. But then the desert and Francis' breathing returned. I realized, sadly, that I could not yet join the joyful dance of the end of time that Pilgrim had shown me and understood what Francis must have felt when the invisible barrier kept him from the eternal valley. Then I slept, until the brilliant sun of the desert morning exploded over the distant range of mountains and woke me.

[Elena's note in the margin of the manuscript] I knew Frank was deep but what a vision! I wish he and I could have discussed this. Of course, his belief is that we'll do that later on, after death. I wish I could believe that. What's stopping me?

Francis was sitting with his back against the rock watching the dawn. He had a peaceful expression on his face and appeared to have slept well because there was light in his eyes that I hadn't seen the day before. He saw that I had awakened and stood and waited for me. As we began walking the morning was delightfully cool.

The desert was fragrant, and I could see now that there was life everywhere in spite of the hardships of living in that place. We ate the fruit of a cactus plant that Francis led me to. He also pointed out plants and small animals that I otherwise would have missed. And, as he gave me an expert lecture in nature's abundance, I only half listened. I was still curious about how he saw God's purpose in the struggle of life. I had seen the final goal of creation in my dream, but not the meaning of the ongoing painful process we were immersed in.

"Francis, you must have had a lot of time to think out here by yourself. Why do you think God is putting you through this instead of bringing you directly into the valley?"

He smiled at me. "You are still wrestling with 'why' Jacob. Be content. God knows what He is doing. We'll understand it all later."

"But God gave us minds. You yourself know what it means to explore."

He replied a bit sadly it seemed to me, "Yet those whom I left behind are already in the valley, and I am still in the desert."

"Surely you're not saying God wants us to give up our curiosity. Look at all the wonderful things man's exploration has accomplished on this Earth. You can't tell me that God is not pleased at our striving."

"Does everything have to be black or white with you Jacob? God is subtle; become more subtle yourself." I didn't give up. "Tell me something then. Granted God's ways are subtle. But what is your insight into the meaning of all this pain and struggle? Why did he make you, me and your friends the adventurers curious, yet frustrate our searches at their ultimate moment by keeping you out of the valley and me from finding my path to the river?"

Francis did not answer; he let the question linger between us. I worked on the answer in my mind. God has some purpose for us: All his actions proved that to me. Yet God allows men extraordinary freedom, so much so that many times his purpose appears frustrated or opposed by man's willfulness. That also seemed obvious to me. Freedom was at the heart of my question. How to reconcile God's purpose for man, with man's freedom to create or destroy? Francis broke into my thoughts at that point.

"Let me tell you a second story as I promised. It may help answer your questions."

"A powerful man had a youngest son whom he loved dearly. Half of everything that was his was promised to his son. Yet the young man was headstrong. Now, Jacob, you'll ask why does God make men headstrong? Maybe God loves risk, and he makes us headstrong to add zest to creation. That's my theory, but maybe I'm wrong. Back to the story. The man was very wise and he understood his son. He knew his son would not listen or be content to let his father simply care for him. He wanted to do things for himself. So, the man prepared his son as best he could to live in the world, knowing full well that one day the youth would demand his share of the father's wealth and leave. That day came and the man did not try to restrain his son but gave him what he asked for and released him.

"Now I said that the man was both powerful and wise; he did not let the son disappear into the world. He had friends observe the son from a distance. Their reports made the man sad: The son was not living as his father had tried to teach him but was wasting everything that he had been given. Things went from bad to worse. The son became a drug addict. He spent all his money and then began to steal to feed his habit; he finally became a male prostitute in order to buy drugs. He was on the way to total destruction. The man decided to rescue his son. He asked his friends to talk to his son and make sure that he knew his father loved him, and that he could return home. But the young man in his hardheaded way rebuffed the friends and insulted them. He wanted no part of his father's way of life. He wanted to be free of restraint, which is how he saw his father's love.

"The man finally sent his oldest son to see his brother in the hope that he could somehow penetrate his stubbornness. The father was horrified to hear that the young addict, in a fit of rage, had murdered his brother."

Francis paused. He knew what I must be thinking, and wanted the point to sink in.

"What would you have done if you were that man, Jacob? Kill your youngest son in revenge? Banish him from your sight forever? Remember, the man loved his youngest son dearly. No, despite his horror and anger at what his son had done the man wanted him to return home to his care, and to still receive everything that was his inheritance."

I saw the point Francis was making. My choices had led me into the situation I was in, but God forgave me and was teaching me. But what could the father do to change the son who was so hardheaded? Francis continued.

"The man saw that his son was a prisoner of his own self-will and knew that unless the young man saw that for himself there was no hope for him. Some intervention was needed in his life: to wake him up before he destroyed himself."

I thought of the chasm—and of the sleepwalkers. And I thought of my own rescue.

"The son had been arrested for murder after killing his brother and was confined in prison in a nearby city. The father visited him and made the following offer: He would restore his inheritance if the young man performed two tasks.

"First, the son had to write an honest confession of his life up to that time and give it to his father. Second, the son would have to remain in prison for the rest of his life to satisfy the demands of justice. While there, his task was to work with the other prisoners and do what he could to help them solve their problems.

"The son was very angry. How could his father leave him in such a terrible place for life? Why didn't he use his power to get him out? He couldn't understand his father's logic about the inheritance at all. He would receive it, but how could he use it in prison? The man assured his son that with patience he would see ways to use it to help the other prisoners. In other words, Jacob, the son would receive the promised inheritance only if he overcame his own selfishness and gave away everything that his father gave to him."

Francis stopped talking and looked at me. What could I say to him? The story was pointed—about both of us. It was the one answer to my constant 'why' that I didn't want to hear.

Francis touched my arm gently. "I hope you'll forgive my directness, Jacob. That story was told to me years ago when I was still struggling to find my own way back to the valley, and it seemed appropriate to your situation now."

"I feel numb. Like a prisoner of my own self-centeredness and hard-headedness. Always questioning everything."

"Oh, don't regret your stubborn nature. That is God's way of using your strength and curiosity to bring you toward Him."

"But my whole life I have been…"

I was lost for words. I could only be silent and try to learn from Francis' story. I wondered who the other prisoners were that I had to help. Lost in thought I failed to see that somehow we had crossed the desert and had arrived at the base of the mountains.

[Elena's note in the margin of the manuscript.] After reading this last story, I feel drained. Something is wrong in my life because I couldn't possibly write such things. I don't feel guilty about anything, but I don't feel at peace either. I wish I could talk to Frank about this.

Chapter 6

The River of Change

I was taken aback by the massiveness and grandeur of the mountains that confronted Francis and me. From a distance through the desert haze they had appeared insubstantial but now up-close they were genuinely awe-inspiring. The lower slopes were heavily forested and higher up, above the tree line, there was year-round snow. We walked out of the barrenness of the desert and up a broad grassy mountain meadow. Francis spied a stream and we drank our fill of the icy mountain water. After that Francis' pace grew even livelier, and I knew he was excited about returning to these mountains.

"How far is the valley, Francis?"

"As I recall, we should be there by evening. After we reach that forest above us, we follow a path through a pass that leads us into the heart of the mountains where the valley is hidden."

I was a bit worried about this tiny old man. "Why did you decide to leave the desert today after so many years?"

He smiled at me, placing his hand on my arm in comfort, "Last night, as I prayed; I knew it is time."

I sensed that there was more that Francis could tell me, but I was reluctant to ask. We walked across the meadow in silence enjoying its life and beauty. But I could not resist a question.

"Francis, are you saying that it's time for you to enter the valley? Doesn't that mean...?"

I stopped because Francis held up his hand to interrupt me. He was listening to something that I had not heard. Then I did hear it: a faint sound almost indistinguishable from the whispers of the meadow.

"What do you think it is?"

"Adversary, no doubt. It knows that I am on my way into the valley and at the end will try to block the way. We must be on guard, especially in these final hours."

We continued up the meadow toward the edge of the forest. I felt I was entering another place of mystery like the cave and I was filled with nervous anticipation. My concerns

410

about Francis soon vanished. He was radiating strength and joy and I felt more confident too. Francis and I were walking toward an encounter with Adversary with God's power surrounding us like a mighty army.

I had known exhilaration like this once before, when I walked through the gate into the kingdom. Everything around us was silent; even our steps were cushioned by the soft rich soil of the forest we entered. The air was almost cold and smelled strongly of pine with a faint highlight of earth and wildflowers. We had gone a mile or so when we heard the sound again. It was much closer and more distinct. Now I could make out the sound of men arguing. Although we could not distinguish any particular words or voices, there seemed to be several men in a heated discussion. Francis looked at me. "I think I recognize those voices." We came to a clearing where we saw three old men seated on the ground, engaged in a heated conversation. When Francis saw them he broke into a wide grin and ran forward. "Those are my friends, the other three adventurers, who were with me the first time we encountered the valley." The three men saw him, and their manner changed instantly to one of delight. I followed Francis into the clearing. The four old men were shaking hands and pounding each other on the back. I stood quietly at the side until Francis remembered me.

"Jacob, I'd like you to meet my friends."

He introduced each man in turn. A tall esthetic man with a sparse white beard was Albert the Scholar. Next to him was a shorter, heavier man with a florid face named William of Goode-Work. And last there was Thomas the Mystic, extremely frail, and easily as old as Francis.

The three nodded at me as Francis introduced us but they seemed anxious to get back to Francis. The most assertive of the three, Goode-Work, led Francis to a place in their midst and motioned for me to come too. The five of us sat facing each other in a loose circle in the forest clearing.

Goode-Work pressed on with the conversation. "Francis, it has been at least forty years since you left us the day we discovered the valley. Where have you been? More importantly, have you found a way into the valley like you said you would?"

Francis smiled at him. "I'll be happy to tell you what has happened to me, but if you don't mind, I'd like to hear about you first. Jacob here is an adventurer like us and he can profit from your experiences."

Each of the three old men quickly told what he had done since the four had split up after encountering the mysterious valley. Each of them had gone down the same initial path as Francis: each retracing his life to try to find some clue about the valley that they might have missed. They found no one who could help them, and each came to the same decision that Francis had. But where Francis had prayed for help and waited, the other three were more decisive. They each selected what seemed to be the most likely way to gain entrance to the valley and pursued it vigorously for forty years, until this very day when they met again, by chance, on their way back to the valley. They had been arguing about the different paths they had followed when we found them.

Goode-Work spoke confidently. "It is obvious, Francis, that doing good is the way into the valley. Look at the family and friends each of us saw inside. They all stayed behind while we explored. They must have spent their lives helping others. So, I chose to do good works for the past forty years to earn my way into the valley."

Albert the Scholar explained his approach next. "And I say that all four of us were good men and helped many with our wealth before we ever found the valley. Still we were unable to enter. Logically, doing good is not the key to the valley. I say that it is wisdom that opens the valley to men. For many people only a little wisdom is required to enter but for us, with our capacities to understand, God required that we truly understand him before we could enter. Man was created to know God, and that is why I have spent the last forty years studying philosophy and theology. Now I know what God is and how to enter His valley."

Thomas the Mystic shyly looked down at his feet when he spoke. "You are both making the same mistake. You are describing God as if He is a human who is interested in our works or our knowledge. I say that God is unknowable; the best that man can do is seek a mystical union with God. There are proven ways to calm one's mind to try to sense and unite with what is beyond us. I believe they are the secret to entering the valley. I have spent forty years perfecting my ability to concentrate and meditate to be able to approach godliness. I hope that I am ready now."

But Goode-Work wouldn't drop his point and aggressively continued. "God created us and put us here to do something with our lives. He didn't mean for us to be selfish and spend all our time studying or contemplating our navels and seeking mystical relations with the cosmos. And though we had some good works to our credit before we first found the valley, they just weren't enough. We each had great capacities for good that weren't being used. I spent forty years trying to overcome that deficiency and I confidently expect to be able to enter the valley."

Thomas the Mystic didn't give in. "And I am confident in my hope as well. I have developed my ability to sense the mystical nature of the cosmos to the point that I am ready to proceed onward to its ultimate source."

And, not to be outdone, William the Scholar added, "I have completed my studies and understand everything that man knows about God. I have used my intellect to its ultimate capacity. So I am confident I can enter the valley."

The three were close to another angry argument. Each was vehement in his belief that he had done what God required to enter the valley. I felt they had some good points, and that they were obviously well-meaning men sincerely trying to find God's way. Yet none had mentioned finding the gate into the kingdom. Were there many ways past the chasm besides the gate into the kingdom?

Francis had been listening carefully as each man told his story. He nodded frequently as if he too had experienced what they were telling us. Yet I thought I detected sadness in his face as well. He obviously liked these men and sympathized with their efforts to enter the valley. At the end, however, he disagreed with all three.

414

Francis spoke gently to the three old men. "Brothers let me tell you my own experience now. I'm afraid each of you may have been misled."

Just then I thought of Adversary; we had heard it as we approached. I could sense its presence nearby. Francis began to tell his story; in much the same way he told it to me. At the end he surprised me because he told not only his own story but mine as well! The three men looked puzzled.

William the Scholar was curious about my story. "So, Jacob. You found this so-called 'gate' like Francis, by praying and waiting. without studying?"

And Goode-Work added, "Unlike us, you hadn't really done much to help others. In fact, you hurt others, including your family. That doesn't seem logical."

And Mystic concluded, "And somehow you have had experiences that sound mystical without knowing how to meditate. I think you are misleading yourself, and just dreaming."

I was a bit nonplussed by all these arguments. "Francis told my story accurately. I am an ordinary person who suddenly realized what a mess my life was in; God rescued me and brought me through the gate. That is the truth."

[Elena's note in the margin of the manuscript] Frank's life a mess? No way. He's one of the best people I ever met.

Francis saw that I was struggling a bit and stepped in to support me. "And that's the point of my story too. Until I gave up the notion that I could somehow get into the valley on my own I was helpless to enter it. I had first to turn to God for help. I'm afraid the three of you have not yet admitted that to yourselves."

I waited for the three adventurers to reply to this challenge. They sat silently for several minutes. Obviously, these men respected Francis and were taking his point seriously.

Thomas the Mystic replied first. "In a way Francis you really are agreeing with me. One must strive to remove all barriers from one's mind, even the desire to enter the valley, before one can achieve the proper state to enter the valley. I believe there are many so-called 'gates' Francis, and my way of concentration and meditation will lead me into the valley as well."

Francis looked at him sadly. "Thomas, you have missed my point entirely. We cannot possibly enter the gate or the valley on our own! God carries us in, not any skill or capability we possess."

Thomas answered, seemingly certain of his position, "But I cannot accept that God is so particular. Surely a good God will not turn me away because I strive to enter the valley in a manner different from you and Jacob?"

Francis answered, "I don't dare judge you; God will decide the answer to your question and tell you directly. I can only say that everyone I have met who entered the gate was first rescued by God because they were helpless to go though by themselves."

Next William of Goode-Work replied to Francis' challenge. "Am I to be rejected because, rather than sitting helplessly like you, I took my fate into my own hands and tried to earn my way into the valley with a good life?"

Francis also looked at him sadly. "William, I would never reject you. But I must say you sound a trifle proud of yourself and your achievements. Are you so certain that you measure up to God's expectations? In your own words: He didn't seem to be satisfied with our good works once before. Why should He be satisfied this time?"

Goode-Work responded "I don't spend a lot of time worrying about what God expects. I see people who need to be helped and I do it. Let God judge me."

Francis grimaced, "And no good God could possibly reject you, right? Are you not willing to admit to yourself, even a little, that you might have fallen short in your life?"

Goode-Work, sighed and answered, "I've done my best, and that's all I can say."

Albert the Scholar spoke last. "I agree with William. Everything I have studied points to an underlying law in the universe: Do good and avoid doing evil to others. I perceived the good I could do was to add to man's knowledge of God, and I did my best. William pursued good works, and Thomas, meditation. Do you think God will find fault with us for that, Francis? We honestly tried as best we could."

Francis nodded. "I'm not God, Albert. The three of you are convinced that you know what God expects. I suppose the final proof is whether you can actually enter the valley. Again, I am only cautioning you; everyone whom I have encountered in the kingdom was rescued by God. It seems to me that you are taking a terrible chance of possible destruction by being so certain of your righteousness. I'm trying to point another way to you. Why not rethink where you now stand, and sincerely ask God to rescue you from your possible blindness? Why not do that? Honestly admit to yourselves that you just might have it wrong. I'm your friend and I guarantee God will rescue you if you genuinely need his help."

> [Elena's note in the margin of the manuscript] Why don't I ask God to rescue me? Because I'd be lying to myself. I don't need to be rescued from anything. I'll get another job. I can build a new life for myself.

I thought Francis made sense; why would they refuse to listen to their friend? These men were so self-confident; it seemed almost a denial of God. I remembered what Evan had said to me before I entered the gate: You have to enter on God's terms, not your own. That's the way it is, period. These three old men in their hard-headedness were missing that point. It is God's river and His valley, and he is free to set the conditions for entry. I noticed that the shadows were lengthening and that sundown was near.

> [Elena's note in the margin of the manuscript] This is really hard going! Frank is clearly saying that God has conditions that we had to meet if we were going to be able to 'cross the river' when we die. It's drawing a line between the chasm described by Adversary and the

418

other side of the river described by Francis. This makes me both anxious and a bit angry. God seems a little like my father, telling me what to do. I want to be free to live life as I see fit. That was one reason (not the major one) that my father and I haven't spoken for over fifteen years. But then, there is the possibility that Frank (and Father Mac) are right. They are both good men and believe we choose now between the chasm and God's valley on the other side of the river. That makes me a little anxious. If I trust them, I'm going to have to go through what Frank and Francis went through. I think I'm beginning to understand what 'finding God's path' means in Frank's allegory.

Finally, Francis looked at his three friends and said, "You asked when I first arrived if I had found my way into the valley. I have and am on my way there now. Why not come along and see for yourselves? We'll stay here tonight, and you can come with Jacob and me in the morning."

The men seemed to flinch at that suggestion, as if they were not quite ready to test their ability to enter the valley. But they didn't argue with Francis' suggestion, and invited us to share their supper. We had a friendly conversation about travel and mutual acquaintances. After supper each of us found a place to spend the night away from the others. I spread some pine needles on the ground and, as well as I could, bundled myself in my summer clothing—the night was cold in the mountains. My mind was filled with the adventurers' stories. I thought again of the shopping mall and the people who apparently were ignoring the ultimate questions of life, unaware of the chasm. These three were different. They took life seriously; each made a commitment to fulfill God's purpose of life as he saw it. How could God reject their sincere efforts even if they were wrongheaded as Francis seemed to believe? I was confused again about what God expected of men. I dropped off to sleep.

I awoke with Pilgrim standing over me. Everyone else was asleep. "Jacob, come with me. I want to show you something." He started walking down the path through the woods and I followed him.

"Once I came through these same mountains myself on the way to the river of change. I encountered a vision that is important for you to see. It's close by. Some shepherds showed it to me."

"Pilgrim, my friend Francis hasn't mentioned the river but speaks only of a valley. Can you explain that to me?"

"Everyone has to pass through the river of change to enter God's final reality. Many good people have no knowledge of how to enter that reality. They are surprised when they arrive at the river, but if they have come through the gate God helps them across."

We continued for a short while on the path through the forest, and then turned off into thick underbrush. Pilgrim led me to a rocky wall on the side of a mountain, which had a small iron door in the rock. He opened the door and told me to look. It was dark inside and the air was tinged with smoke. I could hear muffled noises from far down inside the mountain. They seemed to be like a fire burning out of control, consuming a forest. I heard cries and whimpers as if trapped animals were caught in its fury. I shuddered; I had heard of this place.

"Is this place what I think it is? Is it real or am I only remembering a childish nightmare?"

Pilgrim looked into my eyes. "The shepherds told me that this was a side street of hell and the final reality for those who shun God. They said Judas, who betrayed God's Son, and others like him are here."

I didn't want to hear this. "They came through the gate into the kingdom and ended up here?"

He nodded. "The shepherds only told me that everyone in this place at one time honestly had searched for God and then rejected Him. They did not say any had actually passed through the gate into the kingdom. Perhaps they had not yet entered the gate, or perhaps they had, and then strayed away from God's way. I cannot say."

I swallowed hard. "But the three men, the friends of Francis…"

"That's correct. They are honestly searching, but they are caught in their own pride and may be at risk to end up in this place. That's why I came to you."

"But what can I do? Francis has tried to warn them already."

Pilgrim looked at me searchingly. Perhaps, if you told them of the chasm again, and of this place…"

I could see that even Pilgrim could go no farther. As we walked back to the path, I was thankful to leave that place. Pilgrim left me at the clearing, and I fell asleep again. In the morning I felt a strong urge to plead with Francis' friends but held back. Why would they listen to me? I was afraid of being rejected, or worse: being laughed at for my gullibility. So, I said nothing, but continued to be troubled.

Francis seemed unusually bright and cheerful that morning. I remembered that today was the day he would enter the valley. The five of us set out on the path through the woods. Everyone was silent, waiting to see how the mystery unfolded. We walked for about an hour and emerged from the forest into a narrow rocky pass. Mountains towered on both sides of the path. Suddenly, we were stunned to see our way blocked by a hideous monster that stood in the middle of the narrow path. I shook my head to see if I was still asleep, but the vision was real and the monster approached us.

It was at least twelve feet tall and vaguely like a large lizard, but upright on two legs. It held an enormous sword in a massive human-like arm and its savage face leered at us in anger. Francis held up his hand to stop us, as if we needed encouragement. "Adversary has sent this last test to me. I must overcome this beast by myself."

He left us, and as he walked forward, I was surprised that I could now see that Francis was dressed in armor. Using both hands he was holding a bright shining sword, and he looked like he knew how to use it. When he was about twenty feet away from the beast he stopped and shouted in challenge.

422

"What is your name, son of the evil one?"

The monster opened its mouth and roared in answer, and I could see rows of sharp teeth and a forked tongue. It seemed to spit its answer at Francis.

"You know my name, Francis. You also know my strength because you have fought me your entire life. I cannot let you pass. You will die here and, unless they flee, so will your friends."

Francis didn't flinch. "I challenge you to reveal your true name to me before I defeat you."

"Bold words for such a weakling. Should I reveal to your friends just how weak you are, Francis?"

Francis bared his teeth in anger. "This armor I wear is God's own strength. That is why I challenge you to reveal your true name."

"So, at the end you have found strength? We shall see."

In an instant the monster vanished, and a frail young woman appeared in its place, looking sadly at Francis. I could not see his face, but he must have known that we understood who the woman was: the wife he had deserted years ago. He seemed stunned for a moment and stumbled slightly. But then Francis rushed toward the woman, with his sword high over his head. She saw his attack and instantly the monster was there again in her place. Francis stopped a few feet away from it.

"What is your name? I demand to know before I kill you."

"I am Unworthiness, sent to bar the way of all who seek to cross into the valley of life. No one can defeat me of his own strength."

Francis nodded. "So, I face my own Unworthiness. And you know my weakest spot, my selfishness and cruelty toward my wife. Well, I am unworthy, but God has already forgiven me for all in my life that I did wrongly. He has given me this armor of righteousness so that I can enter the valley of life. You must yield or die."

With that last challenge the monster vanished. I was relieved because I did not know if I were a match for it. The other three men looked worried and confused. They had heard Francis' boast about God's armor but apparently could not see it as I could. Had they begun to sense that their own preparations were inadequate?

We continued through the mountain pass and came at last to the crest of a ridge. A magnificent vista opened before us. I knew this must be the place where Francis would cross the river of change.

How can I do justice to the scene?

We had arrived at a deep valley surrounded completely by mountains. Below us a wide river flowed diagonally across the rolling green meadow. The five of us stood quietly in awe as if we had entered a holy place. The other side of the river was shrouded in a dense ground fog. We could see the tops of distant mountains above the fog with the morning sun brilliantly lighting their snow-covered peaks, but closer to us the mist was thick enough to block our view. It was as if God had discretely dropped a curtain to hide the other side of the river from unworthy eyes. Finally, Francis broke the silence.

"The valley on the other side of the river looks just the same. I don't remember the river but it looks crossable to me."

The four of us looked at Francis. By their puzzled faces I knew that, like me, the other three could see only this side of the river. I said, "You can see the other side? What about the fog?"

Francis asked, "Can't you see the valley on the other side, Jacob?"

Thomas the Mystic answered for me. "It seems none of us can, Francis. What do you see?"

And Albert the Scholar added, "What do you make of the fact that the wall has disappeared?"

William of Goode-Work asked, "Can you see any people on the other side?"

The three had obviously become a little worried. I knew that they sensed now that they had been given an answer—and not the one they had expected.

Francis looked back at us. "Let me describe it for you. There are rolling hills and patches of woodland on the other side. I can see a gap in the mountains in the distance where the river exits this valley and it seems open and unusually bright beyond that point. And, yes, I can see people. They are

425

a long way off, but a group is moving toward the river. Everything looks exactly as I remember it forty years ago."

Albert the Scholar still hadn't got his answer. "What about the wall Francis?"

"Apparently it blocked us years ago because we wanted to climb into the valley only out of curiosity. But today, because the wall is gone, it seems we are all being summoned to the final test."

Francis was looking intently at his friends. I wondered how I could possibly be ready to cross the river, even with my experiences in the cave and the desert. But then I saw that Francis was talking only to his friends, not to me, trying to make them see the truth about themselves. For me this was another warning—like the chasm. The message was—Whom do you trust to bring you across the river? And I knew at that moment that despite what I had said to Evan before I entered the gate, I did not yet trust God with my life. Here in the valley with Francis and his friends, God was patiently giving me another obvious lesson, one that I couldn't possibly misunderstand. *He* would decide when I was ready to cross the river. Suddenly I knew I needed more time and I wanted to leave this place.

Francis continued, "Now I can see a man leaving the group of people and coming to the edge of the river. He wants me to cross over."

Francis turned to his friends. He looked at each of them and seemed to want to tell them something more, but he did not speak. He went to them and embraced each man in turn but said nothing until he came to me. "Jacob, I know the man on the other side. It's my father waiting for me there. Remember this day when you are called to cross." He turned and walked down the slope to the river. At the edge he paused for a moment, and then he waded in. I was surprised that the water was shallow; to me the river looked very wide and somewhat threatening. But Francis walked through the river without difficulty and was soon lost from our view in the mist. I felt a surge of joy at what I knew he must be experiencing at this moment—seeing his father again and the others who were waiting for him. But more than that, finally being across and safe. I thought I could hear distant shouts of welcome and rejoicing, as if a large crowd was hailing someone whom each admired and who each had been waiting a long time to see.

Thomas the Mystic spoke up. "Well, I for one am going to try to cross. I have spent as much time as Francis preparing for this day. I believe I have the strength to make it."

And William of Goode-Work agreed. "Francis showed us how shallow the river is, and the wall has disappeared. I think that is a sign that we too can cross."

But Albert the Scholar was uncertain, for the first time since I met him. "You may be right, but now, being here, I have lost my confidence. It is a sign that we cannot see the other side as Francis could. I am going to wait until I am more certain. All of a sudden it seems I may have taken the wrong path."

Thomas the Mystic looked at him scornfully. "You are losing your courage. We are as welcome as Francis on the other side."

And William of Goode-Work pleaded with Albert: "Come with us; we won't let you sink. Let's all go together."

But Albert the Scholar would not be persuaded, and I think his reluctance almost persuaded the other two not to try to cross. In the end they left us and walked down to the river. Suddenly I remembered that I hadn't told them about the vision of hell that Pilgrim had showed me. I started after them, but it was too late. They had paused, like Francis, but then William of Goode-Work stepped into the river and started to wade across. Thomas the Mystic held back for a minute to watch. As Goode-Work went farther he began to sink and struggle. The river seemed deeper and the current swifter than it had been when Francis crossed. Mystic saw Goode-Work in trouble and went into the water to try to help his friend. I watched them with a sinking feeling of my own and with growing dismay. Why hadn't I told them about my vision of hell when I had the chance? When they were lost to our view in the mist, I heard nothing else—somehow the silence seemed an awful lesson.

Albert the Scholar looked at me hopefully. "I think they made it, don't you?"

"I don't know." I didn't want to admit my worst fears. "The river seemed different for them than for Francis."

"But they were good men…"

I could think of nothing to say. I simply didn't know what went on in the river of change if someone entered it without trusting anyone but himself. I didn't want to think about it; it reminded me of the chasm. But it was more tragic; these two men had not been sleepwalkers. Why hadn't I tried harder to stop them? Had they truly gone to their destruction? Would God mercifully rescue them anyway, from their foolish pride? I felt only sadness when I thought of them and Francis' attempts to persuade them earlier. Why did they insist on their own way? And lurking at the edge of my thoughts was the realization that I too had failed, in my faintheartedness, by not warning them. I would have to live with that, and it would surely become part of my own battle with Unworthiness.

Albert the Scholar finally broke the silence. "What are you going to do now, Jacob?"

"I'm going to leave this place. I don't know where to go, but I know I'm not ready to be here. What about you?"

"I'm going to stay here awhile, away from my books. I think that I'm beginning to understand what Francis was trying to say to us. I need to be alone, to think and listen."

I wanted to tell Albert something that might help him "I ought to tell you one other thing that happened to me. Right before the gate to the kingdom opened for me, as I sat outside the wall waiting, I heard my name called. I think that it was God because right after that I found the gate open. You're doing the same thing—sitting quietly, waiting, and listening. God answers those who need Him even if they can't speak."

429

He nodded sadly, "I don't know how to find the gate; that's why I can only wait."

"I think, by admitting that, you just took the first step on God's path."

I shook Albert the Scholar's hand. He took both my hands in his and for a moment I thought he would try to keep me from leaving. But he let go. As I turned to leave, he sat facing the river. I walked back toward the rocky pass we had come through earlier with Francis and the others. Just before I entered the pass, I looked back to wave goodbye, but Albert was still facing the river. I walked back into the pass and away from the river. I had a strong feeling that the next time I came this way I would be a very different person.

[Elena's note in the margin of the manuscript] I have to ask Father Mac about this whole chapter. Frank seems regard God as a kind of law and order judge. Do what I say or you're damned. That repels me.

Chapter 7

Finding God's Road

Now, alone after the scene at the river, I was adrift in a sea of uncertainty. I knew that I was still in the kingdom, but I could find no signposts pointing toward the road God wanted me to take. The lesson at the river had simply said, Trust Him. But what did that mean in these circumstances? With that question swirling in my mind I found my way back to the clearing where the five of us had spent the previous night. Where was I to go next?

It seemed that I had two choices: Wait here until God gave me some unmistakable direction, or think through my situation, prayerfully, and decide for myself which way to go. I prayed for even a small hint, and the silence of the surrounding forest seemed to answer me. There would be no signal from God; I would simply have to trust that He would be with me as I decided which road to take. That seemed as if it were another test. Perhaps Adversary was leading me down the wrong path like it had led Goode-Work, Mystic, and Scholar. The longer I wrestled with this choice, the more anxious I became. I longed for God to give me certainty. How easy it would be to stay here and wait. And how dangerous all the possible wrong paths in the world seemed at that moment. If I didn't wait, my usual impatience was likely to lead me into trouble. Yet I knew the answer was in the forest's continuing silence. This was not where I belonged. Reluctantly I left the clearing and walked out of the mountains, back into the desert. This time I filled Francis' water bag at a mountain stream and took it along. I had no idea how long I would be in the desert. Perhaps forty years like Francis?

I walked aimlessly along the edge of the mountain range. When evening came, I found shelter next to a rock ledge and stayed the night there. I slept uneasily but did not dream. When I awoke, I was hungry and to my relief I found that cactus has an edible fruit.

For the next few days, I walked and waited for something to happen. Nothing did. I went over everything in my mind, again and again. No new insights came. I felt like I was alone in this barren place and that God was waiting for me to discover something on my own. What could it be? My imagination was as barren as the desert. I had no insights, no

432

sense of God's wishes, not even any direction of my own. It seemed my fate was to stay in this desert and be forgotten.

One day as I wandered along a barely perceptible sandy path, I saw a shack in the distance near the mountains. I hurried toward it. I thought this might be where I would experience a sign from God. I wondered whom I would meet. When I got closer, I could see it was only an empty ruin. In disappointment I sat in a small patch of shade next to what remained of one of its walls. I wondered who had once lived in this desolate place. Maybe Francis had built this house for other searchers to use for shelter. It didn't look as if it would survive much longer. It came to me that I could repair this shelter while I was here, as a kind of a memorial to Francis. So much of his life had been spent in this desert. The idea seemed right somehow, and I began looking for materials to patch the roof and walls. There was nothing on the ground near the house; I walked toward the mountains hoping to find something I could use. After a long walk I came up on another shack in much worse shape than the first and decided to salvage materials from it to repair the other shelter. I spent the next several days dismantling one shack and carrying materials across the desert to the other. I wedged wood into the holes in the walls and roof of Francis' house—as I came to call it. The hard work made me sleep well, and at the end, when I had done as much repair as I could without tools, I felt a sense of satisfaction like I had not known from any other work. I had helped a friend's work live after him by providing shelter for others who might come this way. The repair work on the shack held a clear message for me. It was

433

a sign about the work that God wanted me to do on my way to the river.

That night I knew for certain I was right because I dreamed about Francis. I saw him standing near me in the desert, looking at the work I had done on the shack and smiling. The approval from God was unmistakable.

I thought at first that now, knowing God's path to the river, I would leave the desert immediately. But I could not see any way out. I continued to walk along the edge of the mountains. After several days I came to another small house, not in need of repair. Inside I found something that Francis must have left behind years earlier: An old and well-used Bible. I knew immediately that I had been led here too, and I hungrily began to read the Bible. The words leaped off the page as I read, and I understood, finally, what the Bible was: A clear message to everyone who searches for God's path. Why had I not understood that before? I cannot express the elation I felt that day. I finally saw God's living signposts. It was as if I were actually at the feet of Jesus while He patiently explained everything to me. My life before seemed like struggling up a difficult mountain in the fog but now God had led me in his light to the peak. I can't describe the experience of being spiritually blind and of being healed through a gift of understanding that enlightens everything. That is the gift I received that day in the desert.

[Elena's note in the margin of the manuscript] So Frank was a staunch Christian when I knew him. He didn't act like one and never tried to convert me. Why was that? I thought that's what being a Christian was all about: trying to 'save' people.

I left the Bible in the shack; someone else would need it. I walked toward the mountains, confident that I would find the path to my family and to the rest of my life. I soon came to a narrow pass that led directly to the place where I first met John Waters in the hills above the Goodman's farm. I found my camping gear and went down out of the hills.

Chapter 8

The Road to the River

After I left the desert, I stopped by to see Peter and Martha. They were delighted to see me and we spent several days together, retelling our stories—how God had led each of us to find Him. God's presence is obvious in people like the Goodmans. The encouragement and hope which flowed out of those good people helped me make a fresh start when I returned home.

I tried to mend our marriage, and so did Rachel. There were times when it seemed that God was about to step in and transform our relationship, but my fantasies about easy miracles were always short-lived. God answered my prayers by <u>not</u> miraculously fixing everything. He used discontent as a lever to open my heart, to break through the barriers I had erected against love. This was a painful process.

Nor did Rachel follow the road I had chosen. I itched to take matters into my own hands before she was sleepwalked into the chasm. Adversary continually urged me to 'twist her arm'. After years of tortured argument, I realized that coercion isn't God's way. When I handed Rachel's safety over to Him, God gave me a new measure of peace. But even now I can't remember any gifts Rachel received from our difficult marriage before we split up, and for that I'm truly sorry.

How did God break through the walls I had built around my heart? He caught my attention with flashes of His presence. He left clues for me, often in the oddest places. I began to see why the Goodmans sought Frank Simpson's company in prison. I constantly tried to explain this divine serendipity to others, but they just shrugged it off. I had to learn that the changes in me were His work, not mine. I was His; and He delighted in shaping me.

There were long periods when He seemed to leave me alone in darkness: where I could learn that I had to trust His power to lead me along the right path, and not take things back under my own control. Doing the repair work He gave me in the desert began to pull the fragments of my own life together. In hindsight it seems as if my attempts at repairing the brokenness God showed me were clumsy and produced nothing; I can claim only persistence. Patiently, He breathed His life into me as I struggled with His work.

God kept leading me back into the desert, again and again. There were other things I had to experience. One was that I was in prison but I was in solitary confinement. I had walled myself off from Rachel and my life became gray, lifeless. How could I learn to love in solitary? He solved this problem with a flourish in the person of Elena, a special friend. She burst the walls of my prison, with her energy and drive.

> [Elena's note in the margin of the manuscript] This makes me feel very warm! At least I was a special friend. But God had a hand in our meeting? It happened when I asked him about the breakfast he was eating, in Double Bay. I just felt an urge to know what he was eating. OK, I liked his looks too. And our relationship seemed quite natural to me, rather than divinely inspired. He was married too; would God push us into a relationship in that situation? Very perplexing.

I can't end without telling you the other meaning of the stories Francis told me in the desert. He said that his journey—leaving his home to explore and finally finding his way back to the valley—was an allegory for every person's journey to God. We are all God's innocent sons and daughters when we enter the world. Like Francis, we insist on leaving his safety, and become broken by our experiences. But God never forgets us and sends his Son and Spirit—in the persons of our human brothers and sisters—to rescue us from the emptiness and destruction of the destiny we try to create for ourselves. However, and this is the thing that we cannot seem to understand, rescue is impossible, even for God, unless we learn to rely on his strength and safety, not just our own. We must find our original innocent trust in him before he can bring us safely across the river. It sounds simple, yet we are blind until God confronts us, with 'storms and dead-end roads and chasms,' or impassable walls like Francis encountered. Even these warnings can do little to penetrate our hearts until God, disguised as Pilgrim, Evan, Frank Simpson, or innumerable others enters our lives to rescue us. Even when we 'murder' him with our rejection he continues to seek us in the prisons we build around ourselves until at last we begin to listen! When his patience and love revive our trust, we again remember who we are, his sons and daughters. Then he shows each of us our special work on the way to the river—so we can heal our own brokenness by caring for his other sons and daughters who are broken.

Rachel, I hope you will read this someday. Perhaps you could drive to the Goodman's place and spend some time with them; I know there is a wonderful adventure waiting for you there. Every day I pray that you take the side road when the storm comes into your life.

[Elena's note in the margin of the manuscript] I really like Frank's vision of God! I'd like to believe in such a God.

EPILOGUE

I awake from my dream as the sun begins to set below the mountains. How strange: I can see another brilliant light, brighter than the sun, in the distant gap where the river exits this valley. And now, the mist across the river lifts. In the twilight, I notice a small crowd of people, waving at me to come across. My heart leaps as I realize it's time, and my legs tremble as I walk slowly down the grassy meadow to the edge of the water.

The river appears deeper and more dangerous than it should. Suddenly I'm afraid and know that I need help. A figure in the crowd sees me hesitate and leaves the others to wade into the river to be with me. I step into the water and it isn't as swift or as deep as I feared. In an instant my fear is taken away, and at that moment I begin to know the unfathomable depths of God's love and mercy. Rachel is the one wading out to greet me. We reach each other in the middle of the river and smile in recognition.

[Elena's note in the margin of the manuscript] I am stunned. Obviously, Frank didn't actually know what would happen when he wrote this before his death, but this was how he imagined and hoped for it. For him and Rachel, a happy ending. I feel robbed of something but can't say what.

Book 4   Elena's Story Part II

I trace the rainbow through the rain

And feel the promise is not vain

That morn shall tearless be.

Oh Love That Wilt Not Let Me Go by George Matheson

Chapter 1

When I finished reading Frank's manuscript, sometime after midnight, I looked out the window at the sleeping apartment along the side street next to my hotel. It was quiet in my room, although I could hear the faint throb of traffic on Park Lane. Like others in London, I couldn't sleep.

I felt numb. His book had been so unusual, so unexpected. I couldn't relate to what he had written about himself, thinly disguised as Jacob; I didn't know *this* man; Jacob was lost, guilty and religious, searching for a God that seemed to ignore him. A law and order God. But Frank had imagined mercy at the end. I needed to ask Father Mac about this.

The Frank I knew was in control, not lost. How could he be guilty of mistreating his wife when his relationship with me was so respectful? If he was searching for God, he never mentioned it to me. On the other hand, there was that surprising statement near the end. I had 'burst the walls of his prison!' Why hadn't he written more about that, if it was so important to him? He could have at least told me as he lay dying. In-Elena had nothing to say.

I had heard such God-talk before and rejected it, as well as the people who talked like that. But Frank wasn't like them; I was certain of that. Still, he told this story about himself. I couldn't swallow his almost instant acceptance of finding himself in what he called the 'kingdom.' He seemed to believe it was real. How could a pragmatic engineer and problem-solver like Frank believe that? He described the experience as if a switch had been thrown and he suddenly saw everything differently. Not how real life works I thought.

Obviously, since he asked me to read his manuscript, he wanted me to take his personal experiences of God seriously. But he hadn't wanted to directly discuss them with me. I kept coming back to that sticking point. Why? If he believed these things so strongly, why had he kept them hidden them from me? I thought, Frank, I feel like you're slipping away from me! The person I remember seems more and more remote.

I also wondered about Rachel, Frank's wife, about whom I knew nothing. Had he been thinking of her during those last days when I was with him? A pang of jealousy gripped me. I could understand her reactions when he came

448

home from being 'rescued' as he called it. I felt the same skepticism, with a tinge of revulsion as I read about his experiences. But I was certain I wouldn't have reacted to him the way she had, and I was pretty sure I wouldn't have rejected him. What had he done to deserve such treatment? He certainly felt guilty about the way he had treated her and his children. I couldn't imagine the Frank I knew abusing his family. But I was deeply touched by her forgiveness when she came to his aid in the river at the end.

After a fitful sleep, something happened the next morning, in the shower. As I was rinsing my hair, I thought, Father Mac said Frank thought I was 'special.' Click. He said that Frank loved me. Click. Frank told Father Mac that discussing the manuscript with me was the 'wrong thing to do.' Click. Frank said I was special in his manuscript. There I stood, a dripping, naked woman with an insight. It was suddenly obvious—I need to see everything, including myself through Frank's eyes, not my own. He loved me and thought I was special but didn't think he ought to talk to me about his book. That made perfect sense in his world. If I entered his world I would understand. But how could I do that? I had a new puzzle to solve. How could I see myself through Frank's eyes? In-Elena breathed a sigh of relief. I had finally gotten to the crux.

As I ate breakfast in the Grosvenor House café something else, something far more exciting occurred to me. I had encountered my own chasm, like the one Frank described at the beginning of his book! I couldn't get past the puzzle that Frank had created for me in his manuscript. Could his allegory be true? I suddenly felt a deep certainty that I had

449

arrived at a unique time in my life, a time of unanswered questions. Frank's story implied that I had to stay in these questions until some unusual 'spirits' visited me. I recalled Jacob sitting in his car trying to figure out whether to return to the familiar highway he had been on before the chasm. Was I facing that choice, here in London, whether to finish my vacation and go back to finding a new marketing position somewhere and reconstructing my life as it had been, or set off on a very different path? For some reason I thought of Winifred's smile. Why did her smile keep nudging me? Like Jacob facing the chasm, I was suddenly immersed in a mystery.

Somehow, I felt like a burden had been lifted from my shoulders. I didn't have to try to figure out why Frank hadn't wanted to discuss his manuscript with me. In his world, he wasn't responsible for propelling me into the journey that started at the chasm. I had to encounter that myself, after reaching a dead end in my life. I thought with a grimace that I had certainly done that. I had no job, no home and no relationships! Frank believed that this spiritual journey was central in everyone's life. His manuscript gave me some clues, but I had to be ready to understand them, which meant understanding and applying the hints buried in his allegory. Father Mac suddenly seemed liked a great person to help me with this. I could hardly wait to see him.

I was so filled with energy that I couldn't wait in the hotel until the time came to visit him. I walked across Park Lane into Hyde Park. It was a gray summer day in London but not very hot. There were a few others wandering around the paths in the park but basically, I had it to myself. The empty park with its diverging paths was a good metaphor for my journey right now. I didn't have any destination so I didn't need to decide what path to take. I could just wander. After a while, I came to Princess Diana's Memorial Fountain along the Serpentine. Suddenly, it felt like I was meant to be here, my journey joined with her journey somehow. Her memorial's constantly changing water in an unchanging granite channel was a message. Boris had said I was trying to write on flowing water, and to relax. I didn't have to figure it out, just experience it, and see it through Frank's eyes. I sensed him saying, and In-Elena nodding in assent: Diana is giving you a gift—don't constantly try to figure everything out.

I walked back through the park, savoring the peacefulness of Diana's Memorial, aware that others walking past me were oblivious to my experience. For them, Hyde Park was an expanse to walk across, on their way to work, the shops or museums. I felt special and wished they could realize they were special too. At least that's how I sensed Frank would have felt if he were here. After a while, I crossed Park Lane again, and walked down Mount Street, to the Farm Street Church rectory.

Father Mac greeted me at the front door and took me to his office. It was a tiny cubicle barely large enough to hold a standard steel desk and office chair, and two overstuffed chairs covered in worn leather. There was an almost overwhelming disorder, of piles of books and papers, spilling over the top of his desk, in the chairs and filling the bookcases that surrounded everything, and a vague musty smell of age. How could he work in such disorder?

He smiled wanly. "Please excuse the mess. I know it puts people off and I mean to clean it up but there never seems to be an opportune time." He lifted the papers off the chairs and motioned for me to be seated. He walked around his desk and retrieved a small book but didn't offer it to me. He came back around and sat in the other chair.

"Elena, I've been looking forward to seeing you. I said a prayer for you today at Mass."

I wondered if his prayer was connected to my insights this morning, then I thought what an odd idea for me to have.

"Thank you Father, I've been looking forward to our conversation as well. I think we were meant to meet because some unusual things have been happening to me since I read Frank's book." He nodded but didn't speak like the good listener he was.

"I finished it last night. It was interesting but, I guess a bit off-putting." He smiled at me.

"I want to ask you about one thing in particular, that really bothers me. Frank seemed to have a very law and order view of God. Two of those three good men, friends of Francis, were condemned apparently because they didn't follow God's demand to trust him. Can you explain this to me?"

He looked down for a moment then looked at me. "Frank and I had long conversations about how people would react to God after reading his book. He was focused on a 'wake-up' call to those people who absolutely refused to think about God. I understood that and tried to tell him that the

Hell-and-damnation-approach didn't work anymore, but he thought it would. His intentions were good but, in my opinion, his approach was flawed, as demonstrated by your concerns. The image of God he created in his allegory isn't attractive and is, for many people threatening." He paused, considering something. "Elena, I'm a Jesuit, which means I belong to the Society of Jesus. It's painful to me that you and I can't directly discuss Jesus, but we can't. You're not yet able. But let me assure you, Jesus is definitely not a 'law and order God' as you put it. God *is* love. God also accepts that people can freely choose to go their own way and refuse to accept his love. As Frank said, some people may choose to 'sleepwalk into the chasm' and be lost. In his allegory of Francis's two friends and the river, he was trying to dramatize the risk people run when they ignore the fact of death and God's role in life after death. I'm sorry if you're confused." He smiled at me, hoping his explanation helped more than it hurt.

He was getting too deep into God-talk and it made me uncomfortable. I appreciated his sincere explanation but didn't want our conversation to continue in this direction and told him that. I think he was relieved.

I told him that I now understood why Frank hadn't discussed his book or his spiritual journey with me. I also described my experience at Diana's Memorial Fountain. He nodded. Go on.

I described my feeling that I had reached the chasm Frank described in his book and that I didn't know how to get past it. I raised a practical question.

"Should I stay here in London, and wait, like Frank did?"

He answered immediately. "Why stay in London? Go south, go somewhere with lots of sunshine. The south of France. Go back to Australia."

I shook my head. "I don't want a holiday in the sun and I certainly don't want to go back to Australia."

He nodded. "Do you mind if I ask a few questions? I'm sort of your travel agent for the first stage of your journey past the chasm." He grinned. I smiled OK.

"What do you think the chasm means Elena?"

What immediately went through my mind was, 'What are you up to Father?' I suppose that came from my habit of protecting myself from people prying into my life, not because he was a priest. I had no bad experiences with priests or nuns or religion, like others I knew, who had hair-triggers when it came to anything to do with religion. So, it was easier for me to take the risk of trusting a priest. Still, I wanted to retain control over the conversation.

"Do you mean what did Frank mean by that metaphor?" I asked. He smiled.

"No, what it means to you? What it feels like. You told me you felt like you had arrived at the same chasm that Frank wrote about."

I had too. But what *did* it mean?

"I'm not sure. It seems like my mind isn't able to see beyond where I'm at right now into the future. Before I just made decisions and acted. Life was simple: Work hard, play hard. Now, I'm not sure. Work? Why bother working hard; look what it gets you. Play? Been there, done that. Is that all there is? I'm in a strange place where my world doesn't mean anything. In fact, I feel like I'm all by myself in a vacant world. Today I had a glimpse, briefly, of something at Princess Di's Memorial. I felt a sense of peace, like I didn't have to figure things out." As I said those words, I remembered the poem I had read on the plane and saw another meaning for it. Down below the hurly burly of life is not death but something calm. But I wanted excitement and adventure and challenge of life. I liked the hurly burly!

He asked the question again. "Can you sense what the chasm signifies, perhaps about the future?"

"It's just a temporary block, a place that I will leave when I'm ready. That's a hint Frank left me. I suppose that says that it doesn't make much difference whether I'm here or anywhere, does it?"

He grinned, "As your travel agent, I'm trying to find that out. Here's another question. Is there anything you'd like to do in the next few weeks or months? Sleep all day? Tour? Go to shows? Don't think about it; just blurt out the first thing that comes to your mind."

For a moment, there was nothing. Then something surprising popped out of my mouth. "Saint Winifred. I'd like to visit Wales where she came from." That shocked us both.

"Anything else?"

"I'd like to go to some good shows here in London. I think I'm answering my own question. I'd like to go visit Wales, then come back to London and stay for a while. Maybe, after some time passes, I'll get some other ideas. I'd also like to have dinner with you occasionally Father. My treat. You make the chasm feel, I don't know, more manageable or at least not such a bad a place to be."

"So, I guess I'm a pretty good travel agent. See what happens, who you meet. Go with the flow. Let me look up Saint Winifred for you."

He went over to his computer and googled Saint Winifred of Wales. "Much easier than searching through my books here in my office," he said. "Here is a Wikipedia entry. I'll print it out for you." He brought a couple of sheets of paper back from his printer and gave them to me. "Later, I'll have to find out why we have a statue of Winifred in our church." I noticed that there was a shrine to Saint Winifred in Holywell Wales called Saint Winfred's Well. The Wikipedia article said she died in Wales in 660AD. I wondered what a shrine was. More curiously, why was I suddenly interested in a woman who lived well over a thousand years ago, who was called a saint by an ancient church that I could care less about?

"Father, why does your church call Winifred a saint?"

"Well, the simple answer is that Winifred led a very good life and, after she died, some miracles happened when people asked for her help. My church likes saints because they are good examples for people to follow. Like Winifred. She was brutalized by her fiancée who tried to kill her when she refused to marry him. But she survived and went on to be the head of a monastery. She can give battered women hope. That's how it works."

A long-submerged memory tried to emerge, but I pushed it out of my consciousness. But, for an instant, I knew exactly why I was attracted to Saint Winifred. *That* was eerie! Father must have noticed something cross my face, but he didn't say anything.

Then, as on an impulse, he gave me the little book that he had found when I first arrived.

"Frank gave me this book a number of years ago, and we both read it." He handed me a thin paperback book with yellowed pages and kept talking. "He used to say that the East has some good ideas when it comes to spiritual things. They treat spirituality as part of ordinary human life, not as some extraordinary add-on like the West seems to do. I think this book must have influenced his manuscript. Why don't you borrow it for a while, at least while you're in your 'chasm.' I'd like it back eventually because it means a lot to me, but I feel like Frank is urging me to give it to you."

It was *Siddhartha* by Hermann Hesse. Inside the front cover, Frank had written, 'To Edwin, a dear friend on my journey. Thanks for listening to my ramblings. There's a lot to be learned from this little book. Frank.'

I touched his handwriting and caught Father Mac—Edwin—watching me. He smiled and I smiled back. We both missed Frank.

457

"I really couldn't take this book Father. It's too precious. What if I lost it? I'll buy a copy." He shook his head. "No, you must have this copy. It has some vibes built into it that you can't buy in a bookstore. Frank gave me his copy. You'll see a few places that he underlined. I really want to you to take it. I'm not worried about getting it back."

I sat quietly for a long moment, holding the book. I wished Frank had given it to me and inscribed it. He must have had a close relationship with Father Mac.

"Father, can I ask you a couple more questions about Frank's story? For one, what does he mean by the 'kingdom'? Is that a Christian term?"

He took a while to answer. "That's a complicated question Elena. In fact, for a Christian, Frank's manuscript has lots of complex ideas in it. I think that you'd be better off not worrying about the deeper meaning of words like kingdom. Just accept the allegory at face value. But, in simple terms, a kingdom is a metaphor for a place that is ruled by a king or queen. If you want my opinion, what Frank meant in this case was that after he left his old world, he arrived in a new one that was ruled by a very different set of assumptions. Do you get where I'm going?"

"I think so. It's like a fairy tale. Kingdom means there is power in that place that can make things happen when you enter. Like magic. Is that right?"

"Good analogy Elena. Frank was searching for the magical in life, so he would like that idea. That brings up another key point. Frank didn't mean to describe things

458

precisely in his book. He meant for you and other readers to use their imaginations to discover what his allegory means to them."

"There was that strange section in the cave, where Jacob had all those visions. What does that mean?"

He shook his head. "I'll give you an overall hint Elena but, if I explain his manuscript to you, I'd be doing exactly what Frank didn't want to do himself. Here's my hint. Chapter One takes place as Frank's 'old world' comes to an end. Starting with Chapter Two, the rest of the book is about Frank learning to see things differently in the new world he enters. And, as he learns to see differently, he faces new problems that he never encountered before, which he has to solve. OK?"

I wasn't OK. Like Frank, Father Mac was very frustrating. Why not explain some of the metaphors and images? What would that hurt? He was watching my face and must have seen my irritation.

"Elena, don't get too upset. Frank's book is meant to stimulate your imagination. That's why I won't and can't explain it. What it means to an elderly Catholic priest is probably very different than what it means to a young woman like yourself. All I'd do if I explained it is frustrate you in another way. You'd end up saying, 'What does that have to do with me?' and the truthful answer would be, 'Not much.' At least at present."

"I'm really stuck Father, on some of the images Frank uses. Can't you give me any help?"

"Go back and read those parts with my clue about seeing. Then, after you've read *Siddhartha*, it may become clearer to you. I'd rather not try to explain anymore. OK?" I nodded and thought, 'You aren't going to yield on this one, you old so and so.'

"Can I validate some of my own explanations with you?" He looked worried but nodded yes. "The three adventurers who refused to see things like Francis and Jacob. The way Frank wrote that part, it sounds like he was playing God. He seemed to say that the three men, who had tried so hard their whole life, wouldn't be able to cross the river. Isn't Frank going too far here, pretending he knows how God will treat people?" I returned to the topic because it really bothered me that God might be a tough judge. I guess I wanted more reassurance.

I knew he was going to answer this one because he shook his head vigorously. "Again, Frank and I debated that section when he was writing it. I tend to agree with you Elena. It's too easily misunderstood. I know what Frank meant but he didn't quite hit the nail on the head. He was trying to deal with one of the central mysteries about God, so we must forgive him for falling short. Lots of brilliant people down through history have debated this point." He paused, trying to decide whether to continue.

"I'll violate my own rule here and give you another hint from Christian theology for this section. Jacob, and Frank for that matter, were wrestling with a very difficult question. Can any person find their own way past death, using their own strength, or is life after death a gift from God? The

Buddha achieved Nirvana on his own but Jesus was raised from the dead by God. That's the debate that men and women a lot smarter than Frank and I have been having for many centuries. Frank had Francis and his three friends engage in that debate. That's about as far I as I want to go with this with you, at least right now."

My head was beginning to hurt, with all these ideas so I nodded as if I understood. He hadn't actually helped me.

"Well, I guess I'll have to think about all this, and reread a few parts of Frank's book Father."

We chatted about London for a little and I promised to call him to schedule another dinner. He walked me to the door, and I walked back to the hotel. Suddenly I was tired and wanted to take a nap.

Chapter 2

That evening I had dinner in the hotel restaurant, and brought chapter one of Frank's book with me, to reread. I was really bothered by one passage.

The scene shifted, and I watched my wife and children walk out of our house and toward the same gate that I had seen Pilgrim enter. To my horror I then saw myself run up the hill, roughly grab my wife and drag her away from the gate. The children ran after us crying and frantic because they thought I was hurting their mother. But the final horror now emerged. I pulled my wife by the arm, past our house and over a small hill, until I saw the chasm! I dragged my wife down toward the chasm, with the children following, and I had a look on my face that haunts me to this day. I was asleep and peaceful. I was doing this terrible thing as a sleepwalker! There was no hope that my wife's or the children's cries of terror could bring me to my senses before I dragged them all into the chasm

The allegory's meaning was obvious. Frank had been unconsciously cruel to his wife. He was so self-centered that he hadn't even seen the malice in his actions. How could I trust such a man? And if I couldn't trust him, then how could I trust his story? Then I saw that that was exactly what he wanted to happen: for me to decide (or not) that I trusted him as well as what his allegory meant for me.

I paused and thought about trust. On the one side was my history *before* Frank, where I had basically trusted no one except myself. On the other side was my history *with* Frank— our deepening friendship and growing intimacy. There was no question in my mind now that I loved Frank, but did he really love me? If the answer was yes, then I could trust him. There was absolutely no evidence, except this one passage in his manuscript that Frank was cruel or untrustworthy. I was confident that Frank was nothing unless he was honest. Yes, I believed he loved me in a special way. And I trusted him because of that. Suddenly I felt ready to try to understand his spiritual journey, wherever it led. In-Elena smiled.

Now I knew precisely why Frank hadn't wanted to talk about the book with me. He wanted me to have a crisis of trust, to get beyond only having faith in myself. As the Chinese say, crisis is composed of two characters—danger and opportunity. My crisis of trust placed the danger of only relying on myself against the opportunity of opening myself to trusting others, even perhaps God. I had to leave self-reliance behind (like Francis' three friends) in order to find my way past the chasm. I wasn't yet ready to follow Frank that far, but I was ready to begin a new (for me) journey of pushing the boundaries of trust. I knew I'd be thinking about this new perspective of my life for a long time. Thank you, Frank!

I remembered Jacob's joy at his reunion with his wife Rachel at the end of his story, as he crossed the river of death. It was obvious that Frank hoped that would happen to him; that wasn't just an allegory. I suddenly realized that I had wanted the story to end differently, for Frank to split up with his wife. At the end find the love of his life, me of course. But he hadn't imagined it that way. In fact, he must have known that I would be upset when I read this. I almost groaned out loud as I sat by myself in the restaurant. Why did I insist on punishing myself with this silly romantic view of our relationship? My trust in Frank wavered but didn't break.

There *had been* something special between us; I was certain of that. I was still grieving, not only for Frank but what I had never experienced with him. I wanted something in my life that Frank could have given me but didn't, and that opportunity was lost. Of course, it really wasn't; I was still a young woman and could meet someone else, but I was feeling jilted by Jacob's meeting Rachel at the river. I couldn't get past the way his wife still captured Frank's attention, and I hadn't.

In-Elena asked me a question. 'So, the only reason you're reading Frank's manuscript is to catch glimpses of Frank? He'd be disappointed in that don't you think?'

She saw right away what my problem was. Up to now, I wasn't being much of a detective. I had fallen in love with the author and lost sight of the main game of solving the mystery in his story. Father Mac had given me a clue. Frank's story was about encountering new assumptions and then trying to figure out how to live afterwards. *That* was my problem! I was still trapped on this side of the chasm and hadn't completely committed myself to trusting someone besides myself. I couldn't go back to my old world and I didn't know how to go forward.

As I sat eating with all these thoughts swirling through my mind, all of a sudden, they were swept away by an insight. I needed to go to Wales *immediately* and see Saint Winifred's Well. It felt like an unseen magnet located somewhere north of my hotel had been abruptly switched on and my internal compass was now fixed on it. Winifred was such a strange character; perhaps she was one of Frank's messengers. Maybe the 'gate' past the chasm was located near her well. In that moment my inner conflict about Frank's relationship with me and his wife, and even my sense of frustration about being trapped in the chasm vanished. My next step was perfectly clear. I would get on the internet immediately after dinner and plan my trip! I'd have to cancel the remainder of my three-month trip as well.

I found the sheet from Wikipedia that Father Mac had printed out and read Saint Winifred's strange story. She was the daughter of a rich man and had decided at an early age to dedicate her life to God and remain a virgin. A local nobleman had been infuriated when she resisted his advances and cut her head off. Another saint, Saint Beuno, came upon the scene and cursed the man, who disappeared in a puff of smoke. Saint Beuno then rejoined Winifred's head to her body and brought her back to life. Where her severed head had fallen on the ground, a well sprang up, which had magical properties. Ever since that time, people had made pilgrimages to visit Winfred's Well, located in the appropriately named Holywell in eastern Wales, and many had experienced cures and other miracles. Several kings visited the well and asked for Winfred's help, most notably Henry the fifth before the battle of Agincourt, the great victory celebrated in Shakespeare's play. Winifred had died in 660. Now, almost 1400 years after she lived, I was reading about her!

I had been struck by her statue in the Farm Street Church but why did I feel the urge to go visit Saint Winifred's Well? What did this ancient woman have to do with me? You could hardly imagine a greater contrast. Woman of the world and virgin nun. The daughter of a shopkeeper in Australia and the daughter of a rich man. A famous saint and…? What was I? Still there was something about her that attracted me. Her statue's smile for one thing. I wanted more than ever to visit her well. Was I looking for a miracle? Help on finding a way past the chasm? Was I on a pilgrimage?

I looked up 'pilgrimage' on the internet. A journey to a holy place, undertaken for religious reasons. Well I certainly wasn't on a religious pilgrimage. Why did I want to make this trip to a remote part of Wales? To follow my inner compass and maybe meet one of Frank's strange 'messengers'? I wouldn't want any of my friends to know that. I was already in uncharted territory, even before I set out for Wales. I had the concierge make a booking at a small hotel in Holywell for the following evening and reserved a car. I went to bed with many conflicting thoughts swirling in my mind.

Surprisingly, I had a peaceful dream that night. I was floating in a swimming pool, dangling my arms over the sides of a plastic raft, moving them languidly through the warm water. I knew I was a little girl again because the brilliant Australian sun was overhead, in an endless cloudless blue sky. The water in the pool shimmered, and the raft bobbed gently. A voice at the edge of the pool called me to get out and come home. I was so relaxed I was unable to lift my head to see who was calling me. I wanted to stay exactly where I was, floating alone in dream world. The voice kept calling me, and I lazily wondered who it was. That was all. When I awoke I felt refreshed.

Chapter 3

I decided to begin the long drive to Holywell after the morning rush hour. I killed time by eating breakfast slowly and browsing through *Siddhartha*. I noticed immediately that Frank had underlined a number of passages, things that must have interested him. Another person had written notes in the margin, next to a few of these passages. I knew it was someone else because of the way the first note was written. Frank had underlined, 'One must find the source within one's own self, one must possess it.' The note was, 'Frank, what is beyond possessing?' Frank wouldn't have written that to himself. I thought Father Mac must have written it.

I felt like an eavesdropper on an intimate conversation. Frank had given a close friend a book that was heavily underlined and meaningful to him. It wasn't simply a gift. Was he suggesting an agenda for their discussions? The Frank I knew wouldn't be so direct. And then Father Mac had written his notes in the margin. Of all Frank's underlined passages, why had he chosen these? Another puzzle was addressing Frank by name in his first note as if they were having a conversation. That didn't make sense. Then an intriguing possibility occurred to me. Perhaps the two of them were marking up the book for someone else. Frank had asked Father Mac to give me *Siddhartha* after he died, apparently after I had read his manuscript. His underlining and Father Mac's comments were intended for me! They were both giving me clues about a mystery that I had to solve for myself, each in their own way. They were encouraging me to examine all the possibilities: my relationship with Frank, his manuscript about his own journey, and the hints in *Siddhartha* they created.

For an action junky, this was far too much information, almost enough to make me throw up my hands in despair. Fitting all the clues into a coherent pattern like a real detective was beyond me. But that was exactly what it meant to be confronted by the need to find one's way past the chasm. Then In-Elena whispered, 'Follow your instinct at Winifred's Well' and I felt a sense of peace flow into me again. I remembered my dream from last night. That reassured me too. The faint ripples in the pool were touching me and someone was calling me to come home.

Finally, it was time to leave on my 'pilgrimage.' I had packed my small suitcase with things that would last me for a week, just in case. I checked my large case at the hotel. I made a reservation back here starting a week later. The car rental agency brought a Mini Minor around to the side entrance on Upper Grosvenor Street and I was on my way.

Following the yellow highlighted route the agent had drawn on the rental car map, I easily found the M1 which would take me to the M6 to Birmingham. Taking a bypass, I would go West to Shrewsbury, then follow smaller roads north through Wales to Holywell. Depending on traffic, the trip would take four or five hours if I went straight through. I'd be in Holywell in time for dinner. The Mini was fun to drive and I was looking forward to seeing a part of the world that was new to me.

In less an hour I was clear of London's crowded northern suburbs, doing 60mph. It was a gray day, but I felt wonderfully free and excited about my little adventure. I wondered how the pilgrims who had walked from London to Holywell hundreds of years ago felt. This gently rolling farmland must have been more of a challenge when you were on foot. Soon I was passing Nottingham, wondering if pilgrims of the thirteenth century had to worry about Robin Hood robbing them.

Robin Hood. Winifred of Wales. Why had such characters been remembered for such a long time? Why didn't people make 'pilgrimages' to visit Sherwood Forest? Was Winifred marketed better than Robin Hood? Princess Diana had been very well marketed, but there was something else

471

about her. Her tragic death? Unfulfilled promise? My mind was playing detective as I sped northwest. There was something about Winifred and Robin Hood and probably Princess Diana that endured, some quality attached to them, something that tugged at our memories when we had even the smallest encounter with them. Princess Di's Memorial in Hyde Park; Winifred's smile; Robin Hood's quest for justice. What was going on? Was my internal magnet attracted to Winifred because she was like Princess Di and Robin Hood in some strange way? Is that all it is? If so, I didn't have much interest in going to her well to experience some phony well-marketed saint.

I was so lost in thought that I didn't hear the faint thumping sound that the Mini was making when one of its tires went flat. At 60mph, I was glad that it was a rear tire because I was able to easily steer over to the shoulder and stop without much difficulty. Damn! I got out and looked at the rim of the left rear wheel resting on the asphalt shoulder. I didn't need this snag in my adventure. Things got worse when I discovered that there was no spare in the boot. I got back in the car and looked at the rental contract. There was an emergency number to call. Grrr! I punched in the number on my mobile—thank God there was coverage along the M1 and was connected to a young woman. She patiently listened to my anger about the missing spare then obtained the details about my location. It would take about an hour for the emergency road crew to reach me. Please stay with the car!

After about fifteen minutes, I got out of the Mini and stretched my legs. Of course, this attracted a trucker to pull over and ask if he could help. I told him thank you, but help was on the way. He looked relieved that he didn't have to waste time and drove off. About fifteen minutes after that, a police car pulled over and a young constable also asked if I needed help. When I repeated my story, he said he'd wait until the emergency crew arrived. "There are some strange characters on this highway." He went back to his car to notify his dispatcher. I stayed by the Mini to make sure the emergency crew didn't miss me.

He came back and stood beside me. "Where are you headed?" He had a friendly face, so I answered, "I'm going to Wales, on a holiday."

"What part?"

I wasn't sure I wanted to tell him about Saint Winifred, so I said, "Holywell. I'm going through Shrewsbury and then taking some side roads through Wales on the way."

"You ought to go see Saint Winifred's Well while you're in Holywell. It's the oldest shrine in the UK and well worth seeing."

I looked at him sharply. An insight flitted through my mind, but I didn't catch it.

"That's why I'm going there, to visit the shrine as you call it. Have you been there?"

He shook his head. "No, I haven't. My mother made a pilgrimage there when I was a boy and told me about it. There's another Winifred's Well in Woolston, just past Shrewsbury. You ought to make a short detour and see it. Not as grand as Holywell but special in its own way. The story

473

goes that when Winifred's relics were being transferred to Shrewsbury, the procession stopped in Woolston. Where they laid her body down another miraculous well appeared."

He was looking at me very directly. It almost made his suggestion about Woolston seem like a command. Then my insight surfaced again. Was this young policeman a messenger? Was I being guided on my journey like Frank described in his story? Before Frank (Jacob) found the way past the chasm, he had encountered several messengers who pointed the way forward. How can I tell if this ordinary looking constable is some sort of mysterious messenger? It occurred to me that this was a *very* strange internal conversation for Elena Gaunt!

"This is a coincidence. Of all the people who could have stopped to help me, it was a policeman who knows about Saint Winifred. A little like *The Twilight Zone*. Do do do do."

He grinned at me. "Oh, it's not a coincidence. These things happen for a reason. People cross each other's paths for a purpose."

That destroyed all my tough guy images of policemen. I had to know if he was a messenger.

"And what is your purpose in meeting me do you think?"

His grin got even broader. "Oh, that's a secret Elena."

How did he know my name? We hadn't introduced ourselves. Then I remembered his call to the dispatcher. He must have checked out the license of the Mini and gotten my name from the rental contract.

"Since you know my name, what's yours?"

"Frank O'Connor." If he had said Michael the Archangel I couldn't have been more surprised.

My shock must have shown on my face because he said, "Is something wrong?"

How could I explain? "I had a dear friend named Frank O'Connor who died a few years ago. Indirectly he is responsible for my being on this trip."

"Sorry. I don't usually have that effect on people. Where was your Frank from? Maybe I'm related to him."

"I don't think so. He was from the USA but lived in London."

He nodded. "Probably no connection. There are lots of O'Connor's in the world. If you don't mind me asking, where are you from? I can't place your accent."

"I live in Hong Kong but originally I was from Australia, near Sydney. Have you been there?" He gave me the standard 'I'd like to go there someday' answer.

"So Frank, getting back to your purpose in crossing my path. I'd really like to know why you think the universe arranged our meeting."

He looked up the road. "Here comes your service truck Elena. Woolston is on your way. Take the A5 past Shrewsbury, and just past Weirbrook, before you come to

West Felton, take a left on Woolston Road. Woolston is about three miles. Someone in the village can tell you how to get to Saint Winifred's Well. It's just a short distance outside Woolston. I'll write down the directions for you while the man repairs your tire."

The tire was efficiently replaced with another by the repairman. Frank O'Connor handed me the directions and I got back on the highway.

I couldn't get my thoughts straight. Had this Frank been sent to me? Why was it important to go to Woolston? I drove there with my thoughts more confused than ever.

Chapter 4

"What brings you to Woolston?" The barman at The Green Knight pub, a rather tall older man with a ruddy face, short gray hair and a pleasant manner had just poured me a lemon lime and bitters after taking my order for a plowman's plate.

I had followed Frank the policeman's directions and found Woolston easily. It was a tiny rural village with a few houses, a grocery store and one pub. I was killing two birds with one stone: getting directions to the local Winifred's Well and eating some lunch.

"I'm on my way to Wales but a friend suggested I see Winifred's Well. Is it nearby?"

"Right up the road. I'll draw you a map because it's a bit hard to find. Not much to see there though. I think the cottage is locked up." He got a blank piece of paper and a ballpoint pen. "Here's where we are." He put an X in the center of the paper. "Here's the road out front." He drew a slightly curved line and pointed off to the left to orient me. "You go this way about five hundred yards, and you'll find a path off to the left, down between two lines of bushes. You might think they're trees but they're not." He drew another wavy line off the first one and then put an X at the end. "That's where the cottage is. It's a timber house. The well is behind it. You can't miss it. I wouldn't go down into the water though." He smiled at me.

"I have no intention of getting into the well. Is that what people around here do?"

He smiled even more broadly. "Oh, we don't do that. It's the visitors. Some of them jump in, hoping to get a cure or something, I guess. Not many come anymore. Must not be too many cures."

"So you don't believe in the power of Saint Winifred?"

"Well, I guess I don't, do I? Never seen anyone cured, so why should I?"

I had to agree with him. It wasn't the promise of seeing a 'cure' as the barman called it that lured me to go to Holywell. It was Winifred's mysterious smile. Not like the Mona Lisa's but a peaceful and welcoming smile, as if Winifred wanted me to find my way out of the chasm. I hadn't thought of that before.

While I waited, I thought I'd find out about Woolston. "What else is there to see around here?"

Suddenly the barman perked up. "Now that's an interesting question. I have lived in Shropshire my whole life and still I haven't seen it all. Do you know that you are in the center of probably the most important place on Earth, at least for the last five hundred years?"

I didn't expect this. Woolston and the part of Shropshire I had driven through looked like a backwater to me.

He could see the skepticism on my face. "I'll explain what I mean. Not twenty miles from here is where the Industrial Revolution started, in Coalbrookdale. It's where they first made iron the modern way, because we could dig good coking coal more easily. It's where we built Watt's steam engine and invented modern engineering. It's hard to imagine that the modern world, with its giant factories and corporations started here a little over two hundred years ago." His face was shining with pride.

"And that's not all. You only have to go about hundred miles East to get to Cambridge. That's where Newton and others really started modern science. It was those ideas that changed the way that we think. Here in Shropshire, we took that science and did something useful with it. That's why we're so important."

It was fascinating. Here was a man who had possibly never been to London, believing that he lived in one of the most important places on our planet. Little did he know that he was talking to a woman who was a citizen of planet Earth but who didn't think any place was worth bragging about, let alone being called one of the really 'important places' in human history. I wondered how we had gotten to such different places in our lives.

"Let me ask you a question. I was born in Australia and now live in Hong Kong. I travel all over the world. There are so many different ideas and inventions that make our world the way it is today. How can you say Shropshire is the most important place?"

A woman— it thought it must be the barman's wife— brought a china plate out of the kitchen and set it on the bar in front of me. "Now Frank, don't you be bothering the young woman with your crazy ideas." She smiled at me as if saying, 'You understand how it is with men, I'm sure.'

Another Frank! Another messenger? This one sure had lots to say, that's for certain.

He waited until his wife went back into the kitchen then answered my question.

"Here's the way I figure it works. It's where you start that determines where you end up. We started the whole world down the track that it's on today. That's why."

That got my competitive juices flowing. I chewed on a bite of cucumber, tomato and cheese and swallowed before answering. "So, do you think the world is still carrying out the Industrial Revolution? What about communications, television, computers and the internet? Has that made some other place more important than Shropshire now?"

He shook his head. "No, all of them depend on engineering making science useful. That's what we did here, for the first time." He looked at me triumphantly.

This was going to be harder than I thought. "So are only things that are made by engineering important?" I was panicked for a minute because I couldn't think of anything where engineering wasn't involved. Finally, I said, "What about politics?" As soon as I said it, I regretted it. This would open up a whole new can of worms for this home spun philosopher! But he surprised me.

"Now that's a tricky question. Here's how I see it. What is a country? A collection of people who live together and help each other by making things. If you listen to the politicians, what do they all talk about? The economy and taxes. There is no economy and no taxes to collect without making things and that takes engineering!" He stopped wiping the bar and waited for me to respond.

"Look, I can see your point. Engineering is very important to all of us. If modern engineering got going here in Shropshire, I can see why you're proud. But there's a lot more to life than making and buying things."

"Like what?" He leaned forward and rested his arms on the bar in front of me.

Suddenly, it occurred to me that I was advocating that something besides working and making money was important. But what *was* more important than that? He had me backed into a corner.

He grinned. "I get them going on this too, in the evening after work. Never lose."

"Give me a minute Frank. You've had more practice than I." I grinned back at him and he walked back to the refrigerator. "Would you like another lemon lime and bitter?" I nodded and he opened another bottle and gave it to me.

I thought, if Frank was here, the real Frank O'Connor, he would ask the barman a question that would change the direction of the argument. Come on Frank; inspire me.

"Let me ask you a question Frank. I'm traveling around the UK because I lost my job 'making things' as you say. Do you think I should just find another job as quickly as possible so I can keep on making things for the rest of my life?"

"Now that's an important question! I need to think about it. Do you mind me asking, what did you make in your job?"

What did I make? "I was in marketing. I guess marketing makes ads and other materials that persuade people to buy what other people make. I don't know if we use 'engineering' like you mean the word."

"So, your question is should you get another marketing job making ads. Or what should you use the rest of your life making? Is that what you want to know?"

All of a sudden Frank didn't seem like some argumentative barman, trying to win the debating game they played every night in The Green Knight because they had nothing better to do. He seemed more like another Frank I remembered, who always tried to make me think for myself, leading me somewhere that only he could see.

"Yes, I think it is. What ought I do with the rest of my life? What should I make that's worth spending my life on?" I thought of Frank's manuscript. He found his life's work after he got past the chasm. Maybe I didn't have to go through that. I could just decide what I wanted to do, set some goals and pursue them. But wasn't that just turning around and going back to the 'highway' that I was on before, the same choice that Jacob faced and rejected?

I must have seemed to be somewhere else because Frank didn't speak for what seemed like quite a long time. When he saw me come back into the room, he smiled at me.

"I don't hear such questions discussed very often in The Green Knight. In Woolston, our lives are pretty well set. We know our place. The ones that don't accept this, they leave, mainly the young people. It's strange; your coming here, to this place, asking these questions. You seem to have lots of options, yet you can't seem to find your way. Maybe your problem is too much freedom?"

Are all barmen amateur psychologists I wondered? Freedom was a pretty deep topic. Again, my Frank seemed very close.

"Frank, why do you think I have a problem? I lost my job; I'm trying to decide what job to take next, while I enjoy taking some time off."

He shook his head. "I didn't mean a bad problem; I meant something more like an opportunity. You said you might be trying to figure out what to make the rest of your life."

"OK, when you put it that way, you're right. I haven't told you a lot of the background. There's more going on than just what work should I do." He didn't say anything. "I'm wrestling with something that I can't easily describe, even to myself. It's like all the rules that I used previously to make sense out of things don't work now. Do you know what I mean?"

"I think I do. Do you know the story of Sir Gawain and the Green Knight? I have printed it up for visitors who want to know what the name of this pub refers to." He went over to drawer under the cash register and found a brochure. "Here. It isn't very long." He handed it to me.

The story begins in Camelot on New Year's Eve as King Arthur's court is feasting and exchanging gifts. A large Green Knight armed with an axe enters the hall and proposes a game. He asks for someone in the court to strike him once with his axe, on condition that the Green Knight will return the blow one year and one day later, at his own Green Chapel. Sir Gawain, the youngest of Arthur's knights and nephew to the king, accepts the challenge. He severs the giant's head in one stroke, expecting him to die. The Green Knight, however, picks up his own head, reminds Gawain to meet him at the Green Chapel in a year and a day (New Year's Day the next year) and rides away.

As the date approaches Sir Gawain sets off to find the Green Chapel and complete his bargain with the Green Knight. His long journey leads him to a beautiful castle where he meets Bertilak de Hautdesert, the lord of the castle, and his beautiful wife; both are pleased to have such a renowned guest. Gawain tells them of his New Year's appointment at the Green Chapel and says that he must continue his search as he only has a few days remaining. Bertilak laughs and explains that the Green Chapel is less than two miles away and proposes that Gawain stay at the castle.

Before going hunting the next day, Bertilak proposes a bargain to Gawain: he will give Gawain whatever he catches on the hunt, on condition that Gawain give him whatever he might gain during the day. Gawain accepts. After Bertilak leaves, the lady of the castle Lady Bertilak visits Gawain's bedroom to seduce him. Despite her best efforts, however, he yields nothing but a single kiss. When Bertilak returns and gives Gawain the deer he has killed, his guest responds by returning the lady's kiss to Bertilak, without divulging its source. The next day, the lady comes again, Gawain dodges her advances, and there is a similar exchange of a hunted boar for two kisses. She comes once more on the third morning, and Gawain accepts from her a green silk girdle, which the lady promises will keep him from all physical harm. They exchange three kisses. That evening, Bertilak returns with a fox, which he exchanges with Gawain for the three kisses. Gawain keeps the girdle, however.

The next day, Gawain leaves for the Green Chapel with the girdle. He finds the Green Knight at the chapel sharpening an axe, and, as arranged, bends over to receive his blow. The Green Knight swings to behead Gawain, but holds back twice, only striking softly on the third swing, causing a small scar on his neck. The Green Knight then reveals himself to be the lord of the castle, Bertilak de Hautdesert, and explains that the entire game was arranged by King Arthur's sister and nemesis Morgan le Fay. Gawain is at first ashamed and upset, but the two men part on cordial terms and Gawain returns to Camelot, wearing the girdle of shame as a token of his failure to keep his promise with Bertilak. Arthur decrees that all his knights should henceforth wear a green sash in recognition of Gawain's adventure."[20]

I thought for a few moments. What did this have to do with my struggle with some deeper, unknown issue? For one thing, the parallel with Winifred's story was obvious. Her head had been cut off by a knight, but her life was restored and her head rejoined to her body.

"Frank, can I ask you a question? Did you decide to name this pub after the Green Knight because Winifred's Well is close by? You know her head was cut off but miraculously restored."

"No, I bought the pub from another man. I don't know why he named it The Green Knight. All I know is that the story makes for some good conversation. People find lots of things in it. You see Winifred's miracle in it; others see other things."

I said, "Isn't it obvious to you? Winifred and Gawain both retained their honor despite being tempted. Both are rewarded for this by keeping their life despite the threat of death." How is my honor involved in my journey to Holywell I wondered?

He nodded. "Yes, that's how some of us hereabouts see it too. But we see other things, as I said. In a way, the story is about life." He paused to let that idea sink in. When he saw my interest, he continued.

"Remember, King Arthur and his knights knew the whole thing was a game, right from the start. When Gawain, the youngest knight accepts the Green Knight's challenge, he agrees to play the game—but he doesn't know the rules or the consequences! That's typical of all of us, isn't it? We jump into the game of life, take some hasty steps, cutting off the Green Knight's head so to speak without really understanding what we are doing."

He stopped and removed my plate from the bar. Without asking, he gave me another lemon lime and bitters. I was thinking about how I had decided to play the game of life without really thinking about the consequences. Look what it had gotten me. In a way, my head had been cut off in New York and now I was trying to figure out how to put myself back together. Why hadn't I just gone out a found another job? Something was pulling me to go deeper. My honor? No, it seemed more like my inner authenticity, being comfortable with my life's direction, or something.

Frank added, "Gawain has one thing going for him: his commitment to his ideal of what it meant to be one of

King Arthur's knights. He would keep his promises and he wouldn't violate his ideals. He resists the lady of the castle's advances and saves his life. Pretty much the same thing that Winifred did. So, what do you think?"

I was trying to put together a lot of things. My own life and Winifred's and the mythical Gawain's decisions. I couldn't, other than to see once more that I was standing next to a chasm where such questions were asked but not answered. I also realized that I had encountered another messenger in Frank the barman. The Green Knight was why I had been told to come to Woolston, I was certain of that.

"I'm trying to think what Gawain's story means to me Frank. It's all a bit fuzzy."

He smiled again. "The Green Knight does that to people. I mean the pub and the myth. They both make them a bit fuzzy." He laughed at his own joke. "Oh well, it will come clear, I'm sure. Hadn't you best be going? You have a long drive ahead of you to get to Wales."

I paused. Had I told him where I was going? I couldn't remember and anyway, as a messenger he would know that. I paid the bill, thanked him for his hospitality, and got back into the Mini. It was only a short drive down the road to the bush-lined lane that led to Winifred's Well. It was too narrow for even the little Mini, so I parked on the shoulder and walked to the cottage.

There was no one in sight. The cottage was surrounded by trees. It was small, made of horizontal dark timbers with white plaster in between. I walked around the back and found Winifred's Well. It wasn't very impressive. It was about eight feet square with stone sides and dark water down below. There was a place where you could sit and dangle your feet into the water, but the day was a bit too cool for that, and the water didn't look very inviting.

What do you do at a holy place I wondered? I thought of how the well got here. It was said that it magically appeared when Winifred's body was being carried from Wales to Shrewsbury in the twelfth century. This water had the power to heal, so the legend went. What do you have to do to be healed I wondered? Get down in the water? I certainly wasn't going to do that.

I remembered Winifred's smile in the Farm Street Church. She was leading me along this journey. I smiled as I looked down at the water. She had told me that it didn't matter if I got into the water. I felt peaceful in this place. Maybe my healing was already underway.

I walked back to the Mini, drove back to the main road and continued to Holywell.

Chapter 5

The drive from Woolston to Holywell was uneventful. I took the risk out of the trip by staying on the main highways and not winding my way through the Welsh mountains that rose in the West. The pilgrims of the past probably didn't look for the easy way to Holywell. I remembered King Henry the fifth, who walked twice to Winifred's Well: once before Agincourt and a second time after the famous English victory over the French. I wondered how long his pilgrimage took. From Woolston, my journey took less than two hours but then I wasn't on a pilgrimage. My idea was to get to the destination as quickly as possible. That had always been my way of operating.

I arrived at the hotel the concierge at the Grosvenor House had booked, just as the sun was setting. The Glan Yr Afon Inn. He had made a good choice. It was a quaint two-story stone building with a garden in front and looked delightfully rustic.

Now that I was here, I wanted to see Winifred's Well immediately. I left my suitcase in my room and drove through the small town of Holywell. I spied a small sign saying 'To Saint Winifred's Well' pointing down a road to the left, and there it was. It looked like a small stone castle or church, with a souvenir shop next door. I parked in a parking lot across the street and walked into the shop, following the directions on a sign in front that said, 'Purchase tickets here for Winifred's Well'. Oh well, a little free enterprise is OK.

I paused briefly in the shop's entrance and wondered what I would encounter inside. There was a young woman about my age with purple streaked hair sitting behind a souvenir counter, reading a newspaper. I walked over and picked up a free brochure. She didn't look up. I thought, 'This is just a boring job to her.' Winifred was no one to her, completely irrelevant to life nowadays in a small out-of-the-way Welsh town.

I walked up to the woman and asked to buy a ticket. "Fifty pence," she said, scarcely looking up from her book. I handed over the money and she gave me a ticket torn off a large roll and fifty pence change. I walked around the shop briefly to see if there was anything I wanted as a souvenir. There was a little copy of Winifred's statue at Farm Street Church, but it was very cheap, like everything else in the shop.

I saw a children's book called The Patron Saint of Wales—Saint Winifred. I paged through it. There was more information on the internet. I left the shop through the door marked 'To Saint Winifred's Well'.

It was late in the day so the stone façade of Winifred's Well almost looked black. I walked down a path marked with a low white chain fence and approached the entrance. Off to my right was what looked like a small swimming pool with four faded cabanas. That must be where people changed into their bathing suits to go into the holy waters. The water looked almost black, probably because the pool's sides and bottom were constructed of the same dark stone as the shrine. Not very inviting but I guess if you are a believer you don't expect a resort.

I entered the shrine and immediately saw a statue of Winifred standing in a small alcove. There were dead bunches of flowers scattered at her feet. She had the same small smile on her face, and almost looked embarrassed to be seen amid such tawdry surroundings. There was a kneeler in front of the statue, but I couldn't make myself kneel. I stood and looked into her face. 'Winifred, you have led me here for some purpose. Please help me to understand what it is.' She just smiled her little smile at me as if she were saying, 'It's up to you to figure it out.' I knew that wasn't what she would say; it was probably my own cynicism whispering in my ear.

I walked around the shine, wondering how old it was. At least eight hundred years old I thought. There were faded mosaics in the walls, and another small pool in the center with steps leading down into the dark water. On one wall there

493

were photographs of the shrine taken many years ago. One of them showed stacks of crutches thrown away by the crippled people healed here, I guess. A note on the photo said a Catholic Bishop had ordered the crutches to be removed to maintain the dignity of the shrine. I thought, good on him. There were also a number of letters and notes posted under Plexiglas—testimonials from people who had experienced miracles. One especially struck me, from a protestant not a Catholic. "I am not of your faith, but I want to pay tribute to you. My son had a very bad motorcycle accident and was paralyzed, confined to a hospital bed for many months. I was desperate and came to your shrine and prayed for your help. From that day, my son began to experience sensations in his legs and now has healed to such an extent that he is able to get around on crutches. We remain hopeful for a full recovery. Thank you."

I waited patiently in the shrine for about ten minutes, for some sign from Winifred but nothing happened. I slowly walked outside back toward the shop. An old couple was slowly making their way toward the shrine. He was very stooped, using two canes to slowly hobble. She was carrying a little plastic jug, to get water from the well I supposed. But she was mumbling something as they walked past me. It sounded like "Winifred pray for us," said over and over but I couldn't be sure. I suddenly felt like an alien. I didn't belong here.

Why had I come? Had I expected to encounter Winifred? Suddenly the smiling statue of her back in London seemed like some kind of trick, to con gullible fools like me into…what? Father Mac was part of the scam. I shook my head. No, that couldn't be so; a friend of Frank's couldn't be that cynical. But this place was so, well, tacky. I felt deflated, disappointed, let down, by the dirty dark water in the pool, the garish souvenir shop, the odd old couple I passed on the way out. Even Winifred's statue seemed second-rate, maudlin.

As I sat in my car in the parking lot across from Winifred's Well, my mood was leaden and gray like the Welsh sky. A large van pulled up nearby and a woman dressed in a track suit opened the sliding side door and began unloading. She unfolded a wheelchair next to the cargo bay, and helped a boy laying on blankets drag himself across the floor and wiggle into the chair with difficulty. His head slumped as he sat, and I could see he had Cerebral Palsy. She said something and two younger children got out of the van and the four of them headed for the crosswalk and Winifred's Well. She knew why she was here. I wondered how many times she had gone through this ritual, patiently waiting for Winifred or her God or whomever to cure her son. I thought, maybe I should go back into the shrine to see what would happen this time, but I just started the engine and drove back to my hotel.

I ate dinner, went to bed early, and put Winifred and her well out of my mind by thinking about where I would go next. I could return to London. I could go somewhere else and…what? I still had no idea of where I wanted to go on my vacation, let alone where I wanted to work and live. Those two were inextricably tied together, and not just because I needed money. I had lots of activities I did when I wasn't working but they were just time fillers. The only part of my life that seemed real was when I was at work—and now that seemed empty too

Winifred had known what she wanted to do with her life, and had her head cut off pursuing it. The woman with the disabled child invested her life in seeking a miracle. I had this vast expanse of future life in front of me, with nothing worthwhile to invest myself in. I could hear Frank saying, "Listen to In-Elena," and I suddenly realized that she had been silent during my pilgrimage to Holywell.

I went over to my suitcase, got Frank's manuscript and read the opening again.

"One summer, more than a few years ago, I encountered a mystery."

I turned and looked at myself in the mirror. Like Frank's, my life had been interrupted by a chasm that I couldn't find a way around. Winifred's Well seemed like a disappointing dead end to me. Now what? When did my new beginning start, like the 'kingdom' Frank had encountered? My head was swirling with ideas and I couldn't go to bed, so I went down to the hotel bar and sat by myself in a booth. Several men looked at me, but I looked away. No thanks guys; you wouldn't want to be with me tonight. I fiddled with the drink in front of me and wondered what Frank would say to me if he were here? He already had spoken; 'Listen to In-Elena' but she didn't seem to have much to say right now. I opened my purse to get a Kleenex and saw The Green Knight's sheet about Gawain and read it again. The ending caught my attention.

The Green Knight swings to behead Gawain, but holds back twice, only striking softly on the third swing, causing a small scar on his neck.

Something occurred to me. Winifred had a thin scar around her neck where her head had been reattached. The Gawain story had been written many centuries after Winifred lived. Were these two myths related? Suddenly I saw the meaning. Winifred, like Gawain, risked death when she denied her rough suitor—in service of her God. Innocent self-denying service. That is why she (and Gawain) have been celebrated down through the centuries—in the King Arthur myth and in the Church's pantheon of saints. I took a sip of my drink, proud of myself that I had deduced this connection. Both of these stories were meant to teach simple people how to live their lives.

But what had any of this to do with me? Innocent and self-denying definitely don't apply to me! I decided to go to bed. It had been a long, puzzling and disappointing day.

Chapter 6

That night, in a dream, I experienced a spiritual visitor. I know, that's a *deus ex machina*, a too easy resolution of my dilemma. Hear me out; you'll see it wasn't that simple.

I tossed and turned for about an hour and couldn't get to sleep so I reread part of Frank's manuscript, where he was very frustrated by his inability to figure out what was happening, after he had been visited by the two spirits.

When I awoke, I looked for Pilgrim to ask him about the dream, but he was gone. The sun was up, and I went outside the farmhouse. My car was there, and the road; but more wonderfully the chasm was gone! I felt exultation and got into my car to drive away from the place. Then I remembered what Pilgrim had said about the decision to return to the highway or not, and I didn't start my car.

I sat in the car for a long time before I went back into the house. Several times I got up and started back to the car, in mounting frustration and anger. "What do you want from me?" I asked no one in particular. Only silence answered me. I wrestled that day with the visions and especially with Pilgrim's dream that pointed to the mysterious gate. Of all the possible meanings I considered, only one made any sense: I can avoid death if I find Pilgrim's gate and walk through it.

It seemed that this was the clear message of the dream, but it made no real sense to me. Why the mysterious way the message was delivered? In fact, Adversary had tried to mislead me. Why? Why was the gate hidden, not right out in the open where anyone could see it? Try as hard as I could, I did not have satisfactory answers to many troubling questions. I discovered that I had spent the day struggling with these questions. Tired and hungry again, I ate more bread and honey and fell asleep.

I thought, this is exactly how I feel. I'm at here in Holywell, to discover a new way forward, and I'm frustrated. I haven't encountered Adversary or Pilgrim. But maybe I have. The encouraging cop on the motorway, and the bartender in the pub were my pilgrims. What messages were they giving me? Keep on going; you're on the right path.

Maybe my Adversary was my disappointment in Winifred's shrine, telling me I was on the wrong road, with a lot of people believing in mumbo jumbo. But how did I know what that old couple, or the mother of that invalid boy believed? Like it had done with Frank, Adversary was trying to mislead me. Why did Adversary have it in for Frank and me? For that matter, why were the cop and bartender and Winifred on my side? I turned off the light and closed my eyes thinking about these questions.

I had a familiar dream that night, one that I had told Frank years ago. I was in an empty London theater, sitting near the stage, which was bare. I became aware of someone sitting behind me and when I glanced back, it was another me, smiling at me. Then I realized I had to go up on the stage, so I walked over to the steps near me and went to center stage and looked out at the empty theater. My other self was still there, watching me. I didn't know what I was supposed to say or do. Then I noticed something I had hadn't seen in the dream before. There was *another presence* in the theater, high up in the balcony, sitting in the near darkness, also watching me. I was afraid of it and looked away. Then I woke up.

I was really spooked and turned on the room light. Years ago, Frank had said that the other me in the lower part of the theater was In-Elena, and that had been an important step in encountering her. But who (what) was the other presence? I felt goosebumps that it might be Adversary. I had never taken ghosts seriously before but that night I did. I lay there with the light on and was afraid to close my eyes. Finally, I dropped off to sleep and didn't dream again.

I woke up to the sound of a hard-driving rain hitting the window in my hotel room. I got up and looked out and saw that the trees behind the parking lot were dancing and being bent by strong gusty winds. That makes my day, I thought. I'd be stuck in the hotel unless I wanted to be drenched because I only had a small folding travel umbrella and no raincoat. I lay back down on the bed and tried to decide what to do. Should I go back to London? That seemed like running away from something that I had been led here to find. I'd have to find a way to occupy myself in the hotel today. They didn't even have cable TV in this primitive place. I got up, showered and went down to breakfast. At least that would occupy a little bit of the day. Maybe it would clear up later. I took along *Siddhartha* to have something to read while I ate.

There were only a few glum looking people in the dining room. I ordered the Classic English Breakfast and coffee. While I waited, I thought about my dream again. The mysterious figure in the theater balcony put a different slant on what had been a wonderful moment of discovery for me— the time when Frank had first told me about In-Elena. What did that figure signify? Can you hear me Frank? Give me one of your insights. But nothing came, except the realization that the figure frightened me somehow.

The waitress put my breakfast in front of me. "I won't have to eat again all day; this is huge!" I said. Two fried eggs, two large sausages, bacon, mushrooms, a big dollop of baked beans, two grilled tomatoes, a large heap of fried potatoes and, on another small plate, four slices of toast. I bravely began to eat, and opened *Siddhartha* to keep myself entertained. I paged through it looking for Frank's underlined places and Father Mac's (I assumed) notes in the margin. About a quarter way through the book, there were a number of underlined passages and notes, almost like Frank and Father Mac had been conversing.

[Frank's underlining] But you, my honored friend, don't you want to walk the path of salvation?

[Father Mac's note in the margin] Siddhartha wasn't ready to follow his friend's example. Salvation is a mysterious need that must come to the surface, like a sprouting plant.

[Frank's underlining] And over and over, Govinda urged his friend, he should tell him why he would not want to find refuge in Gotama's (the Buddha) teachings.

[Father Mac's note in the margin] But the Spirit moved Siddhartha otherwise.

[Frank's underlining] This is why I am continuing my travels—not to seek other, better teachings, for I know there are none, but to depart from all teachings and teachers, and to reach my goal by myself or die.

[Father Mac's note in the margin] Siddhartha's strong desire to be saved is good but how one finds the right path is the crux. Whose strength does one depend on?

I put the book down and wondered when Frank and Father Mac had this conversation. Did Frank read *Siddhartha* before he wrote his own story? Certainly, the image of choosing the right path was one of the central themes in his manuscript. Or had Frank finished his book already and he and Father Mac were comparing his journey to that of Siddhartha? And then another possibility occurred to me. Frank and Father Mac had been discussing me and my yet to be undertaken journey. Father Mac had insisted I take this copy of *Siddhartha* when I suggested buying my own copy. Clearly, he wanted me to see how he and Frank had marked up this copy.

I finished my breakfast, charged it to my room and went to sit in the hotel's lounge. I found an easy chair facing a window and watched the rain and wind with thoughts and questions swirling in my mind like the wind was blowing them too, causing them to flit in and out of my attention. I needed to slow down and think about the last twenty-four hours. That urge to reflect was a new one for me and I didn't know how to do it—so I grabbed a thought as it went past and started there.

I had been so excited about coming to Winifred's Well, and it was a big disappointment. What had I expected (hoped?) to see? I mentally listed the possibilities: Winifred herself; a person who was my own Pilgrim or Evan, like Frank's story; some kind of miracle; a sign that would lead me to find what Frank had found? None of these seemed to fit my experience thus far. That was important. Thus far. Jacob (Frank) had to wait and learn some patience before he could find the gate into what he called the kingdom. Waiting is part of what I'm going through. Thinking that, it made being stuck here in the hotel seem like it might be part of my journey.

But what of that strange figure in my dream? What did In-Elena think of it? I sat quietly and waited for her to speak up. The rain and wind seemed to intensify. Why was she silent? Either she didn't know or wasn't saying. I thought she knew; she always seemed to understand what I was going though. But maybe the presence in my dream was beyond her. Or maybe she knew but wasn't saying; I had to answer the question about that figure on my own, for some unfathomable reason. This was a little like Siddhartha. He had to leave wise teachers and find answers on his own. And it was like Frank's insistence on finding God. Maybe the presence was a sign to me that I couldn't use any of my life experiences on the path I was on. I remembered Father Mac's note in the margin to Frank: Siddhartha's strong desire to be saved is good but how one finds the right path is the crux. Whose strength does one depend on?

I suddenly had an insight. I realized I had a strong desire to see something mysterious here in Holywell, having been led here by Winifred. And I had! The figure in my dream. In a way it had posed a question to me, like Adversary had to Frank. A question about the purpose of my trip, not just to Holywell but my entire life's journey. The ultimate question: "What do I believe about finding the path beyond the chasm?" Father Mac used the strange term 'saved.' Sounded too religious for my taste but it meant 'rescued.' The crux was (and Frank's story clearly pointed at this), did I need to be rescued, and did I trust God or anyone to rescue me? Anyway, who am I that God should care about me? Isn't the cosmos only godless, mindless, purposeless energy and matter? Those were questions I had never asked before—and probably why I had been led to Holywell!

Elena Gaunt didn't need to be rescued, of that I was sure. Up until a few hours ago. I could solve the problems of what I wanted to do with my life on my own—my next job, my career, where I wanted to live, and even my future relationships. But I couldn't solve the mystery signified by the dark figure in my dream by myself. I was helpless, just as Frank had discovered. I could either ignore the sign I had been given and return to London to continue my life as before, or I could 'live in the question' and see where I was being led. For the first time I felt like I was making Frank's journey myself, not just trying to figure out what his manuscript, and *Siddhartha*, meant. I began to feel in my heart that I might need to be rescued—but who could do that?

It was only 10 am. What was I going to do the rest of the day? I could sit and reflect; I had plenty to think about. But I was itchy to do something. I finally decided that I would actually read *Siddhartha*, not only Frank's underlined part and Father Mac's notes.

The book was fairly short, only a hundred and fifty pages. I took my time, stopping every so often to think about what Siddhartha was going through, comparing his story with Frank's—and seeing a few parallels with my own life. Even so, I finished the book by mid-afternoon.

One particular point in the book struck me. Siddhartha had encountered his own form of chasm. "Siddhartha noticed that the bright and reliable voice inside of him, which had awoken him at that time and had ever guided him in his best times, had become silent."

The only bright and reliable voices I had ever experienced were Frank and In-Elena. Frank was gone and In-Elena had been strangely quiet. There was no one to guide me! I really needed a guide right now. Siddhartha had eventually found his way forward, as had Frank, to a sense of being in the hands of something beyond himself. Wasn't that the whole point? Trust in something beyond this world, in God? I kept coming back to this same point and facing the same barrier. God was not real to me; how could I trust some cosmic force or religious myth? In a way, like Frank I kept saying, "Show yourself to me God so I can believe in and trust you." I had never said this very clearly to myself. Either I could choose to seriously search for God, or I could say to myself, suck it up Elena; there is no God. The only one who can save you and get you out of this dead end you have created for yourself is you. I could just get on with my life—get into my car and get away from the chasm.

How does one make such a choice? What evidence is there that a God who rescues people from the chasm exists? My analytical mind tried to attack the problem of God like any other problem. Then I remembered a story Frank told me, about a NASA engineer in Houston he once knew. That man had tried to figure out the meaning of his life using engineering problem-solving techniques—and almost driven himself crazy. He had finally simply decided to wait for some insight to emerge. One evening he was sitting at the edge of a pond watching swallows swooping in to catch bugs on the surface of the still pond, creating ripples in the surface as they fed. He suddenly realized that he was creating a ripple in the surface of the great 'pond' of reality—and that his purpose was to understand what he was creating and try to change his own ripples so they'd help other people create their own ripples. His life had meaning in so far as his ripples made the 'pond' a better place for everyone to have meaningful life.

The meaning of Frank's story was clear. All I could do was stop wrestling with this problem in my usual way and let some insight emerge. As in his manuscript, God (if he existed or cared about me) would send messengers and helpers to trigger insights and help me find the path past my current roadblock.

I must have had a very strange expression on my face as I sat there thinking about these things because an older woman sitting near me came up to me. "Are you alright dear?" she asked.

Pulled out of my thoughts, I answered, "Oh, I'm…fine. Thank you."

She looked to be about sixty years old, like someone's grandmother. She was wearing slacks, a rough sweater and what looked like hiking boots.

"I couldn't help noticing you dear, sitting here all by yourself, reading *Siddhartha*. I read that book long ago. It helped me find my way." She stopped and looked at me very directly.

Okay God I thought. That was quick. She's a messenger.

She continued. "Are you here by yourself?"

"Yes, I am. I came to see Winifred's Well. I went there yesterday."

"I've been there too. A little disappointing don't you think?"

"That was exactly my reaction too." I stuck out my hand. "I'm Elena Gaunt."

"Penelope Jones. People call me Penny."

She seemed to be sizing me up for a moment, then asked, "I'm hiking to Basingwerk Abbey tomorrow, if this storm passes. Would you like to come with me? The walk won't be too hard, and you'd get to see some of the most beautiful scenery in this part of Wales. Saint Winifred used to roam this same area."

I immediately thought of Frank's story, of Jacob Newman encountering the angel, hiking up into the hills, meeting John Waters and then being led to the cave where he had all those incredible experiences. Whether Penny was an angel or not, I couldn't refuse such a potentially important hike.

"I'd love to. But I need some walking shoes. Would you help me pick them out?"

We went to a small shoe store in the shopping district of Holywell and bought a pair of hiking boots and thick socks. I was ready to see what Penny had to show me, or so I thought.

Chapter 7

The next morning it was still drizzling so we decided to shorten our hike by driving to Saint Winifred's Well and using the park trail to the Abbey. I drove my Mini and Penny was impressed.

"I have an old Land Rover, a big clunky beast. I love your little car."

"I can't claim any credit; it's a rental and the price was right. I drove it up from London. It handled very well on the road until I had a flat, which pissed me off. You'd think the car hire agencies would check out their cars before renting them. They did send a service vehicle right away though." I thought of the young constable, who I thought was another messenger. I decided to probe into Penny's background to see why she might have been 'sent' to me.

"What brings you to Wales Penny?" I glanced over at her as I was driving. She was turned slightly in her seat looking at me.

"Oh, I love Wales and come here every chance I get. I hadn't seen Holywell or the Abbey before. It isn't much of a trip from where I teach, at The University of Warwick. I'm a Professor of Philosophical Anthropology in the Global History and Cultural Centre. Have you heard of that?"

I thought, you've got to be kidding. I not only hadn't heard of Warwick university but I had no idea what she did. I responded, weakly, "No but I have spent most of my time in the Far East. The last ten years I worked as a Marketing Director in Hong Kong."

"Oh how interesting! My main focus has been on Western civilization. You'll have to tell me all about China."

"If you want to know about the consumer habits of Chinese and other Asians, I can tell plenty about that, but I don't know much about history or culture."

Just then we pulled up to Saint Winfred's Well and we stopped chatting as I parked the car.

She asked me if I wanted to go see Winifred's Well again. "No," I said. "Let's get going on our hike."

"How far is it to the Abbey?" I asked.

"Oh, not very far. Only about a mile or so. Of course, we'll have to walk back to the car as well, after touring the Abbey."

We set off down the tree-lined path. She set a good pace, but I had no difficulty keeping up. The drizzle had slacked off, but the day was overcast. Wales on an overcast day seemed dark and slightly sinister.

After a little bit, she asked me a messenger-like question.

"Why did you come to Saint Winifred's Well Elena? What did you expect to find here? Seems like an unusual place for a woman like you to visit."

How could I summarize my motives for her? I didn't want to tell her about Saint Winifred's statue and her mysterious smile. In fact, why had I come here?

"I was in London, on kind of a sentimental journey. A dear friend of mine had died there a few years ago and I wanted to see some of his friends. One of them was a priest and there was a statue of Saint Winifred in his church. One thing led to another and I decided on impulse to come see where Saint Winifred had lived."

She stopped for a moment and looked at me.

"Have you found what you were looking for?"

What a blunt question! I hardly knew the woman. My feathers got a bit ruffled and I guess my face showed it because she quickly said, "Elena, you looked so forlorn yesterday afternoon when we first met, I guess I have overstepped my bounds trying to help. Sorry."

Her honesty reminded me of Evan, the first visitor Jacob had met before he found the gate. I knew why Frank unburdened himself to Evan even though he hardly knew the man. He needed help in finding his way.

"It's okay. I'd like to tell you what's going on, if you don't mind a convoluted story."

She pointed at a picnic area near the path, so we went over a sat down, on either side of the concrete table.

"Fire away Elena."

So I told her about Frank and our relationship, losing my job, being homeless and then encountering Father Mac and Frank's book. I tried to hit a few highlights from his book, including how messengers influenced his journey. I finished by telling her about my trip here, the messengers I thought I had encountered, and *Siddhartha*. She listened to all this, which took about fifteen minutes, without interrupting.

She looked directly at me.

"Do you think I'm one of Frank's so-called messengers Elena?"

I stumbled over an answer. "Well, I don't…I mean, it had crossed my mind."

Penny grinned broadly. "Why don't we pretend that I am. What kind of message would you like to hear?"

"It doesn't work that way Penny. The message comes as a surprise and leads me to a new part of my journey."

"So, you believe you are on a journey, but you don't know where you're going or why?"

I thought about it for several moments. Jacob (Frank) had recognized he had to make a journey when…what? Maybe he finally accepted it when he went home and his wife rejected him, and his office seemed strange. That led to meeting Jack Waters and hiking to that strange cave where he had all those visions. How did that relate to me?

I finally answered her. "I guess I am on a journey of discovery but you're right, I don't know what I'm looking for or where I'm going. In Hong Kong I wanted to go to London to find Frank's manuscript and I accomplished that. Then, after I read it, I felt I had to visit Winfred's Well, almost on impulse but that hasn't worked out. Now I'm here with you, walking toward some ruined Abbey that I never heard of. It all seems rather aimless doesn't it?"

"No, it doesn't sound purposeless at all Elena. It reminds me of something I read once. *The Hero with a Thousand Faces,* by Joseph Campbell I believe. Yes, that's it. Every human being in Campbell's view has a main myth they follow in their life. It's not done consciously. He believed that there are deeply implanted archetypes in all of us, which shape our individual myths. One of these is the hero's journey. Listening to you I thought that might be what you are experiencing: the emergence of your main myth of a journey into your future life. Would you like to hear more?"

We weren't going to see the Abbey any time soon I thought.

"Yes, I'd like to." She began, looking up above my head as if recalling what she could about Campbell's work. Then she took out her iPhone and began entering some information. "I'm googling the hero's journey."

She scrolled down several times then read from the screen. "Campbell describes a number of stages or steps along this journey. The hero starts in the ordinary world and receives a call to enter an unusual world of strange powers and events (a *call to adventure*). If the hero accepts the call to enter this strange world, the hero must face tasks and trials (a *road of trials*), and may have to face these trials alone, or may have assistance. At its most intense, the hero must survive a severe challenge, often with help earned along the journey. If the hero survives, the hero may achieve a great gift (the *goal* or *blessing*), which often results in the discovery of important self-knowledge. The hero must then decide whether to return with this blessing (the *return to the ordinary world*), often facing challenges on the return journey. If the hero is successful in returning, the blessing or gift may be used to improve the world (the *application of the blessing*)."[21]

She looked at me, waiting for me to react.

"Why does Campbell call the person on this journey a hero?"

"Oh, the term hero comes from classical literature. Each culture has important stories that exemplify their ideas about what life is about, the struggle and its meaning. The main characters in these stories are called heroes (or heroines). For example, the Greeks had Achilles and Ulysses and the Jews had Moses. But all cultures have such myths and Campbell analyzed them and saw the deep similarities, which he called archetypes or monomyths. That's what he based *The Hero with a Thousand Faces* on."

"How do you think all this relates to me?"

"Well, Campbell and others believe that every individual has the structure of the hero's journey embedded in their unconscious, or perhaps other archetypical myths. It sounded to me like you might be starting to realize that you are in a mysterious place. I thought that might be the beginning of your heroine's journey. You won't know, of course, until you get further down the track."

I suddenly realized that Frank had taken his own hero's journey and written about it. And that's why he hadn't discussed his manuscript with me. He knew I needed to begin my own journey in my own way, at the right time. If he explained everything to me up front, there was a great risk that not only wouldn't I understand but worse, not actually begin my journey. He was afraid he would be providing a comfortable place for me to stay in the status quo, a powerful excuse for me to avoid my own journey.

It certainly seemed that Penny was a messenger. She had led me to the entrance of the cave Frank had described, where everything would be unfamiliar. Like Frank, I would face tasks and challenges before I received the promised blessing. I was excited by the prospect. It was the first time I had felt so energized in many, many years.

I looked at her, trying to discern whether she had some deeper purpose, in approaching me back at the hotel and inviting me to hike up to the Abbey. She must have seen the question in my expression because she shook her head. "I don't have anything up my sleeve Elena. It just happened that we met and that your situation triggered a memory in me, about the hero's journey. Why don't we continue walking toward the Abbey?"

I nodded and we returned to the path. But my mind was still working.

"Penny, do you think there's any validity to this myth stuff? Why should I believe that I'm on a mythical journey?"

"Now you're getting into my field of study Elena, Philosophical Anthropology. I study the origins of insights into the deepest questions that have puzzled human beings since the beginning of recorded history, and almost certainly before that too. The simple answer to your question is that the quest for answers to these questions has always existed—and that myths represent each culture's way of telling stories about their answers. The myths are considered valid because they not only exist, they endure. And, as Campbell saw, all these myths have much in common across all human cultures. They seem to be woven into us as humans."

I thought about what she had just explained. There is an unknown, even mysterious part of me that understands the hero's journey and wants to follow it. Suddenly In-Elena said, "Your dream about being on a stage, and not knowing what you were supposed to do. And the stranger in the audience watching you. What does that mean now?"

We walked across a little bridge over a stream.

I answered In-Elena in my mind. "I think I had this dream originally so I could meet you. But then I had it again after I read Frank's book. The empty stage represents my life going forward. I don't have any real idea of what I want to do. The strange presence in the balcony, looking down on me on the stage and In-Elena in the seats is probably Frank waiting to see if I finally understand that my way forward involves the hero's journey. He didn't want to suggest it or force it on me. I have to decide to go on my own. That all fits."

Penny kept walking, waiting for me to respond to her original question.

I knew what the obvious answer was, but I kept walking silently. I felt like I was being manipulated somehow, into committing to a journey that I hadn't chosen, that was imprinted in my unconscious. That's not how I ran my life. I made rational choices and didn't act on whims or impulses. But In-Elena wouldn't let me get away with that. "You followed your intuition to come to Winifred's Well didn't you?" She was right. But I still couldn't commit.

Penny must have known what was going on in my mind because she said. "Don't break your head over this Elena. Let's just enjoy our walk. The drizzle has let up and the Abbey is just ahead."

519

Chapter 8

The Abbey was in ruins. Penny told me its history as we walked around. It had been built in the 1100s and then, in the reign of Henry the eighth, it was confiscated from the monks and its lands sold. It gradually went into decay with no monks to maintain it.

The grounds were quite peaceful, a collage of well-mown grass and gray stone walls and other remnants of the old Abbey. I thought about the hopes and dreams that had inspired men to build it. For that time, the construction was quite elaborate. I imagined they thought it would last forever, as a monument to their God. Then the world, as it usually does, destroyed their dreams. I wondered where that bleak thought had come from. Probably, some residual anger over my life having been disrupted by being fired. But my dreams hadn't been destroyed; I'm not sure I ever had any. That's another insight I thought. I stumbled over a low ruin of a wall.

"Watch your step Elena. Be careful" Penny said.

I turned and looked at her. She had that crooked grin on her face again.

I felt like Jacob arriving at the cave. Jack Waters could only take him so far and had warned him that things might be hard if he entered. Penny knew I was still wrestling with whether I wanted to commit to the hero's journey. She had taken me as far as she could. We could spend some pleasant hours at the Abbey and hiking back but she wouldn't and couldn't make my choice for me, or even make it any easier to decide.

I wanted to get back to the hotel and spend some time thinking but I didn't want to be rude, so I focused on the Abbey and chatted about everything except the hero's journey. When we got back to the hotel it was about 4 pm, so I told her I was tired and wanted to take a nap.

I paged through Frank's manuscript to remind myself about what happened after he entered the cave. He had visions then exited the cave and met Francis in the desert. He walked awhile with him until they met Francis's three friends and then they all went to the river where Francis crossed over. After that Jacob (Frank) wandered around until he finally understood his life's work. Then he tried to cross the river of death and Rachel rescued him. I still felt a twinge of jealousy when I read that.

Did I want to commit myself to such an intense adventure? It seemed to involve finding a different path for my life, and not returning to the one I knew now. Siddhartha had experienced the same choice and it radically affected his entire life. And there was a spiritual dimension in both Frank's and Siddhartha's story that I had avoided my whole life. I wished I could talk to Frank—but I knew he would not push me one way or the other. This had to be one hundred percent my choice. I remembered that a hero's journey had difficult tasks and challenges associated with it. This choice was certainly one of my challenges!

In-Elena said, "Don't overthink this Elena. Just do it. Take a first step." That was a good idea. I recalled an old Chinese saying: A journey of a thousand miles begins with one step. I laughed. What would a baby step be?

Why not go back to Winifred's Well? That was why I came here in the first place. I called Penny on the house phone to see if she wanted to go but couldn't reach her. So, I decided to go alone in the morning.

Chapter 9

It was raining again the next morning, so I took my time eating another large breakfast. Penny wasn't in the breakfast room. I thought about my expectations from a second visit to Winifred's Well as I ate.

What I wanted was some kind of signal—that God existed or at least what I should do next. Frank's book was about his search for God. He finally accepted that God wasn't present like any other thing in our experience, even in our imagination. In-Elena couldn't help me see God. She (and all the messengers I met) could encourage me to keep seeking, but they had no words or ideas that would paint a picture in my mind about God. And, anyway, that wasn't what I wanted. I didn't actually know what I wanted.

Finally, I admitted that I was lost. The only possible answer was that God (if he even existed) had to reveal himself to me in some manner. That was what I was hoping would happen when I visited Winifred's Well again.

The weather cleared a little, so I left the hotel and drove back to the shrine. I thought about all the people who had experienced miracles—and Henry the Fifth, who believed God would help him triumph over the French. They all had something I didn't—the ability to pray to a God they believed in. I just had my hope that God existed and would help me find my path. I wasn't a hero like Penny described. I was a woman who was lost.

I bought another fifty pence ticket and walked back to the shrine. I saw Winifred standing in the dim light and stood for a while looking at the detail of her statue. I felt an urge to kneel in front of her. I also felt resistance; I had never knelt down in a religious sense. In-Elena or some other voice said I was being silly; go ahead and kneel! I looked around to see who might be watching but the shrine was empty. I bent down and as my knees hit the kneeler, I felt a rush of emotions: embarrassment, a bit of anger that I had to do this, and relief that I was able. Now I was much closer to Winifred's statue and I studied it. The colors were dim; the statue must be very old. I looked up at her face. The artist had captured her mysterious smile, which I first saw at the Farm Street Church. I thought, why is she smiling? At my silliness? A non-believer kneeling in front of her? I imagined I heard her say 'I smile because I'm happy.' I asked another silent question. Why had I wanted to visit you here in Holywell? She replied, 'because you are lost and unhappy.' A lot of other questions swirled through my mind, but I didn't think Winifred could answer them. I did ask one final question of her that day. How can I believe in God as strongly as you do? I waited for an answer, and all she revealed was her mysterious smile. I suddenly realized that I was experiencing the same frustration that Frank had described in his book when he was searching for God. Suddenly I recognized that I was asking a serious question about God, which I had never done before. That's why Winifred had led me here!

I knew I needed to talk with Father Mac. I checked out and drove to London. When I got back, I called and invited him to dinner, my shout.

I picked him up at the rectory and we strolled over to his favorite restaurant. I summarized my trip, the messengers and Winifred's words to me. I didn't tell him my question about God because I was afraid that he'd jump at the occasion to convert me. I should have known by then that that wasn't his approach. Frank must have learned his indirect questioning approach from Father Mac.

After we were seated and had ordered, I asked him if he would tell me more about his relationship with Frank.

"Elena, let me try to help, by giving you some background. I first met Frank in the mid-1980s when he moved to London. He was living apart from his wife and children and was quite upset, so he came to see me, hoping, I think, for some emotional support. We talked a bit but I'm not sure it helped. He came to Mass but didn't receive Communion. I suppose he felt guilty for leaving his wife; he never said. After a while he went to confession but, of course, I can't tell you about that. Anyway, he started receiving Communion again.

"We began going to dinner regularly after that. He had started writing his book and tried out various ideas on me. He was wrestling with a number of issues, and finally decided to tell a prophetic story of his life—from the present forward to his death—laying out what he imagined would happen in his future, and God's influence. I'd call him a prophetic mystic—two complicated terms that simply mean he had a deep desire to encounter God and a powerful vision of how that would affect his life and death. I think, in terms of his book, he had already experienced the chasm, and his first encounter with entering God's presence.

"If I can try to summarize, Frank was wrestling with three questions in writing his manuscript: *What* God is, what God was asking of *him*, and the *meaning* of his own life and death. To him, God was mysterious, always just out of reach yet a powerful force in everyone's life. He imagined God had a particular purpose in mind for each person, and an appropriate way to fulfill that purpose on the way to death. Frank wouldn't accept easy answers to these questions; that's why his story is so interesting. He imagined what would happen as he searched for these answers, and then, I think, began to live out what he had imagined."

Father Mac paused. I must have sent some signal that I was getting overwhelmed. Too much information. I couldn't take it all in.

"Father, I met Frank in 1988. Do you think he had finished his manuscript by then?"

"Oh no. He first gave it to me to read in the mid-1990s. I think he was only sketching parts of it in the 1980s. He would have been keeping notebooks of ideas I think but I never saw them. I know he read *Siddhartha* back then. I can't recall any specific issues we discussed but maybe they'll come back to me."

So Frank was writing his book while we were having out conversations. I couldn't see where I had had any effect on the manuscript. That made me sad, but it was Frank's way, to thrash things out for himself and not ask for help.

"Father I can see the main questions you outlined in his manuscript. The encounter in the cave was wrestling with what God is, where God is. His encounter with Francis was probably him wrestling with what God was asking of him, in comparison with Francis. And, at the end, he discovered his purpose: healing wounded institutions, even individual people. He never resolved his broken marriage—yet he had a profound hope that it would work out in the end."

He smiled at me. "Very good Elena. Perhaps now you know why Frank never revealed his spiritual journey to you."

I sat there not saying anything, waiting for some idea to emerge. And, slowly, it did come to me that Frank respected me too much to tell me about his broken marriage, which was at the heart of his story. Perhaps he was afraid of what that would lead to, to a level of intimacy that he wasn't prepared to participate in. He wanted to be a friend and nothing more. And he knew my attitude toward God-talk, so he honored my choices there too.

After a while, I asked "What do you think I can learn from Frank's journey Father?"

He took a sip of wine and smiled at me. "What do you think Frank wants you to learn?"

I think I scowled at him. More questions; never direct answers. In-Elena said, "It's the best way for you to learn Elena." I answered her "But I don't have to like it!"

Father Mac just waited.

"He seemed to act in response to each situation he encountered. He seemed to trust that he was being led to discover the answers, not trying to always figure things out for himself. That would have been hard for him, I think. He was a natural problem-solver. So, I need to relax and go with the flow so to speak. Trust that I'm being led somehow, even if I can't see it. Put Winifred's smile on my face and appreciate the journey. To let God find me so to speak."

"Sounds good to me Elena," he said.

"So, you think God is leading me where I need to go?"

"Yes, I do. And you're getting pretty good at recognizing his signals. Like identifying messengers. They were not angels, just people who crossed your path with something you needed. But you were alert and saw that there was something significant in your conversation with each of them."

That reminded me of the Green Knight for some reason.

"I didn't tell you that I had gone to a pub on the way to Winifred's Well called The Green Knight. The pub owner gave me a sheet about the myth of the Green Knight. I didn't really get any message from that. Do you have any ideas of what the message might be?"

"Maybe just the fact that it's a myth. That you don't have any myths in your life. Myths contain deep meaning in the cultures that create them. The power of the Green Knight myth in its time would have sent very strong messages to people. It doesn't anymore because our culture doesn't place any significance in myths in general. Rollo May, a famous psychologist said in his book *The Cry for Myth* that many of man's current issues and unhappiness comes from the lack of myth. Perhaps your encounter with the Green Knight is saying to you that you need to find a myth that gives meaning to your life."

He stopped and looked at me. His face communicated that this was not just a casual answer; it was a very important point.

"Father, did you give me *Siddhartha* because you thought it was a myth that might help me?"

"Very good Elena. Yes, there is something in *Siddhartha* that has a mythic meaning that helped Frank, and I think it might help you. Obviously, I'm not trying to convert you to becoming a Buddhist. Neither am I trying to persuade you to become a Christian though I think that would be a good life choice for you. There's something that you need to find on your journey before you start any specific religious search. Reflect on what Siddhartha encountered in his journey and then you may see the mythic dimensions of your journey more clearly."

Without directly talking about God, somehow, I knew we had. In Father Mac's opinion, God was leading me down this path and would find me. He wasn't engaging in God-talk with me because he knew it wasn't intelligible to me, where I was at the moment.

We finished dinner and walked back to the rectory. Father said "Good luck Elena. Stay in touch. I'll pray for you. Come see me anytime if you need me."

Chapter 10

I moved from my hotel to a serviced one-bedroom apartment near Harrods, on upper Sloane Street. I had a three-month lease, which was as far ahead as I could see right now. Over the next two weeks I did London: Museums, landmarks, theater. After that I settled into a daily routine: sleep late, walk down to Chelsea and browse, have lunch, walk some more, have tea, go home and take a nap, go to dinner, watch telly and go to bed early. Boring. Little stimulation. Plenty of time to think and wait for God to find me.

I reread *Siddhartha*, looking for what Father Mac had referred to as its mythic meaning. What was below the surface of the mere facts of the story? Siddhartha gradually withdrew from the world. At the end his friend Govinda asked him to reveal something that would help him along his journey. That's like me I thought. I want someone—Father Mac, Frank, Winifred, even God—to reveal something useful to me on my journey. Govinda had experienced a vision, of everything cycling and recycling, and had felt great love, great joy at the vision that Siddhartha enabled. Suddenly I recognized that my emptiness yearned for this experience of love and joy. I had looked into Winifred's face and seen her smile of peace and joy. That's what I wanted!

The myth of Siddhartha concerned his journey to find deep love and joy. I was on that journey too. Not a hero's journey but an ordinary person walking a confused path, lost without a goal in mind, but with a yearning that had only begun to emerge in the last month or so. Like Frank in his story, sitting on the edge of the river after watching Francis cross and his two friends disappear in the water, I could only sit and wait for some sign to go on, some new direction to take. That was a new experience for me, an action-oriented person.

Somehow, I knew simply analyzing all the hints I had been given wouldn't work. Govinda's vision just emerged, after he gazed at Siddhartha's face. What was I to gaze at? I walked over to Farm Street Church and sat near Winifred's statue in the quiet emptiness. I tried to empty my own mind of thoughts to match to silence of the church. I wanted to do this so badly that it made things worse. My self-criticism destroyed my silence. Then, I seemed to get an inspiration that said, "Don't struggle. Don't worry so much. All will be okay. Just wait."

That afternoon I sat quietly in my flat for about a half hour then left. The next few afternoons I did the same. I kept criticizing myself, "Stupid Elena, you can't even sit quietly and wait." But then I heard, "Don't worry Elena." And I knew somehow that message wasn't from In-Elena but somewhere else. I hadn't made it up, even in my inner self.

I went to dinner with Father Mac and told him what was going on. He encouraged me to continue sitting in silence and waiting. There were no special things I had to do; it would be done for me.

My days continued in much the same routine as before, but I noticed I was becoming more aware of my surroundings. There were small fenced parks in Belgravia on one side of Sloane Street. Some were locked, for residents only but a few were open. I began sitting in them and noticing the peaceful flow of life—birds waiting and feeding, squirrels darting and digging, older people sitting and dozing. Sometimes I sat and dozed myself. Why not; there was nothing driving me to action anymore. I noticed I was feeling more peaceful, a new experience for hard-driving Elena.

One day while walking on the high street in Chelsea I walked into a bookstore to browse. I wondered if Neil's book was available and went to the inquiry desk. All I could remember was his first name and the book's title *Dangerous Undertaking*. The customer service person looked up the title and there were only two listings, one by a Neil A. Schmidt. That must be it. I ordered a copy and left my contact details.

I decided to try to contact Neil, to say hello. I wasn't sure I had the right email so I googled his name and found an entry for general manager, Apex Electronics in Reston Virginia. That surely must be him. It had a contact, so I sent him an email.

> Hi Neil!
> We met in Hong Kong while you were writing your book. I have just ordered a copy.
> I'm in London for the next few months. I'd love to chat. Send me your contact phone number and I'll give you a call – if you'd like to catch up.
> Regards
> Elena

I heard back in two hours.

> Elena
> I am the right Neil Schmidt and I'd love to chat,
> My mobile phone number is +15715551111 in Reston Virginia.
> Please call me in the late afternoon, which should make it evening your time. My secretary will interrupt me to take the call if possible (I usually forward my phone to her during working hours.)
> I'm delighted you got in touch.
> Warm regards
> Neil

I waited a couple of days and called Neil on a Saturday morning his time. I didn't want to interrupt him at work. I got his voice mail and left a message and my phone number. He called me about three hours later.

"This is Elena Gaunt."

"Hi Elena. This is Neil Schmidt. Good to hear your voice again. I was playing golf when you called. How have you been?"

"Doing fine Neil. I'm in London for an extended holiday. I was laid off from my job in Hong Kong and am taking time to consider my options." I wanted to tell him about Frank's manuscript but felt I should lay some groundwork first.

"That's too bad. Do you miss Hong Kong?"

I thought, not at all but didn't want to sound like a homeless waif so I said, "Hong Kong is great and, for the right job I might go back there. But right now, I'm enjoying myself in London. I have taken a serviced apartment on Sloane Street for three months, not too far from where Frank lived in Belgravia." I mentioned Frank to break the ice on where I really wanted this conversation to go. He bit.

"Good old Frank. I really miss him. You said you bought my book. It's my story but in a way it's Frank's story too. How he affected me, and you too for that matter. I'll be anxious to hear your thoughts on how I handled your story after you read my book. I stayed with what Frank told me and didn't speculate. You may have different memories." He paused, then went on.

"Look, I'm going to be in London three weeks from now on business. Maybe we could catch up and have dinner. What do you think?"

"Neil I'd love that. By that time, I should have read *Dangerous Undertaking* and we can discuss that. But there's something else I need to tell you. Frank left me a manuscript that he never got a chance to publish. It's his own story. I won't tell you anything about it. I think it would be great if we could also share our ideas about his book when we have dinner. Should I send you a copy of his manuscript?"

"That's fantastic. I mean having dinner and discussing Frank's story."

"Okay then. Text me the address to mail you the manuscript and I'll send it Monday morning by express post. You ought to have it the same week. Let me know which hotel you're staying at, and I'll pick a restaurant nearby."

He sounded enthusiastic. He added an idea, which gave me something else to think about. "Elena, we need a marketing person to cover Asia for us. Wouldn't have to be based in Hong Kong. Would you be willing to chat about that? No worries if you're not interested. Just thought I'd ask."

Why not I thought? Can't hurt to have a chat. "I'd like that Neil. I'll enclose a copy of my resume in the package with Frank's manuscript."

"Great. By the way my wife Connie is coming with me for a holiday. Maybe you could tell her some good places to visit."

"I'd love to meet Connie. And I'd be happy to show her London if she wants company."

"Sounds good."

"I've got to run Neil. I have a theater ticket for tonight. I'll text you my apartment's address. Talk to you soon. Bye."

The next day I took Frank's manuscript to be copied, after whiting out my comments in the margins. The store also offered a mailing service, so I paid for express post. They said it would be in Neil's hands the same week.

Two days later, the bookstore sent me a text that Neil's book had arrived. I walked down to Chelsea and picked it up. I liked the cover—a mystical road leading into bright light—and the title: *Dangerous Undertaking; The Search for Transformation*. I couldn't wait to start reading it.

Let me summarize my thoughts about *Dangerous Undertaking*. On the whole, it was about Neil's hero journey guided by Frank. Neil was accurate in reporting what happened between Frank and me. He got a few things wrong, or maybe it was Frank that was wrong about what he told Neil about me. I'd set Neil straight on those when I saw him. I learned a lot about Neil's journey. He had some experiences like mine. I'd be interested in hearing more about his views on what he meant by transformation. And Frank? Neil brought him back to life. I had a lump in my throat quite a few times when Neil discussed their conversations. He wrote that Frank said he loved me, with a "courtly love." That was bitter-sweet; I thought Frank was keeping his distance from me. Still, I relived my encounters with him and realized how much I missed him. I wanted to reminisce with Neil about Frank, and yet I was reluctant to do that. It might hurt too much.

For the next few weeks, I mainly lolled around the apartment and waited for Neil and Connie to arrive. I reread sections of *Dangerous Undertaking* and made a few notes to discuss with Neil. I also thought about going back to work, as well as returning to Asia. I was interested in what Neil might offer me. I'd rather not return to Hong Kong and wasn't sure where to suggest putting Neil's Asian headquarters. Tokyo? Shanghai? Maybe Singapore, but too tropical for me. Sydney? That might be nice, but I'd have to deal with my parents again.

Neil called me from the Westbury Hotel in Mayfair the next Tuesday about noon. He said he and Connie were worn out from their flight and suggested we go to dinner Wednesday evening, in the Westbury's restaurant. His treat. I said that would be fine, and that I'd treat the next time.

It was a nice evening, so I walked over to the Westbury, just over a mile. I detoured a little and went past Farm Street Church. I wasn't sure why. I hadn't seen Father Mac in a few weeks. He must have been on my subconscious mind. In-Elena said I was right, and I'd should call him after tonight's dinner.

I called Neil on the in-house phone and he and Connie got off the elevator a few minutes later. Connie was a very attractive young woman—significantly younger than Neil and dressed rather casually for the Westbury's restaurant. (meow). Neil had on a dark suit and looked exactly the same as he had in Hong Kong.

"Connie, this is Elena. She and I are both close friends of Frank O'Connor. Nice to see you again Elena." He stuck out his hand and I shook it. Connie smiled at me and said,

"So nice to meet you Elena." I held out my hand to her, but she gave me a hug. In-Elena liked that; I was more sedate and still, suddenly I liked Connie. Neil suggested we go in the restaurant and have drinks at our table.

We were seated in a secluded corner booth, which Neil must have arranged. We ordered drinks—Connie a glass of white wine, Neil a draft beer, and I ordered a Bombay Sapphire gin and tonic in a tall glass. What can one tell from what people drink? In-Elena said relax!

I asked, "How was your flight?" Connie answered, "I never sleep on airplanes, so it was a bit long for me. Neil conked out immediately. He travels so much; he must be used to flying." I replied, "You have to be able to sleep on planes when you travel a lot. I went from Hong Kong to London quite often when I worked there—all in all a fourteen-hour trip—and I had to work when I arrived. So, I had to sleep on the plane." Neil didn't join in our opening gambit about travel.

Connie and I continued to chat, about London, what to buy, and had she been here before? She had, once, and was looking forward to being on her own while Neil had his business meetings. I said I'd be happy to help her and maybe we could do coffee tomorrow. She readily accepted so my promise to Neil was taken care of.

Neil said, "You and I also need to have a coffee and chat about Apex in Asia Elena. I'm tied up tomorrow, but could we have coffee on Friday?" I said yes and that took care of point number two on my agenda. There were only two other points, but they would take more time—Neil's book, and Frank's manuscript. I figured Neil would be interested in my reaction to his book, so I broke the ice.

"I really enjoyed your book Neil." Neil's eyes lit up and Connie smiled at me.

He said "Really? What did you like particularly?"

I thought, I should have written a review and given it to him.

"For one thing, I liked your title. *Dangerous Undertaking.* How did you think of that?"

"Oh, I didn't come up with that. One of my friends read the manuscript and suggested it. She thought it summarized my struggle to change. I did come up with the subtitle, *The Search for Transformation.* What do you think of that?"

"It was provocative. Made me want to know more. What do you mean by transformation?"

He took a sip of beer. "To me it means something new, unthought of, a higher plane of living. I was cruising along with 'Perform, Achieve, Succeed' as my roadmap. I had no idea that there was something beyond that, love for instance. Frank helped me begin to search for that." He smiled at Connie and squeezed her hand. "Transformation is living life on a different level. That's what Frank's manuscript is about too."

Suddenly, Neil had merged the two agenda items together, using transformation. I was thrown off balance and

542

my mind was swirling with fragments of ideas. I need to get control of the conversation.

"Neil, I want to talk about Frank's story, but can we stay with yours for a while? Like Winnie the Pooh, I'm a 'bear with a small brain'."

Connie put in her two cents worth. "Neil always does that. He makes things complex. Tell Elena why you picked transformation and not happiness or love to search for." She smiled at him to soften her criticism.

"Sorry Elena. Why transformation? It just seemed broader and deeper to me. We are used to being ourselves and then, one day, we experience something that shows us we could be so much more. Capable of much more love, able to be happier, and able to use our talents more wisely. The old example of the butterfly's transformation from a larva seemed to sum up the human journey for me. We can't fly, never dream of flying as our normal everyday selves, then one day we get a glimpse of what we might be destined to become, and that we will fly someday. That's kind of the thought process that inspired me."

I thought Wow! Neil's much farther along his journey than I am. In-Elena said stop competing.

Connie asked, "Neil should we order?" I was disappointed; I wanted to continue to try to find out when Neil realized he was on a transformational journey. I also thought of Frank's story and wondered when he had begun to consciously envision his future. After Neil signaled, the waiter appeared with the menus and announced today's specials. We ordered and after that the sommelier appeared with the wine list and after much discussion, Neil ordered an expensive Australian Shiraz, in honor of me I suppose.

While we waited for our first course, I asked Neil about his journey.

"Neil, in your book, it's not clear when you first became conscious that you were searching for transformation. Obviously, it happened after you met Frank. But do you remember exactly when you began to see life as a journey of transformation?"

He paused. I could almost see his mind flipping through the pages of his book—or was it his memories of Frank?

"It's hard to say. I know that I didn't see it that way before I met Frank. And initially, when Frank was asking me his provocative questions, I was focused on finding answers. I didn't have a larger perspective, even though Frank told me that was his goal with me: to help me find a different perspective on life. I began to sense something was expected of me by the way he kept exposing me to different stories, like Parsifal (who wouldn't ask questions), and Frank's experiences of discovering the Yes-World. But my mind couldn't find the key to applying what he was telling me to my own life. Even In-Neil could only encourage me to keep reflecting. Of course, Diane was also working on my concept of myself as a leader."

Connie broke in. "Elena, Diane is one of Neil's managers who has a unique style. She doesn't accept that he is some high and mighty poohbah and tells him exactly what she thinks. I like her a lot."

Neil added, "Yes, Diane is someone I trust to always tell me the truth. And come to think of it, I think she may have been the trigger for me to finally see that I was on a journey to some mysterious future, not only business success. After Frank died, I thought a lot about all his ideas and began to try to apply them to myself. On a business trip to Australia, Frank had met a homeless man who recited a poem he had written. I remember it perfectly because it seems to apply to me too.

> *God, you must have heard me,*
> *Shouting over the years,*
> *Yet you never answered,*
> *And gave me the gift of waiting."*

Neil paused, and I thought I saw a glimmer of tears in his eyes.

"I told Diane about this poem and she lent me a book, *The Upanishads*. That triggered a new phase of my life. I saw, for the first time, that there was a mystery connected to life, which was important to me. I didn't yet think of it as transformation— that insight came while I was writing my book. Looking back, it seems that I just had to be ready to see this other dimension. Frank knew that and kept telling me stories to pull me closer to seeing. He was always patient with me."

The three of us sat quietly. Neil's revelations seemed to stop conversation somehow, as if our minds needed to respect what he said and needed time to honor his experience.

Finally, I asked, "What has happened since Neil?"

"Oh, life still seems to be carrying me along. I haven't connected with Frank's Yes-World yet but I'm still hopeful. My job has many challenges that keep me busy. In-Neil sends me signals that I'm not paying much attention to. In fact, this dinner is the first time I have seriously focused on my journey since I wrote my book. That makes me feel a bit ashamed and sad. The journey seemed so important then. I'm not sure why I haven't progressed. Probably because I don't know any different steps that would fit with my life, and my life seems to be on the right track on the whole."

Connie said, "I second what Neil is saying. He is awfully busy. We don't have enough time as a couple either. Not complaining but success creates demands."

The dinner came and we began to eat. Our conversation wandered off the topic and I began to tell them about London. After a while I also shared how I ended up in London, and how I found Frank's manuscript. I didn't share Father Mac or my encounter with Winifred, I don't know why. Maybe it was because Neil might become my boss and I didn't want to reveal too much before I knew I could trust him.

Over coffee, I continued my assessment of Neil's book. I gave him good marks for capturing Frank's style and making his story flow, keeping my interest. I did tell him he got me basically right but missed on one point.

"When you reported Frank's summary of what happened to me after I encountered In-Elena, you said that Frank thought I had changed. He thought I became gentler, sharing my story with anyone who would listen and saw telling my story as my mission in life. That isn't what happened. I suppose that I experienced what you just talked about in your life. Life got busy again and I basically forgot In-Elena. What I remember is Frank himself and how I miss him. Frank must have hoped that he had changed my life—and he certainly would have if he had focused on our relationship—but that couldn't happen, could it? He was faithful to his wife, as his manuscript revealed to me."

I felt I had gone far enough. I was over Frank now. I didn't want Connie and Neil to think I was carrying the torch for him. In-Elena said, 'That's exactly what you're doing Elena.'

Neil said, "Since you have brought Frank's story up, what do you think of how he told it Elena? I have read it and it puzzles me."

"It puzzles me too Neil. I keep trying to translate his strange encounters into what they really meant in his real life. The chasm allegory is easy—he encountered something in his life that forced him to think about where he was going. But then there is the cave, with all those terrible scenes. And the monster that confronts Francis on the way to the river. I found it hard going at times."

Neil added, "I agree. But the overall idea was his search for God and then his search for what God wanted him to do in his life. That was pretty clear."

I nodded. "Yes, I got that. It made me think I was one of his projects, a person to whom he was sent. I don't know how I feel about that."

"Yes, I felt the same way. When he met me on the plane, he seemed to evaluate whether to begin working with me. Was I ready to be one of his projects? Well, speaking for myself, I'm glad I qualified!"

We both smiled when we remembered Frank's way of guiding a conversation—and our learning—using provocative questions.

Neil said, "The end was very touching, when his wife came to help him cross the river. I had the feeling that they never got back together in this life."

That ending had shattered my dream that I had experienced a special relationship with Frank. I couldn't think of anything to say.

Neil must have recognized that he had made a mistake bringing that part up.

"Something else I wondered about. Who was that old man Francis? What do you think Elena?"

"My theory is that Francis wasn't a real person. He represented Frank's internal conversation about what life would be like after he encountered God. The desert represented his life's emptiness now that he had encountered

God. The rest of the book is his mind wrestling with that emptiness. Francis's story of his journey was Frank's imagination about his own journey going forward."

Neil added, "That makes a lot of sense. And he wove in one of Jesus's parables about the Prodigal Son without mentioning Jesus. What do you think his three friends represented?"

"They were three choices of direction he was exploring—study, good works or contemplation. He decided that none of them, by themselves, were the right path for him. He had to leave that in God's hands. He finally saw that the work he was called to was repairing damaged buildings in the desert. I think those building represented people and institutions who had built their life without God."

"That's very confronting, don't you think Elena?" Neil had a frown on his face.

"Well, I'm just trying to interpret what Frank wrote. And it is confronting. But in his interactions with us he was never confrontational about God. At least not with me. In fact, as I remember our conversations we never talked about God. And your book remembers him the same way."

Neil agreed. "I wonder why, if he had that mission from God, he didn't practice it on us?"

"I don't know. I have thought about it but don't have an answer."

We had finished discussing Frank's book and wrapped up the evening, confirming Connie and I would meet the next day, and Neil and I the day following, to discuss Apex. I caught a taxi back to my apartment. I hadn't really learned anything new, other than Neil's journey had stalled. How could such a significant thing in life get set aside, with busyness as an excuse? In-Elena said, 'Watch out that it doesn't happen to you, if you go to work at Apex.'

Chapter 11

I picked up Connie at the Westbury at 10 am, and suggested a game plan to her: Shop on New Bond Street and the galleries near her hotel, then catch a taxi over to Harvey Nicks near me where I'd treat for lunch, then to my flat so she could see it, then the rest of the afternoon kept open. She was happy with that. She bought a few things for herself, and a stylish tie for Neil from Hawkes and Gieves, on Savile Row. I hoped he'd appreciate the elegance. We stopped by her hotel to drop off the packages and freshen up, then caught a taxi to Harvey Nicks, where I'd made a reservation at the plush fifth floor bar. She was suitably impressed.

We started off with a glass of pretty good champagne. I didn't really have an agenda, but I think she did. After a few opening volleys about London and the weather, Connie asked me about Frank.

"You know Elena I'm kind of jealous of you and Neil. You both knew Frank well, and all I know is what Neil wrote in his book. He seemed like an extraordinary man." She paused and looked at me, hoping I'd pick up on her lead.

It would have been rude to just sit in silence and look at her. I actually didn't want to share anything intimate about Frank with anyone, not just her. But I liked her, so I opened up a tiny bit.

"He was very special Connie. I miss him still, though he's been gone for several years. I knew he was special the first time we met in Sydney. He wasn't particularly good looking, but he had a good mind and a way of stimulating conversation that pulled me into new topics I rarely thought about. He wanted to know how people thought, and asked questions to help you reveal yourself. Neil got that aspect of Frank spot on in his book."

Connie nodded. "Neil told stories about Frank leading you into new places in your life, toward transformation. How do you feel about Neil revealing that in his book?"

I wondered if she thought I was upset with Neil. "Neil reviewed what he was going to put in his book with me before it was published. I was okay then, and I am now, generally. Now, as I read his book, I can see the larger context, and it all seems plausible to me, in terms of my memories. I'm generally happy with what he wrote, except the part I told him about at dinner last night. So, if you're at all worried that I'm offended Connie, don't be. I'm very pleased with Neil's rendition of the relationship between Frank and me. Did he ask you to ask me?

"Oh no Elena. I just was checking myself because I could sense last night that this is a sensitive area with you. Sometimes Neil misses signals, and I wanted to check."

"No, it's all good Connie."

She asked another question. "I haven't read Frank's manuscript. Did you enjoy it?"

She was asking me to reveal some more about Frank and myself. I couldn't just give an objective book review to her. She knew my feelings.

"His manuscript surprised me. It is fundamentally about his religious journey. We never talked about God or religion at all. So it shocked me a bit, to find out what had been going on in his life at the same time that I knew him." I paused.

She commented, "But that's pretty common, I think. Even Neil and I don't get into our inner feelings about our religious beliefs. Most people keep that area of their life private."

I nodded. "Probably you're right. But still, Frank and I had some pretty intimate conversations—about my dreams and what they meant for example. I wondered for a long time why he didn't tell me he was writing a book about his own journey. Only recently have I begun to understand why he might have kept it from me. I really don't want to get into that please."

I suppose the way I reacted put a damper on more intimate conversation because we just reverted to idle chitchat. When we finished our meal, I paid. Connie said it was later than she realized and she needed to go back to the hotel and get ready to go out for the evening: dinner and the theater. She and Neil were going to see Agatha Christie's *The Mousetrap*. I had seen it many years before and told her it was great. I walked with her to get a taxi and we hugged before she left. I then went home

The next day I met with Neil. He surprised me by going immediately into the Asian job, describing what he wanted me to do for Apex. He talked as if his mind was already made up. We chatted about how I'd approach things. We never talked about money or title. He said that, within reason, I could locate my office wherever I wanted in Asia. Lastly, he asked me to come to the US as soon as I was able to learn more about Apex and to discuss a contract of employment. I said I'd love to come over and would seriously consider his offer once he made one. We had no more discussions about Frank.

I went home felling exhilarated and a bit overwhelmed at Neil's speed. I called and made an appointment to see Father Mac. He had time the next day, so I arrived at his office at 10 am and went straight to the point. I wanted to get his advice about the inner journey I was on and whether he thought I ought to take a job right now. He was really the only friend I could talk to.

"Father, I am struggling right now, with all the new experiences I have been having. I feel like I've started on a journey like Frank was on, but he started at a different point. He believed in God and was a Christian. I'm not at that point. I'm lost, trying to find my way to even begin Frank's journey."

Father Mac smiled at me sympathetically. "I know it's an uncomfortable place to be, like you've left your familiar surroundings behind and your mind hasn't learned how to interpret the signals it's receiving in this new environment. It's not something you can control. You can't say to yourself, 'I believe' and make your mind instantly work in a new way. Do you get what I'm talking about Elena?"

I was so confused that even his simple words didn't make sense. "Sorry Father, I still don't get what you're saying. Can you give me an example or something that might help?"

"Here's an example. Have you ever tried to break a habit? Say, biting your nails?" He looked at me, waiting for an answer. No, I never bit my nails. I tried to think of a bad habit I have.

"I don't bite my nails, but I do interrupt people when they're talking. That's something I'd like to stop doing. It's seems like I have good intentions, but I can never quite get out of that habit."

"Great example Elena. You know you'd like to behave differently but you can't seem to master your habitual way of acting. You even recognize what going on, but your mind seems to have automatic control and you don't know where your control panel is to change its setting. Are you beginning to see any comparison with your current situation?"

I thought about it. My mind had a set of beliefs about God. I didn't know how to change its settings to become a believer. Did I even want to?

"Yes, that's helping me. I'm feeling confused about two things. How do I reset my mind to become a believer—and do I even want to? I read Frank's manuscript and have had what seems like some similar experiences. What you're saying is I can't really decide to take Frank's journey with my current mindset. I'm getting mixed signals and am questioning what I am doing because I don't believe in God. I don't even know who's asking those questions!"

Father Mac looked delighted and I felt like a good student.

"Elena, you are very quick. I think you are beginning to see why Frank didn't give you his manuscript while he was alive or talk to you about his beliefs or journey. He knew that you had to become ready—and that you had to walk the path toward readiness alone with God. That's what you've been doing. Of course, you think you are alone, but I believe God is walking with you. I've been praying for that."

"I remember Frank's frustration in his manuscript. Why does God hide from us and make things so difficult? I feel that way to, but I don't think that God is hiding from us. I don't think much about God at all."

He smiled again, broadly. "Of course, God doesn't hide from us. The God I believe in is present all the time. Your gut feelings are right on target Elena. All I can say is keep walking and you'll see eventually that God is quite active in your life."

"So, you're not going to quote the Bible and tell me what to believe?"

"No, it would be like describing a symphony to someone who's deaf. First you must get past your deafness then we can listen to the symphony together. Lots of wonderful things I'd love to share with you Elena. Sometime soon I hope."

That seemed to be his last word on the subject. So, I told him about Neil's job offer.

"I might be going back to Asia, Father. Neil has asked me to come over to the US and learn about his company. If I'm interested, I think he might make me Head of Marketing for Asia. I've said I will go to the US, but I haven't agreed to take the job. I wanted to talk to you first. Do you think I ought to hold off getting back into a demanding job while I'm struggling with this other journey I'm on?"

He smiled again. "What are your feelings telling you Elena? What is In-Elena saying to you?"

Father Mac and Frank—never give a direct answer to a question!

"My feelings aren't clear, and In-Elena is quiet right now, only saying 'Trust yourself Elena'."

"So, tell me the different feelings that seem to be in conflict."

"I am excited about the challenges, and about choosing where to live in Asia. Neil said he'd trust me to pick where my office would be. I don't really have any negative feelings, just uneasiness about whether I need space in my life right now, to sort out this other journey."

Father got up from behind his desk and came around and sat on the other chair next to me.

"Elena, the other journey as you call it happens as we live our lives. For some people that means withdrawing from the world to focus intently on this inner journey. Others find ways to make the inner journey while in the world. You seem like the latter type of person to me. So, if you generally feel right about going back to work, especially in a position that will challenge you and fulfill you, I'd say do it. You won't be alone. You can always call me to chat."

I felt very close to him at that moment. It was very much like the feeling I had for Frank. He was someone on my side, wanting the best for me. I reached over and squeezed his hand and smiled. He squeezed back, and that was basically the end of our conversation.

I left for the US a week later.

Book 5   Diane's Story

"I am shut up in a world of consciousness."

George MacDonald[22]

Prologue

After reading Neil's book, I must write a prologue to my story. Neil described the bare facts of our relationship correctly but not who I am. His Diane seems a bit too self-assured, challenging him (her boss) and easily finding ways to change him. Some sort of corporate heroine. That's not me. I'm no hero, although I'm pretty sure I'm on Joseph Campbell's 'hero's journey'. So, who am I?

I'm Diane Twomey. I was raised in a middle-class American home. My parents were both churchgoers and God was a natural part of their lives and mine.

When I was seven, in the first grade, I began to realize that I was a bit different than other kids. I have a distinct memory of standing at the edge of a large playground, watching other kids run and collide and have fun. I felt safe on the sidelines, but a bit lonely and left out. Later, I did join in their fun but my habit of keeping others at a distance, of feeling separate and alone stayed with me. Resolving this introverted mindset is part of my ongoing journey of transformation, of becoming who I am meant to be.

At university I took a course in spirituality, an unusual choice for a marketing and sociology major. The professor asked us to recall our earliest memory of a spiritual experience. As I concentrated with my eyes closed, I saw a scene of darkness, with a pinpoint of light. I was with my mother at the rear of a dark church, before I was in school. Although I don't specifically remember her next to me, it certainly wasn't my father, who never went to church. I was trying to see what was happening in the front of the church but couldn't make out anything. As I related this memory to the class, I added that I thought the vision represented my early sense of the presence of God.

In my later years at university, I felt like I had a 'calling' to do something special. I liked hero stories. A woman pilot risking her life to save someone. A screwed-up world and a lone woman struggling to save it. Not their achievements but their daring, living life beyond the ordinary. There was something missing in my university routine. I concluded that I had to get away from the path I was on if I was going to find adventure. After praying about it, I decided to leave school and become a nun, a Carmelite, in a cloistered order of nuns who live separate from the world and largely keep silent. A completely different path than I was on! And it certainly was an adventure.

The Carmelites are not stupid. They don't just let you immediately commit yourself for life. Some people enter for the wrong reasons (me) so they make newbies go through preliminary steps. I lasted fourteen months, after which I returned to university and finished my degree. During my time with the Carmelites I learned two extremely valuable things. One, my calling was to be a 'special' person in the ordinary world. Two, I began to be able to see God's presence in my life more clearly, (and in others too), and to experience his love in many ordinary situations, which makes me a 'mystic' I guess.

My 'calling' after joining Apex was and is about doing well in the job they gave me—and about taking on the cultural system they have created—one that seems to me to not value people as it should. Neil's book gives a pretty accurate view of that side of me. I also think that Frank would have called me an innocent fool. I agree with Frank's transformational view of bringing love and the Yes-World into organizations.

Lastly, I'm especially interested in wanderers and seekers, people who sense something deeper (or higher) in life that is just beyond their reach.[23] Like Frank O'Connor, I want to help them change their perspective. I want people to reflect on the wonderful reality that they are conscious of themselves, and the fundamental question which that implies. Is their consciousness the result of an incredibly sophisticated naturally evolved brain 'computer', or are they spiritual beings gifted with unlimited consciousness? That's why I try to nudge people into rethinking the ideas about consciousness on which they base their life. So far nudging Neil seems to be gradually working. He did sponsor the Indonesia project and my team has been allowed to openly pursue its values. More about Neil in what follows.

I'll begin when I first encountered Frank's allegory. His story resonated with many of my beliefs. I liked the way he explored different aspects of the spiritual journey. Reading Frank's manuscript also nudged Neil further along his journey, and Elena as I'll relate.

Chapter 1

Neil handed me a thick manila envelope addressed to him, with several UK stamps on the upper right corner. I wondered who he knew over there and turned it over. From: Ms Elena Gaunt, Sloane St, Kensington. Elena. Her name sounded familiar.

"I'd like you to read a manuscript I received, written by Frank O'Connor. You've read my book *Dangerous Undertaking*. This manuscript is a book written by the Frank in my book. I read it and I need to discuss it with you. Would that be okay?" He looked at me, but he wasn't really asking a question. When your boss says, "Would that be okay?" he really means "Do it please."

Oh, *Frank's* Elena. I opened the envelope and saw a thick stack of paper, about a hundred and fifty pages, single-spaced.

"When do you need me to read this? I've got a lot on right now."

"Oh, just do it after work, when you have time." Another mixed message. Neil was famous for these.

I looked at him, without saying anything.

He got my message. "Look, if it doesn't interest you, just stop reading and let me know. I think you'll like it though."

I still didn't say anything.

"What if I take you to dinner at the 1789 restaurant in Georgetown? We can discuss it over a meal and a bottle of red."

"Okay, I'll read it. But I get the dinner even if I stop reading it, right?"

He grinned. "Diane, you are one tough negotiator. Maybe I should transfer you to Contracts."

I nodded, gave a brief smile and left his office. I started to read Frank's manuscript that night after work, got hooked and finished it in two evenings.

*

Frank wasn't a stranger; I had read about him in Neil's book. As I read his manuscript, I saw right away what he was trying to do. He was attempting to describe the mysterious process of experiencing God. His own hero's journey exploring consciousness and its limits. I loved heroes, risking everything to find some Holy Grail.

Why did Frank use an allegory to tell his story? I guessed it was to cut through the daily tidal wave of Facebook posts and media sound bites that fill most people's lives to make them engage their imaginations.

His personal allegory reminded me of *Pilgrim's Progress*. When Bunyan wrote his book in the late seventeenth century, people were very engaged with religion. It was a matter of life and death in England, depending on which side of the Catholic versus Protestant religious war you were on. Today, most people are more interested in which form of 'spirituality' you practice than which church you go to. Still, it bothers me that people don't seem all that interested in what seems to me to be an important religious topic—how does the way you live affect your afterlife? Frank certainly didn't dodge that question in his book. That's another reason I liked it. Maybe it would light a fire under some people, such as Neil.

Neil avoids spiritual discussions. He told me he's a fan of Frank's gentle revolution and the Yes-World. But it seems he is only for change if it stays away from him and his organization. I don't waste time debating with Neil; I tell him what I think. That seems to be gradually working when it comes to adjusting Neil's style of leadership but it doesn't seem to be working when it comes to his personal beliefs, no matter what he wrote in *Dangerous Undertaking*. You're wondering why that is any of my business. I'll let you chew on that question for a while.

A few days after I finished reading Frank's book, I went by Neil's office to tell him what I thought about it. He wasn't there so I left the manuscript with his assistant, with a note. "Finished the book. Let me know when you'd like to discuss at 1789. D". I got an email from his assistant saying Neil was in London so she scheduled a meeting in two weeks in his office. Neil must have forgotten his offer of dinner.

When the time came for the meeting I waited outside his office until he was free. When I entered, Neil asked me if I'd like a coffee, came around from behind his desk and sat on the couch, motioning me to sit next to him him. I could see he was trying to establish rapport. It was right out of *How to be a Successful Boss in 10 Easy Lessons*. At least he was trying. Not like the old Neil who would have stayed at his desk and worked on something else while talking with me.

"So, what do you think of Frank's book Diane?"

"I've been thinking about it a lot and wondering why you want my opinion. His book isn't about business."

He looked like he was trying to remember why he had asked me to read it. "I value your opinion Diane. You're a straight shooter. The book puzzled me. There were some things I didn't understand. I know you're a Christian and I thought you could explain what he meant by some of the experiences he described: his visions in the cave, the encounter with the monster on the way to the river. The river itself. I know this is an allegory about Frank's life, but I don't understand the references."

I thought about how to answer? Should I just give him precisely what he asks for? Or wander around a bit, to explore the possibilities? I decided to start slowly.

"Neil, as you know Frank's book is complex. We only have a half hour scheduled here. I'm not comfortable just answering your questions. An allegory isn't about details; it's about perspective. Could we schedule some time out of the office, when we could relax and have a more wide-ranging conversation?" Maybe he'll remember his promise of dinner at 1789.

He looked at me. I could see his mind working. I'm the boss versus this subject is personal. Personal won. "How about coming to my house for dinner? It would be more relaxed, and we've been meaning to invite you over. I'll call Connie and see what works for her, and let you know. Is that okay?"

It was more than okay; I was delighted. I'd rather go to his home than 1789 and get to know him and Connie better. I told him I'd wait for his call and left his office. After lots of back and forth we managed to all get together on a Tuesday evening a week later.

Connie and Neil lived on Lake Anne in Reston Virginia, in one of the townhouses. They had obviously refurbished it since it was originally built in the mid-1960s. We sat in a comfortable conversation pit looking out on the lights reflecting off the lake. Neil and I sat facing each other and Connie continued working in the kitchen.

"So, what did you think of Frank's book Diane? I've been very curious to hear your thoughts."

"First, tell me about Frank. I know you have mentioned a few things about him in passing, but I want to know more about him. It will help me understand more about why he wrote his book, the audience he was addressing, and so on."

I thought I heard Neil sigh. Typical Diane he probably thought.

"Frank is, well, hard to describe."

"I agree. But I want to hear how he came to write an allegory about his spiritual life. Did you know he was working on it?"

"No, it came as a surprise to me. I don't think Elena knew about it either."

I encouraged him to continue. "I know you and Frank talked about your In-selves and Elena's too. How does that relate to his book?"

He frowned. That stopped him. What does being in touch with your In-self have to do with one's life journey and God as Frank had described?

"Tough question Diane." He paused, and Connie called out from the kitchen. "Neil, you and I have talked about this. You remember Diane loaned you a copy of *The Upanishads*."

He called back to her. "Of course, I do Connie. But I'm trying to answer Diane's question about Frank."

Connie walked over to where we were sitting. "Honey don't get defensive. There's no right answer to such questions. Diane just wants to hear what you think about Frank."

I looked at Connie and thought, Go girl!

Neil looked at her, nonplussed.

"Neil, I just want to understand more about Frank's beliefs before I tell you what I think of his book."

He relaxed. Connie stood looking at him for a moment then went back to the kitchen.

"Frank and I never discussed his religious opinions. He never asked about mine and I followed his lead in our conversations. I felt that his belief in each person having an In-self was based on psychology or something like that. He never said where he got that idea."

"Interesting. You followed his lead. Where was he taking you, do you think?"

Neil squirmed and crossed his legs. "Ummm. Pretty hard to sum up years of conversations and letters. Well, I suppose his main idea was opening my mind to new possibilities. You know, like 'Life is a quest, not a contest'."

He smiled at me as if he had a secret, which he might or might not share with me.

That aphorism came from the opening of *Dangerous Undertaking*. Maybe he thought he could be as puzzling as Frank.

"Dinner is ready," Connie interrupted. She had made a curry, which smelled delicious. Neil poured each of us a glass of red wine and raised his glass in a toast. "To Frank and wherever he's leading us." We all clicked glasses and took a sip. Nice wine.

Connie asked, "What do you do at Apex Diane?"

Neil said, a bit irritably I thought, "Connie I'd like to stay on Frank's manuscript."

Connie and I looked at each other. We both knew he didn't mean to be rude. I began my summary.

"Here's what is interesting to me about Frank's manuscript. First, Frank wrote as if he knew what would happen the rest of his life, even after death. In his prologue he is in the hospital, waiting to die. In his epilogue, after death, he meets his estranged wife Rachel as he struggles to cross the river, which is the boundary between death and eternal life. Those two parts of the manuscript were clearly in the future. That raised the question for me: how much of his journey had already happened and how much was he imagining? I think only the first three chapters had happened to him before he wrote the book. He had entered the kingdom as he called it and had experienced Rachel's rejection of his encounter. But after that I think he was imagining what might happen, as he went forward." I paused.

Neil broke in. "Diane you know that Frank and I discussed encountering our In-selves. Do you think that's what he meant by going through the gate into the kingdom? Is entering the kingdom simply Christian terminology for meeting our real In-self?" He looked at me intently.

How was I to answer such a complex and loaded question? You'd have to have a degree in theology and psychology to understand all the implications and nuances of the human encounter with the beyond. Is it strictly an internal encounter or is some outside agent active as well? Beyond that, I didn't want this conversation to get side-tracked into Christian beliefs; Frank's experience and current beliefs are what is important at this moment.

"Neil, I think they are deeply related. You don't have to be a Christian to encounter your In-self, but Christians believe that that encounter is part of a larger reality, God's quest for us." Connie was watching Neil to see his reaction.

Neil sat quietly as both of us waited for him to digest what I had said. I was getting edgy and almost spoke when Neil looked at Connie and then me.

"Thank you, Diane. I have felt before that something deeper was going on concerning my In-self. I could never quite put my finger on it. You know I'm not a Christian, or even a believer in God. When you gave me *The Upanishads,* it resonated with me somehow. Enriched my mysterious experience in Sydney, and Frank's Yes-World. People had been thinking about things like this for thousands of years. I was part of that." He paused and took a sip of wine.

"Why do you think Frank wrote his manuscript Diane?"

"Good question Neil." I wondered if I even knew. "I don't think I know Frank well enough to guess. What do you think?"

Neil shook his head. "I ... I ..." He was lost for words. Suddenly it seemed like he had lost all interest in discussing Frank or his manuscript. He looked at his watch.

"Sorry Diane, I just remembered I have an early appointment. I'm interviewing Elena Gaunt for a job tomorrow. Would you have a chance to give her an interview after I finish?"

His abruptness jolted me. Connie looked a bit upset. I said I'd be delighted to meet with Elena and we said our goodbyes. I imagine Neil and Connie were having a few words, and not about Frank. I was disappointed that he had ended the conversation, but that was his choice.

Chapter 2

The next afternoon I sat in a conference room I had reserved for the interview, waiting for Elena to arrive. It was going to be an interesting meeting. I assumed she had read Neil's book. Each of us had read about ourselves through his eyes. Would we continue to project our public personas, or would we be honest about who we really are? What motivations did each of us have in this meeting? Elena was trying to get a job with Neil as her boss, I assumed. What was my motivation? Was I just fulfilling a task assigned by Neil? Doing a routine interview? Or did I want to get to know Elena more deeply? Was that part of some bigger plan?

And then there was my curiosity about Frank. Elena knew him directly. I only knew *about* him, through Neil's

577

experience of him and Frank's odd telling of his own story. I would love to have Elena tell me more about the real Frank.

Why did I want to know more about Frank? I wanted to understand why he engaged, like me, with helping seekers find their way. Could Elena give me any insights into his inner life? But she might not have any data about Frank's inner life. I'd have to play that by ear.

There was a knock on the door. I could see Elena's fuzzy outline through the frosted glass wall of the conference room. She was not as tall as I had imagined, but her red hair was as Frank had described it to Neil, flowing, down to her shoulders.

"Come on in Elena." She opened the door, smiled at me, and said. "Hi Diane," offering her hand to me. I stood up and shook it.

I started by describing my role and what it was like working at Apex, trying to encourage her to consider joining us. I made no commitments, but Neil wouldn't appreciate it if I didn't tell her how great Apex is.

"Why did you leave your last role, Elena?"

"The company I worked for was downsizing in Asia." She paused as if there was more to it but didn't continue. We would have to check her references.

"Can you tell me how you feel about joining Apex?" I was very surprised by her answer. At first, I thought it was naïve to be so open in a job interview, but then I remembered she had read Neil's book and also knew a bit about me.

"Can I be honest Diane? I'm not actually sure why I'm here interviewing for this job."

"Did Neil say something that has caused you to feel this way?"

Elena shook her head and replied, "No, it's not Neil. It's me. I'm stuck Diane. I can't seem to let go of constantly questioning myself and what I should do with my life. I know that isn't a very good recommendation for me as Marketing Director, but it's what's really going on right now. I need to be honest with you and Neil."

I recognized, suddenly, that Elena had arrived at her own 'chasm' in Frank's terms. I sensed that God had selected me as one of her companions in this 'dangerous undertaking.' All this was clear to me in an instant.

I asked her softly, "Do you mind telling me a little more about what's going on? I might be able to help you sort things out, about taking this job or not."

She told me the story of what happened when she went to London, about finding and reading Frank's manuscript and meeting Father Mac—then about Saint Winifred and all the messengers she had encountered. She confirmed that she thought she had encountered Frank's chasm in her life, and couldn't seem to find the way past, like Frank had. Father Mac had tried to reassure her that taking another job was okay, but she still felt something wasn't right. She had to resolve this nagging doubt before she could move forward.

When she finished, I asked her, "You're using Frank's spiritual journey to measure your own. Right?"

She nodded then said, "I'm not comfortable with saying I'm on a spiritual journey, but yes, I guess I am tracking myself against Frank. I think that's one reason he gave me his book."

"But maybe you're being too black and white, too literal Elena. You journey doesn't have to exactly match Frank's. Yes, you both encountered a chasm. Frank quickly found himself in the kingdom as he called it. Then he met many messengers in his search for God. Is there another way that you could better line up what's been happening to you with what happened to Frank?"

She looked at me blankly. I could see she was wrestling with that complicated question. She was accustomed to reflecting before answering, from her interactions with Frank's provocative style I thought. At last she seemed to find an idea.

"There is a basic difference between Frank and me Diane. It has a profound influence on our journeys. Frank was a Christian when he encountered the chasm. But he realized that he didn't know God or how to find him. I'm not a believer so I don't even know what I'm searching for."

Good answer, I thought.

"Good summary Elena. I'm sure that Apex ought to hire someone with your ability to recognize patterns and find solutions!" She smiled.

I paused for a moment, to decide where to go next.

"You know, using Frank's story, I'm either giving you a shoulder to lean while you wrestle with the chasm, or you're about to enter the cave and I'm also here to help. Which do you think fits you?"

Again, I could see her mind working as it tried to find the answer that was authentic for her.

"Diane, you're certainly easy to talk to. But I think I'm further along in my journey, even though I haven't found the gate yet. If I use cave as a metaphor, it is dark, and filled with mystery. So where am I—and who are you? My instinct is to say I need support right now to find the gate. I also need help to enter myself more deeply—go into the cave. And these experiences aren't necessarily sequential. They may be happening in parallel, influencing each other. But, like Frank's characters, you *are* a messenger. I'm very sure of that now." She smiled at me, and that is how our relationship went from two personas in an interview, to companions on our journeys.

I felt as if I needed to follow my heart and help her a bit more before we finished our meeting. I silently said a prayer and asked God to help me help Elena to find her way.

"So, let's talk about the cave first. What does the darkness represent to you Elena?"

"What occurs to me immediately is In-Elena can't see. Even in the deepest, most trusted part of myself I can't ask the right questions. I'm just lost, still on the wrong side of the chasm."

"If I may, please don't judge yourself Elena. Don't say wrong side of the chasm. You're doing the best you can. You're waiting to find out which questions to ask."

"Point taken. Thanks. So, what do I do?"

"Take a minute and imagine you're in a cave. Do you see anything?"

Elena closed her eyes. We both sat quietly, for what seemed like a very long time.

Finally, she opened her eyes. "I see a boulder, with a small yellow flower trying to get out from underneath."

"Excellent. Does that mean anything to you?"

Again, she paused, as if listening to someone explain the metaphor.

"The rock is my heart, or at least my feelings. The flower is something subtle trying to attract my attention.

"Did you analyze the rock and flower to come up with that explanation? Or did it just come to you, like it just appeared in your mind?"

She answered immediately. "No, it wasn't me analyzing. It just kind of came to me, like someone whispered in my mind."

"Was it In-Elena?"

"It just came to me like someone wanted to help me."

"Let's just call it an insight and leave it at that. So, why do you think that your heart might be like a rock? Are you hard-hearted? Do you block your feelings? What is your sense?"

She paused for a very long time. I thought I might have pushed her too much, but then she answered.

"Thinking about Frank, I probably hid my feelings from him. But he did the same to me. Maybe that's it. And the flower was love trying to grow between us. Maybe we both were in a dark place where we couldn't open up to each other. I don't know."

She sighed softly. She was out of touch with her feelings, which was a barrier she'd have to overcome in life, including her spiritual life. I thought I could see why she had a hard time believing in God. Believing to her was a mental exercise, unrelated to intimacy. Pretty hard for a largely rational person to know God, or at least develop a feeling of God's closeness. That was my struggle too, so I recognized it in her.

"Do you think the chasm might represent your mind's inability to imagine God?"

She looked at me, expressionless.

"Elena, can you relate the rock and flower to God, who is outside the cave where you can't see him?"

She continued to stare at me. I wondered what nerve I had hit.

Then she spoke. "Sorry Diane. When you said the word God, my mind went blank. I don't talk about God. I really don't know how to relate God to the rock and flower, or to my chasm. I know Frank's question was 'Where is God?' but, being as authentic as I can, using the word God in conversation just doesn't work for me. I don't feel negative about God. I just don't know enough about God to relate myself or my feelings to him."

I paused. She clearly said she doesn't want to talk about God. Where do I take this conversation next?

"Maybe we should wrap up our meeting and leave this conversation for another time and place. What should I tell Neil the result of our interview of each other is?"

She nodded and said, "Thank you Diane. Tell Neil I'm very excited about what I've heard about Apex. That I'd like to mull things over for a few days. In the meantime, maybe it would help if he pulled together a specific offer and give it to me. I don't think I'll need very long to decide after I receive his offer."

That all made sense to me. We chatted a few minutes about what she might want to see in Washington, then we both left the conference room.

I told Neil our meeting went well—not about the spiritual journey part—and he said he'd take over from here and arrange for an offer to be pulled together.

The following day, Elena dropped by my office and asked if I'd like a coffee. We went out of the Apex Building to a nearby Starbucks, where we both ordered a Mocha Grande, no whipped cream. We found a table and Elena smiled and said, "Thank you for listening to me yesterday Diane. I thought about our conversation and wanted to make sure you were OK with the interview. I didn't seem too flaky?"

I could see she was a little anxious and reassured her, "Not at all Elena. I like people who don't mince words and share their feelings."

She seemed to relax and then we just chatted and drank our Mochas. She said she planned to be here for a couple of weeks before returning to London—and I invited her to dinner at my house, on a date to be confirmed. We finished our coffees and she went back to her hotel.

The next time I saw Elena was at Neil's house, at a dinner he'd invited both of us to attend.

Chapter 3

I picked up Elena at her hotel and we drove over to Neil's house. He greeted us at the door.

"Hi Elena. Glad you could come. Connie's in the kitchen. Come on in and I'll fix you a drink." He nodded at me, including me in the invitation. After he brought us our gin and tonics we chatted a bit. He didn't directly ask about Elena's and my conversation. He was playing it subtle, for once.

Neil looked at me. "Diane, we had quite a good conversation about Frank's manuscript last time you were here a few weeks ago." He paused, for me to respond.

"Yes, very enjoyable." If you want to make a point Neil, go ahead.

"Elena, you knew Frank as well as any of us. I hope we can discuss his manuscript a bit more tonight."

She looked at him. I could almost hear her thinking, 'Do you want to see whether I'd be focused on Apex and not my spiritual journey?' But she responded quite openly.

"Neil, I love discussing Frank and the general subject of inner journeys. I've read your and Frank's journey. You probably want to know more about mine. And Diane's too." I liked her directness.

"Oh, that's not necessary really." He paused and thought. "But yes, I think it would be interesting to explore the subject. There is so much data we have access to. It's like a detective trying to look at all the clues and discern a pattern. In our case, there hasn't been a crime. Only a puzzle. I have a life puzzle to solve; Frank had one. Probably you and Diane also have one. We can learn from each other." He stopped and seemed rather proud of his summing up. Just then Connie called us to the table.

We began to eat Connie's lovely curry, the same one I had last time I was there.

I could see that Elena was itching to take on Neil's challenge, to find a pattern in all our puzzles. I looked at her, expectantly waiting to hear Miss Marple's opening situation summary, and she didn't disappoint me.

"Neil, to your point about patterns in our conversations. There are five of us involved. The four of us here and Frank. He remains unknown to us, except as he chooses to reveal himself. Like John Galt in *Atlas Shrugged*, Frank is a central character in my life story and yours Neil, but still is hidden, to a significant degree. Diane, you never met Frank and only know him though reading his story and by how he changed Neil. Connie, you also only know Frank by his effects on Neil, and I assume you haven't read his manuscript. Have I summarized our individual situations correctly?"

Everyone nodded. I was impressed by the way Elena led the conversation. She certainly wasn't hurting herself in the job department, in my opinion.

"Why does Frank continue to puzzle us?" We were all silent, trying to think of an answer. She continued. "I think there are three ways in which Frank is a mystery. First, his manuscript is an allegory, which is open to various explanations. We can't get closure about what he meant. I'll come back to that. Second, Neil and I experienced Frank's unique way of teaching, which involved raising questions and not giving final answers, leaving it up to each of us to decide what we believe. Why did he teach in that way? I'll also come back to that. Finally, there is the deepest mystery of all about Frank—who was he? Oh, I know, he was Frank the former NASA employee, the management consultant, and our close friend. But who was he, actually?" Elena paused.

No one moved. That question stumped us.

589

Elena continued. "Let me ask that question a different way. Who was In-Frank? Neil, he revealed that to you directly and he also revealed it in his manuscript." Neil didn't respond.

Elena answered her own question quite softly.

"He was a kind, decent person." Now Neil responded.

"He was a gentle but powerful person. I knew he only wanted the best for me."

So, Neil would be the one to play Frank's Socratic game with Elena.

"And how did you know that Neil?"

"The way he treated me with respect."

"If he was respectful, why didn't he tell you that he was writing his life story?" She smiled at Neil to let him know she was on his side.

Neil looked at me, but I didn't help him.

Elena led him a bit. "He respected you, you said. He was gentle. How was withholding the story of his spiritual journey gentle and respectful?"

Neil looked out at Lake Anne. He was trying to assemble an answer from many fragments of memories and reflections about Frank.

"I don't know. Maybe he thought hearing his actual story directly would have the wrong effect on me."

"And how might that be so?"

Again, a long pause.

"He didn't want to overpower me, to force me to listen to things I might not be ready to hear. That wouldn't be respectful." He nodded, to himself.

"And now, after reading his manuscript?"

He frowned. "I'm still not sure I want to hear what Frank is saying in his manuscript."

Elena nodded to him and looked at me.

"Diane, what do you think?"

Elena was using my normal challenging role with Neil on me. I didn't answer and looked at Connie. Elena looked at her.

"What do you think Connie? You only know Frank by his effects on Neil. What does that tell you about him?"

She looked at Neil and smiled.

"Oh, that's easy. I wouldn't be married to Neil today if it hadn't of been for Frank. I didn't much like the old Neil. He didn't need me or anyone else. But when Frank lured him into encountering himself, and realize that his life was empty of intimacy, Neil came to me for help. That's when our relationship started. So, I see Frank as a kind of doctor, helping people heal themselves of whatever keeps them from knowing how to relate and care for others."

She had been looking directly into Neil's eyes as she talked. Now she looked back at Elena. "That's who I think

Frank was—and still is. A good influence on Neil's life, and my own."

Neil spoke up. "That's exactly right Connie. Neil helped me change my life. As Elena said, he was a good and decent man—and more. He wanted to help people become who they really are. To recognize they might be innocent fools. Come to think of it, that was his life's work, which he described in his allegory. Just like Francis, he had to go through a long hard journey to find that."

Now I needed to say what I thought about Frank. I took the lead from Elena.

"All that is true, yet there is another dimension to Frank, which he revealed in his manuscript: his understanding about life and death and God. Frank was not some guru writing about the power of positive thinking. He despised gurus. His story was basically about going from independence and self-sufficiency—which hadn't worked very well for him—to a different place. In your book Neil, Frank discussed trust with you. Who do you trust your life to? Do you see what I'm pointing at?"

All of them were frowning now. I had brought the elephant in the room out into the open and they didn't want to deal with it. Too big of a leap. I tried another tack.

"Let me go back to the other ways Elena mentioned that Frank is a mystery. Why did he write his story as an allegory, open to various explanations? You can't read an allegory literally. Why did he do that?"

The conversation was getting more difficult, requiring some serious thinking.

Neil said, "Can we take a break Diane? Does anyone want another drink?"

As we drank our wine, the energy seemed to go out of the room. I suppose they had tired of playing detective. In any case, Neil, Connie and Elena didn't seem to have the drive or whatever to pursue the questions I was raising. We all quickly made our polite excuses and I drove Elena back to her hotel. She sat silently, watching Reston slip past. "Thanks for driving me Diane," and she entered the hotel lobby. I wondered what she was thinking about the evening.

When I got home, I felt the need to understand what happened that evening, like a detective creating a whiteboard showing all the suspects and their relationships.

I realized we were all on very different paths. Frank and I were on the path of faith; Neil, Connie and Elena were not, at least not yet. I believed that they could only see what their reason allowed them to see, while, with the assistance of faith, as well as using my reason I believed that I could see the tremendous eternal reality that God showed to believers. We were at an impasse—a crossroads actually—where one side or the other had to change its assumptions to find a way forward.

How could we discuss our individual spiritual journeys in a mutually understandable way, with such different mindsets? I went to bed with that question on my mind.

Chapter 4

Up to this point, our conversations had wandered around many different points of view aimlessly, driven by curiosity or whatever. Frank seemed to be involved in many of them even though he wasn't present. Our different views of him colored our discussions and made them richer somehow. But we didn't seem to be getting anywhere. I began to realize that I needed to guide our conversations more, with a goal in mind, much like Frank had done for Neil and Elena.

You may think we should all respect the beliefs of others and not try to convince them of the truth of our belief, letting others find their own way on the journey of life. Hands off. Is that what you believe? Then how do you explain what

Frank did with Neil? Was he intolerant? Didn't he guide him toward questioning then changing his ideas? Did Frank have in mind any goal for Neil to achieve? And why did Frank write his allegory about his search for God?

I'm asking you these questions because I am leading you to consider that there is a goal worth seeking in life, 'a pearl of great price' waiting to be found. Frank had found the pearl and he wanted to help others find it as well. That was what I now concluded. I wanted to shift our dinner conversations to seeking the 'pearl.'

I knew I could just ask each of them what they were seeking, but that probably wouldn't work. They might not yet even see themselves as seekers. They were lost, looking in the wrong places as St Augustine put it.[24] Their motivation, often lifelong, came from some vague mystery they wanted to solve, something beyond their grasp, which couldn't be formulated into specific questions, goals or intentions.

In a flash of inspiration, I thought of our group's discussions in a new way. Our small group was exploring *seeking* itself, and our *motivations* about why we felt pulled to solve some unknown mystery. We needed a common language that we could use to describe our ideas about these things. Then, perhaps, we might be able to begin to discuss the goal of our seeking.

We needed a shared concept of how the human mind thinks about such things. What would that model be like? It had to be simple to understand but based on science.

I had to simplify the best findings of neuroscience and sociology. I had read some seminal works in each area. Could I actually do that? I mulled that question, again overnight.

The next morning as I was getting ready for work an idea popped into my head. I imagined the mind as being like a computer. I then realized computer software has two levels: The User level and the Settings level. What you can do at the User level is determined by how you set up the Settings level. Suddenly with excitement I saw the solution to discussing how we think—use an iPhone to represent our mind. We use our minds (iPhones) every day and, over time, we learn to use more of their features and change our mind's settings (mindsets) that enable us to see things in a new way. In a rush I wrote down my ideas as they came to me.

I decided on the following approach. I would host two dinner parties—the first to prepare Neil, Connie and Elena to discuss human thinking using my iPhone example. I had to introduce this idea during the first dinner in such a way that it got enough buy-in so they would believe it represented the way their minds work. During the second dinner, we would discuss seeking and our individual journeys in the light of this iPhone model. I was excited that we would finally begin to get somewhere in our conversations. I could hardly wait to get started.

They all arrived at my apartment right on time for the first dinner party. I served mushroom risotto, my specialty, with a dry white wine. They were soon eating hungrily.

597

Out of the corner of my eye I saw my cat Chewy (named after Chewbacca in *Star Wars*) watching us from the hall. I knew he was hoping we would have some cheese. He had his own agenda for the evening. Chewy always overcame his shyness when it came to begging people for cheese. I wondered what vibes he was picking up; cats read people's minds, I'm sure. He was patiently waiting to see what developed.

"Let me tell you about an idea I have for our conversation tonight, to see if you all agree. We each have been wrestling with what Frank's manuscript means, and how it might relate to our own journeys. I think our conversation has raised some interesting questions. I was thinking about those two things the other night—Frank's book and the importance of questions—and had an insight. Where are our questions leading us? Is there some common element to them? It occurred to me that we are all trying to learn something from our questions but cannot quite see what the goal is. Rather than directly trying to discuss what that goal might be, I propose to examine the process of questioning and what it does for our awareness and thinking. This may sound a bit academic but are you willing to go along with me for a while and see where this leads us?"

All three nodded as they continued to eat. Chewy swished his tail at the sound of my voice.

"First of all, why do we ask questions? Anyone?" Neil nodded and swallowed a mouthful of risotto. Then he said, "It's obvious. There is something we don't know that we'd like help with."

"Good, that's one reason. Anyone else?"

Connie responded. "Well Frank asked questions that he knew the answer to, to make others think about things they probably never considered. To get a new perspective as you said in your book Neil."

"Very good Connie. Yes, the so-called Socratic method of teaching. Any other thoughts about questions?" They seemed stumped so I gave them a clue.

"Why didn't Parsifal's mother want him to ask questions?"

Neil said, "Because if he asked questions, he would see the world outside the forest and leave her?" Neil ironically answered my question about questions with his own question. I don't think he got it.

"Very good. So, Neil, what is a question in your example?"

Neil kept going, like a bright student on a roll. "A change stimulant. Questions themselves, before they are even answered, begin to build up a desire to know. That creates a desire to find an answer."

Elena added excitedly. "The chasm in Frank's book was a question in a way. It created the energy that drove him forward to find out how to see God." Chewy fixed his gaze on Elena.

"Excellent! So, our conversations and questions have been creating energy driving us to find something. We could try to directly discuss what that might be, but I'd like to use that energy in a different way. Okay?"

I felt they really wanted to go directly to the answer, but I knew that wouldn't get very far. There were so many difficult barriers in the way.

"There is another word for the type of questioning that leads to change. Seeking. I see all of us as seekers. What do you think?"

Connie said, "I don't know that I am. I don't seem to have the continual desire to question, to seek new ideas that Neil does."

Neil replied, "That's what I love about you Connie. You are so centered. You know who you are and what you want." She smiled at him in silent thanks.

I said, "Connie, that's a great insight. Not everyone, at least on the surface, seems to be seeking. So, maybe we should only call people seekers who are actively curious like Frank. Such people seem to ask more questions, be more dissatisfied, want to find something more intensely than others."

Elena said, "I feel like that. I have been seeking like Frank was, at least since I lost my job and started searching for his manuscript. I really became serious once I read it. Maybe, thinking more about it, I started being a seeker earlier, when I first met Frank. Before that I was satisfied to float along in life."

Neil nodded. "I became a seeker when I met Frank. Definitely."

"So, if you are a seeker, do you want to learn how to seek better?" They had arrived where I wanted to guide them.

They all nodded. Who wouldn't want to improve their chances of finding what they were seeking? Chewy rolled over on his side and stretched. Too many words. Where's the cheese? I had to get to the point quickly.

"That is what I propose to help us do—improve our skills as seekers. Then we can return to the questions we have been asking with new tools to help us find answers. Okay?" Step by step I wanted their buy-in. Again, they nodded yes. Now I needed to tell them how I would do that.

"What we actually need to talk about is how the minds of seekers work. If we understand that, we can find ways to seek more effectively using the basic capabilities of our minds." They nodded now, almost as if I had hypnotized them into a buy-in process.

"Here's my idea. I have read a lot over the years about the sociology of learning and neuroscience—how the mind works and matures. But all those ideas are too complex to learn quickly. So, I'm going to simplify and assume that our mind is like a computer, specifically an iPhone. Then we're going to talk about how our minds work like an iPhone.

That's as far as we'll go tonight as I don't want to overwhelm you. Then we'll have another dinner in the next few days while Elena's here and discuss seeking and other things using the iPhone model. That's what I propose to do. Any questions?" I saw that there were a lot of questions on their faces.

Neil asked, "This all sounds pretty complicated Diane. How much time will it take? Isn't there a simpler way? Can't we just continue our conversations? They are fun." Good old Neil. Always looking for a quick fix.

Elena said, "Tell me how you're going to explain the mind is like an iPhone"

I decided not to answer Neil. "I'm not going to discuss the hardware at all, just the software. You all have iPhones or Androids? That's the kind of software I'll describe: Apps. You all have experience of that kind of software. Okay so far?" Elena nodded. So did Neil. "There are two ways we use phone apps—as Users and when we adjust their basic Settings. When you first get an iPhone or a new app, you have to set it up. That's what I'll call the Settings level. For example, when you set up a mail app you have to define what account details you'll use, who is your mail provider, etcetera. It defines the basic capability of the app. Then as you use it, you make other choices of which parts of the app you want to use. That is the User level. For example, in the mail app, do you want to look right now at mail input, sent mail, saved mail, deleted mail or would you rather just see new mail messages.

Those ideas about Settings and Users are basically all you'll need to understand."

Elena said, "That sounds simple enough. But I can't see how that relates to how our mind works."

"You will, believe me. In just a minute."

Neil said, "Tell me again, why we have to do this? What is the value of your model?"

"Great question Neil." He smiled. "The value of any model is it is a simple way to understand something that's complex. The findings of neuroscience and sociology are quite complex. My model will allow you to apply these findings and understand how your mind works somewhat like an iPhone. You will be able to use your 'Seeker' app better, okay?"

Again, he nodded slowly. I asked them, "So, let me explain how our minds are like an iPhone?" I paused, to get them focused.

"When we are born, our brains have only the most basic software. Our minds (our iPhones) come with the factory settings. We automatically know how to turn our head and suck to get food, and cry when we want attention. Then gradually, as we get grow up we program our Settings to make our mind work better. We enable our iPhone's Wi-Fi setting—we take in other people, and words, and what feels good and what doesn't. We learn to use our brains (iPhones) to think in simple ways."

Elena clearly got it. She was nodding and smiling. Neil had a frown, like he couldn't quite keep the metaphor straight. I continued.

"Somewhere around the age of six, we change another setting in our iPhone. We learn to choose new apps from a wide range we discover in the world. We go to school and learn new skills. We make new friends and hear different ideas. We disable some of our parents' ideas and try out new apps. Our world expands. Our iPhone has quite a few apps on it. Our thinking becomes more and more sophisticated."

Now Neil was smiling. I guessed he was remembering some of the 'apps' he experimented with as a boy.

"Then, around thirteen or so, we change another setting in our mind. We learn to turn off a lot of our parents' tracking and advice on the iPhone and make our own decisions. After changing this setting we try lots of apps and some don't work very well. We make mistakes, some of them serious. But we learn to live in the world following our own settings and apps. This is when we form our mindset that we will use for much of our life. We keep the mindset settings we learn as teenagers and young adults until the next major point where we may change another iPhone major setting— enabling our deeper consciousness. This is as if our Wi-Fi connects to another set of inputs."

They were all wrapped up in my simple story of human development.

"Enabling this feature on our iPhone is eye-opening. It is like suddenly discovering that all the information and videos and games on the internet our iPhone connects to are being created by marketing 'magicians', who want to sell us something. Up to this point in life, we all buy into the conventional version of the world that we are "sold." Gradually, however, we begin to see what those magicians are doing. We become aware that the internet itself isn't real—it only shows us what the magicians want us to see. This happens, many times in our forties, when we become disenchanted with life. The apps we invested so much time in—Facebook, Twitter, Google, work, success, and so on, no longer seem so important. But what lies beyond what we have been sold? What is the truth beneath the surface of what we're experiencing every day? That's when some people, like you, download the Seeker App."

I checked out Elena's reaction to my marketing magician analogy. Was she insulted that I said we are all being manipulated? She didn't seem upset, just pensive. She trusted me enough to find out where I was going.

I waited. Elena looked at me, then Neil. I thought she was wondering how much of herself to reveal. Then she spoke.

"That's exactly where I'm at right now Diane. All the old apps and the ideas I thought were so important, now seem, I don't know, kind of trivial, I guess. And I don't know another app I can download to help me get on with life."

I admired her more than ever. She got it!

Connie looked at Neil, waiting for him to react, I guess. When she saw he wasn't going to respond she asked, "Diane, can you explain what actually happens in our mind when we begin to see life as being like a game, manipulated by magicians? Does that always happen? If so, why does it happen?"

Neil looked at Connie, a bit shocked I thought. She had asked very penetrating questions, which I could answer but didn't intend to.

"Great questions Connie! Imagine Frank were here. How would he answer them?"

She paused and that gave Neil an opening to answer.

"Frank wouldn't answer. He'd probably tell a story, to get us to supply our own answers. Can you do that Diane?" He was challenging me, trying to reassert his...I don't know what. I felt his response was visceral, not thought out. But I decided to tell a story, nonetheless, one which would puzzle them and lead them to new ideas I hoped.

"Ok, Neil. Here is a story a Zen Buddhist friend of mine told me. A man went to a Zen master and said, 'If I work very hard, how soon can I be enlightened?' The Zen master looked him up and down and said, 'Ten years.' The fellow said, 'No, listen, I mean if I really work at it, how long—' The Zen master cut him off. "I'm sorry. I misjudged. Twenty years.' 'Wait!' said the young man, "You don't understand! I'm—' 'Thirty years,' said the Zen master."

I stopped again, and like the Zen master I waited for the story to work. I think Neil took the story personally because he had a frown on his face. Elena looked at Neil, then me, and spoke up.

"Realizing that you don't understand your own perspective is the beginning of the journey. Enlightenment isn't mainly about striving. Right?"

I nodded but remained silent. Connie spoke next.

"I asked you what triggered our minds to begin to see life as a game created by magicians. That wasn't the right question, was it? The questions we ask lead may lead us down the wrong path. Is that right?"

Again, I nodded, and remained silent. Neil finally spoke.

"I am like the man, wishing for a master to teach me the answer to life. You are like the Zen master and Frank too, knowing the answer but wishing me to discover it on my own. But I don't know how. I have limits which block me, which I must find a way past. That's the only way I can become a true seeker isn't it?" I nodded but did not answer him either.

I felt the seeds for the next dinner party had been sown and didn't continue the conversation. I served some cheese and Chewy jumped up onto my lap, purring contentedly as he finally got to taste the triple cream brie. We stayed a bit longer, chatting about nothing, staying away from seeking and apps and figuring out the Zen story. Then Neil and Connie went home, and Elena followed shortly afterwards.

Chapter 5

Neil called me into his office on Friday, the day before my second dinner party was scheduled, ostensibly to talk about Elena.

"Diane, I just wanted to get any final input you might have before I make an offer to Elena. Anything I should know?"

"She's a good fit for our culture. That's certain from how she engaged in our conversations. She was open and upfront with her opinions. I can't really say much about her marketing competency; that's not my area. In her last job she seemed to have a similar level of responsibility as our Director of Asian Marketing. You need to check her references. My vote, if I get one, is hire her."

He looked at me, probably trying to think of a way to get to what he really wanted to talk about.

"I've been thinking about your Zen story. Very interesting." He paused. I just looked at him.

He continued. "It made me think." I nodded appreciatively.

He slowly shook his head. "Why is it so difficult to talk with you sometimes Diane?"

I opened my eyes wide. "Me? Difficult? What do you mean?"

He shook his head in frustration. "You know and I know that you know exactly what is going on here. I feel like you're manipulating me somehow."

Was I? I didn't think so. I was just trying to help him to say what was on his mind. I wondered if he ever listened to In-Neil.

"Do you mean about Elena's hiring? Why would I do that?" Now he had an angry grimace on his face. Definitely not In-Neil.

"You know exactly what I'm talking about. This iPhone model of yours, and your dinner parties. You're up to something. I'm your boss. I don't have to play this game."

Now I had to respond. He had revealed his real concern. It wasn't about our boss-employee relationship; that was fine and he knew it. It was about his lack of control over where the dinner conversation might lead. He wouldn't be pushed or manipulated as he called it into moving forward on his own spiritual journey.

"Sorry, Neil. You know me. I'm a pretty straightforward person. I didn't mean to manipulate if that's what you think. You're probably bothered about where the iPhone discussion might go. Is that right?"

He nodded. "I'm comfortable with the way my personal development is going right now. You said this iPhone model would help me become a more effective seeker, as if I'm not doing it well at present. Who are you to judge me?"

I briefly paused to let silence do some healing. Then I said, "I apologize if I gave you that impression Neil. Who am I indeed? To be very clear, the limit of what I'm trying to do is give you and Elena and Connie a new perspective on what it means to be a seeker. If you were to ask my hopes for where our conversations go from here, I hope only for growth and expansion of capabilities, not any particular outcome." I didn't mention I had put what happens in his and Connie's and Elena's and my own life in God's hands. He wouldn't get it and might even be offended.

"Okay. I just wanted to clear the air. I do trust you Diane. I'll be happy to participate in the conversation tomorrow night, wherever it takes us." Hello In-Neil!

*

Elena, Neil and Connie arrived at 7 pm on Saturday evening and the conversation began almost immediately. This time Chewy stayed out of sight.

Neil said, "What about emotions? Why aren't they important in your iPhone model of the mind? I think they are relevant." Connie nodded and Elena added, "I have the same question Diane. Your model should discuss emotions, and memories too. They are both important."

"Hang on. Let me get you a drink before we begin." I ushered them into my living room. The gin and tonics only took five minutes to make and serve. During that time, I planned how I would answer their questions about emotions and memories.

Returning from the kitchen with the drinks on a tray, I said, "There are two answers to why I didn't include emotions and memories in the discussion. First, I wanted to concentrate on 'rational' man—how we consciously use our minds to think and control our behavior. Yes, emotions and memories are important. Ultimately, emotions and memories can have a significantly good or bad effect on our thinking and acting. Ask any cognitive therapist about automatic thinking and behaviors controlled by emotions connected with old, out-of-date memories. But rational behavior involves sorting out the effects of emotions and perhaps inappropriate memories and making the best decisions we can in our current situation without those influences. I want us to think and act rationally. Does that make sense?"

Connie replied, "I see where you're going Diane. But are you being realistic about human beings? Are you turning us into computer-driven robots without feelings? It still seems like your model leaves out something very important." The others nodded.

"No, I'm not denying these are important aspects of being human. That brings me to the second reason I left them out. I wanted to use the simplest model for a human mind I could imagine. If I brought in emotions and memories the model becomes far more complex. It is better to look at how we think rationally first, then add on emotions and memories, than to make the model far more complex and difficult to use. My belief is that we are rational beings with emotions, not emotional beings with reason. My request is to use my simple iPhone model as the starting point. I think you'll find it's easy to bring in emotions and memories, as we use it."

Connie said, "OK Diane. I trust you. Let's try that. The idea of simplicity is good. But let's remember that Einstein said, 'Everything should be made as simple as possible, but not too simple'." Connie and Einstein? I'd like to spend more time with her!

Neil said, "Could we try an example, just to see how this works? For example, as I begin to think about changing my mind's settings, I might feel anxious about what might happen. That emotion of worry would affect how quickly I made decisions and acted."

"Good example, thank you. You're thinking then you get anxious. Your thinking app triggers emotions (or brings up memories) which slow down or influence your decision app and action app. That's the way your mind works, isn't it?" He nodded slowly.

"So Neil, are you okay on emotions and memories being introduced as influencers on a particular thought, decision or act? To deal with them as secondary effects after dealing with rationality?"

He said, reluctantly, "Let's see how it works when we try to use your model to discuss our journeys as seekers." The others nodded their agreement.

Elena asked, "Where does psychology come in?"

"Another good question Elena. The basic answer is I suggest that we agree to defer psychological discussions in our conversations. First, none of us is an expert in that field. We'd be using a lot of pop-psych arguments with no real basis. Second, even experts would want to wait to understand the specific circumstances and situations surrounding our rational thinking."

Elena tilted her head, quizzically. "So, are there so many complexities and environmental factors left out of your simple model that it is basically useless? It's just too simplistic?"

I felt proud I had recommended Elena to join the Apex team. She gets to the heart of things very incisively.

"Elena, may I try and answer your question by using an analogy?" Elena nodded. "Good. Newton's Three Basic Laws of Physics are simple, but they allow modern engineering to calculate accurate orbits, build strong bridges, etcetera. Quantum physics brings in more complexity but at a very deep level of reality. So, just because something is simple and doesn't take into account all the complexities of reality, doesn't make it a useless tool. Understand?"

She nodded again. "What you're saying Diane is that your model is useful for discussing how the human mind works, especially for seekers. You're not trying to create a new scientific model for reality, which the scientific community agrees fits everything. Is that right?"

"Exactly. Are there any other general questions about whether the iPhone model is valid?" No one spoke so I said, "Okay, let's go through to the dining room. I'll serve dinner and then we can begin to use the model to discuss our journeys."

Once they were seated and I had served, the first question came from Neil.

"Maybe we should talk about Frank's journey first since we three have read his story. Sorry Connie, I know you haven't read it. Is that okay?" Connie and the rest of us nodded so he continued. "It's obvious that Frank was a seeker. Right? How had he set his iPhone consciousness? Do you think he put any limits of his consciousness?" Couldn't have said it better myself.

Elena answered, "Frank was obviously beyond the chasm and examining his perspectives because he was asking questions about why his consciousness seemed limited—

where was God and why couldn't he see him? I also think he was seeing the mystery in his life, not just trying to think his way into a new perspective about God. All the mysterious incidents in his story show that. It makes sense to me at an emotional level too. I knew there was something different about Frank. He wasn't just another management consultant trying to improve or even reengineer the existing system." But he wasn't ignoring the system either, I thought. Neil and Frank had an extensive discussion about organizations as ecosystems, and how to transform them.

Neil added. "I agree Elena. Frank had a different perspective and he wanted me to examine my own. He never mentioned a higher level of consciousness or his own spiritual journey. But I could sense something was there, beneath the surface of our conversations. I would have said something deeper, but now I'm not sure that's right. Maybe the right word is broader or more expansive. His allegory seems to define a bigger world beyond our own everyday world. For example, he included what lies beyond death—the other side of the river—implying there is reality beyond death. And his visions in the cave embrace vast cosmic dimensions and historical eras. He doesn't just see the here and now as being the only reality, the only thing affecting him. I'm reaching here but I sense his perspective was quite different than my own everyday perspective and experience. He and I had different consciousness Apps."

I smiled and added, "And, obviously, his language included God. What does the iPhone model say about that?"

I was worried they thought I was advocating my own Christian position, but I needn't have been concerned.

Connie said, "Good point Diane. Frank obviously had some concept of God in his iPhone mindset and knew something about Christian language. That's interesting. I've always thought that Christians weren't seekers. That they thought they had all the answers. But Frank didn't think like that. What do you think Diane? You're a Christian."

I didn't want the discussion to get off on a sidetrack, but I had to respond. "In my experience, many of the Christians I know are seekers. Like Frank, they may have a concept of God, and some religious language they learned as a child, but many don't actually 'know' God experientially. They struggle with expanding their consciousness and perspective. That drives them to seek God in new ways. Just like Frank."

That seemed to satisfy Connie, and I think the others. I wasn't there to convert them. I believe, as I said before, that their finding God was between them and God. They just had to be open to downloading a new consciousness App.

Neil wanted the floor.

"When I read Frank's book, I kept referring back to my own book and my experiences of Frank and his effect on my journey. If that sounds complicated, it really wasn't. I began my book with where I was before I met Frank, contrasted with where I am now, in one sentence—Life is a quest, not a contest. That summarized my own journey, right up front, in my story." He paused to let us assimilate what he said. Then he continued.

"I think Frank was writing about his personal experience of transformation in his allegory. Even the name he chose for his character—Jacob Newman—points toward that. He felt like a new man. When Jacob goes through the gate into the kingdom in the first chapter, that is his first experience of being transformed. The kingdom is where Jacob, through a new iPhone app, begins to be conscious of everything, including God, in a new light. I know Frank was also using 'kingdom' in the Christian sense, but I think he was mainly writing for those of us who don't share that language or mindset."

"At the beginning of the second chapter he describes how, in the kingdom all his senses were heightened, and he saw things differently. A little later he says that becoming a new man isn't reversible—the gate has disappeared, and he couldn't return to his old way of thinking. But, the rest of the book deals with his journey *inside* the kingdom. His initial transformational experience of being a new man is just the beginning of learning to see with his new heightened consciousness App."

"In his former world, Jacob (Frank) had heard *about* God. In this new kingdom, with his new App he experienced God more directly. The rest of his book was about his personal journey to search for experiences of living in God's presence. That's what I think Frank was telling us in his allegory."

He paused. This was a lot to take in.

I thought that Neil had a pretty sophisticated understanding of what consciousness and seeking mean. I wondered if that knowledge was helping him seek any better.

Elena said, "When I think about Frank, it was like he saw things more clearly than I could see. But he never brought God into our conversations. I see now that I was at a different level of consciousness than Frank was. I wouldn't be able to understand his language about God, so he didn't use it. I haven't yet become a new person like Jacob did—but I can see now that I'm beginning to hope to become one. To find a way to access a new level of consciousness on my iPhone."

I thought Elena, in this conversation, may have gotten past the roadblock of her chasm, and was beginning to sense she wanted to become a new woman. I felt happy that I had been privileged to witness this.

Neil went on, "Frank didn't criticize people, so don't judge yourself Elena. He knew everyone was on a road leading to transformation. His mission was to support and encourage us."

I loved the way the conversation was going. Here were two ordinary business people talking about seeking a higher level of consciousness in a matter of fact way, even hoping it might happen to them.

I asked another question. "What did the cave and desert represent in Frank's allegory?" Interestingly, Connie responded. She obviously had picked up some ideas during the conversation.

"I think Frank was probably describing as best he could, using the cave, what his sense of ultimate reality looks like from inside his new level of consciousness." She stopped.

I had misjudged Connie. She was far more insightful than I had pegged her for being. That'll teach me to judge people on appearances.

I said, "That was a great insight, Connie!" Neil smiled proudly.

Elena then asked, "Then who is Francis, the old man Jacob met in the desert? He told stories about how he had come to live in the desert, and led Jacob to the river of death, where he crossed over. What does all that represent?"

I responded, "Let me take a shot. I think Francis represents Frank wrestling with wisdom. Francis's great age represents the wisdom of the ages. Francis's long journey, and the other three adventurers represent the acquisition of wisdom and man's historically different perspectives about how to live a good life.

"Ultimately, however, Frank learned that having wisdom wasn't enough to cross the river. Neither were his own decisions or power. Jacob watched Francis cross the river only after he admitted his own helplessness to cross under his own power. That was the central lesson Jacob learned in his journey."

Neil asked, "So, self-sufficiency, even wisdom doesn't work?"

I answered, "In some things, no it doesn't."

Elena then asked, "But what can we do? We can't depend on ourselves and we can't depend on the wisdom Frank outlined—knowledge, good works, devotion to understanding God. What can we do?"

I answered, "Frank said, at the end, all we can do is trust and wait, to be carried by God's love and mercy across the river." They were silent, thinking about this.

Neil then said, "So then, Diane, why have you put us through all this trouble, learning about how our minds work? Why not just sit and wait for God to act rather than seeking?" Great questions Neil.

I answered, "Why did I do it? I wanted to help all of you learn language for the growth process of consciousness and mindset change that everyone goes through. The different capabilities of our iPhones at different ages. Life is about striving to mature, to run the race well as Saint Paul said. We all start as children, shape our different mindsets, then explore the world, like Jacob and his friends. Eventually, in one way or another, we all arrive at a chasm—a recognition that 'magicians' (only humans after all) are behind the apps which shaped our mindset, and they cannot help us find certain dimensions of life, especially what happens after we die. We can either refuse to think about this stark reality, or we can continue to seek. I wanted to help you learn to seek.

621

What you find is up to you and, in my belief, up to God too. Here is probably a good place to share more about my own journey."

They seemed very alert, wanting to hear more so I continued. "I'll describe what I see from my current vantage point."

"For a short time, I lived in the Mojave Desert, on the Western slope of a high, barren ridge. Everyday, before dawn, the sky above the ridge became bright but the sun didn't directly strike me yet. That Mojave Desert experience is what it is like to be human. We all have hints of what the world would look like in full daylight (our everyday valleys are still in deep shadows) but not the actual experience. The valley is created by our own ideas yet lit by light which is out of our sight and understanding. My life has been a gradual awakening to the source of the light in my valley—which I believe is the presence of God."

Neil was leaning forward, engaged with my metaphor. Elena had a slight frown. I had to keep my explanation short.

"So, what is it like, believing in God's presence in my life as I do? If you and I are both living in a valley where the sun is hidden behind the mountains, what's different for me?"

I paused, hoping one of them would answer. Elena didn't disappoint me.

"Your iPhone has a setting ours doesn't?"

I replied, "Well, maybe, but from what I know about your stories I would say that all of you have begun to see the light in your valleys. Your iPhone is set up to receive it. What else is different?"

She sat silently, puzzled. Neil said, "Do we have a different setting somehow? Therefore, we have a different mindset and different ways of thinking about the light?"

I smiled. "Excellent Boss. Right on target. So why don't you believe that the light comes from God? Where did your setting and apps come from?"

He thought for a minute then said, "I guess I downloaded all my apps myself. I chose what to believe or not believe. Thinking about Frank's story, when he was searching for God, he believed there was a God but he didn't see the light in his valley coming from God. God was remote, not real to him. And that's actually something like where I'm at now. I guess I believe in a God but not a God who touches me. Maybe a God who is the source of the light, located behind the mountain, a great distance away."

That was a major step forward for Neil. Elena looked like she had just had an insight, so I asked her, "Does that trigger something for you Elena?"

She nodded, "Yes. All the hints and messengers I've encountered, and my encounter with In-Elena too. I think Neil's idea applies to me. These things weren't my own creations; they came to me from somewhere. I guess I'm getting more comfortable with believing they came from God. Yes, now, all of a sudden, I can say without hesitation that I believe there is a God! Thank you, Neil, for sharing your insight. It helped me realize what I believe."

What had just happened was a miracle to my way of thinking, a gift from God to Elena and Neil. But they weren't past the chasm and in the kingdom yet.

"I'm really happy that you both have gotten that from listening to my story. Maybe we should stop now and let you digest what just happened."

Neil immediately replied, "No, I want to hear more about your journey Diane. Maybe we'll encounter more insights. Using your valley metaphor, I can see that there probably is a God beyond the mountains. I'm not sure what God has to do with me—what I'm experiencing in the valley. In fact, things here in my valley seem to be run by the 'magicians' we discussed a while back. God doesn't seem to be active in the world." He paused, then added, "At least that's how it looks with my mindset. I'm willing to believe that, with a different mindset, I might be able to see God's actions. They must be very subtle though, or they would be obvious even to non-believers. Believing in God doesn't guarantee that you can see him. That was Frank's situation."

Elena added, "I think I might be willing to go a little further than that Neil. I encountered a statue of Saint Winifred in a church in London. Her smile attracted me, and I visited her shrine in Holywell in Wales. There I realized what attracted me to her: she seemed to want me to be happy. Maybe God was behind all this. And behind my meetings with my priest friend Father Mac and all his questions. I can almost see that these are gifts from God. But I wouldn't be truthful if I said I believed God had taken a personal interest in me. Or that I knew him and had a relationship with him."

What was happening was remarkable. The openness and energy that Neil and Elena were expressing. I felt sure that their seeking would lead them to the gate Frank had encountered. I didn't want to go any further in the conversation and knew I had to draw it to a close

"Neil, you said you wanted to hear more about my journey. I went from *knowing about* God, to *knowing* him. It didn't take as much thought and reflection as Frank but eventually I found my way through the desert. Now, I think I need to let each of you find your own way from here on."

They sat silently, respectfully. Neil nodded, as if he already knew my story. Elena didn't quite let it go and asked when I had encountered the chasm.

"I suppose it was when I knew I had to leave the convent and live in the world. I don't know if all of you know I used to be in a Carmelite convent. I left there after a few years. It wasn't my calling. There were many nuns (advanced souls) relating with God in silence. I felt that wasn't for me, but I couldn't say why. That was my chasm. My questions were, where is God if I leave this sheltered world? Why was he calling me away from the convent? The most basic question I kept asking myself was, like Frank's—what is God's goal for me? It has taken me many years on a difficult journey to begin to answer that question."

I stopped talking, and we all sat quietly for what seemed a very long time but was probably no more than a minute or two. The others were probably already thinking of their own journeys and comparing them to Frank's and mine.

They were probably raising very personal questions, ones which they didn't want to discuss with the group. Telling them about my spiritual life had felt very personal; I guess the others felt the same, because they didn't continue the conversation. In any case, my dinner party broke up soon afterwards.

*

Two days later, Elena appeared at the door to my office. She seemed a little on edge.

"Can I see you for a minute Diane?" I waved her in. "Sure. What can I do for you?"

"I wanted to tell you I just met with Neil and turned down the Apex job. He was a bit put out. I wanted to warn you; he might think it had something to do with you and our dinner conversations. In a way, it does. But not really. If anything, you gave me a great example of someone who is on a spiritual journey but also being a success in a difficult job. No, my decision was based on personal issues, which I haven't discussed with anyone."

I was utterly surprised.

"Elena, I'm stunned! I had myself convinced you'd be joining us. I was looking forward to many more conversations with you, about business and our journeys. If you don't mind me asking, was there some particular turning point?"

She thought for a moment. "I think it was when I thought of Frank after he left the river, not knowing where to go next. He didn't feel it was right to leave the desert so he continued to wander around until he was certain about his way forward. I came to realize that I wasn't certain that Apex was my way forward right now. I need to leave space for wandering around, staying alert for signals, just waiting. I need to face the river squarely. I have avoided it my entire life. I didn't even go to Frank's funeral for God's sake." She paused, to collect herself. "When I realized that, I was certain I couldn't go back to work in a demanding job right now. That's how it happened. Also, I need to go back to Australia, to straighten out some personal things. Over the past few months, I also recognized that I'm homeless, with no close relationships in my life since Frank died. I need time to heal." She looked at me, almost pleading for me to understand.

I paused, momentarily speechless. I felt her turmoil and loneliness. Then I recovered. "I understand Elena. And I'm sure you'll meet whatever or whoever you are seeking. Stay alert for surprises. And please stay in touch with me. I'd love to support you anyway I can." I didn't want to start a conversation. It was time for her to listen, and not to my words.

We hugged and she left.

An hour later I wandered down to Neil's office. He was sitting with his back to the door staring out the window.

"Am I interrupting? Can I come in?" He turned and saw me, and waved me in.

"Did Elena stop by and see you?" He paused. "I guess she did, judging by your nonverbals. I'm really disappointed. I thought she'd be great in Asia. I thought we had her!"

"So did I Neil. And I was shocked too. But, once she explained why, I agree with her decision. She said it was personal, and she just didn't feel like now was the right time for her to risk leaving her journey for a fast-paced job. I think we ought to value her honesty."

He looked at me and nodded.

"I guess you're right. I was just thinking how, in a way, I envy her. I wish I could go to some lonely desert and sit and think. Find out what the Yes-World really means. It seems like my own journey has been pushed into second place by this job." He looked at me, for reassurance I think, that everything was okay. I couldn't give him that.

"Neil, you trust me, don't you? You know I'm always dead honest with you?" I paused. He looked like he felt he had made a mistake opening himself to me.

"You need to listen to that voice inside you."

Chapter 6

I didn't hear from Elena for several months, after the COVID pandemic had struck globally. She got back to Australia before international air travel had ceased, passing through London to see Father Mac. She didn't share that conversation with me, but I gathered from her email that Father Mac had explained what she had to do to become a Christian. She must have convinced him that she was ready to hear this.

Here is the email she sent me from Sydney.

Dear Diane,

I'm in lockdown here in Sydney, isolated in a hotel room, so, as I have plenty of time, I thought I'd drop you a line to let you know how things are going on my journey so far. Not that I didn't want to talk to you before, but I guess I wasn't ready.

I didn't get held up by all the travel disruption caused by the pandemic, landing in Sydney from London in early February before it hit here. The *Diamond Princess* fiasco became a big problem here in New South Wales several weeks after I arrived.

At Father Mac's suggestion, I hooked up with a Catholic priest here in Sydney, before the pandemic made such meetings impossible. I like Father Brendan. He's interesting and a sensitive person. He gets where I'm at on my journey and doesn't push me. We have yet to figure out how to continue our conversations while the pandemic is our constant companion.

So, where am I on my journey? Frank's gravestone had an epitaph that read 'Once I Was Lost.' Now I understand what he meant. I was lost for much of my life, wandering aimlessly, searching for something—Frank's love, a purpose in life, I don't know. Now I realize I actually wanted to find God but hadn't acknowledged it—and couldn't find God, like Frank. But God found me and sent me some wonderful guides like you, Father Mac and Frank, and now Father Brendan. So, my current status is, I'm beginning to find my way.

Isolated in my hotel room I think a lot. The other day I had this thought and wrote it down: I have an absolute ability to change my life—but I have given it over to God.

This seems very profound to me. When I think about my abilities, they are extensive, yet I know I can't find what I yearn for. So, I have given the choice of how I should change my life over to God. It seems like this is the lesson Frank learned, so I'm in good company.

I hope you are keeping well.

Love Elena

Neil is in isolation like the rest of us. I suspect he's still thinking about how he could take time off and go into his own 'desert'. For some reason he doesn't see this time of enforced isolation as an opportunity to do that. Probably he's focused on how to save our business. Same old Neil. What should I do to help him? Do I have permission to help him in his inner journey? Do I need permission?

I am learning the mind of God in these matters. His infinite patience and his yearning for someone like Neil to find his way home. The pain of being ignored. No anger just waiting to be noticed. I have so much I could share with Neil and others, yet I don't. That's how God feels, I'm sure. So I wait for Neil to do the 'one thing necessary.'[25]

And me? Now that I have almost finished this abbreviated story, I'm wondering how much more to reveal. Up to now, I haven't told Neil or Elena or anyone about my inner life. In some ways I'm still that little girl feeling lonely, separated from the other school kids at the edge of the playground. No one would understand. Yet, I know that I am understood by God.

As I said in the beginning of this book, I'm no hero. You have experienced my flaws—abruptness, impatience, sometimes manipulative, trying too hard to get people to change their perspective. It's too easy to say I'm working on these. I have been this way for a long time, but I am learning to forgive that part of myself because God doesn't judge me. I guess I'm a work in progress.

"We are God's work of art, created in Christ Jesus to do good works, which God prepared in advance for us to do."

Saint Paul's Letter to the Ephesians 2:10

Afterword

By James Harlow Brown

Those of you who are Christian will likely note the almost total absence of mentioning Jesus by name in this novel. Jesus is "our living icon of transformation" as Richard Rohr states. Why did I write a book about transformation with so little emphasis on Jesus?

Why didn't Frank emphasize Jesus in his story? Why did I have Diane, a Christian, give Neil the ancient myth of *The Upanishads* and not the Bible? The same question applies to Elena. Why did Father Mac, a Catholic priest, not tell her about Jesus and the church's wisdom in the beginning and, instead, gave her the same book *Siddhartha* that Frank had given to him? Was it that Father Mac and Frank and Diane aren't good Christians? That they (and I) think it doesn't matter what you believe?

My approach has to do with my assumptions about the readiness of my audience to hear Jesus's story *in their unique situations.* In simple terms, my Christian characters and I are following good marketing practice—know your audience and tailor your message to them. Saint Paul said, "I have become all things to all people, that I might by all means save some." [1 Corinthians 9:22] Jesus knew that many of his audience would be unable to hear his message, so "With many such parables he spoke the word to them, as they were able to hear it." [Mark 4:33] Both these holy men recognized and struggled with the entrenched mindsets of their audience. Jesus, with all God's power available to him, wouldn't violate human freedom to overwhelm us with grace and make it easy for us to change our mindsets. He wanted his hearers to struggle with their own beliefs about who he was. So, in this novel Father Mac and Frank and Diane (and I) have led you to places where you *might* begin to ask questions and to seek God.

I based my characters' journeys on a familiar fact of religious experience—we almost always encounter God in his silence, indirectly experiencing grace through its ambiguous evidence. This especially applies to experiencing Jesus in our current cultural situation. Our general mindset is we only trust the evidence of our senses. We don't generally trust that our consciousness can operate accurately beyond the evidence of our senses. That means we are generally oblivious to mystery: that we are mistrustful of becoming 'mystics'.

The Canadian philosopher Charles Taylor put our modern situation this way. "We are all skeptics now, believer and unbeliever alike. There is no one true faith, evident in all times and places. Every religion is one among many. The clear lines of any orthodoxy are made crooked by our experience, are complicated by our lives. Believer and unbeliever are in the same predicament, thrown back upon themselves in complex circumstances, looking for a sign."[26]

So, how do ordinary people like you and I attempt to encounter a deep mystery? Literally, how do we experience the living, risen Jesus before his Second Coming? That is the unseen goal toward which my characters are struggling. Especially Neil and Elena who, even at the end, do not yet fully (authentically) believe in God's presence, let alone possess the unique faith of Christians. I have attempted to represent what it was like for four very different people to struggle with their modern situation and this unseen goal, in an era that has become almost completely oblivious of the mysterious presence of God.

The ancient people who wrote *The Upanishads* were reaching as far as they were capable at that time into the reality beyond ordinary life. *Siddhartha* is another story of man's early struggle to reach into mystical reality. Some modern people will listen to these ancient sages but not the Bible. Why?

The problem with modern man's mindset is that, in our culture, religion has a bad name. Many people simply aren't ready to listen to anything that sounds the least bit religious. But they are ready to listen to history and man's ancient search for explanations of reality. Why? Because they think these beliefs can't hurt them or try to ensnare them. Modern man believes they have advanced beyond *The Upanishads*, which makes it safe to read. These texts have lovely thoughts which support the Humanist view that each individual must construct something to believe in. The ancient Hindus had some good ideas that can be included in one's self-constructed belief system.

But Jesus is different, not to be taken casually in constructing one's own belief system. Why? Jesus excluded the possibility of including his sayings in constructing an eclectic individual belief system by claiming to be the one and only God and thus truth—"I am the way, the truth and the life." His claim of being *the* truth makes it impossible for someone to construct their own version of truth about God.

Some Christians claim that only by believing in Jesus can any human being be saved and live with God forever. Others, while believing that Christ is the way to heaven, believe that his mercy will make allowances for men of good will of all beliefs to be saved and cross the river. To preach Jesus to many modern people means to immediately become involved in arguments about salvation, religion and truth. So, Father Mac, Frank and I—all of whom want to help you find Jesus in your personal search—walked with you part way along your journey, hoping to help you choose to make some changes in your mindsets, and become more open to hearing Jesus's message. Frank's allegory went the farthest along the path of Christian belief, in his talk about his search for God. But he didn't discuss Jesus's claims about being God or the source of salvation. He hoped that those reading his allegory would be people who had progressed along the journey and would have questions and engage in conversations about his story, leading them closer to God, and eventually Jesus. So, our hope (and prayer) is that we have been good company in your journey, and that you will encounter Jesus in your seeking and come to know him.

Is my approach theologically correct? I have followed the path of Karl Rahner in approaching conversion and an encounter with Jesus. Rahner famously said, "In the days ahead, you will either be a mystic (one who has experienced

God for real) or nothing at all." He also said, "The number one cause of atheism is Christians. Those who proclaim Him with their mouths and deny Him with their actions is what an unbelieving world finds unbelievable." I did not want to have my Christian characters (Frank and Diane) be hypocritical Jesus people. I wanted to present what I felt any thoughtful Christian would do in their interactions with non-Christians, knowing that they too are only on the way to finding him.

In his *Foundations of Christian Faith*, Rahner organizes his arguments in ascending order, from below as it is often called. He starts with the nature of human beings and ascends to how they reach a knowledge of their own transcendence. From that point, he continues upward to knowledge of God, then Jesus Christ. My book stops short of Neil and Elena reaching knowledge of God—but they begin to sense their own transcendence, at least as a question. That is the crucial beginning of true seeking. Admitting to oneself that you are a creature unlike any other, transcending physical reality and human logic, being drawn toward some mysterious goal. That is what Francis helped Jacob (Frank) to see.

Finally, this novel is only a beginning, a hint about the riches that exist once one embarks on a serious search for who you are and who God is. Humans are both finite and infinite; opening our consciousness to this mysterious reality is one of the important tasks we undertake on life's journey. Frank hinted at this when he described the In-self. He knew that he couldn't begin to describe the meaning of In-self, even to himself, let alone Neil and Elena. And that means that I, the author, realised that I had to draw the line in what I included in this novel. Beatrice Bruteau calls it "the great mystery of the intersection of the finite and the infinite." [27] I have put many hints of this mystery throughout the five Books. If you reread these stories, look for and reflect on these hints. They are God's gift to you and me.

AMDG

Ad Majoram Dei Gloriam. For the greater glory of God. The motto of the Jesuits

Sources and Further Reading

Mystical Reality

Beatrice Bruteau, *Radical Optimism*, Boulder Colorado, Sentient Publications, 2002

John Bunyan, *Pilgrim's Progress*, Digireads.com book, 2009

Ilia Delio, *The Unbearable Wholeness of Being*, New York, Orbis, 2013

Chretien de Troyes, *Arthurian Romances*, London, Penguin Books, 1991

Herman Hesse, *Siddhartha*, London, Pan Books, 1988

Karl Rahner, *Foundations of Christian Faith*, New York, Crossroad, 1985

Joseph Cardinal Ratzinger, *Introduction to Christianity, 2nd Edition*, San Francisco, Ignatius Press, 2000

Richard Rohr, *The Wisdom Pattern*, Cincinnati OH, Franciscan Media, 2020

Stephen Wigley, *Balthazar's Trilogy*, London, Continuum, 2010

Scientific Reality

Peter Berger and Thomas Luckmann, *The Social Construction of Reality*, New York, Anchor Books, 1967

Gerald Edelman and Giulio Tononi, *Consciousness*, London, Penguin Press, 2000

Brian Greene, *The Fabric of the Cosmos*, New York, Vintage eBooks

Thomas Kuhn, *The Structure of Scientific Revolutions*, Chicago, University of Chicago Press, 1970

John H. Miller and John E Page, *Complex Adaptive Systems*, Princeton, Princeton Uinversity Press, 2007

About the Author

James Harlow Brown graduated from Marquette University with a bachelor's in electrical engineering, served as a Marine Corps officer, joined IBM and worked at NASA, graduated from The Catholic University of America with a master's in applied physics, became an executive in IBM and Satellite Business Systems, got a Certificate in Theological Studies from Georgetown University, became a Management Consultant, specializing in Organizational Transformation after leaving IBM. He has written two other books *Imagining Rama, a brief guide to exploring the universe, mystery and meaning* and *Living Well in the Presence of God; Everyday Spirituality in the 21st Century.*

Acknowledgements

Many people contributed to this book. To acknowledge them all would certainly leave out someone. So I'll just acknowledge my wife Hacy, who continually reinforced and supported my desire to write and share my views about life.

644

Endnotes

1. If you haven't read *The Lord of the Rings* or seen the movies, you may find some of Neil and Frank's references puzzling. Gandalf was an old and very wise wizard who opposed the evil Lord Sauron. Sauron planned to conquer the world (Tolkien called it Middle-earth) by gaining control of a lost Ring of Power, and he used a mighty army of mindless creatures called Orcs to do his bidding. But there was one flaw in Sauron's master plan that Gandalf could exploit to defeat him. The Ring of Power was hidden, and Sauron couldn't find it. It was in the possession of Frodo the hobbit, a good guy, one of the little folk. Hobbits were peace-loving, insignificant people that the rest of the people in Middle-earth ignored. Gandalf is Frodo's friend and mentor, and helps him go on a dangerous but vital quest: to take a long and difficult journey to defeat Sauron's plan to dominate Middle-earth. To do so, they must destroy the ring.

2. The prefix "In" is linked to powerful words about the human spirit: Insight, Innovate, Inspire. Innocence also begins with "in" so that is probably why Frank used this name for the inner person.

3. Many cultures have pointed toward this dichotomy between our interior life and our external persona. The Japanese use the terms hen'na (façade) and tadasho (who we actually are). The mystics saw it as the place where the infinite and the finite intersect.

4. See Sources and further reading at the end of the book for a selection of books from Frank's library.

5. Aragorn represents Tolkien's ideal leader. Aragorn never uses his power unwisely, but uses it only to serve others.

6. Aragorn's test was simply to serve Frodo and not try to destroy the ring himself, to prove himself worthy to be a king even though he was the rightful heir. His father had attempted to take the ring for himself, and this selfish act led to Sauron's current war on Middle-earth.

[7]. It may seem strange for Frank to use the term 'myth' when referring to science. Isn't science based on facts? The study of how humans determine what fact is (and what science is for that matter) involves another human storytelling device called philosophy. The problem is there is no absolute foundation for any human knowledge. We only have our philosophical story about knowledge to tell us what is true and real. Therefore it is appropriate when Frank calls science one of the human 'myths' about knowledge.

[8] Peter Vaill used this idea in his preface to *Maslow on Management*: "It is not espousing values, a mission statement, and a corporate mantra while pushing motivational techniques that do little more than manipulate employees. [It] calls for fundamentally altering the system, revamping the organizational DNA in order for the human side to flourish."

[9]. In biology, a tag is a part of something living that makes it attractive, which attaches to another living entity. See Clippinger *The Biology of Business* in the bibliography

[10]. This isn't a new idea. Buddhists call it being aware and mindful, and the Jesuits call it reflective action. Even the Green Movement is based on thinking globally; acting locally." These emphasize the fundamental human desire to create good; not only for oneself, but for the entire world.

[11]. This is well documented by Chris Argyris in his work on organizational defensive routines and Model 1 behaviors. See *Flawed Advice and the Management Trap* referenced in the bibliography

[12]. Robert K. Greenleaf, *Servant Leadership*, New York: Paulist Press, 1991.

[13]. The quotes in the story about Speer are all taken from Joachim Fest's *Speer: The Final Verdict*, London: Wiedenfeld & Nicolson, 2001.

[14]. Thomas Berry, *The Great Work*, New York: Bell Tower, 1999.

[15]. Edward O. Wilson, *Consilience*, New York: Vintage Books, 1998, p. 325.

[16]. Neil based his three approaches to leadership on Melanie Klein's model, taken from 'Mourning, Potency and Power' by Laurent Lapierre in *The Psychodynamics of Organizations*, Philadelphia: Temple University Press, 1993, pp. 26–31.

[17]. The statue is called 'Pioneering Mankind' and is located just up the path from Saint James train station, across from the Sheraton on the Park where Frank first met Elena.

[18]. *The Upanishads*, trans. by Eknath Easwaram, Tomales: Nilgiri Press, 1995, p. 115.

[19] The roles we play in life create one side of us, our persona. We construct mental boundaries to protect this façade, because we know, at some level, that it isn't who we are. There is another side to us, a mysterious strong and true presence within us. Frank O'Connor used 'In-Self' to describe it, linking it to powerful words about the human spirit: Insight, Innovate, Inspire. Because innocence also begins with 'in,' Frank called people who are particularly attuned to their interior reality 'innocent.' The Japanese use the terms hen'na (façade) and tadasho (who we actually are) to describe these two sides of all human beings.

[20] Wikipedia article on Sir Gawain and the Green Knight

[21] Wikipedia article about *The Hero with a Thousand Faces*

[22] C S Lewis, *George MacDonald*, (87) Incompleteness

[23] 'In this life, we are searching for God and soul, but we do not know what we are doing, and thus get lost in the realm of forgetting by attending to the outside.' Terence Sweeney, *God and the Soul: Augustine on the Journey to True Selfhood,* The Heythrop Journal, 2 July 2014

[24] 'I walked through dark and slippery places, and I went out of my self in the search for You and did not find the God of my heart.' [St Augustine in The Confessions] The person walking through dark and slippery places is lost but still wants happiness. They are looking for God and themselves in the wrong place, but *they are looking*. This looking, as a kind of

restlessness, is a clue. The person may not know this, they may have almost totally forgotten themselves, but they are looking.' Sweeney, *Ibid*.

[25] Luke 10:42

[26] Cited in Paul Elie, *The Life You Save May Be Your Own*, New York, Farrakhan, Strauss and Giroux, 2003, p. 427.

[27] Beatrice Bruteau, Radical Optimism, Boulder Colorado, Sentient Publications, Chapter 4.

www.ingramcontent.com/pod-product-compliance
Lightning Source LLC
Chambersburg PA
CBHW070536030726
47505CB00001B/54